I0819955

CHRISTMAS DAYS IN THE MORNING

Christmas Days *in the* Morning

The Life Events of Jesus and His Wife to Age Ten Years Old

The Dawn from on High
BOOK I

BY ANNE M. DUDLEY

Foreword by Lou Hammann

RESOURCE *Publications* • Eugene, Oregon

CHRISTMAS DAYS IN THE MORNING
The Life Events of Jesus and His Wife to Age Ten Years Old

Resource Publications
An Imprint of Wipf and Stock Publishers
199 W. 8th Ave., Suite 3
Eugene, OR 97401

www.wipfandstock.com

PAPERBACK ISBN: 979-8-3852-0972-9
HARDCOVER ISBN: 979-8-3852-0973-6
EBOOK ISBN: 979-8-3852-0974-3

04/29/24

All photos taken by the author in April 2009.
All diagrams and maps created by the author.

CONTENTS

FOREWORD

It is clear from reading the (first) novel by Anne M. Dudley that she can be trusted with reliable familiarity with the **New Testament** text. Her use of biblical quotations is always appropriate and contextual. Her self-confidence, in what I prefer to call "expertise" in literature and history, is impressive. It gives her an authority in *reenvisioning the argument* of a book in which many people often depend for personal guidance in matters I dare call "spiritual."

I venture to appreciate how well she has accomplished what above I referred to as "reenvisioning." This is true, notably of the text but also of the argument that has rendered the book indispensable for many who would understand a highly specialized history. Her quite systematic interpretation of some of the more obscure and demanding of the texts as revelation is more than just clever. She helps her readers "translate" the personal value of this or that aspect of the "story" as a whole. The Bible as a record of ordinary history as well as spiritual education has given its readers insight that might otherwise elude casual attention.

Perhaps one episode in the biblical New Testament story of Jesus prompted her skill at reenvisioning in effect that surprising venture may have been off-putting for some readers and a virtual revelation for others. Simply read that aspect of Dudley's novels and judge for yourself its effect on your consciousness.

Somehow this first episode in the Jesus story is engaging and even puzzling. How historically true is it? Surely the author cannot claim it as an authentic episode in Jesus' life that deserves unhesitating acceptance. Still, it is an aspect of what may have been authentic history. But why not? There are still aspects of his personal history that are at least imaginable. I leave it up to the readers to cope with what seems at least almost a paradox: believability "wrestling" with uncertainty.

It seems to me that we may trust the author's decision to include the above in her story/history. Much of this novel reminds its readers of Anne's professional role in marriage counseling and, of course an alert reader cannot miss her aptitude in biblical studies. Indeed, the novel itself is virtually dependent on a commitment to *biblical* studies. And her autobiography and her scholarship should prompt the reader to recognize a story that is at least consistent in its believability; there is little reason to see this episode as less than a reliable possibility.

Please understand that giving credibility to this aspect of the Jesus story does not come to us without a sense of ambiguity. Many aspects of this amazing biblical story may or may not bear the mark of being true or authentic. I say again, I trust this author's integrity as a writer, given her learning, sincerity, and open devotion as a person.

Dr. Louis Hammann
Professor of Religion, Gettysburg College
(1957-2008)

MY FATHER'S ENDORSEMENT

4/20/07—Comments upon reading the first forty-four pages of this narrative . . .

- It's pleasantly interesting and instructive to experience the natural realities and relationships that surround the people and events mentioned in early writings of the New Testament Gospels.
- The very natural and human unfolding of events in people's lives reveal God's plan, God's will, and God's presence in the interplay of human feelings and emotions of these created people of God.
- God's miraculous power and God's loving plan for his creation is revealed in the everyday events and lives of human beings. . . . This, in fact, is why God came to people . . . This is why God could not possibly expect people to come to him . . . and God came in the understandable terms of human realities, not divine mysteries.
- This is good writing, alive with imagination but never presumptuous in terms of human emotions and events.
- I would encourage you to continue pursuing this writing.

Dad
Rev. Theodore Pelikan
Lutheran pastor for fifty-six years

PREFACE

IN 2003, I EMBARKED on a journey of study, research, and reflection to satisfy my personal desire to better understand the life of Jesus as the son of man. I wanted to know what Jesus' childhood was like; what kind of relationships did he have with his parents, his relatives, his friends? What made him laugh; what made him sad and angry? What kind of games did he play as a child and as a teenager with his friends, cousins, and siblings? Did he fall in love with one special woman? How was he able to become such a great teacher, one whom we think we know today, though more than two thousand years have passed since he lived on the earth? And among other things, what meaning does his brief and remarkable ministry have for me and others in the twenty-first century who are also seekers?

I'm not a theological scholar or seminary-trained minister, although the men in my family of origin were, as the women in my family were biblical scholars in their own right. However, I've always been drawn to follow Christ, and I have loved people in my life and work as a teacher, youth minister, and counselor therapist for individuals, couples, and families. I am also an avid seeker and wanted to know and understand the life events of Jesus more closely and accurately than what I learned in Sunday School and church. My most prominent question began at age four and stayed with me until I could accurately answer this question: Was Jesus married, and if so, who was his wife and from where did she come? I was always encouraged and inspired by Jesus' words as recorded in the Gospel of Matthew: "Ask and it shall be given you; seek and you shall find; knock and it shall be opened to you." So, at the age of forty years I began a formal personal study, researching and seeking to find the accurate, definitive answers to my questions in 2003. In my seeking I encountered and applied a remarkable, guiding force from an ancient rabbinic discipline known as the halakic principle. This principle guided my study and searching, requiring me to accept all points of view—not an *either/or* approach to the world and the life of Jesus, but a *both/and* state of coexistence of thought, faith, and reason. Naturally, accepting opposing and challenging points of view often resulted in personal tension and confoundedness—but it was in this very state of contemplative tension that I experienced a deeper, transcending understanding of Jesus, his life, and his being. I gained revelatory insights, different from what I had been taught and had casually accepted. It was difficult, but surprisingly, all turned into a great blessing for me and *my faith, and, more importantly, I found answers.*

While my seeking and researching spanned twenty years, I wrote an autobiographical book recording my search, research, and the process and sources of information. I entitled the book *Another Way.* But it was not enough. Simultaneously, I was compelled to write the story of Jesus' life events with his wife (yes, spoiler alert: Jesus was married, though traditional Christendom and Christianity subtly subdued this fact to the extent that most Christians don't know or care about this fact). I intertwined his and his wife's life events closely with the reporting of the Gospels in the Bible and research. Writing their story ended with eight historical novels! All the novels have been completed, owning their own titles but included together under the main entitlement of *The Dawn from on High*. Book 1, which you hold, is entitled *Christmas Days in the Morning*, published and released for your reading.

I think it is important for you to know that I have considered myself a dedicated Christian, attending church for most of my life until recently, having had trouble remaining part of a religious Evangelical Christian title; but I have read and studied the Bible, implementing meditative personal discipline on Christian teachings and principles. I have come to accept what Jesus taught and hold a genuine love for him and our God. Of course, my faith and discipline have been shaped and influenced by my life experience, of which my family has been one of those greatest influences. My father, my grandfather, and great-grandfather were all dedicated Lutheran pastors. My only paternal uncle was also a Lutheran minister/historian, but his brilliance landed him in Yale Divinity School as a graduate professor and writer of Christian history and theology. I feel blessed to be a part of these great men in my life and hold close to them and my maiden's name of Pelikan.

But then I unexpectedly reached the place where I could no longer accept the concept that seemed to grip most religious institutions that one *either* believed the Gospels fully, and in their entirety, as presented in the Bible's New Testament, *or else* . . . one was not a Christian, nor a worthy child of God or a creditable recipient of redemption. My father, grandfather and uncle always portrayed the power of grace *alone* for *all* and encouraged me to ask, seek and knock. Fortunately, they impressed upon me that there were, and continue to be valuable ideas beyond the lessons from *both* the

Christian Bible, the teaching of the Christian church, and the many Christian denominations. But they also impressed upon me that all religious disciplines of the world *and* other historical sources, recent archeological discoveries, other writings, other points of view, even one's own imagination were just as valuable in any faith journey.

So, what you are about to read may in many ways be very different from what you may have learned in church or Sunday School, different from where your own faith has come to rest. You may be shocked and offended by parts of the long, comprehensive story about the life of Jesus and his wife. Your faith may well be challenged at the very onset! But I believe this story is informative and valuable, and had to be told. Therefore, I encourage you to accept my challenge. So much more information is included in the books I've written, and it will give you a broader perspective of this incredible, remarkable man named Jesus who lived more than two thousand years ago. Fortunately, if you keep your heart and mind opened, the Spirit of God shall carry you through to see and understand beyond your expectation. I think you will benefit from incorporating *both* your current understanding or faith *and* the story I present, as you continue on your own faith journey of asking, seeking, and knocking.

In conclusion, my work is based upon disciplined research and study, and information never before included in the consideration of the canonical Gospels of Matthew, Mark, Luke, and John. If you can't accept some of the information presented, don't give up! I hope my series of books telling the story of Jesus' life with his wife will provide an understanding from another enriching perspective. You may note how closely my story parallels the Bible, and I hope you will enjoy how I have written of the missing years of our Lord Jesus' life. It may bring completeness of understanding, knowledge, and blessing into your life.

Thank you, and may God bless your faith journey.

Sincerely, Anne M. Dudley

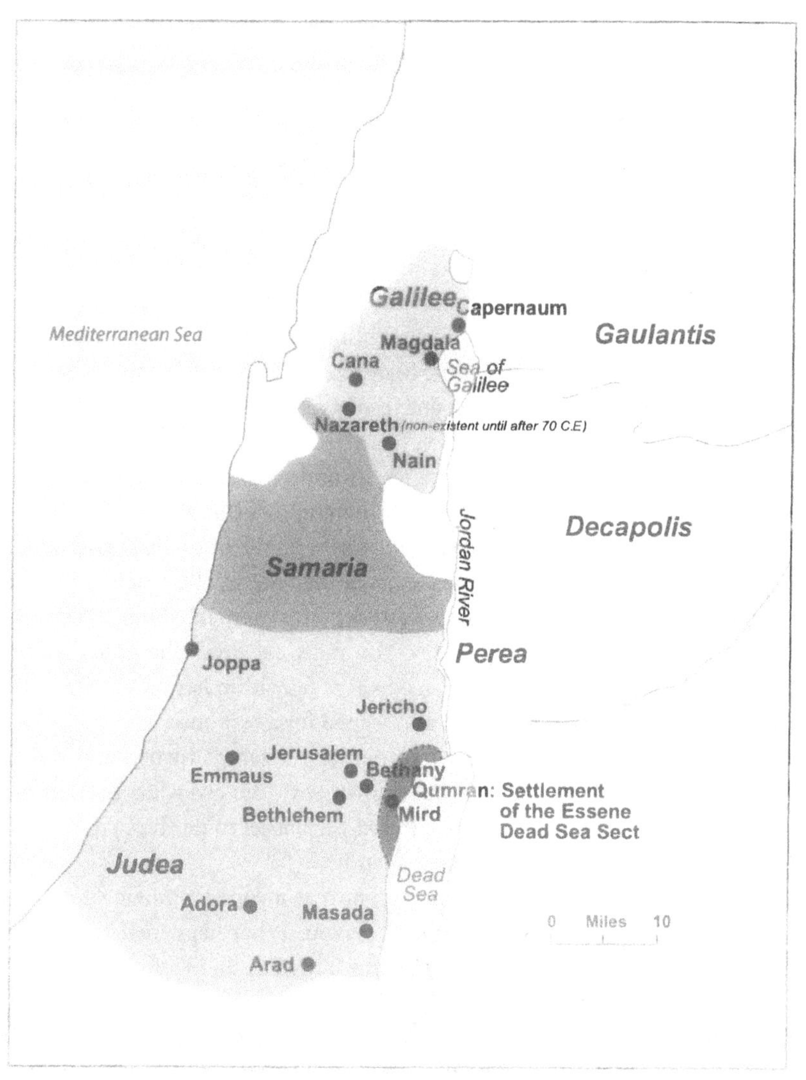

Palestine at the Time of Jesus's Ministry

THE QUMRAN SETTLEMENT

Elizabeth was concerned. There sat Mary, gazing out the window again. Looking to the west, she occasionally rested her head on the windowsill. Otherwise, she assumed her role as sentinel. This was the third sunset she had watched from her hours of the early mornings. She didn't move her gaze except for the bits of time she spent resting her head on the sill, eyes closed for brief moments.

Elizabeth paused at the doorway, wondering if she ought to disturb what seemed to be one of those brief moments of Mary's rest. Finally, she placed the basket she had been holding down on the dusty floor and walked silently into the room and stood close to her niece. She reached out and placed her hand gently on Mary's shoulder. Mary remained unresponsive.

Elizabeth spoke softly, "Mary. You must eat this." She pulled Mary's hand from the windowsill and placed a ripe fig within her palm. She closed her niece's fingers around the fig and waited for a response.

Mary's hand let the fig drop to her lap. Elizabeth turned and walked back to her basket of figs and bent down with the awkward motion of a pregnant woman at full term. She raised the basket to her hip, paused, and glanced back at Mary, a motionless shadow.

"I have known you as a child and now as a young woman. Mary, how I see you here is not God's purpose for you. What happened to you was devastating, and traumatic . . . but now you hold a child within your womb. We are all waiting for your son to be born."

Mary looked up from resting on the windowsill and spoke with despairing anger reflected in her voice, saying, "And what if my child is a girl? What then? Will she share my fate? What then of our hopes and dreams?" Her head fell to the sill again. "I wish I had been stoned to death. I can't bear this child."

At these words, Elizabeth purposefully dropped the basket, scattering the figs. "Yes! You can bear this child! I believe you *are* pregnant with your first son, but if you birth a girl we will still rejoice!" With determination she stepped up to Mary, lifted her by the shoulders, and guided her to stand. "Open your eyes! Something awesome is going on here! Great events are happening right before us!? Mary," she took a step back, "look at me . . . look at me! I'm an old woman and I'm pregnant! Your uncle is in the next room and can't talk! He's a rabbi. He loves to talk. He never shuts up. He's dumb! Why would God allow a rabbi to be struck dumb and make him a father in his old age!? Don't you see! Something is happening! Something great is happening!"

Mary fell into the arms of her aunt and wept. Her voice shook as she asked, "And why would God allow me to be raped!? Did God allow the soldier to strike me to the ground and tear my garment? Why was no one there to help me? . . . Elizabeth, he hurt me! I felt like he was tearing at my insides like he tore my garment. And now I am bringing a child into the world with no husband, no father. What good can come for the baby . . . or me . . . or our future? And you talk of something going on, as if enough hasn't happened already."

Elizabeth turned toward the window and the western horizon. "We will love you and the child. We will not abandon you." She looked down and stroked Mary's head and whispered, "God will not abandon you or any of us . . . God loves us." As Mary began to cry, Elizabeth looked up and once again gazed out the window. The birds were flapping and flying around the tree. They chirped and sang with an excitement that did not seem appropriate to the humans' circumstance. "I don't understand everything, but I know God loves us."

Elizabeth didn't know how long she held her niece in her arms, or how long she gazed out the window, but when her conscious focus returned, Mary was sitting on the chair by the window eating the fig.

Pounding could be heard from the other room. Elizabeth's husband, Zechariah, was calling for her. He would pound his staff against the wall, or a pot, or the wooden leg of a table to get Elizabeth's attention. Elizabeth gathered up the figs and responded to her husband's bidding, leaving Mary sitting alone in the room.

Mary ate the fig with ravenous appetite. She wondered when she had eaten last and realized that this was not good for her unborn child, or for herself.

While still chewing on the last bit of the fig, a gentle but distinct movement of air brushed against her cheek. She looked up and around the room expecting to see someone, but the room was still. It must have been her imagination. But no, again a warm wind, like the breath from a living fire, brushed passed her face and body. She sat still and waited. This had happened before. The warm breeze stirred her memory. It was when she had been home, harvesting figs from the trees in a grove near her father's house. She couldn't recall if it happened before or after she had been ravaged by the horrific crime of rape three months earlier and had told no one, but she was still scared. At that time, she had sat on the flat boulder by the path that ran through the fig grove on the east side of the settlement. How many generations had used the same flat boulder as a sort of bench, she wondered? How many had contemplated the tragic madness and harshness of life? She had been raped by a Roman soldier. She wondered when the frightening images that replayed in her mind would end.

A sudden wind had jolted her then, and she had turned left to see the trees on that edge of the grove waving wildly. The wind moved in a strange way, blowing the trees in an unnatural swirl of motion. It was odd then. It was odd now, sitting in the quiet of the room. While in the fig grove at home, she had turned to her right, shifting her position on the boulder, and was startled to see a man on the path, not ten paces from her, at least she thought it was a man; what else could it be? He was leading a laden donkey on the track toward the cluster of homes toward her village.

To be alone again, and with a stranger approaching, might have produced a reaction of dread. Instead, and somewhat remarkably, her feeling was of irritation and challenge.

As the stranger drew closer, Mary stood. The stranger, yes, it was a man, stopped, and looked kindly upon her.

"Greetings, favored one," he spoke. "My name is Gabriel, and I give you greetings from the city of God."

"You are from Jerusalem then," she had replied.

"Ah, you have heard of Jerusalem?"

Mary remembered thinking, "Why the jesting?" but instead she had said, "Yes, of course, even here, in the Qumran Settlement, we know of all the cities of Judah."

He smiled, "I am not often at home though," he stated, "I am a traveler. My trade is honing and repair. I carry my stones on my friend's back here, and sharpen tools and knives, traveling from village to village. And because I travel, I am also something of . . . a messenger, some would say even a teller of fortunes."

He paused for a response, but Mary stood silent at that time.

"It's funny about the sharpening trade, you know," he continued. "My stones are abrasive, and they remove small pieces of the blade, and the process is noisy, but when the edge is smooth and sharp, the tool is ready for any job, and the user of the tool is safer than with a dull blade."

"And what message might you have for me, Gabriel the sharpener and fortune teller?" Mary asked challengingly.

He stepped closer, looked her full in the face, and with a quieter voice said, "The Lord is with you."

It might as well have been a slap. Her reaction was such.

"What could you possibly know about me or the Lord, stranger?" her voice rising.

"Do not be afraid, child. You are right, of course. I do not really know you. However, I do know that sometimes the Lord uses the strangest things to fulfill his will. Doubt, disobedience, captivity, even violence . . ."

Mary stood unmoving, her mind waving like the branches of the trees.

"Do not be afraid, young woman, Mary, is it? You have found favor with God. Well, I've got more sharpening to do. Perhaps you'll walk with me to your village?"

She remembered she had acted against her better judgment and walked beside him. He hummed an old shepherd's tune and told her things she felt she just dreamed. However, she remembered that as she walked with him, somehow, her step seemed lighter. She also remembered feeling that something had been revealed to her and that, in essence, she had accepted a message. At the time she had not told anyone, but she felt she was going to become pregnant even though she and her betrothed husband, Joseph, had not celebrated their first wedding ceremony. But the message didn't seem upsetting to her then.

Now, her reality was different. It seemed as if her life was over. So, it wasn't surprising to her that this time she initially felt uneasy about feeling the warm breath of something she couldn't comprehend.

It was a mystery. Mary stayed still and waited. Suddenly, she felt incredible peace. She felt something was going to happen to her again, and she felt it would be good. After a while—she didn't know how long—the warm presence departed, but her sense of peace lingered. She looked out the window. The sun had sunk below the Judean hills. Mary stood and walked to the room where she, her aunt, and uncle ate. Both Zechariah and Elizabeth were sitting at the table eating in silence. Mary stepped forward, bowed her head in prayer, and sat at the table. Elizabeth reached out to take Mary's hand in a strong grip that somehow conveyed a sense of hope and joy. Mary reached for the bread and began to eat.

After the first bite she felt a terrible hunger. Without speaking, Elizabeth placed a platter of meat and fruit before her. Then she poured a brimming cup of wine that Mary had to delicately balance as she raised the cup to her lips. She ate and drank her fill. For the first time in a long time, she felt sated, and didn't experience the anxious nausea that had become common.

Uncle Zechariah looked over to Mary with an approving eye. He reached out and patted her hand and smiled. With that he rose from his chair and walked to the other end of the table where Elizabeth sat. He bent down and kissed his wife on the top of her head as she reached for his arm and drew it over her shoulder and to her chest. Zechariah's hand moved to the roundness of her belly, and he grinned as he felt the certain movement from the child within.

"You know what is strange?" Elizabeth asked. "I don't wish to disrespect, but in the past, there were many times I longed to hear your voice silenced or that your talking would be still. Oh, Zechariah, now I long to hear your voice again. I long to know what happened to you the day you entered the holy of holies room in the temple, and for you to tell me what you heard or witnessed."

Zechariah reached over and picked up a crude slab of slate and a dried piece of clay. He wrote: "We will all understand in God's time." He returned the slate board to the table and walked out of the room with a smile upon his face and in his eyes.

Yes, Elizabeth thought. We will all know in God's time. She stood up and began carrying pots, plates, and other implements from the table to the large carved-out wooden bowl that held precious water. There was not much water in the Qumran Settlement. To the east, three or four miles from their modest home, lay the shimmering Dead Sea. It was well named because there was no life in this sea. The salt content was too great, too toxic to sustain life. As a child, Elizabeth remembered going on trips with her family to the Dead Sea. There was one trip she never forgot. She had been about Mary's age then. It was then when she and her little brother Micah were playing on one of the cliffs rising up from the water like the pinnacles of the Jerusalem temple. Closing her eyes and remembering the event still filled her soul with fear. Micah was to stay close to her if she were to allow him to climb to the top of the cliff, but instead, the thrill of the climb led him out of her reach, and in terror she watched him tumble down the dusty cliff and disappear into the blue-green water below.

"*Miiiccaah!* No, Micah." His body hit the water and disappeared below the surface so quickly. Horror gripped her as she thought for sure he would drown. There was no way to traverse the descent down the cliff and pull him out before he drowned. There were no pieces of wood or fallen branches to throw out to him to grasp and grab if he bobbed to the surface. There were no trees in this place, only red-brown crusts of shriveled earth. In a flash, Elizabeth had remembered feeling anger toward her parents for bringing them to this godforsaken place to live, but it had not overshadowed her terror as her brother resurfaced from the water's grip. Her little brother Micah was going to drown if she did not do something fast!

Elizabeth's mind snapped back, and she found herself standing at the wooden bowl filled with fresh water and pottery to clean. She closed her eyes and took a deep breath. She kept her eyes closed and continued remembering when Micah popped above the surface of the water. She felt she had to reach him before he went under again but, unbelievably, he had not sunk under the surface of the water again. He floated above, coughing and spitting out the salty water.

"Micah! Can you swim?"

"No!" he had cried out with childlike delight and surprise at the realization that he wasn't going to go under the water again and drown.

"How are you doing that?"

"I don't know!" as he laughed and giggled with glee.

"Push your way to the shallow shore, right now!"

"Elizabeth, come on in. It's fun!" he had yelled in childhood pleasure.

Remembering the event with her brother, Elizabeth opened her eyes to find herself in the kitchen, and she felt the presence of her mother, standing next to her in that moment as she had stood next to her on the shore that day Micah fell into the Dead Sea. Elizabeth remembered stumbling down the cliff in desperation and panic as Micah splashed and kicked, playing in the water. She ran to the side of her mother, who was already peacefully waiting for Micah to step to the shore, and she was still visibly shaken with the terror of possibly losing her brother.

"Micah. Listen to your sister. Come to the shore and get out of the water." Her mother's arm wrapped around Elizabeth's shoulders, and for the first time Elizabeth noticed that she was as tall as her mother. "Elizabeth, you are a good sister. You will be a good mother someday. Always remember that you cannot save or control any life. You can only remain faithful to your God, yourself, and other people placed in your life to love."

Micah had stepped onto the shore. His flowing garment was drenched. "That was fun! I want to do it again."

"No, Micah," their mother had said. "This has been enough excitement for one day. Go back to our campsite and hang out your garment to dry."

Elizabeth found herself standing by the wooden sink again. She turned around and saw only Mary sitting at the table. "I feel the presence of my mother here . . . I was just remembering something that happened many years ago when my brother Micah fell down a steep cliff and into the Dead Sea."

Mary sat quietly and listened to her aunt as Elizabeth placed the pots and plates in the water and returned to the table to sit across from Mary. "When that happened, my mother told me that I would be a good mother. Here I am. An old woman who has mourned many years because I was barren . . . and now the child in my womb will be born soon . . . I remember being shocked that day when my brother didn't drown. My mother seemed to appear out of nowhere on the shore. It was if she knew I needed her. She said something I will never forget . . . She said, 'God always provides' . . . And she went on to explain that because the Dead Sea is so salty, a living body remains buoyant and *cannot* sink . . . One couldn't sink even if they wanted to . . . I asked her, 'Why do we live here? Why can't we live in Bethlehem, or Bethany, or Jerusalem?' She told me that we had accepted God's calling to be set apart. 'Elizabeth,' she had said, 'we are Essenes, and we *cannot* forget our calling to faithfully live in this place.'" Elizabeth was silent for a moment and added, "I often still wonder why I live here." Elizabeth sighed with a heaviness that often presents in the last months of pregnancy.

Mary rose from the table and began to finish the cleaning of the plates and pottery used for their dinner. "Just sit, Aunt Elizabeth. I'll get these finished." Mary worked in silence and finished the cleanup. She returned to sit across from Elizabeth.

"I'm young, and I don't understand a lot of things. I admit that I am most puzzled by my parents' choice to remain in this settlement. Nothing about living here has seemed worth the trouble. Not until I learned that Joseph wanted me for his wife did I begin to think about life in a different way. Now even that is not to be." Mary looked intently at the grain in the wood of the table before she looked up and continued by asking, "Aunt Elizabeth, did you think Joseph was too old to be my husband? Maybe that is why this has happened to me. I wasn't sure I wanted to be the almah of such an older man."

Elizabeth chuckled. "To me, Joseph is a young man. He is no older than thirty years, and you are asking this question of a woman who is pregnant for the first time and looking at an age nearing seventy-five years."

Mary and Elizabeth looked at each other and began to laugh hysterically. They laughed until their laughter tapered into short breaths and soft whimpers. Lastly, Elizabeth looked at Mary, reached for her hands across the table and said, "It is late. Go and receive a restful sleep. May the Lord's countenance shine upon you and give you peace."

Mary stood up, feeling the sadness of her situation rudely creep back into her soul. She tried to hide her sad emotion and walked around the table to hug Elizabeth. She walked to the opposite doorframe where she knew her uncle was sitting somewhere in the darkness, listening to everything she and her aunt spoke. "Good night, Uncle Zechariah," she called out. Three taps of his staff against the stone wall expressed his evening salutation to Mary.

Mary walked into the darkness of her room and lowered her body to her sleeping mat. She thought of Joseph and began to cry. She prayed and asked God why she was not given the opportunity to fall in love with this man . . . Joseph. She could easily picture his face. She could see his dark eyes, and his dark curls, falling over his handsome face. His beard could not hide his beauty. His stature was formidable, but his gentle way was engaging. Through her tears, Mary thought she could have truly loved him. She wondered if he truly could love her, even now. Her sadness enveloped her like a cold dark cloud. Enough! No matter what, Mary knew her pregnancy was shrouded in inexplicable reality. She had come here to live with her aunt and uncle in the Judean Hills until the baby was born. She had left her mother and father's home and took with her the shame of her circumstances. Maybe, she thought, her first child could be born in the safety of her relatives' home. There would be so many more decisions to make upon the baby's arrival but she was determined to be the mother to the child beneath her heart. She would do it without a husband . . . without love . . . without Joseph. Each night always seemed an eternity. She cried for the hopelessness of her future, and cried for the suffering her child was sure to endure. She thought of Joseph. She knew they would not be married. They would not have children together. They would not see years together. They would not be a family. No.

Then, in the silence of the night, she heard the voice of a man. It was a low, soft, comforting voice. Someone was here! Here, in the dwelling. He was in the next room beyond her door. How strange. It was not her uncle's voice. He was struck dumb upon her aunt's conception. "Oh, God, am I hearing things?" she wondered. "It sounds like a familiar voice. I know this voice. But I know it is a voice I will not hear again."

"Mary," she heard the voice say. She ran from the mat to her door. She flung the door open. Light blazed in, and all she saw was the silhouette of a man she immediately recognized.

"Joseph!"

"I had a dream, Mary." He opened his arms and drew her close. "I don't understand everything, but I do know that I love you. I'm here to take you home, home to live our lives together. God will help us."

Mary sank her face into his mantle, turning her head to listen to his heart beating rapidly in his chest. She began to cry softly. She thought she could cry no more, and yet tears came, saying, "But the rules . . . What about the rules? What will happen to us, Joseph? What will happen to this child?"

"We will continue to live in faith." He gently took her head into his hands and turned her tearstained face to his own. "God is greater than anything. He is greater than rules. Love is greater than rules. This is out of our control now. I dreamed that I was supposed to love you and the unborn child . . . I have faith that God lays no rules against love. Mary, we are more important to God than rules. My love for you is greater than rules." He drew her close again. "I'm taking you home with me."

Joseph led her back to her sleeping mat and removed the blanket, cloak, and mantle from his shoulders and spread them out on her mat. He helped Mary down to lie upon them. They were soft. She lay down, and Joseph lay next to her and pressed his warm body closely against her. "To-night, we shall sleep together," he said.

Zechariah stood at the doorway to Mary's room and watched as they fell asleep. He smiled and turned, returning to Elizabeth who was also asleep. "What a day," he thought.

Peace encircled Mary. Joy filled her and Joseph as they slept. At one point Mary woke up in the darkness of the night. But through the window from where she was lying, she saw a bright morning star in the west. She thought she was dreaming when she saw Joseph asleep by her side, and then remembered. She moved closer to Joseph and whispered, "I will love this man and now shall love this child."

ELEAZAR'S HOME IN BETHANY AND THE BIRTH OF MARY (MIRIAM)

LITTLE MARTHA HUDDLED IN the corner of the room next to her big brother, Lazarus. Their mother was screaming, and both she and Lazarus were terrified. They felt invisible as women they didn't recognize rushed about their dwelling carrying rags and clay pots filled with steaming water. Sometimes the rags they held in their hands were stained with fresh red blood. Every now and again her brother would release a terrified whimper that frightened Martha even more. Even at the young age of four years, Martha knew something was terribly wrong, and her terror caused her own crying and whimpering.

Finally, she tugged on her brother's arm, and through her fear she asked, "What's wrong with Mommy? Why is she screaming? Where's Daddy . . . I want my mommy!"

Lazarus was young himself but at the age of seven years he understood more. He wrapped his arms around his sister, and they clung to each other. "Mommy's having a baby," he whispered. That is all he said while he continued to hold his sister. He understood something was terribly wrong. He remembered when his sister Martha was born and recognized there was a great difference in the behavior of the other women who were here to help his mother have this baby. He remembered his mother had screamed out then too, but the talking of the other women had been filled with expressions of anticipation and joy. Today his mother's cries were different. She was screaming in desperation and pain. Something was wrong. He hung his head and began to cry. He thought his mother must be dying, and he wanted to see her. He wanted to be next to her and hold her but he knew he dare not move from the room where he and his sister were told to stay. His body shook violently at the next horrible shriek. Then there was silence, which seemed worse.

Martha jumped to her feet and ran toward the room that housed their mother's bed, crying, "Mommy . . . Mommy!" Lazarus grabbed her hand and drew her back into their space by the corner of the room.

"No, Martha! No. Stay here with me. Dad said for us to stay here!"

Martha allowed her brother to take her back to the corner of the room and cried on his shoulder. "I want my mommy . . . I want my mommy. She is supposed to feed me now. I'm hungry!"

Lazarus tried to comfort his little sister by offering a handful of raisins. "Eat this now and don't cry, Martha. You'll be alright. Come now and eat these."

Martha sat up. She didn't reach for the raisins her brother offered but rather began to stare at a spider on the wall crawling slowly up, up, up. After a while she turned her blank stare to her brother who once again offered the raisins. "Here," he said, "Take these and eat them."

Martha shook her head slowly and returned her stare to the spider. Lazarus dropped his head and prayed a simple child's prayer. "God, please help my mommy. Please help my sister. Please help me."

He didn't think to pray for his father. His father was a Pharisee and was probably in the temple praying anyway. Lazarus believed his father was close to God, too far from them to hear their mother's screaming or his children's whimpering. He didn't believe God or his father could see them and hear their cries.

Lazarus was suddenly aware that there was no sound coming from anyone or anywhere. The women who had been rushing past their room were no longer moving or talking. It was so quiet. And then, the still, small cry of a newborn infant was heard. Lazarus felt no joy even though he knew this was the cry of a new brother or sister. Martha didn't move but continued to stare as the spider made it to the top of the window where a warm breeze came through, and in its embrace, she cuddled next to her brother more closely, and they both fell asleep on the dusty floor.

When the children awoke, night had fallen. Lazarus sat up and saw his five-year-old cousin Levi's mother, Aunt Rachael, standing over them. She spoke with a serious gentleness he was not used to hearing from his aunt. "I'm going to lift Martha and carry her to her sleeping mat. You can go to your mat as well."

"Is my mother dead?"

His aunt took a long time before she simply said, "Yes." After carefully lifting Martha from the floor, she walked toward the door and turned. "You have a new sister. Her name will be Mary."

Lazarus remained alone in the corner for a time and finally rose to go to the sleeping mat in his own room. He passed his mother and father's room and saw no one lying there. There was no sign of his mother anywhere. Down the passage to his left, he saw the flicker of an oil lamp lighting the table. There sat his father with his head bowed in his hands. Lazarus walked toward the light and his father but stopped when he saw that his father was weeping. It frightened him. Lazarus turned to return to his room, lay down on his mat, and fell asleep. In his deep sleep he dreamed of his mother.

* * * * * * *

Note: At this time in history, almost half of females in Palestine were named Mary. The newborn baby in this chapter was also named Mary. She grows up to be known as Mary of Bethany. Later in life, as a grown woman, she is referred to as Mary Magdalene. In this series, *The Dawn from on High*, Jesus called her by her Hebrew name, *Miriam*.

THE QUMRAN SETTLEMENT

THE NOISE OF BIRDS woke Joseph. Their chattering was a sure sign that spring would follow soon. They were busy singing their songs to each other, alerting, and announcing their new-claimed homes in the bush trees. Joseph looked over to his sleeping almah. "We will have a home also, Mary," but she didn't stir from her sleep. He looked at her brow and tried to gently smooth out its furrow. "You are so troubled," he whispered. "We will go home today. We will live together in the safety of our families. There is nothing of great concern today except God's love for us."

Mary stirred and opened her eyes. She looked over her shoulder and saw Joseph, who sat up and uttered, "Good morning."

"It wasn't a dream? You're here."

"Mary, I'm the one who had a dream . . . remember."

She turned to him, and they embraced. "The birds are sure singing up a storm."

"It's a sign that spring is on the way." Joseph moved away from Mary and stood up and walked to the window. He stretched his arms and body and said, "Mary, we will be going to my home today to live together." He turned to face her, ready to receive her response. Mary stared back at him. "I know it is not according to the rules of our discipline but . . ."

"But what? Why would you not take me to my father's house?"

"Your parents know I came here to take you back to my home to live with me. I know it is out of order but given your circumstance . . . your father doesn't want to let you go back to live in his home until we have celebrated our first marriage ceremony as is the custom of the Essene discipline. But I cannot leave you here to have your baby. Rather, your sister is planning to come here and stay with your aunt and uncle for a while until their baby is born. It will be hard for your aunt, and she will need help because of her age."

Mary remained silent, looking in disbelief at Joseph. Confused, she wondered why her father would treat her this way. And then a terrible thought came into her mind and she blurted out, "Six months ago I took the journey from home to here. It was on that journey that I was raped! Is my father now going to let his next daughter travel here to also be raped! What a stupid man he is! I wouldn't want to go home to him even if he begged me to come home! I hate him!"

Joseph walked quickly from the window to Mary, crouched down, and looked at her as if he could see straight into her soul. "Mary, you don't mean that and you must not think that." After a long gaze into her eyes, she began to cry. Joseph flopped over to sit with his arms over the top of his bent knees. His hands dangled out above his feet. His head fell as if he spoke to the floor. "You are no longer your father's daughter but you will be my wife. After the baby is born you and I will celebrate our first marriage ceremony according to the marital rites of our Essene sect. Together, we will raise your firstborn child." Joseph looked up and over at Mary. "I am taking you to my home today. I will travel the short distance from my home to your father's house and accompany your sister back here. Then I will return home to you. I will not let your sister travel alone through the narrow passages between her home and here, even if it is within the Qumran Settlement's boundaries, and only a distance of two hours traveling time." Mary said nothing. Joseph sighed deeply. "I must tell you something more . . ."

Mary looked at him and waited. He seemed to lose his courage and didn't speak. "What is it? I'm ready to hear." She lied.

"Your father spoke to me, saying he could not have the disgrace of your circumstance in his home . . . You are dead to him . . . Your younger sister now bears your name . . ."

Mary sat frozen, expressionless. Joseph remained next to her in silence until Mary spoke. In a trembling voice she said, "I will travel home with you Joseph . . . I . . . will be your wife. I will learn to love you more as I witness your goodness and strength . . . please bring my sister safely through the passages from our home here to my Aunt Elizabeth." Then Mary took his hand and asked, "And now . . . what is my name . . . what will my name be to you?"

His voice was low and soft and strong when he spoke her name again, "Mary."

BETHANY AND JERUSALEM

Lazarus woke up to the sound of his sister Martha wailing. Aunt Rachael was speaking softly over Martha's cries. He rose from his sleeping mat and intended to walk to his sister's room but he was confronted at the door by his father, Eleazar. Lazarus looked up, and his father seemed as if he were a giant. It reminded Lazarus of the story of young King David, when he slew the giant Goliath. For some reason Lazarus didn't know why he felt unsafe around his father.

"You and Martha will be staying with your Aunt Rachael for a short time . . . long enough for the grief and disruption of your mother's death to settle."

"I want to stay home . . . here."

"Lazarus, it's time for you to be a big boy now. You have no choice, and you need to help your aunt care for all of you. She has a son of her own, and the two of you can help."

"Aunt Rachael has a husband. Won't he help?"

Eleazar seemed irritated with Lazarus when he responded with "Pack clothes that you will need."

"I don't know what I need. Mom always took care of us, our clothes, our food, our . . ." Lazarus was struck with the memory of his mother's voice, the gentle touch of her hands and arms holding him as she helped him eat and dress and get ready for sleep at night. He could almost hear her voice singing a familiar song. Suddenly, he burst into tears and lunged forward, grabbing his father's legs. "Don't send us to another mother! Let us stay with you . . ."

Eleazar tore himself away from Lazarus. He shook him gently but firmly. "Stop it. Stop it right now. Your mother is dead. This is what God willed. You have a new baby sister, and Aunt Rachael needs your help."

"Did God want us to have a new baby?"

"Yes."

"Can't *God* help us with the new baby?"

In a rage fueled by his grief Eleazar slapped Lazarus across the head. "You are not to question God Almighty! Do you understand? Get up, stop crying, and pack your clothes to go to Aunt Rachael's." Eleazar spun around on his heels, placed the prayer shawl on his head, and left the house abruptly.

He walked quickly down the streets of Bethany toward the temple in Jerusalem. He didn't notice anyone or anything as he walked a pace that would take him to his destination in less than ten minutes. He was consumed with guilt and confusion. He knew he should not have impregnated his wife again so quickly after her delivery of their stillborn third child. He justified himself, dismissing this new fourth child's importance and significance. It was a girl. He had no use for another daughter. Martha was enough. The stillborn son, born after Martha, was not what he had prayed for, and that was why he imagined it hadn't lived. It was not aligned with his own will. Surely that is why his third-born child was stillborn. No matter.

Eleazar stopped in his tracks. He looked around, surprised to see the temple and the Jerusalem city wall a stone's throw away. He ran his hand up the other sleeve of his robe to pull the fringes of his phylacteries down. It made him feel important and reminded him of his status as a Pharisee. It would be good to be in the temple with his colleagues. But when he stepped into the temple's sanctuary, he found himself alone.

He called out, "Simeon . . . Nicodemus . . . !" Where were they? After standing motionless for what seemed to Eleazar a long time, he became overwhelmed with guilt and grief again. He couldn't shake the words of the law from the Torah instructing husbands to refrain from sexual intercourse with their wives until after the time of purification. If a male was born, the time of purification was to be seven days and the mother was unclean, not to be touched. No sexual intercourse was to follow for a time lasting thirty-three days. If the newborn was a female, the time of purification was to be fourteen days with no sexual intercourse for sixty-six days.

Eleazar was plagued by the knowledge that he and his beloved wife were the only two people who knew of their engagement in sexual intercourse before the designated time of the law. What tortured his soul was that she was not in agreement with having relations so close after the birth of their stillborn son. His wife had told him she didn't feel well and pleaded with him to be faithful to the law for her sake. He knew the law well . . . there in Leviticus. And now she was dead . . . Leviticus racked his brain and consumed his thought . . . And now he also had another, living, healthy daughter. He suddenly realized that it would not take long for the women to add up the months and know his crime. No! He had to justify his action. He was her husband. He was entitled to his conjugal rights . . . those old busybody women were evil. He was glad they would be out of his house now that the baby was born and its mother dead. The *baby* had killed his wife . . . yes, it was the baby's fault . . . ! In despair, Eleazar raised his hands to cover his face. His breath blew loudly through his fingers, and it seemed to echo in the empty Court of Israel, matching the great beat of his heart. He rended his cloak and fell to his knees. He cried out . . . "Why God? Are you not a God of mercy? Why have you taken my wife from me?" He wept with deep gulps of air. He felt as if he were drowning. "Must I live the rest of my days with this? I *cannot* . . . I *cannot*!" He fell and lay prostrate against the hard, cold stone floor . . . "Oh my God! Help me for I *do not* know where I can find peace . . . I *do not know* where I can find peace . . . !"

* * * * * * *

Note: The next chapter takes place in the home of Elizabeth and Zechariah, the high priest at that time. According to the Gospel of Luke, Mary, pregnant with Jesus, went to their home, which had been located east of Jerusalem in the Judean Desert Hills, most likely within the boundary of the Qumran Settlement of the Essenes. (See map, p. 1.)

THE QUMRAN SETTLEMENT

UNCLE ZECHARIAH PLACED HIS arms around his niece and held her in close embrace for what seemed too long. Mary looked over her Uncle Zechariah's shoulders and saw her Aunt Elizabeth smile back at her. As Mary looked at her aunt, she thought surely Elizabeth was to deliver her firstborn child soon. Even at her young age, Mary knew the baby had dropped in her aunt's womb . . . it was obvious. When her uncle finally let go of his embrace Mary stepped back to see that he was crying and smiling at the same time. She patted her uncle's hand and said, "The baby will be here soon. All will be well, and my sister will be here to help. She will be better help than I anyway," as Mary patted her own round belly.

Uncle Zechariah reached quickly for his slate and clump of clay, writing, "I am content."

"Well, I'm glad he's content. If this baby isn't born soon, I will be in a mood that won't give my husband cheerful contentment."

Zechariah walked close to Elizabeth and stood next to her displaying a broad smile that Mary knew she would be able to recreate in her mind for the rest of her life.

Joseph seemed a bit embarrassed and said, "Come now. There will be time to ogle over babies soon. If I am to get Mary to my home and her sister back here, and then back to my home again, we need to leave now."

Mary stepped forward, out of Joseph's way, as he prepared the burro for the trip, and both she and Elizabeth embraced. Mary jumped back and said, "Did you feel that? The child in your womb must have done another somersault. Even I felt that."

With a dreamy expression Elizabeth said, "It is as when you entered our home three days ago. I'm not surprised. Something very important for us and the world, and the stars, sun, and moon is happening here." Elizabeth clutched Mary's face in her hands. "You are blessed, and so is the fruit of your womb. We have a mighty God. Don't ever forget that, Mary."

Joseph helped Mary onto the burro and turned to Zechariah and Elizabeth. His message was short and genuine. "Thank you."

Slowly the burro began to walk, and Mary was glad the chill in the morning air had lifted somewhat. The sky was a deep blue, promising to be a beautiful day. Joseph walked before the burro, leading it down the narrow dusty path that connected the settlement to Jerusalem. Mary looked back and saw that her aunt and uncle were no longer standing in front of their door. There were other dwellings that dotted the slope beyond her uncle's home. They looked like little white-and-gray bricks under the brilliant reflection of the sun. The land was barren. They passed only small clumps of bushes and every now and then a rare, short, twisted tree that defiantly survived the harsh elements. Mary didn't like the unnatural distance between the sparse vegetation but she was thankful for the shining of the sun and the warmth it gave today.

Mary turned back around to look forward. The path led down toward the familiar red-and-brown hills and cliffs. She wondered again about why her family had chosen to endure the harshness of Essene living. It was too barren and wasn't safe. She felt a nervous feeling rise in her blood. Her heart began to race, and she felt little beads of sweat dampen her forehead. She knew it was because they would have to pass the place where she *did not* want to pass. When she had passed this way alone six months ago, she had spoken of her trepidation to her father, but he had ignored her with a grunt. So, she closed her eyes and forced herself to think of home while she hummed the tune tof a lullaby her mother sang to her as a child. She thought she would do the same today when they came close to the place of her violation. Mary kept her eyes closed tight and hoped their trip to Joseph's home would pass quickly with little anxiety.

Not too far ahead, the path dipped down and narrowed, leaving room for only one burro or horse to pass at a time. Although Mary kept her eyes closed tight, she smelled the dust and felt the coolness of one of the many caves the earth had hollowed out. There had been a violent earthquake in this area years before, and many fallen boulders and sunken pits carved out such hollows that led to dead ends. The smell and the feel of this place revealed to Mary where she was. She raised her hands to cover her face but images flashed in her mind. Her heart beat faster as she relived seeing the handful of Roman soldiers round the path.

"Well look what we've got here."

"Leave her alone, Panthera, she's just a kid."

"In this godforsaken place she looks like a pretty, delicate Jewish flower." Mary remembered they had all laughed, and she had become more frightened because she didn't understand their words. She had only recognized the word "Jewish" and knew they were Roman. The terror visited her as if it were happening again.

"Come here," his voice ordered, and he grabbed her by the wrists. "You're going to like this." He looked around and then let her wrists go. He unfastened his belt. It fell to the ground along with his short sword. He walked to the side of the path and gently laid his standard, a tall pole topped with various insignia and symbols significant to his legion, onto the ground. Mary was terrified but believed she had no chance to escape from these big, strong men. Panthera approached her again, and his sheer size caused her to crumble to the ground. It was clear that Panthera was a proud Roman career soldier, and although he was of Greek descent, he held his position and job as a Roman soldier with unfaltering pride.

This time when he grabbed her wrists, Mary tried to pull away from him but he was strong, and he lifted her up. She began to kick and scream. She lunged at his face with her nails and scratched his cheek. It made him angry when the other soldiers laughed.

"A pretty, delicate, Jewish flower, hey, Panthera"

Panthera threw Mary over his broad shoulder and walked around a boulder to a hollowed-out cave and flung her to the ground. "Now I'll show you how I scratch . . . you little Jewess."

She started to cry in fear. "No, please, no. Don't hurt me . . . don't do this." Mary looked and saw she was trapped, and her cry turned to a terrified whimper. Panthera came close and with no effort held her to the ground and sat on top of her, straddling his legs around her hips. He grabbed her cloak at the neck and tore it open. The little bit of light underclothing Mary wore ripped easily. Panthera paused and took his fill of looking upon her nakedness. Then he took a large remnant from her torn cloak, ripped it into a strip and bound her arms together and held them above her head by her wrists. He placed the remaining remnant over her face to blind her. In an instant she felt the weight of his body and the smell of his sweat as if it would suffocate her. With his own strong legs, he forced her legs open, and Mary felt a sharp pain stab at the center of her body. He jabbed his body into her over and over. All the while she thought to herself that this was not really happening. This was just a terrifying dream. She knew she would wake soon.

Panthera took the blinding remnant of her cloak off her face and grabbed the back of her hair, pulling her head to face his own face. "Look at me! Look at me, you whore! Don't ever forget who rules in this place!" And then he hit her on the side of the head and left her to lie in the hollow, alone.

"Let's get going, Panthera. You had your fun."

Panthera bent down to strap his wide belt to his hip. One of the other soldiers remarked, "It's amazing. You left your sword and standard out here and still got the job done." The other soldiers rolled with laughter.

Panthera lifted his standard and in anger yelled, "Shut up before I ram this down all your throats." He retrieved his sword and placed it in its sheath. They all went on their way in silence while Mary huddled in the small cave, afraid they might return.

From the burro Mary screamed with terror, "Help me! Help me!"

Joseph was next to her in a flash. Mary opened her eyes and didn't perceive Joseph standing next to her. She began to strike out at him, and Joseph caught her before she fell to the ground. "Mary! Mary! It's me. It's me, Joseph." Her arms stopped flailing, and she collapsed into a ball on the ground, weeping. Joseph held her and placed his cloak over and around her to keep her warm. He sat with her on the dusty path for a long time. He sat listening to Mary's cries, and he changed his plans. He decided he wouldn't accompany Mary's sister back to her aunt and uncle's home. That would be her father's responsibility. Joseph decided that when he arrived home with Mary, he would stay there with her all night and visit Joachim the following morning.

Mary lifted her head from the dust of the path. She brushed her hair from her face and looked around in an effort to acclimate herself to the surroundings. She saw the burro off to the side of the path, nibbling on the leaves of a lifeless juniper bush. She turned her gaze to Joseph, who sat by her in silence, and said, "They'll eat anything, won't they?"

Joseph smiled. "They don't know better. All they know is that it's time to eat." Mary displayed a faint smile and leaned forward into Joseph's arms. "Are you all right, Mary?" and he gently stroked the back of her head just as she remembered her Aunt Elizabeth had done when she had fallen into her arms with despair the day before.

"What's happening to me? I feel so scared and confused?"

"I'm here with you now. Don't be afraid. I will do everything I can to keep you safe. You must have remembered something terrible that happened to you when we came around that narrow pass." Joseph looked back. "We're past it now. Are you alright to continue our journey to my home?"

Mary looked up to him and leaned back away from him with a strange expression upon her face. Her tears had left streaks of dust that had dried like muddy little streams down her cheeks. Joseph stood up, reached for the water jug, sat down next to her again, and dampened the corner of the cloak he had wrapped around her.

"Do you know when I first knew I loved you and desired that you would someday be my lifetime partner? You were just four years old." He took the damp part of the cloak and gently wiped the dusty streaks from her face. "I was standing in the doorway looking down into the courtyard of our homes, watching all of you children play in the rain. You were all having fun, and the adults didn't stop your splashing in the puddles. Rain is so rare in the settlement, and they dared not deprive the children of their play." A rumble of thunder echoed through the canyon, and Joseph paused to listen as it tumbled from the top of its distant cracking sound to its deep low vibration. "When the lightning struck and the thunder rolled, all the children ran to their homes and mothers. Not you. At first, you crouched down and tried to clean a stain of mud from your little tunic. But then you jumped up with pure joy and successfully cleaned the stain out by dancing in the rain that fell directly from the sky. I saw your happy beauty and your tenacious attitude. I still see it in you today."

Mary stared at him. He looked at her and said, "I suppose it sounds silly to you . . . but that's when I knew I loved you . . . and I have waited for you. My prayer has been that you will be able to love me also." He looked down and talked as if he were talking to the dust. "Mary, I want to kiss you . . ." and he looked up . . saying, " May I kiss you?"

Mary felt awkward and was still feeling shaken and nervous. Suddenly there was another flash of lightning followed by the clash of thunder that rolled into a lowness of pitch that vibrated within Mary and Joseph.

"It's going to rain," Mary said.

"I don't care, I still want to kiss you . . . may I kiss you?"

And then the rain came. Mary lifted her face up to the sky and felt its cold. She wished it were spring and warmer. She wished the baby was born. She wished she had not been raped. She wished she was married . . . she wished Joseph would kiss her.

As if he had known her thoughts, Joseph tenderly placed both of his hands on the sides of her face and gently pressed his lips to her mouth. He drew back and said, "I love you, Mary. I've loved you for many years. Please find the strength and love for me too. I can't bear to see you lost in sorrow, fear, or despair. I *cannot bear* to live without you."

This time Mary reached around his neck and drew him to another kiss while their bodies shivered together in the cold rain of January.

BETHANY

THE BABY WOULD NOT stop crying. Lazarus and Martha watched from their chairs by the table as their Aunt Rachael tried to feed their baby sister some mashed hummus. Baby Mary spit and gagged as the food was placed into her tiny mouth. Martha and Lazarus could see that the baby couldn't eat the hummus because she was not swallowing. Martha scooted off her chair and gingerly approached her frustrated aunt. "My mommy let me drink milk from her . . . her . . ." and she innocently reached for her Aunt Rachael's breasts. They felt soft and warm.

"No, Martha. You don't understand. Milk is there only when the mommy gives birth to her own baby." The baby screeched with painful hunger. Rachael tried rocking her in her arms and began to cry. "I don't know what to do, little one, I don't know what to do!"

Lazarus' cousin, Levi, aged five, walked into the room and realized the seriousness of his mother's situation. He looked over to Lazarus and asked, "Is Baby Mary going to die?"

Lazarus noticed that his cousin was holding a blown-up bladder of a goat his father had made for him to play with as a ball. He remembered that he and Levi had been playing with it yesterday when Levi would fling it up and the two of them would run to keep it popped up into the air. The game was over if the air-filled bladder touched the ground.

Lazarus grabbed the bladder from Levi, who assumed they would go outside to play. Instead, he asked with an intensity and urgency, "Levi, where is your dad?" Levi stared back at him. "Levi, tell me. Where is your dad?"

"He went to work. He's at the market." Lazarus' uncle, Levi's father worked there every day with Dan, and for some reason, Lazarus had temporarily forgotten this fact.

Lazarus ran out of the house and down the street toward his uncle's market stand. Levi followed close behind, yelling, "Slow down, Lazarus. I can't keep up . . . Where are you going?"

Running down the narrow streets of Bethany, Lazarus remembered exactly where his Uncle Benjamin's market stand was. Why did he waste time asking Levi? He turned the last corner and accelerated down a long, steeply descending street. At the bottom, he ran directly into the arms of his Uncle Benjamin.

"Whoa, whoa, you're going to run into someone. What's your hurry, Lazarus?"

Just then, Levi turned the corner and skidded in the dust to stop but fell anyway. His father couldn't help but laugh to watch his son. He bent down and helped Levi up and began to brush the dust from his clothes.

"Your mother won't be happy to see this dust brought into our house. Now, what's going on here?"

"Uncle Benjamin, the baby is starving!" Lazarus cried with urgency. "Aunt Rachael is trying to feed her but the baby can't swallow. Yesterday I stood over Baby Mary and I touched her cheek with my finger. She turned her head, and her little mouth latched onto my finger, and she sucked like she could suck my blood out. Could you come home and make a bladder like this? You could make a small place shaped like a finger. We could fill the bladder with goat's milk for her to suck and drink!"

In a moment, Benjamin took his apron covering off and yelled back to Dan. "Dan, I'll be going home for a little while. Take care of the market, will you? I'll be back later this afternoon," and with that he and the boys ran up the narrow street toward home.

Dan looked around the corner at their backs, saying to himself, "You're the boss . . . do I have a choice?" Dan shook his head and picked up Benjamin's apron lying on the ground where he had dropped it.

As Lazarus, Levi, and Benjamin entered the house there was an eerie quiet. There was no baby crying. When they walked into the room where Lazarus and Levi had left Rachael holding the baby, Benjamin saw Martha sitting in the corner. She was sitting with her knees tucked tightly against her chest. Her arms were wrapped around her legs, and she was rocking back and forth, back and forth. Benjamin moved to Martha, bent low, and said very gently, "Martha. Martha, where are Aunt Rachael and Baby Mary?"

Martha didn't respond. Then, faintly they all heard the weakened cry of an infant coming from the bedroom. Benjamin stood up quickly, and the boys followed him as he headed toward the sound.

There, they found Rachael sitting with the baby close to her breast. She looked up with tears in her eyes, "I am dry. I have no milk to give her. She's starving before our eyes."

Benjamin instructed the boys to stay with Rachael and the baby. "I'll be right back. Rachael, let the baby suckle at your breast for comfort."

Benjamin disappeared and was gone for what seemed an eternity. When he returned, he held a goat's bladder filled with goat's milk. When he placed it in Rachael's hand, the warmth of the milk permeated through the bladder and felt like her breast. Benjamin turned the bladder over to expose a protrusion that leaked milk from its end.

"Feed her," was all Benjamin said.

As Lazarus, Levi, and Benjamin watched, the baby turned her head and latched onto the protrusion with her tiny mouth. She knew exactly what to do. She was not strong but she sucked with a power that squirted milk into her mouth and over her tiny face. Little sounds of gulps assured her aunt that she was swallowing the milk. And then Rachael cried. "What made you think of this, Benjamin?"

"I didn't. Her big brother Lazarus thought of it."

Lazarus beamed for a moment and then remembered Martha. He ran to where she sat in the corner. "Martha! Martha! Don't be sad. Baby Mary is going to live! She's eating right now! You ought to come and see. She's going to be fat." He grabbed her hand and led her to the room where their Aunt Rachael held their new baby sister, Mary, whose little mouth was filled with milk.

Martha stroked Mary's head. "Mary. You found a way to eat." She turned and jumped into the air and laughed. Levi grabbed ahold of his father's hands and skipped in a circle. Lazarus grabbed Martha's hands and joined his uncle and cousin's dance, circling round and round while Rachael looked on in peace.

JOSEPH'S HOME IN THE QUMRAN SETTLEMENT

Joseph was worried. They had been traveling wet and cold for over two hours. He was mostly concerned about Mary. As he continued walking, he looked back at her, and she smiled. "Don't worry," she said. "I am not cold."

He also was not cold, although the elements would not dictate this, yet he felt a warm wave that sprang from his loins and surged to his heart. After all that Mary had suffered, he continued to believe that Mary could come to love him as her husband. How unbelievable it was for him to realize that he was taking Mary to his home to be his wife.

Finally, he could see the cluster of homes that was their village. Mary's father's home was a ten-minute walk from his home, and Joseph was glad that his home was the closer of the two. He was also glad they would not pass Mary's father Joachim's home. Joseph couldn't understand his soon-to-be father-in-law. Although Joachim was a simple farmer and an ethical man of God, Joseph felt he possessed a pride that would not bend for love. He recalled the night he had gone to talk to Joachim about his daughter Mary's circumstance just two nights before.

"She was raped," he had said to Joachim. "Don't you understand? That was not her fault, or choice, yet you are rejecting your daughter as if she were the perpetrator of this violent crime."

That night Joachim had looked at Joseph with a stone face that *did not* change, saying, "She must have done something which brought this upon her. God is a just God, and we *cannot* see into the hearts of even our children."

"Do you know what I think brought this upon her? Living here! We are not governed by a just God! We are governed by Rome. And now you have abandoned your daughter in her greatest time of need."

Joachim had turned his gaze to Joseph. "Joseph, you are a just and good man. What will you do? Stay betrothed to my daughter or seek another almah?"

Joachim's words had cut into Joseph like a sharp knife. He had become ashamed and felt a deep loss. He knew he had already decided to quietly dismiss Mary from their betrothal, and yet his heart couldn't align with his thoughts. He had looked back at Joachim and had said in shame, "You know what I have decided."

"Yes, I know. My daughter Mary is dead to me also. I *cannot* allow the disgrace of her rape to dwell in my home. Let her be dead to you also, Joseph. You can't allow the disgrace of her rape to dwell in your marriage either. And yet you argue with me. Mary's younger sister now bears the name *Mary*." Joachim had stood up from the table, and his large dark shadow had seemed to cast a cold, deadly grip upon Joseph. "Good night, Joseph."

Joseph had risen from his place in Joachim's home and walked out into the cold air that night. He felt a deep ache, missing his adoptive mother and father who had died before he was seventeen years old. He had no brothers or sisters, and his aloneness was caving in on him. The night sky hadn't mirrored his emotion. Instead, it had shined with the light of a million stars. It had been a new moon that night, so there had been no reflective light to dim the brilliance of the stars. In a very strange way, it had seemed to comfort him somewhat. He remembered an owl had hooted. It continued to hoot and had sounded as if it were always just behind him as he walked the short distance to his own home.

When he had stepped into his home that night, it was as he had left it, and yet he felt as if something had changed within him. He had walked to the oil lamp on his table and lit it with a smoldering ember from glowing pieces of wood in the fireplace. He had let the lamp's light guide him to his sleeping mat in the next room. He had sat on the mat, placed the lamp down, and pulled the blanket over his shoulders. He had sat still for a short while, lowered his head, and wept. He had felt so alone. He had felt forsaken, even by God. He couldn't keep his tears from falling to the floor. They had made perfect little circles where they fell on the floor in the dust. He wondered why he had even noticed the circles at that time.

Suddenly, the flame in the lamp had grown and filled the room with great brightness. Just as suddenly, it had diminished its light to a very small flicker, almost extinguishing the flame, and then back to its original glow. Joseph remembered he had stopped crying and looked at the lamp. After sitting still, looking at the flickering lamp for a long time, he had lain his head down to the mat and fallen asleep.

He had dreamed. It was a glorious dream. He had dreamed a man stood next to him dressed in a dazzling white robe. The man had a gentle, soft voice. He spoke his name. "Joseph, you are not to dismiss Mary from your betrothal. All decisions in life are directed by God to be made from the guidance of wisdom and love. Justice will kiss goodness and mercy. The child in Mary's womb is a boy, and his name shall be called Jesus, Emmanuel, for God is, and has been, with you, Mary, and all of creation for all time."

The next morning Joseph had awakened with a start. There seemed to have been no passage of time from the dream to the morning light. Looking out the window he had realized by the rise of the sun it was not morning. It was noon! How could he have slept so long? He had risen from his mat and packed the burro with water and food for a short journey. He had decided to go to Elizabeth and Zechariah's to bring Mary home with him. But first he had gone back to Joachim's door and shouted for Joachim to come out. Joachim had appeared at the door and looked at Joseph with a puzzled look, saying, "Where do you think you're going?"

"I'm going to get Mary and bring her home to be my wife," Joseph had declared with certainty.

Joachim's wife, Anna, had stepped from behind and pleaded, "But what of my sister Elizabeth? She needs someone to help her in her time of delivery and care of a newborn."

"We will decide that upon my return home with Mary. Mary is also pregnant, and young. She should not be caring for another pregnant woman at this time." Joseph found it hard to believe they could abandon their daughter so easily. "She needs to be cared for herself."

"You're a fool!" Joachim had waved his hand at Joseph in a gesture that indicated that he should go.

As Joseph recalled his possible future father-in-law's behavior, he continued to lead the burro forward and headed up the path. He remembered that at the time, he had anxiously anticipated seeing Mary, but in his excitement, he had misjudged the time of day, and he had left for Elizabeth and Zechariah's home late in the evening, not arriving until darkness had come. He had thought that maybe he *was* a fool.

Joseph looked back at Mary again, riding on the burro. It had been a cold, rainy trip, and she looked tired. "It won't be long now," he said cheerfully. "We'll be home soon, and I'll build a fire to warm you."

Mary closed her eyes and let Joseph lead the burro the last bit of the way. The rocking motion stopped as the burro halted and brayed, and Mary opened her eyes as Joseph was reaching up to help her down. As he guided her off the burro, he grabbed her sopping wet bundle of clothes and turned to lead her into his home.

"Joseph, please take the rest of the water in my jug from the burro. Even though it's raining, I'm so thirsty."

"No need," Joseph said, and he led her into his home to a room with a table and chairs. Joseph lit the oil lamp. Mary could see that the room was used for preparing food and eating. A large piece of cloth hung on one of the walls, almost covering its height and width. The colors were bright and gave the room a very cozy feeling. Joseph stepped over to a large, carved-out wooden basin. He took a wooden goblet from a shelf above and reached over to a tubelike implement hanging over the wooden basin. Mary could see it was made from animal skin and appeared to be hand stitched together. Joseph released a clamp from the tube, and water flowed from the tube into the wooden goblet. He replaced the clamp on the water tube and turned to give Mary a drink.

The water was cold and clean. She drank her fill and slowly handed the goblet back to Joseph. She questioned him with her expression. "It's no trick," Joseph responded. "Didn't you know this village is built on an underground stream? That's why there are more trees in our courtyards. The others dug wells to draw water when they needed it. I thought it would be easier to draw it up from the underground stream directly into this wooden basin. There is a hole with a clay plug underneath, and if there is water that needs to be drained, I rigged it to let the water drain out into the garden."

Mary looked under the basin and saw the same tubing run down and out through the wall. She stood up and stared at him blankly. "That's clever, Joseph."

"Thank you."

"But how does the water come up from the underground stream?"

"Mary, it's been a long day. You're wet and tired. Come to my sleeping room, and I will give you some dry clothing. They may not fit you well but you must get dry."

Joseph took her into his sleeping room, and it, too, had beautiful woven spreads hanging on the wall. In the corner of the room was a fire pit that jutted out with an opening above to release smoke. Joseph walked over to a large wooden storage that had two doors on the front. He opened the doors and pulled out a garment and a shawl. Giving them to Mary, he shyly said, "Remove all your wet clothing. Do not place these garments over any wet or damp underclothing. I will prepare food for us and start the fire in the other room." He handed her his dry garment and told her to wrap the shawl around her as tight as she needed to feel warmer.

Mary stood for a moment, not sure she was where she was. Then she stripped and placed the garment over her head and let it fall to the floor. It was certainly too long but when she tied the shawl around her waist and pulled the garment up over it, to avoid tripping on the hem, she imagined it was an elegant, flowing gown. With the remainder of the shawl, she draped it over her shoulders and back around her arms.

She walked into the room where Joseph had just stoked the fire to a warm, soft glow and asked, "How do I look?" She spread her arms out and twirled around slowly.

Joseph stood up and whispered, "More beautiful than I could have imagined."

"What?"

"Never mind," he said. "Come here and sit down to eat."

Mary walked to the table and felt instantly famished. She sat and began to eat the hummus, lamb, raisins, and figs that Joseph placed out for her to eat.

Joseph stood close to the door and said, "Uh . . . I'm going to unpack the burro and place him in his stall to be fed and watered. I'll be right back. Then I'll get into some dry clothes myself and join you to eat."

Mary stopped eating suddenly. She looked at Joseph and said, "But what about my sister. Weren't you going to take her back to Aunt Elizabeth?"

Joseph stood still by the door, and they both listened to the driving rain against the roof made of sticks, dried mud, and hay. Finally, Joseph broke their silence and said, "No, Mary. I'm staying here with you. Your sister is your father's responsibility, not mine. I'll run to his house and inform him and appeal to his duty as your sister's protector and guardian. I believe he will also realize his responsibility as I have realized mine to you." Joseph turned and went out into the rain as Mary sat alone, staring at the fire that grew into a roaring, warm blaze.

THE HOME OF BENJAMIN AND RACHAEL IN BETHANY

RACHAEL SAT WITH MARY nuzzled against her breast suckling. Benjamin had encouraged her to sit with the baby like this because it seemed to comfort both of them. But she had never dreamed she would actually let down milk for her little niece. It was not until she began to relax, no longer riddled with stress, that she began to be able to nurse little Baby Mary. Who would have thought this could be true. And yet there lay her sister's baby, in her own arms, filling up with nutritional milk from her own breast.

Rachael stared forward blankly and thought of her sister. She ached for her company, her laughter, and wisdom. Her life had been too short. Her eldest child, Lazarus, was such a kind and sweet child. Her daughter, Martha, was a dedicated child who already displayed personality traits that would most likely develop into conscientious service and work for others. Rachael looked down at the baby in her arms, saying softly, "And you, little Mary. Who will you grow to be? Will you fall in love with your husband? Will you have children? Will you live to see great-grandchildren, or maybe even great-great-grandchildren? Will you choose to live here with your father, and brother, and sister? Or will you live in faraway lands across the sea?"

As Rachael pondered upon these thoughts, she noticed Benjamin leaning against the doorframe looking at her. He was smiling. Rachael smiled back and said, "What?"

"You just love babies, don't you? Maybe we should think about making a brother or sister for Levi. You are a wonderful woman, and I love that you love your sister's children as you do, despite your feelings toward her husband, Eleazar."

"Now, Benjamin. We must remember that we are blessed beyond our wildest dreams. We have love, Benjamin. You and I have loved each other since we were children, and then God allowed us to realize our love in marriage. My sister had no interest in marriage, especially to Eleazar. But she was a faithful wife and a wonderful mother."

Benjamin walked to Rachael and sat on the bed mat next to her. He kissed her on the cheek and bent low to kiss the baby in her arms. "She may have been a faithful wife but Eleazar was not a faithful husband. I believe it's because of him that she's dead . . ."

Rachael raised her hand and gently placed it over her husband's mouth. Then she drew her hand away and said, "No, please. We have enough tragedy now. I love my sister, and I miss her so much. I am happy to have her children with us, and I believe she must be aware that great things are yet to happen for all of us. It seems odd though. I feel there is something very special about this baby in my arms." Rachael looked down at the baby and then looked back at Benjamin. She gazed into his eyes as if she could drink his soul in and whispered, "I love you, Benjamin. God has truly blessed my life through you."

Benjamin blushed and was about to say, "I love you too," when Levi ran into the room with Lazarus right behind him.

"What's wrong with you, Dad?" Levi asked. "Your face looks all red."

"There is nothing wrong, Levi. Did you children finish eating?"

Martha came trotting into the room all out of breath. "The boys run too fast, and they never wait for me. Lazarus found a little lizard under the table, and he's using it to scare Levi."

"Is he scaring you with it too, Martha?"

"No, Uncle Benjamin. He can't do that to me."

"Why not?"

"Because I'm not scared of lizards." Martha turned to Lazarus and took the lizard and walked out of the room, saying, "Come on, Levi, I'll take care of you." Levi obeyed and walked past Lazarus with his chest puffed out.

Lazarus approached his aunt and uncle and sat down close to peek at his baby sister, Mary. He looked up at his uncle and asked, "Do you think the baby will live now?"

"There is no question about it. Your baby sister will live."

Lazarus sat still, thinking, and then asked, "Does that mean we will all go home to live with my father?"

Benjamin looked at Rachael and then back at Lazarus. "Do you want to go back to live with your father?"

Lazarus contemplated his uncle's question. He missed his mother and couldn't imagine life in their home without her presence or care. But he loved his father and was very worried about him. He remembered seeing his father the night his mother died, sitting alone at the table with the low, flickering light coming from the lamp. He remembered feeling scared when he saw that his father was crying. He had gone to sleep that night knowing that he could do nothing for his father but love and respect him. He was so happy to be with his Uncle Benjamin and Aunt Rachael, yet he felt drawn to be at home for his father. Suddenly, Lazarus realized that both his aunt and uncle were waiting for an answer to their question. "I want to be home *for* my father. I'm not sure I want to be *with* my father. He seemed so upset and angry when I saw him last. I hope he's feeling better."

Rachael lifted the baby and placed her into Lazarus' arms. The baby was asleep and didn't stir. Lazarus looked down at his baby sister and felt happy. He smiled and touched her little face. "You know, Lazarus, you will have great responsibility in your home with only a father and no mother. But I have watched you these past couple of days and I believe you will be a very good brother to Martha and now Mary. There may be times you will feel sad and unable to do what is required but I also want you to know that I will be close by with your uncle to help you. Even more importantly, God will help and guide you through. Can you remember that?"

All Lazarus could speak was a sobering "Yes, I can and I will."

JOSEPH'S HOME IN THE QUMRAN SETTLEMENT

"Wake up! Mary, wake up!"

It was her mother Anne shouting at Joseph's front door. Mary awoke with a start and ran through the dusty halls to the front door of Joseph's and now her home. She was alarmed and disoriented, having been awakened so abruptly. She wondered where Joseph was and then saw that he had risen to her mother's cries, making it to the front door before her.

"Mary, Mary . . . ! Elizabeth has given birth. She gave birth to a healthy little boy! They plan to come this way together on their way to Jerusalem and the temple for the baby's circumcision."

Joseph stepped aside and said, "Please come into the house and sit down. Tell us everything you know."

Anne stepped into the house and noticed how Joseph tenderly placed his arm around Mary and helped her sit into a chair. He lifted the shawl she had grabbed before running to the front door and pulled it gently around Mary's shoulders and over her back. Anne thought to herself, "He loves her. Joseph really loves her. How can this be?"

"Well," Joseph said. "Tell us about this new baby boy."

Anne sat and began to talk in her excited way. "Your sister reported that Elizabeth had some trouble during the labor but the baby was born, and she is doing fine. The other women were there, and they helped turn the baby before he came out because he was not coming out with his head turned to the ground. His head came out looking straight up to the sky. So, one of the midwives placed her hands in and grabbed the baby's shoulders and turned him completely around. They are learning so much these days. Things they never knew to do when I gave birth. But God was good to me. I never lost one of the seven I birthed. Your brother, Issachar, was the most difficult of the births. He was such a big baby boy, and he was born breech no less."

Joseph looked at Mary and suddenly felt worried wondering about her time for childbirth. He looked at her and thought, "You're too young. What will I do if this baby takes your life in delivery? Why must new birth be so hard and life-threatening to the mother? Is that part of your great almighty plan too, God?"

Mary's voice brought both Joseph and Anne back to the situation at hand. "Mother, please. I'm glad all seven of your babies survived, along with you, but what of Aunt Elizabeth and her baby?"

"Oh, yes . . . well, your sister said that after the baby was turned in the womb, he was birthed quickly. They cleaned the baby off, and your Uncle Zechariah took the baby from the midwife's hands and brought him outside. He raised him up and many of the neighbors, who were gathered in front of the house, rejoiced, and said, 'Blessed be God on high, for Zechariah, son of Elizabeth and Zechariah is born. Well then, Zechariah spoke for the first time since his wife conceived, and you'll never guess what he said! He said, 'No! My son's name is John!' John! Imagine that? I don't understand Zechariah, especially since Elizabeth's pregnancy. Anyway, Elizabeth will be here in five days to share a meal and a night with us." Suddenly, Anne became subdued and sad. "Mary, you cannot come to our home to share the meal with Elizabeth, Zechariah, and the baby." Mary was puzzled. "Your father will not allow you to pass into our home . . . I know Elizabeth and Zechariah will come to see you here, in Joseph's house."

Before Mary could respond, Joseph stood up, pounding the table as he rose. "You should say 'Mary and Joseph's home. Anne, do you also agree with your husband, Joachim?"

"He is my husband. I must abide by his decisions."

"Do you really believe that?! Your daughter was raped and now must birth a child while you and Joachim treat her like a rag, tossed aside! You yourself spoke of life-threatening dangers during childbirth! Are you telling us that you agree with your husband?"

Anne was silent. In anger Joseph blurted out, "This is unjust, harsh treatment, beyond my understanding!"

Tears filled Anne's eyes. "What can I do? I still have children to care for and rear. I can't do it without a husband or without the support of our village."

"No . . . but you have abandoned your daughter and don't give a thought as to how she will survive and rear her child! Do I not speak the truth?"

"Joseph, please don't be so harsh . . ."

"Don't be so harsh, don't be so harsh?!" Joseph shoved his chair away from the table and across the floor. He walked around to Anne. He held her by the shoulders and looked at her squarely. "You and your husband are life partners. You are part of the Essene Jewish sect that holds marriage sacred. Your marriage is of God. Or am I not seeing your calling correctly? You don't seem to hold your love for Joachim with a sacredness that recognizes the blessed gift of life from God in your daughter. Joachim's mind seems possessed by another ethic apart from our God. You are his wife. You must help him see what he is doing here. Or do you not see what he is doing to your own child?"

Joseph released her shoulders, and her head and arms fell to the table in sorrow. She sobbed in a way Mary had never witnessed her mother sob before. "You don't understand, Joseph."

"I think I do. When it is time for Mary to have her baby there will be no midwives to help her. Will there, Anne? There will be no parents or family to support her. Isn't that it?"

"Mother, surely the women will help me have this baby when my time comes? Mother, won't they help me?"

Anne raised her head and said, "No . . . no . . . Joseph is correct." Anne took a deep breath and didn't stop crying as she said, "You must understand, your father, your brothers and sister, and the whole village will not . . . and cannot believe you were raped. They don't believe your story about the wind in the fig tree grove either. They believe you met someone and allowed him to make love with you somewhere in the country. Since we are a family of good Essene standing, they have chosen to let you live and have not stoned you for your deed."

Mary sat in total disbelief. She looked aside and whispered, "Oh my dear God. How can this be?"

Joseph walked to the window and pounded his fist on its sill. "I can't believe this. I just can't believe this. Anne, you are her mother. How can you let this happen? You've got to do something to help your daughter. You've just got to do something!"

Anne stood up very slowly. She didn't take her eyes off her folded hands. She walked to the door to go home but stopped, turning slowly to look at Mary, saying, "My beautiful daughter, I'm so sorry we could not give you a better world. This is your life now. Be a good wife to Joseph . . . for as long as you both shall live. If it means anything to you, or Joseph, I want you to know that . . . I believe you . . . and . . . I love you. I have always loved you. My prayer is that God will be with you now, and forever. As a young woman myself, I remember that our mother said God would always provide in our times of need." She turned to Joseph and said, "Thank you for loving my daughter. God will provide." Anne walked out into the courtyard and down the path toward Joachim's house. She felt dead inside and lifted a prayer that God would also provide what she needed, even though she didn't know what it was she needed. She thought, "How will I ever be forgiven. Who must I ask for forgiveness? Is there hope for my marriage and living with Joachim?" She stopped walking. A sudden, strong breeze blew the trees overhead. As the wind moved the branches, making noise similar to the sound of waves hitting the shore when a storm moves off the sea onto the land, she closed her eyes tightly. She longed for waves, rolling waves that could wash away her hateful thoughts but deep inside, she *could not* deny that in that moment, she despised and loathed her husband.

ELEAZER VISITS BENJAMIN AND RACHAEL IN BETHANY

"I DELIBERATELY CAME KNOWING the children would be asleep." Benjamin stepped aside with the intention of allowing Eleazar into the house. "May I come in?" Eleazar asked. Benjamin gestured for him to enter.

From the joining hallway Rachael walked into the anteroom, addressing Benjamin. "Who's here at this late hour, Benjamin?"

"It's Eleazar."

Rachael paused and waited for Eleazar to speak. Before he spoke, he took a little sack out from under his cloak and placed it on the table in front of Rachael. When it hit the wooden table's surface its sound identified its content.

"There are ten pieces of silver there for you, Benjamin. I appreciate all you've done for the children and me."

"I did it because I loved my sister and I love her children. I don't want payment from you, Eleazar."

"Take the money . . . please." It was hard for Eleazar to encourage Rachael because he possessed no true graciousness. "I have also come to inform you that I plan to take Lazarus home to live with me before the next Sabbath. I'll be here to collect him on the sixth day's afternoon (Friday). So, please have his clothes gathered and have him ready to go."

Rachael stepped forward and sat in a chair by the table while Benjamin stood by the door. Benjamin's expression revealed his disapproval of Eleazar's commands. Rachael sighed and looked at Eleazar, saying, "And what of Martha and Mary? Are you telling me that they are to stay under our care?"

Even Eleazar realized his presumptuous blunder and awkwardly said, "Um . . . forgive me. I cannot take care of Martha and a baby also. I would greatly appreciate your further service in the care of these children until I can make other arrangements."

Benjamin stepped forward and said, "And what are your plans to care for Lazarus? He certainly can't stay in your house alone all day while you are at the temple."

"Lazarus will come with me to the temple every day to begin his studies to be a rabbi. He already knows how to read and he can begin to study the Torah."

Rachael, Benjamin, and Eleazar stood still and silent for what seemed a long time until Rachael stood and sadly stated, "Well then, I will have Lazarus ready to go with you this . . . this seventh-day Sabbath." She walked toward the hallway that led to their bedroom, stopped, and without turning to face Eleazar said, "I hope you understand the importance and need for love in your children's lives. Love from you, Eleazar. As for me, I shall miss Lazarus. He is a wonderful child and son." Rachael walked down the hallway and her tears were overflowing before she reached the entrance to her bedroom.

Eleazar walked to the front door to leave, and Benjamin stepped aside to let him pass. "The peace of the Lord be with you, Eleazar."

Eleazar mumbled a response that Benjamin didn't understand, but he didn't care either.

ROME

Panthera awoke from another restless night. Sleep no longer graced his life. As his eyes opened, he heard the sickening sound of rain hitting the roof of their barrack. He should have been thankful to be at the barracks back in Rome instead of in the usual tent camp he lived in while they occupied whatever territory to which his legion was assigned. This night he could not shake the terrible memory. The memory would visit him in night terrors or flashes in the middle of any given waking moment. They were always images of a trauma he had experienced at the age of four. The event emerged from his memory, terrifying him now as strongly as when he was a child. Years ago, when Panthera was a little child, he had lived together with his father, mother, and baby brother on the rocky eastern shore of the Aegean Sea in Greece. He remembered it as a peaceful, happy time, save for the fact that his father was often absent for days while hunting the pelican.

At that time, rogue Persian soldiers wandered the vast domain of what used to be the Persian Empire. Rome had since successfully established its expanding empire and controlled most of the territory in Greece after the Persian Empire finally crumbled. The final blow came when the Roman commander Pompey defeated King Aristobulus, whose army had retreated taking a stand in Jerusalem. King Aristobulus and his skeleton army attempted, and failed, in one last surge to push Commander Pompey back into what had been part of former Persia. It marked the official end to the existence of the once-great Persian Empire and when it fell, soldiers from the Persian army scattered like treacherous rodents across the land with no place to go and no place to call home. Many wandered for decades. Some crossed the Aegean Sea and fled into the wilderness of Greece. One such Persian soldier found his way to Panthera's childhood home.

Panthera kept his eyes closed as the rain continued to beat down on the roof above. The images of that terrifying day haunted and possessed his mind. He remembered the pounding of the Persian's fist on the door of their home. His mother had pulled him from his frightened, frozen stance in the middle of the room while his little brother screamed in fear. She shoved Panthera into the corner of a small cupboard next to the wall.

He remembered that his mother's voice captured an extreme desperation as she said, "Panthera, not a sound may come from you! Do you understand?! Not a sound, no matter what happens!" She closed the cupboard doors but Panthera could see through the crack of its opening.

The Persian soldier burst the door of their home open, brandishing a sword. His mother snatched up his little brother, who was still screaming. She spoke with great fear in her voice as she said, "There's nothing you want here! Please, please! Don't hurt my child!"

The soldier tore his little brother from his mother's arms and without hesitation ran his sword into the baby's chest. The sound of his mother's scream could not be silenced in his conscious and unconscious mind to this day. He watched as the soldier threw his bloodied brother to the floor and stabbed him again because he cried out and was not completely dead. In terror, young Panthera continued to stare through the crack of the cupboard door as the soldier grabbed his mother and threw her to the floor next to her dead baby boy.

The soldier sneered and said, "Look at your baby one last time." Panthera's mother released a terrified whimper and the Persian soldier fell on top of her. In his own terror, Panthera didn't understand what the soldier was doing to his mother. The soldier stood up. Panthera saw that his mother's clothing was lifted completely around her neck and she was lying like a naked, dead woman. The soldier lifted his sword above his mother and plunged it down into her heart. When he pulled the sword out Panthera saw the bright red fountain of blood pulsing from his mother's chest. He heard a gurgling sound and thought that maybe his mother was still alive and that the soldier would go away.

Instead, the soldier walked to the cupboard. Panthera crouched back further into the corner but he could see the soldier's legs and sandaled feet. The soldier opened the top doors of the cupboard and grabbed bread and fruit from inside. He turned, stepped over the lifeless bodies of Panthera's mother and brother, and left.

Panthera did not move for many hours. He cried for his mother and brother and called for his father. When his father didn't come, he slumped into a ball and fell asleep.

His father's cry awakened him. "Oh, my God! Oh, my God!" Panthera jumped out from his hiding place and ran to his father, who stood dazed in the middle of the dwelling among the horrifying carnage.

"Daddy! Daddy!" He began to punch his father's legs over and over again. "Daddy!" He screamed a high-pitched scream that finally turned his father's dazed stare down to him.

Panthera remembered that his father had lifted him up and had carried him away from his dead mother, brother, and the only home he had ever known. From that time on, he knew his father to be only a ghost of a man. Panthera's father died in despair and bitterness, only months after Panthera turned sixteen years old and left Greece to join the Roman army. Now, at twenty-three years of age, he felt as if life held nothing more than marching and building, building and marching. Every now and then there was killing.

All Roman army recruits were required to serve for at least twenty-five years. He had served in the Roman army for seven years and he felt more despair when he realized he must endure eighteen more years of army life.

The rain had not stopped. He rose from his platform bed of straw and looked back at the crude wool blanket shoved into a ball at its foot. "No wonder I felt miserably cold," he thought. He walked past the other beds lining the long room of their barrack. Trying not to hear the disgusting snores of his "comrades," he walked to the window at the end of the narrow, large room that he and twenty-seven other Roman soldiers called their temporary home. The window had wooden shutters and he could hear the wind whistle through its wide crack. He couldn't bear to hear the wind so he unlatched the shutters and swung them open.

The gray gloom of the first early morning light matched the sick feeling he felt in the pit of his stomach. His head ached and his back felt as if it could not support his body for long. He leaned his weight onto his forearms against the windowsill and felt the cool dampness of the rain water against his skin. He remembered what the Persian soldier had done to his family and he was horrified that he had done the same. He closed his eyes and saw the face of the Jewish girl he raped. He tried to comfort himself with the thought that he hadn't killed her. He could have, but he didn't. "Does that matter?" he wondered.

Panthera hated everything about his life. He hated the regimen of a soldier's existence. He hated the food he ate. He hated the places he traveled only to return to this place that he despised. He hated his patrolling the roads and towns of Judea. He hated having no real friends. Most of all he hated himself.

Today they all would receive their new orders, and if he knew how to pray, or who to pray to, he would beg for mercy. He couldn't bear to be assigned to Judea again. Ever since he had raped that girl, while on tour in the Qumran Settlement, he had not been the same. Mary . . . yes . . . he knew her name and he knew who she was, his comrades made sure of that. They praised him for doing what Rome required. In the endeavor to remain dominant and powerful, he and all Roman legionaries his age were encouraged to rape local young women. In Judea the young Roman soldiers were ordered to rape young almahs, or betrothed young women to Jewish men, for the purpose of biologically fathering "Roman" children and thereby disrupting the cultural practices of the area they had conquered. Rome used this violent action to ethnically infiltrate their culture and presence. Judea was a particular target for this practice because the Jews in that province were always showing defiance, causing unnecessary trouble for Rome.

Panthera dropped his head into his hands. The rain sprinkled onto the top of his head and he shivered as the cold water ran down his neck, splitting and trickling over his shoulders to drip onto the hard stone windowsill. It had been over six months ago and yet he was haunted by her face and the image of her young naked body. "Oh God!" He raised his head and looked out into the gray gloom. He shook his head to rid his hair of the cold water but he felt no better. He spoke out loud again, "Dear God! Where are you? Who are you? Where can I find peace?" He cried as he wondered about the young girl, Mary. Did she know he was not a monster? How could she know he was not a monster when he himself did not know? He wished he didn't know her name. He wished he didn't know the place of her dwelling. He wished he had not been so stupid. What could he have been thinking when he had decided to rape her on that godforsaken day in that godforsaken place? Worst of all, his crime had been witnessed by other soldiers. His particular unit consisted of twenty-eight men and although not all twenty-eight soldiers were direct witnesses of his action, they all knew and spoke of it privately, among themselves. Were they proud of him? Was he becoming a true Roman soldier? No. In his mind they all seemed to look at him accusingly. He was guilty of atrocity.

"Panthera. What are you doing standing here next to the open window? Can't you feel the cold rain blowing in?" It was Jarius, irritated that Panthera disturbed his sleep by opening the shutters this early morning hour. Jarius pushed Panthera away from the window. He reached out and grabbed the wooden shutters and pulled them shut. He gave Panthera a dirty look and then realized that Panthera was not well. He was pale, his eyes were glassy, and he clutched his arms around his chest. When Panthera leaned back against the wall and slid down to his haunches near the floor, Jarius squatted down to Panthera's level. "What's the matter, Panthera? Are you sick? Come, I'll help you to the infirmary. They'll give you something hot to drink and you'll feel better." Jarius looked up at the light that shined through the crack between the closed shutters. He guessed that it was early morning, sometime before the sixth hour. The other soldiers continued to sleep, uninterrupted by Panthera's suffering. Jarius reached for Panthera and helped him up to his feet.

Panthera pushed Jarius away, leaned against the wall and said with fear in his voice, "No. Leave me alone." He staggered to the door, rammed it open to walk out into the rain and wind. Jarius watched from inside as Panthera fell to his knees in the narrow cobblestoned street between the barracks. It did not take long for the cold rain to completely drench him. It may have been delirium, but for Panthera, the rain felt like it washed something away and he embraced the cold that numbed him.

Jarius stood inside the door and didn't know what to do. He decided to try again. He went out into the rain and once again tried to lift Panthera to his feet. As Jarius placed Panthera's arm around his neck and over his shoulder to lift him up, Panthera wrapped his other arm around Jarius' neck. He began to weep on Jarius' shoulder. "I don't know why I do what I do! I'm a soldier. It's my duty and honor to fight, protect, and . . . and . . . obey the leadership of this, this," he raised his face to the gray sky, "this great, glorious, all-powerful Roman . . . state. What a glorious state . . . !"

Jarius used all his strength to lift Panthera to his feet. "Come and lie down, my friend. You have an hour yet to rest. Then we will all go and accept our new assignments." Jarius began to walk Panthera back inside. He could feel Panthera shiver and quiver with subdued sobs. "You are a soldier, and a good soldier. Now walk with me, back to your bed." This time Panthera let Jarius lead him to his bed. He also allowed Jarius to help him lie down and cover him with the wool blanket. The wind whistled and howled as it blew through the cracks of the closed door and shutters. Jarius looked at Panthera and felt glad that his comrade's eyes had closed before he walked to his own bed and although he tried, he couldn't sleep any longer because the wind made too much noise.

THE QUMRAN SETTLEMENT

"OH, ELIZABETH! ZECHARIAH! LET us see this little one named John!" Anne had been watching for their arrival from the front of her house. As soon as she saw them on the path, she ran to greet them. Elizabeth was riding on the burro and Zechariah was walking with his walking stick in one hand and a tiny baby in the other. As soon as Anne saw the baby in Zechariah's arms, she took him into her own arms and led the way back to her house. Elizabeth was helped by Zechariah down from the burro and all entered into the house that had a table set to share a banquet. Anne's children ran up to see their new cousin and they laughed and giggled, as Zechariah and Elizabeth looked on with pride.

"Anne, I never dreamed I'd be a mother. It is more wonderful than anything I could have imagined."

Anne replied with a sobering voice, "Oh . . . Just you wait, it gets better but it also gets worse."

Zechariah sat on the nearest chair. "And where is Joachim?"

Anne's cheerfulness diminished as she replied in a matter-of-fact tone. "He's in the field, harvesting what little winter wheat is left to use for bread."

Elizabeth walked to Anne while the children continued to fuss over the baby. Elizabeth took Baby John from Anne's arms and turned to Anne's son Issachar. "Do you think you're big enough to hold a baby very carefully?"

An enthusiastic yes followed and Elizabeth handed the baby to Issachar. "You and the other children may take the baby outside to show him to your father in the field."

As the children headed out the door, Anne yelled after them, "Tell your father to come home and prepare for our meal."

"Anne, something is wrong. Are you and Joachim having problems?"

"I have lost my love for him. We don't really talk, unless it is absolutely necessary . . . I've lost my love for him because he has lost his love for our daughter. He has disowned her. He and this whole village have disowned her because of her pregnancy." Anne's eyes glassed over with tears. "I know my daughter. She wouldn't ever have made love with another man! She accepted her betrothal to Joseph."

Zechariah spoke up and asked, "Where is Mary now?"

"Joseph believes she was raped. He speaks of having a dream that he was told not to dismiss Mary quietly from their betrothal. Joseph has taken her into his home and plans to celebrate their first and second marriage some time after the baby is born. People in the village turn their eyes from my daughter and Joseph. Even if Joseph and Mary were to establish wedlock, I know the people of this village believe, and know, that Mary should not be living under the same roof with Joseph. But Joseph has no father or mother and my husband will not allow her to live under our roof." Anne paused and looked to Elizabeth. "Joseph may have had a dream that told him to remain betrothed to Mary but he also claims he was told in the dream that the baby is a special baby boy, and that he shall be named Jesus, Emmanuel. Joseph plans to name the child Jesus. Among all these circumstances I believe Joseph truly loves Mary. You should see how he looks at her, and after her. I thank God for Joseph. I feel a love for him as if he were . . . as if he were my own son."

Zechariah stood up and walked close to Anne. "Do you believe Mary was raped?"

"I don't know." Anne seemed tortured by the question.

"I didn't ask you if you knew Mary was raped, I asked, 'Do you believe Mary was raped?' It is often what we believe, rather than what we know, that gives us powerful peace. God's Spirit brings us peace through faith."

Anne raised her head and declared, "I believe she was raped. I also believe her report that she was raped and violated by a Roman soldier. This is our reality. This is the dangerous world in which we live. What I find difficult to believe is that God would allow this to happen to Mary and Joseph. You know as well as I that many in Mird, and this Qumran Settlement of Essenes, are waiting for the birth of the promised Messiah. Mary and Joseph were looked up to by many of us, hoping that they would be used by God to bring the Long-Awaited One into the world. Our village and our neighbors had been all puffed up with pride when some leaders from the Jerusalem temple interpreted from the prophets that God planned to bring the Messiah through us to the world for all time! Not only would the Messiah come from the chosen race of Israel, but he would be born in our settlement, among the Essenes. He would be born as the firstborn to an Essene husband and wife. Their idea grew into a frenzy of belief that had led us all to believe the blessed couple would be Joseph and Mary . . . Look at us now. We can't look at anyone without feeling shame."

Anne flopped onto a chair at the table and shoved the plate and goblet in front of her aside. The goblet fell to the floor and broke into three large pieces. Her head collapsed into her crossed arms. She had cried so much these days and didn't want to cry in front of her sister and her husband at their time of joy over the birth of a son. She began to weep anyway. Through her weeping she said, "Where is our God? All the women of the village will have nothing to do with Mary. They have decided to shun her even when the time for the birth of her child comes. Joachim has forbidden me to help her and he refuses to let her come through our door . . . not even for a cup of water." Anne looked up. "I'm an evil woman, but I cannot deny that I hate my husband. I am completely undone. What am I to do, Elizabeth? I can barely stand to look at him." She dropped her head into her arms again and tried to gain control over her sobbing.

For a little while longer, Zechariah didn't move from where he stood. Then he walked to Anne and placed his hands on her head. "Do not cry for long, my sister. God's purpose cannot be undone. What our lives become is changed and influenced by what we decide to do in the midst of the Great Jehovah's plan. We need to remember that we can find comfort in believing this plan encircles us and carries us to where we are meant to go. In my years as a priest, I have come to learn that the place we all go . . . is back to Him. In our living, and in our dying, we choose our path through faith. There are many paths, Anne. Many different possibilities of experience can be part of our living, but our choices can only alter potential for joy, peace, and love in whatever life brings to us. It cannot take our oneness with God away from us."

Zechariah sat down next to Anne and lifted her face to meet his eyes by placing his finger under her chin and guiding her countenance to meet his own. "The good news is that all potential paths end in the same place, and that place is with God. Your great challenge now is in the choice before you, and in the choice before Joachim. Anne, you can choose love."

Zechariah bent down and picked up the three broken parts of the goblet and placed them back on the table. "These can be glued together and the goblet will be as good as new." He walked away from the table and started toward the front entrance to go outside.

"Zechariah, where are you going?" Elizabeth asked.

"I'm going out to the field to fetch my baby boy and find Joachim, wherever he may be."

BETHANY

LAZARUS AND HIS AUNT Rachael gathered his clothes and folded them together. She took some twine and wrapped it around the bundle so the clothes would stay together efficiently for his little walk home with his father. As Rachael pulled Lazarus' prayer shawl out of the wooden box and shook it, instead of a little cloud of dust, a bundle of dried flowers flew in all directions and fell to the floor in broken bits and pieces. Lazarus stood frozen. Rachael tried to gather them up but both she, and he, knew it was a worthless endeavor.

"Dear child, why were you saving these flowers?" Lazarus didn't respond to Rachael's question. Rachael could see they were important to Lazarus so she tried to tenderly gather the pieces with no success. They crumbled all the more. "Did someone give you these flowers?"

Lazarus nodded his head. "My mother gave them to me last spring when my little brother was born dead. She told me she loved me and thanked God for me and that I was a wonderful son. She said she would always love me. She wanted me to remember her every time I saw these flowers grow outside because it meant spring was near and many new things would begin to grow again."

Rachael dropped the dried pieces of the flowers and reached out to hug Lazarus tightly. "You were born to a wise mother. She loved you so much." Rachael knew Lazarus was crying so she held him in her embrace until she felt him become still. She took him by the hand and led him to the window. She pushed the wooden shutters open and the sun streamed into the room. "Look."

Lazarus and Rachael gazed out over the few scattered houses and beyond to the desert field that stretched as far as they both could see. The hills were covered with red, yellow, violet, and green blooms that covered the landscape. It was brilliant and beautiful. As Lazarus stared through the window at the beauty before him, his aunt stood behind him and placed her arms over his shoulders to hold him close.

Lazarus was stunned. "But those flowers weren't there yesterday. How did this happen?"

"God is so good," Rachael whispered as if she was also dreaming. "It's not magic, Lazarus. The desert blooms like this every spring and it always blooms within one day. But every now and then the desert blooms into this kind of magnificence because more rain falls during the winter season. Recently, these last two months of winter brought much more rain than usual, and look at the beauty we are blessed to see." Both stood and gazed at the vista. "I always try to remember that every spring brings growth and new life to the desert. It's as if God brings us a kind of resurrection every year by restoring life. It reminds me that nothing is ever lost, or gone forever. It only changes. Your mother knew that." Rachael turned Lazarus around to face her. His eyes were glassed over with tears of amazement and wonder. "Lazarus, do you understand what your mother was trying to say to you? Do you understand that the Spirit of God will always provide for you and fill you up? All we must do is remember, accept, and not be afraid."

Lazarus fell into his aunt's arms and he clung to her. "I don't want to go live with my father. I want to stay here with you and Uncle Benjamin, and Levi, Martha, and Baby Mary."

Rachael held him and said, "I know, Lazarus. I know."

Benjamin knocked lightly at the door and said, "Eleazar is here." He saw Lazarus clutch his wife all the harder. He walked into the room and came down to Lazarus' level. "Come now, Lazarus. I know this is hard but we are men. You must be strong like the young man I know you are. I know it is hard. Look at me Lazarus . . . I had a conversation with your father just now. I convinced him to let you spend every other Sabbath with us."

Lazarus looked up from his aunt's arms. "Yes," Benjamin said. "You will be with us every other Sabbath. The rest of the time you will be at the temple to begin your studies to be a rabbi. Lazarus, I really believe you will be a good rabbi. We need good rabbis. You can do this."

Benjamin took Lazarus by the hand and pulled him away from Rachael. He grabbed the bundle of clothes and led Lazarus away from Rachael to Eleazar, who was waiting at the front door.

ROME

The rain and wind had stopped, but the sky remained overcast, giving everything a gray hue. Jarius sat up as the other soldiers began their morning routine to dress themselves. He looked over to where Panthera should have been and saw that he was not there. "What is wrong with that soldier?" He got up and finished dressing himself for report and walked out toward the courtyard.

To his surprise, Panthera was standing at attention, ready, before anyone else had arrived. Jarius walked up to his side and looked toward the platform, which would soon accommodate different centurions announcing assignments by cohorts of legions. Today, four thousand men would be receiving assignments of duty. At first Jarius decided to stand at attention as Panthera stood and then, realizing how stupid this all seemed, he sighed and turned to Panthera.

"What's the matter with you, man?"

"Nothing is the matter with me. I'm just waiting for my assignment."

"Panthera, take a look around. Do see anyone here yet?"

"You're here."

Jarius paused and finally said, "Yeah . . . you're right. I'm scaring myself." He looked back at Panthera and asked, "Come now, are you alright? After the episode this morning I'm . . . concerned for you. Are you feeling well?"

Panthera continued to stand at attention. He finally broke the silence and sternly asked, "Jarius, did you know I raped a girl in Judea?"

"Yeah. Haven't we all raped girls in Judea, and Samaria, and Galilee, and Persia, and . . . What's your point?"

"Jarius, you never raped."

"Well, don't let that get out, will you?"

"I raped a girl in the Qumran Settlement seven months ago. They told me her name was Mary."

"Do you know how many females are named Mary in the Judean area?" Panthera didn't respond. Jarius went on to inform him. "About half, Panthera."

"No, you don't understand. This Mary was betrothed to some man named Joseph, and the Jews in that area believed he and she would be the parents of the Messiah."

"Panthera, since when did you start letting foreign religious superstitions affect your life? They're all Jews in Judea. They're all possessed with crazy ideas that will never amount to anything for Rome. Get ahold of yourself."

Panthera finally relaxed his stance and turned to face Jarius. "I believe you're wrong. I have never been riddled with such suffering. Ever since I raped that girl I have not been able to eat properly, sleep properly, or just feel peace . . . or simple joy. I've decided that if I am reassigned to Judea again, I will find that Mary and Joseph and ask for forgiveness. I've thought about this for more than seven months and I can't live another day in Judea without following through with this plan . . . If I impregnated that young girl, she should be ready to give birth in the middle to the end of March . . . somewhere between March 21 and April 15. If I'm reassigned to Judea I'll be in the area at the time of the baby's birth."

Jarius stared at Panthera in disbelief. "You're not making sense." Panthera returned to his stance of attention. "What if you get assigned to Athens or Ephesus?"

"Then I will know I did not impregnate that girl and I will receive forgiveness from the gods."

"You obeyed Rome. What makes you think you need forgiveness?"

Panthera didn't respond to Jarius at first. Jarius stood still as soldiers began to gather in the courtyard. The time for the announcement of their assignments were about to begin. Jarius felt tension and anxiety. He was not sure if his anxiety was for his comrade or for himself when Panthera said, "Jarius, you're a good friend. Thank you. I know you haven't raped yet so I will say to you that it is not right to rape under any circumstance. I have suffered because of my deed and speak to you in truth." Panthera turned to him and grabbed Jarius' right forearm with his hand and looked at him with genuine love.

The courtyard was full. Four thousand young Roman soldiers stood at attention and they stood in neat, subdivided cohorts of five hundred soldiers. They waited for their centurion to stand on the platform to announce their assignments. There would be two announcements before Panthera's legion received its orders. The first centurion stepped on the platform. Without delay he stated that his group would be leaving to occupy the area of Galilee and Samaria, west of the Sea of Galilee and the Jordan River. The second centurion announced that his soldiers would be occupying Perea, Decapolis, and Gaulanitis, east of the river Jordan, the Sea of Galilee in the north and east of the Dead Sea. Panthera felt numb. He really hadn't hoped for anything specifically, but he could predict where he would be assigned by the fact that all of Palestine was pretty well assigned except for Judea. Panthera's centurion officer took the platform and announced that the 1500 soldiers, including his legion, would be joining forces as tent groups in the Judean area, which included Jericho, the Qumran Settlement, Bethlehem, Bethany, and Jerusalem and the Palestinian land west of the River Jordan.

With no emotion, Panthera knew what he had to do when he returned to the area to which he had been assigned again. It seemed as if the knowledge he possessed about where he was going reduced his anxiety somewhat. He stood and listened as the others received their assignments.

Upon dismissal Jarius looked at Panthera and said, "Well, we still have the rest of the day and night before we depart for Judea again. Why don't you and I engage in something pleasurable . . . like eating."

THE QUMRAN SETTLEMENT

THERE WAS NO SIGN of the children, his baby son, or Joachim. Zechariah felt sure he would find Joachim in the closest field of winter wheat but heard no sound and saw no activity that would indicate their whereabouts. A gentle breeze pushed the grain in ripples of golden waves. The sun shined brightly and gave the field a glistening shimmer of color. The sound of the wind was calming to his soul, and he stood still and listened.

A distant sound of an infant's cry perked his attention to look over the crest of the hill to the west. As he followed the infant's cry, as if it were a guiding compass, he came to the top of the hill and saw Joachim and the children sitting together in the small hollow the slope of the land provided. Zechariah called out. "Joachim," he yelled, "children, stay where you are because I'm coming down there."

Joachim stood up and yelled back, "No, Zechariah, there's a gully just ahead of . . ." It was too late. Zechariah tripped and began to tumble down the hill. His black robes flew around, giving the image of a strange apparition. One could not detect hands, sandaled feet, or face. Joachim was horrified, but the children all began to point and laugh uncontrollably.

Zechariah tumbled down the hill completely. When he came to its end, he sat up with a silly, rather dazed look on his face. Joachim came to his aid first. "Zechariah, are you alright? Do you think you can stand up?"

Zechariah looked up at Joachim and said, "That was really . . . fun."

The children cheered and screamed, "Come on! Let's do it together."

"Yeah, let's do it again!"

Zechariah rose to his feet with Joachim and Issachar's help saying, "No. No, the Lord's goodness and mercy does not need to be tested further. The memory will serve me well for a long time."

Issachar said, "It will serve us well too." And they all laughed again together.

"Issachar, will you and the children take Baby John back to the house. Elizabeth is in the house. He needs to be fed. I'm going to stay here and talk to your father for a little while."

"Come on," Issachar directed his brothers and sisters. "Let's get Baby John back to his mother without tragedy. We know where that gully is, Uncle Zechariah. We won't fall." The small group of children walked up the hill and over its crest, leaving Zechariah and Joachim alone, sitting in the golden waving of the winter wheat.

Finally, Zechariah spoke. "Joachim, something is not right in your household, is it?"

Joachim didn't answer at first and then stated, "Zechariah, you are a man I respect. You are the high priest from the priestly caste of Abijah, a rabbi and one who is holy. But if you're going to talk to me about my daughter Mary, who now lives with Joseph, there is nothing to discuss."

Zechariah said nothing and lingered with Joachim for a long time. The sun began to set and Zechariah noticed that Joachim shivered. "Aren't you thankful for warmth?"

Joachim looked at him as if he had lost his mind. He thought, Zechariah is getting old and after the tumble he took he must be a little off.

But Zechariah asked again, "Joachim, aren't you glad for warmth?"

Joachim shivered again and finally said, "Yes, Zechariah. I'm thankful for warmth," but he had no idea where Zechariah was going with this conversation.

"It's going to get warm again . . . soon. Winter is over and we will experience the warmth of spring and summer again. Every year, the warmth comes . . . Praise God! I keep remembering that passage from Ecclesiastes, 'Two are better than one, because they have a good reward for their toil. For if they fall, one will lift up the other; but woe to one who is alone and falls and does not have another to help. Again, if two lie together, they keep warm; but how can one keep warm alone? And though one might prevail against another, two will withstand one. A threefold cord is not quickly broken.'"

Joachim looked out over the landscape in front of him. He picked a handful of wheat and rubbed it in his hands only to let it blow away in the wind. "Zechariah, speak to me clearly. I don't understand what you're talking about."

"I'm talking about your marriage. I'm talking about your relationship with Anne." Joachim still looked confused but now his feeling was leaning toward irritation.

"What about my wife?"

"She is falling away from you. She has no respect for you because of your treatment of your daughter."

Joachim stood up and waved his hand. "My daughter is dead to me. She made love to some boy she secretly met in the country. Then she went on and lied that she was raped by some Roman soldier. I will not tolerate this abomination. We are a sacred and holy people. I love my God more than a daughter who commits adultery against her betrothed, lies, and brings shame upon all of us!"

Joachim turned his back on Zechariah. The wind caught his robe and blew it like a billowing sail. He turned back to Zechariah and said, "I have other children. I have other daughters."

Zechariah said, "Yes, but you do not have another wife."

"What are you saying?" Joachim almost yelled.

"I'm saying that, apart from whatever happened to your daughter, your wife believes her and is showing signs of increasing hatred toward you because you have given your 'command' without talking about it with your wife. I'm saying, 'Let your heart hold fast my words; keep God's commandments, and live, get wisdom; get insight; do not forget, nor turn away from the words of my mouth.'" Zechariah struggled to stand up and his staff helped him. "'Do not forsake her, and she will keep you; love her, and she will guard you. The beginning of wisdom is this: Get wisdom, and whatever else you get, get insight. Prize her highly, and she will exalt you; she will honor you if you embrace her. She will place on your head a fair garland; she will bestow on you a beautiful crown'" (Prov 4:4-9).

Joachim's heart was hardened and his words spewed out like venom from a viper. "You read too much from Scripture. Why don't you try living in this reality for once?"

Zechariah smiled with kindness and answered, "I understand, Joachim. I just find it hard to live in this reality when I'm seventy years old and I have a new little baby boy."

"Dad," Issachar yelled to them from the top of the hill. "Mom needs for you to come home for the meal that is prepared and waiting." Joachim turned and reached to take hold of Zechariah's arm to help him up the hill.

Zechariah accepted Joachim's support and simply said, "Thank God for youth."

They walked together up the hill and across the small wheat field. When they entered the house, the children and women were properly seated at their places at the table. Anne placed the prepared feast before her family and guests and Zechariah lifted the Sabbath prayer and litany. The meal began and so did the chatter of conversation. It was a happy scene but Elizabeth paused and thought of Mary and Joseph's absence as she nursed her baby and felt sadness as she also noticed her sister Anne's cold treatment of Joachim. Quickly and quietly, she prayed, "May the God of the universe have mercy on us."

In contrast, the Sabbath meal was strained for Joseph and Mary, who ate alone, apart from the rest of the extended family. They ate in silence, not speaking the Sabbath prayer out loud. When they had eaten their fill Mary rose from the table and began to take the pottery they had used to the wooden basin to clean. In previous evenings after supper, Joseph would stand beside Mary and help with this task, but this evening he left the table and walked outside somewhere.

Mary filled the wooden basin with water and placed the pottery in the water to soak and walked outside herself. She didn't look for Joseph. She wrapped her shawl around her shoulders more tightly and although she was chilled, she stood and looked up at the stars. She wondered what they were. Was it just a black dome that covered the sun's light at night? If so, why did the stars twinkle and change colors as she watched them from her spot on the ground looking up? Mary felt filled with awe and sadness. How could such a great God create such an awesome night sky and at the same time allow her to be violated as she had been and then shunned by her family and her village? What good could come of this? She wondered if this was what mystery was in life. Could mystery be the events in life that are not understood? If so, it was all so painful. Suddenly a bright streak of light sped across the sky and the light trailed for at least three seconds. Mary had seen this phenomenon in the night sky before, but never had the light lasted so long. It gave her a sense of ambivalent exhilaration. She stood and watched the night sky for a while longer until the coolness of the night led her to her sleeping mat. The blankets were there, as she had left them in the morning, but Joseph was nowhere to be seen. Feeling exhausted, and sad that she was not a part of her family's meal, celebrating the birth of John and the Sabbath, she lay down and pulled the blankets over her tired body.

She tried to go to sleep, but without success. The previous nights had been spent with Joseph lying next to her. His body had kept her warm and comfortable. She wondered where he was. She became tormented with thoughts that he might be changing his mind about taking her for his wife. She certainly had brought a lot of trouble to their fragile relationship. Mary gave up and allowed herself to cry again. As she lay alone, muffling her crying, she felt a strong, warm hand reach around her middle as her body was drawn close to his. It was Joseph. Mary turned to him and began to explain why she was crying but he just said, "Shhhh-hush. It is time for both of us to sleep." For Mary that was enough and she fell into a deep sleep. In the arms of her betrothed she slept, unaware that he remained awake for most of the night.

Anne had trouble sleeping that night as well. The Sabbath meal with Elizabeth and Zechariah was unbelievably tense. She felt the growing resentment toward her husband. She couldn't eat having to look at him across the table. His arrogance was nauseating. His self-righteous justification for the rejection of their daughter made her blood hot. She would never touch him again or allow him to touch her. She knew she could no longer sleep beside him, so she sat on the ground against the wall of their home that had become just a house to her now. She looked up at the night sky and began to cry beneath the stars that shined in defiance of the seething in her heart. A flash of light flew through the blackness of the sky. The streak of light lasted for what seemed like three seconds. She'd seen this phenomenon before but never with such magnificence. She wondered for a moment and then stood up and walked into the house.

How different the room seemed to her. Looking at the hearth she realized that the fire was dying. She sat by the dying embers and began to feel the chill succumb to the ember's lingering warmth. She bowed her head and dropped her face onto her arms that crossed and rested on her knees. She spoke in a whisper, "Mary, my beautiful daughter Mary. The world will never be able to forgive this deed done to you. You must disappear or your pain and shame must disappear, but I love you, my child. I love your husband, Joseph. God will see into your hearts and save your souls." She lay down on the floor and stared at the embers slowly fade into darkness. She was not aware that her husband stood watching. Neither was she aware that he was crying with her. He finally turned to go. He knew he could not talk to his wife and bring her to his side for sleep that deep, dark night.

BETHANY

Eleazar didn't honor his agreement with Benjamin. Lazarus didn't return every other Sabbath to be with his sisters, his cousin, his aunt, or his uncle. Lazarus stayed at the Jerusalem temple every day and every Sabbath. Eleazar felt it necessary that this routine be established to help his son focus upon his calling to be a rabbi. He believed his son needed to be independent and strong.

Martha missed her brother and asked for him often. Her Aunt Rachael would give excuses and reasons for Lazarus' absence until she could no longer endure her brother-in-law's blatant dishonesty.

"I don't care if he is the father, Benjamin! This is totally unacceptable. Lazarus has been gone for a month and has not returned for a visit. This is his family. He needs to be with Martha and Mary. He also needs to be with Levi. I miss him. Do you miss him?"

Benjamin sighed. He did not do well with conflicts and confrontations. "What can we do? Eleazar is his father. He's the one who decides what happens with his children."

"Ooohhh, Benjamin! We're the ones caring for them. We have been feeding, clothing, and sheltering Martha and Mary since my sister died! We have some say in their present situation."

"Eleazar paid us, Rachael."

"And do you believe that gives him the right to emotionally abandon them and us?! That money sits untouched in my bedroom cupboard. I will not care for children under the rule of money!"

"Well, what can we do?"

Rachael could see her husband's quandary and pain. She reached out to him and placed her arms around his shoulders as he sat in the chair at the table. She knew her words were harsh as she paced behind him. Their harshness was not meant for him.

"Benjamin, you are twice the man Eleazar is because you are gentle, loving, trustworthy, and truthful." She moved around him and sat on the chair next to him. She took his hands into her own and said, "Let's all go see Lazarus. Let's use the money Eleazar gave us to travel and lodge somewhere near the temple. Jerusalem is only two miles away and Mary is strong enough to make such a journey. Let's stay near the temple for the next Sabbath. We'll stay two nights and take Lazarus to the top of the Mount of Olives and through the Kidron Valley. We'll visit the garden of Gethsemane and pray in the temple's courts. We'll eat in the marketplace and watch the sunset at the pool outside the western wall."

Benjamin's expression softened, "That's a great idea! Of course, we can do that. Dan will cover for me at the market in Bethany for three days. I'll talk to him and see if this can be worked out. We'll go when it gets warmer, maybe four weeks from this Sabbath."

Rachael leaned toward him and held him close. She kissed his cheek and whispered, "I'm pregnant, Benjamin!" She kissed his mouth and leaned back to study his expression. His eyes welled with tears as Rachael placed her finger against his lips. "I love you, Benjamin," she said clearly. His arms encircled her and he felt a joy he knew he couldn't explain as he listened to the happy sounds coming from Martha, Levi, and Baby Mary.

JUDEA

THE DAY STARTED POORLY for Panthera. He woke with illness in his bowels. They were to disembark from the ship that sailed them from Rome to Joppa. He knew they would immediately begin their twenty-five-mile march from Joppa on the eastern Mediterranean coastline to the interior of Judea to build a tent camp southeast of Jerusalem. Setting camp for a Roman soldier was like building an instant fortified city. Roman camps were always constructed according to a set pattern, laid out like a city bisected by two streets leading to four gates. It was fortified, surrounded by a deep ditch and then a wall. It was grueling work for the soldiers and, even though they would begin building upon arrival to the designated site, it would take more than a month to complete its construction.

Stepping off the ship, Panthera felt worse. He wondered if the journey would make his illness worsen, prohibiting his personal task of finding Mary and Joseph. This thought did not comfort him because he had promised the gods that he would travel to the Qumran Settlement as soon as he returned to Judea. He knew this meant an additional two or three miles beyond their campsite construction. He felt more than compelled to keep his promise to the gods, even though he wasn't sure who the gods were. He also knew that he had to find Joseph and Mary. If the gods led him to them he could not help but dread the confrontation that would follow. He had no idea how he would even speak to them though he had been practicing saying "Forgive me for what I have done" in Aramaic.

The march began. Panthera made a last check. His blanket was over his shoulder, his hip belt with a short sword in its sheath was around his middle, his helmet was on his head, and his standard, which helped him walk, was firmly grasped in his hand. Today he used it as a walking stick, not an emblem of Roman pride.

After little distance in the march, his bowels screamed to be relieved. They had marched two miles before he had to break rank and trot to the side of the road and relieve himself behind a clump of juniper bushes. He felt humiliated as he put himself together and ran to take his place in rank again. It was as if he took only ten paces and he had to run to the bushes again. When he ran back to his place this time, he found Jarius marching beside him.

"Augustus traded spots with me because he saw that you might need a little support from a friend."

"You are my friend, Jarius." He took another ten paces and said, "I'm so sick. What did I eat last night that would give me this ailment?"

"Panthera, you ate the same things I ate at the same place. I think it's your nerves."

Two or three miles later, Panthera ran off to the side of the road and went over a small mound, out of sight. After a little while he ran to join his place next to Jarius again.

"How far do you think we've gone?" Panthera asked.

"Not far enough." They became silent and didn't talk for a while until Jarius courageously broached the subject about Mary and Joseph again. "You're really upset about this, aren't you?" Jarius said, looking at Panthera, noticing his flushed face.

Panthera looked straight ahead and marched for a long time. Finally, he broke their silence and said, "I found something out about this couple, Mary and Joseph from the Qumran Settlement. The Jews have been waiting for a promised Messiah for centuries. The Mary I raped, and her betrothed husband, Joseph, were to be the birth parents of this supposed Messiah." Panthera ran off to the side of the road behind a clump of bushes. When he ran back to catch up with Jarius he let himself catch his breath before he continued. "I can't shake this feeling like I did something really, really wrong. I don't know what drove me to do what I did. Apparently, Joseph has decided to take her for his wife and be an adoptive father to this child."

Jarius looked ahead as he marched and began to chuckle. He said, "Do the Jews think this Messiah will be a male?"

Panthera was irritated. "Well, of course, he'll be a male."

"Well, what if your Mary gives birth to a female. Will that calm your fears?"

Panthera thought about this and answered, "No. I still believe she was impregnated by me and I am the biological father."

"No matter what, the child will be a poor unfortunate child." Jarius began to chuckle again. "Do you realize that if you did impregnate this Mary, the Jews could have a Roman, Greek, Jewish female for their Messiah?" Jarius laughed out loud but when he looked at Panthera he soberly said, "Come now, Panthera. Don't take this all so seriously."

Panthera ran again to a place of cover to relieve his bowels. When he returned, he said to Jarius, “I think I’m better now.” He took three more paces and collapsed.

THE QUMRAN SETTLEMENT

Mary awoke and turned to touch Joseph but he was not there. She heard voices outside their front door so she rose, smoothed out her hair, and changed her garment for the day. She placed her sandals on and walked quickly to the front of the house where she heard familiar voices. It was Elizabeth and Zechariah with their baby son, John.

"Well, we're on our way to Jerusalem. It will take us a little over four hours. That's less time than from our home, which is north of here, closer to where the Jordan River flows into the Dead Sea." Zechariah always seemed to talk about time and distance and this was no exception.

"Thank you for that information, Zechariah. I'm sure that was exactly what was on Joseph and Mary's minds." Elizabeth winked at Mary, who turned and saw Joseph standing behind her quietly. He looked different. She didn't like the difference she detected in his eyes.

Elizabeth turned to her husband and handed him the baby. She let herself down from the burro and walked past Mary to reach her arms around Joseph's neck. She held him close and whispered soft words to him. He hid his tears. Mary had no clue what was happening. She stepped closer to Zechariah and looked at him with inquisitive eyes.

Zechariah breathed a heavy sigh. "Your betrothed is suffering great emotional pain."

"What are you talking about, uncle?"

"Mary, Joseph is a very gifted and learned man but he has no support. Not from your family, or from this village. His friends have abandoned him and he has no family of his own. Do you understand that you are all he has in life? He is afraid. He may be able to figure out how to bring water up from the ground, irrigate a field of wheat, build the best functioning house in this province, but he does not know how to help you birth your baby. He doubts his ability to be a husband or a father. Mary, you must give him your attention as I am sure he will love and support you the best way he can."

Mary hugged Zechariah gently and bent down to kiss the baby in his arms. As she stepped away from him, Elizabeth was lifted up by Joseph to sit on the burro. Zechariah handed Baby John to Elizabeth.

"Well," Elizabeth declared, "I guess we are on our way to the temple." She looked down at her baby son and said, "This circumcision will hurt a little, John, but it will save you trouble throughout your life and, more importantly, our God commands that it be done." She gently rubbed her nose against his cheek and the baby cooed. "Goodbye, Mary." Elizabeth looked up and Joseph was gone. "Tell Joseph we love him, you, and your baby."

"Yes, I will," said Mary.

Zechariah said, "If I were you, I would go look for that husband of yours. Goodbye, my child. God be with you."

With that they left Mary standing alone. For the first time she realized that she was not cold and it was still early morning. Spring was coming. It felt wonderful to stand in the sun and almost feel hot at this hour. She turned to enter the house, remembering that the pottery from the meal last night still sat waiting to be cleaned in the wooden basin. As she approached the door, she looked down and saw flowers that had bloomed and grown in the bed of soil Joseph must have planted last year. They made her feel excited. Instead of going into the house, she turned and walked quickly down the path toward the desert. When she rounded the bend that opened the desert's expanse to her view, she felt her breath taken away. It was beautiful! The gentle slope leading to a hill that crested before her eyes displayed colors beyond her imagination. She'd never seen the desert look like this before.

She couldn't help but run through the color of the desert, lie down, and rest in its divine beauty. The sun shined, so she closed her eyes to take in all its warmth over her face. She sat up and looked at the different colored blossoms, encircling her like a blanket. She stood up and raised her arms up to the sky and prayed a prayer for her beautiful Joseph. She didn't know how long she stood in its beauty, but a distant rumble of thunder coaxed her to leave and return to the shelter of her home to find Joseph.

The spring storm came faster than she anticipated but she stepped into her home before rain began to fall. Surely Joseph was somewhere in the dwelling. She checked every room. When she looked out the back window toward their wheat field, she saw him in the distance. He was harvesting the winter crop. She stood and watched him from this distance and wished she could see his facial expression well enough to determine his mood.

As she watched she saw that he stopped. He pulled some wheat and offered it to the burro, which ate obligingly. He stood in front of the burro and stroked its neck. He bent down and caressed the sides of the burro's face and neck with his own. There was a great crack of thunder and he looked up at the sky as the burro brayed and jumped in fright. He took his tunic off and placed it over the eyes of the burro and began to quickly lead it back to the shed.

Mary watched Joseph and noticed that he had a strong body. His back was straight and broad, his shoulders and arms were full, and the muscles were well defined. When he came out of the shed, having secured the burro under cover, he started to walk across the yard toward the house, holding his tunic over his own head as a covering when the rain began to fall. It was no use. Rain saturated the cloth of his tunic and washed through to roll onto the top of his head, dripping from his curls over the rest of his body. Mary ran to the closest door. She ran out into the rain and met Joseph and they stood together in the yard. She didn't seem to mind that her garment was wet now too. She began to dance around him with her arms extended toward the sky. She dipped and spun around Joseph and grabbed his hands. "Dance with me, Joseph. Dance with me."

"I don't know how to dance, Mary."

She stood still in front of him and ran her hands up his very wet arms. "Then kiss me, Joseph. Kiss me." He raised his arms up around her, pulled her to himself, and kissed her. They had kissed in the rain before, but this time they were both warm.

As they embraced, they seemed to be in a very distant place from their momentary reality. The next flash of lightning drove them both to the house. Mary turned and laughed at Joseph's effort to use his tunic as a covering. She took the tunic from him and wrung the water out of it over the sink filled with the clay pottery that was still waiting to be cleaned and put away.

Mary turned to Joseph and just looked at his beautiful, soft brown eyes. Bravely and boldly, Mary approached Joseph, threw her arms around him, pulled him close, and passionately kissed him. Stepping back, she wondered if her action was proper or even acceptable to him. She waited, glad to see him remove his soaked loin cloth, moving closer to her to take her into his arms. He kissed her as passionately as she had kissed him. Mary whispered, "This feels better than dancing!"

Joseph laughed, saying, "You shall learn, my beloved, just as I shall learn. But not now, there is a baby to be born first, and then we shall have our lifetime together."

Joseph led her back to their sleeping room and retrieved dry clothing for them both to wear. With no thought or shyness, Mary stripped off her wet garment and raised her arms for Joseph to slip on the dry gown he held over her head. But he paused and gazed upon her for a moment. Mary quickly crossed her arms over her body. "Don't look upon me now, Joseph. You're making me feel shy."

"No, Mary. You're feeling that all by yourself," as he placed the gown over her head and let it fall over her shoulders to the floor. As she slipped her arms into the oversized sleeves, she smiled at him, gazing upon him. Joseph turned quickly and slipped his robe over himself.

When he turned back to face Mary, she said, "Now who's acting shy?"

THE SECOND TEMPLE IN JERUSALEM

Today, Lazarus and all the young rabbi students would witness a circumcision. Their rabbi told them that they all needed to be quiet and reverent. As the baby was put on the holy table, Lazarus' thoughts wandered and he thought of home with Aunt Rachael and Uncle Benjamin. He wondered what Levi, Martha, and Baby Mary were doing. He was so homesick. Worse, he felt the nagging emotion of anger against his father. He knew his father was always in the temple yet he never came to see him.

The baby screamed! The scream shook Lazarus back to his presence in the temple. He saw blood oozing around the baby's penis and he turned his head away until all the prayers were spoken. The baby didn't stop screaming until the wound was wrapped with a gauzelike material and the baby was placed back in its mother's arms.

Lazarus thought to himself, "I will never let them do that to my baby boy if God gives me a son." He walked up to the mother who was holding the baby and asked, "What is your son's name?"

The rather elderly mother looked down at Lazarus and said, "John, his name is John."

JOACHIM AND ANNE'S HOME

"You have not talked to me this entire day." Anne ignored her husband. "Anna, I am telling you to stop this nonsense!"

Anne continued to clean the pottery from their meal with Elizabeth and Zechariah. She looked up at Joachim from her cleaning and said, "All our married days I have requested that you call me Anne, not Anna."

Joachim sneered at Anne. "What does that have to do with anything we're talking about?"

"You mean to say, 'What does that have to do with anything *you* are talking about,' not about what *we* are talking about because you don't even hear what I have to say!"

Joachim was truly confused. He paced the floor behind his wife who didn't acknowledge his presence any longer. Her heart beat with a fury she had never experienced. Her resentment toward him was strong and she just wanted him to go away. Finally, he started to walk out of the room, saying, "What a fine, obedient wife you turned out to be," but not before she turned in a flash and yelled, "Joachim, how dare you speak such words, a man who has abandoned his daughter and his wife!" Anne dropped the platter she was washing and it shattered, shards flying everywhere. She left the room, pushing Joachim out of her way.

JUDEA

JARIUS CALLED TO THE centurion and the medics in the front line, "We've got a man down . . . here!" The men stopped marching but didn't fall out of order as the centurion and the medics came to the aid of Panthera. The medics knew by the feel of his skin and the lack of perspiration that Panthera was dangerously dehydrated. They revived him with smelling salts and made him drink water. They ordered four other soldiers to place Panthera onto a handheld stretcher to carry him. Jarius was ordered to give Panthera water every hundred paces and the march continued.

Panthera was groggy but he realized he was being carried and he was thankful for his fellow soldiers. Jarius followed orders and gave him water every hundred paces. He took Panthera's blanket off his shoulder and placed it over his body to shade his skin from the sun, which had grown strong. Panthera said, "Thank you," through the blanket and Jarius chuckled. Panthera fell asleep.

By midafternoon the legion had reached its destination and the soldiers were given two hours to rest and eat before they began the preliminary construction of the tent camp. After that time, the commander in charge came to visit Panthera. He brought with him two medics to assess Panthera's physical condition. It was determined that Panthera was to be placed under a nearby tree and refrain from the work of digging the trenches and building the walls that would surround the camp. In essence, he had the rest of the day free.

Panthera looked around his surroundings and recognized much of the terrain. He knew the Qumran Settlement was two miles east of the spot he was sitting on. He rested for a little while, picked up the animal skin filled with water, his belt, sword, and standard. He was sure that he was being directed to find Mary and Joseph. He would obey.

He walked a little way and came upon a stream filled to its banks. He stripped naked and dipped his body into the stream and let the water flow over him to clean and refresh him. As he lay in the moving water, he didn't feel sick anymore. Instead, he felt an anxiety he had not felt since he had been four years old, hiding in the cupboard. He had a strong urge to return to his place under the tree but something compelled him to continue what he had set out to do. The gods seemed to be cooperating with him and he obeyed.

THE QUMRAN SETTLEMENT

JOSEPH RETURNED TO THE field to gather the wheat he had cut before the rainstorm. He hoped the sun had dried it enough by this early evening hour so he could store it before mold began to grow. He suddenly felt uneasy. He looked up toward the end of the field and saw a man standing next to the olive tree he had planted when he was a young boy. Today the tree spread out and stood over ten feet tall. Joseph placed the bale of wheat down and walked toward the tree to speak to the man who seemed to wait for his approach. As Joseph neared the tree, he recognized that the man was a Roman soldier. Joseph stopped and said nothing. The presence of a Roman soldier on your property was not a good omen and Joseph was at a loss as to what he should do.

The soldier walked twenty paces closer to Joseph, standing no more than an arm's length away. He finally spoke. "My name is Panthera . . . I am the soldier who raped your wife." In a very poor accent Panthera tried to say in Aramaic, "Forgive me for what I have done."

Joseph was fluent in Hebrew, Coptic, Aramaic, Latin, and Greek. He felt less threatened by this phantom soldier because his attempt at speaking his native tongue was spoken so poorly. Joseph refrained from speaking to the soldier, thinking it best to remain silent. He hoped the soldier would take his leave quickly if he realized there was no way to communicate.

Surprisingly, the Roman soldier didn't leave but rather took a step toward Joseph and ceremoniously laid his standard on the ground. He removed his belt, which held his sword in its sheath, and placed it also on the ground next to his standard. He looked at Joseph squarely, removed his helmet and went down on one knee. He placed his helmet next to his other weapons on the ground and bowed his head to Joseph.

Joseph was completely confused and began to realize he must communicate with the Roman. He bent over and guided the soldier to his feet as they stood and looked at one another. Joseph slowly bent down again and collected Panthera's helmet, standard, belt, and sword. In Latin, Joseph asked, "Why are you here doing this?"

Panthera sighed with some relief, glad he could talk to this Jew, Joseph, saying in Greek, "As I said, my name is Panthera and I am the . . . the soldier who raped your wife eight months ago. I've been plagued with illness and sickness of the mind ever since. I know I must seek peace for my soul. I don't understand forgiveness but . . . but I know I need it desperately."

Something about Panthera's urgent tone convinced Joseph that this Roman soldier was sincere. He stood trying to decide what to do when he remembered Mary. Joseph looked to the house and wondered where she was. He looked back at Panthera and said in Latin, "Come with me to talk to my almah, my betrothed . . . who shall be my wife. I will carry your weapons and helmet."

Panthera obeyed and followed Joseph up the gentle slope to their home and was led into a room at the front of the house. Joseph placed Panthera's belongings on the floor inside another room and hoped he would have time to find Mary somewhere in the rest of the dwelling. He moved quickly down the hall, checking for Mary in every room. The only room he didn't have access to without passing Panthera was the kitchen, where he had left Mary washing the pottery from the night before.

He was too late. When he returned to the front room Mary stood facing Panthera with her hands across her mouth and terror in her eyes. Joseph didn't know what to do. He immediately regretted bringing this soldier into his home. He felt stupid and angry at himself. All he could think to do was pray aloud in Aramaic, "Oh God, have mercy on us all."

Panthera said, "Please, say it in Latin."

Joseph moved close to Mary and placed his arm around her and said in Latin, "Oh God, have mercy on us all."

Panthera suffered from a flashback and remembered the blood spurting out of his mother's chest so many years ago, as he also vividly remembered the bloody body of his little brother lying dead on the floor. In an instant he wondered why he had been spared to live, only to repeat the terror he had perpetrated to this family. He looked at Mary and remembered the terror in her eyes when he had dragged her into the cave and raped her. The same look of terror was in her eyes looking at him now. For Panthera it was too much. He fell down on his knees and began to weep. "I can't live like this any more. Help me! I need to know the forgiveness of your God and I can't find him." He placed his face into his hands that visibly shook. "There is no peace in my heart. Help me! Forgive me!"

As Panthera wept, very slowly at first, Mary lowered her hands, which had covered her face. She lost her conscious reality for a moment and didn't know where she was temporarily. When she did become aware, she didn't know what to do. Panthera's presence caused horrific images to flash in her mind. The images terrified her and left her alone with help only from Joseph. She allowed herself to feel Joseph next to her holding her with his arm. Joseph was strong and his strength seemed to calm her fear and enabled her to look at the soldier's bowed head in front of her. She watched as Panthera collapsed to the floor and curled into a ball, weeping, just as she had on the path when they journeyed here from her aunt and uncle's. Compassion began to possess her soul. Her fear and anger dissipated and lifted like a breath released from the core of her soul. Compelled to do so by a force alien to her, she calmly walked forward and stood over Panthera. She placed her hand on his head and it seemed to quiet his sobbing. She said, "You are so tortured." She turned to Joseph and said, "Joseph, please tell this man that . . . that maybe . . . that . . . sometimes our great and mysterious God breaks through evil and human suffering with blessedness beyond our human comprehension."

Mary didn't remove her hand from Panthera's head until Joseph had finished repeating her words in Latin while he kept his arm around her securely. When he finished speaking there was a long span of great silence. Mary removed her hand from Panthera's bowed head and moved closer to Joseph. She felt no fear, anxiety, or despair. She then moved to take bread, figs, and grapes from the cupboard. Joseph said to Panthera, "Come eat, here is food to share, my brother."

Panthera stood up slowly and walked to the table, sat down, and began to eat. He would not have done this had he not been so starved from the march and the recent illness he had suffered. Joseph sat across from him and said, "I ask you to talk to one last family member about what took place between you and Mary. Will you talk to her father? He has abandoned Mary because he doesn't believe she was raped. If I go and bring him here, will you speak to him? He is a good man and a simple farmer who is on the brink of a ruined marriage over these circumstances."

Panthera looked up from his eating. He didn't know if he could endure such an encounter. He felt emotionally drained and vulnerable. To his own surprise he answered, "Yes."

Joseph instructed Panthera to stay in the house and eat his fill while he and Mary left to retrieve Joachim.

Joachim returned with them believing Joseph that a Roman soldier named Panthera was waiting in Joseph's home ready to confess the truth about Mary's rape, but he didn't believe Panthera would still be there when he arrived.

To their disbelief, Panthera had not left. When Joseph, Joachim, and Mary entered the front room, Panthera was standing and staring out the window. He turned around abruptly as Joachim entered first. Joachim stood speechless. Panthera's words were translated by Joseph as he told Joachim his shameful act and his intention to monetarily support the child until he, or she, reached adulthood. He took a purse from the belt of his garment and placed it on the hearth's mantel.

"Use this money as you need. There will be more." Panthera looked at Joseph and asked for his belt, sheathed sword, helmet, and standard. When Joseph brought out his belongings to him, Panthera looked at Joseph and said, "You will be blessed by the 'gods' for your kindness and for both Mary's and your forgiving heart."

"Panthera, we believe there is only One Almighty God who ultimately cares for the universe. I'm not telling you to throw your trust in the 'gods' away from your spirit if it brings you peace. I'm just suggesting you become aware that there just may be one Divine Creator of the universe who loves you and all of us."

Panthera stared at Joseph and didn't understand his words, even though he spoke them in Latin. He reached out and took his belongings from Joseph, who held them out to him. He walked slowly to the front door and paused, looking awkwardly back. He said nothing, turned, and walked out into the cool evening air. He headed west and knew he would return to the campsite before the sun set. All he needed to do was follow the light.

Joachim walked home in a daze. He looked straight ahead and although his home was just a short walk from Joseph and Mary's home, he wished his journey would take more time. He stopped as he looked in the direction Panthera had left and saw no sign of him walking away in the distance. A warm breeze brushed against his cheek as he turned to walk toward his own home again. Nothing seemed to make sense to him. He truly believed his daughter had lied about a Roman soldier raping her eight months ago. The fact that he was a Roman soldier of Greek descent boggled his mind and strangely frightened him. Mary's baby would be the son of a Jewish Essene mother, a Greek father who was a Roman soldier and citizen. All the talk that his daughter Mary was to be the mother of the Messiah seemed impossible on the one hand. Yet it was incredibly, miraculously, and inclusively likely on the other. The warm breeze brushed him again and he came to his senses, remembering that he was walking home and needed to talk to Anna, no . . . Anne. He remembered she wanted him to call her Anne. For the first time he wondered about his wife's insistence to be called Anne by him. Maybe, he thought, Anna was too much like the name of a little girl and she was a woman. Yes, that must be her reason. Why had he not understood and heard her request before? The warm breeze brushed him again and urged him to go home and talk to his wife. He hoped it was not too late. She seemed to hate him now.

As he walked, he prayed, "God, help me to repent. Give her strength to forgive me. She is my wife, the mother of our children given to us by you. Whatever comes, help me to also accept your will, so that I may continue to live in love, and peace, as husband and wife in marriage together as one."

Joachim found himself standing at the entrance to his own home. He paused, sighed, and opened the door to step inside. The house was still and unusually quiet except for a fire burning in the hearth. Anne was standing over a pot of stew she had prepared, stirring its contents.

"Where have you been? It was late and the children were hungry so they ate without us," she stated.

"You have not eaten yet?" Joachim asked.

"I've not been hungry lately. No, I didn't eat. I've kept it hot for you. Help yourself." She moved from the hearth and headed out of the room. The entire time she talked to Joachim, he noticed she didn't look at him.

Before she reached the hall leading out of the room Joachim cried out, "Anne, please do not leave me here to eat alone." She looked at him. "Please," he said again.

She turned to him and paused before she walked to the table and sat down. Joachim didn't take any food from the bubbling pot of stew but sat across from her.

Slowly, he said, "I was at Mary and Joseph's home."

Anne's expression became mixed with hope and dread as she wondered what Joachim was about to tell her.

"Anne, God truly works in mysterious ways."

Joachim felt faint and reached for the pitcher of water on the table. He poured some water in the goblet and drank it quickly. He put the goblet down and looked directly into his wife's eyes.

"I was wrong," he said. "I falsely accused our daughter of lying. She was raped by a Roman soldier eight months ago. The soldier most certainly impregnated her. This afternoon, while still working in the wheat field, Joseph and Mary found me and implored me to come to their home. I was irritated but I walked with them to their house and while on the way I was told that a Roman soldier named Panthera was waiting to speak the truth to me about Mary's pregnancy. When I stepped into their home the soldier, Panthera, was still there, standing by the window. When we entered, he turned to me. Joseph translated his Latin, explaining that he was seeking forgiveness. He confessed that he was the soldier who had raped Mary. He left money with Mary and Joseph and promised to monetarily support the child into adulthood. He . . . he . . . said he was sorry and that Mary had nothing to do with this crime perpetrated against her. He told me I should not disown my daughter or allow my wife to disown me because of . . . the hardness of my heart . . . or my pride. He left then, after Joseph had returned his weapons and helmet to him . . . he said he would be back . . . to check on our families . . . Anne, please forgive me, don't turn your love from me . . . I cannot bear it."

Joachim didn't take his eyes off Anne. She sat staring at him in a stillness that matched death. But this was a good death. Finally, she rose from her chair and walked to Joachim. Tears welled in his eyes as she knelt next to him and gently took his hands into her own and laid her head on his lap.

She spoke her words softly, "I love you, Joachim, I love you." She kept her head in his lap and he began to stroke her hair. Finally, she looked up at him and with a hint of a smile on her face she said, "So . . . it took the witness of a Roman soldier, no less."

* * * *

Three weeks passed and Mary was very tired of being pregnant. The baby moved often in her womb and she wondered if the baby longed to be born before its time too. If she were to hold the baby full-term, she had at least three more days, maybe seven more days to wait.

The women of the village had not changed their minds about Mary and no family member tried to convince anyone of the truth. Mary believed she would be fine birthing the baby with just the help of her mother and inexperienced sister who continued to bear her name. Joseph was not as confident. As the time grew near to Mary's time for delivery his anxiety increased. If the birth killed Mary, he knew that he could not accept the child as his own but he dared not admit this secret thought to anyone.

It was late in the morning and Joseph was writing in the room he used for the many things he studied. Recently, he had an idea about using water to lift heavy objects too large and heavy to lift with manpower or animals. Like a haunting dream he heard sweet, beautiful singing just outside his window and recognized it immediately to be Mary's voice. But what was she singing? He listened carefully and felt compelled to write the words she sang:

My soul magnifies the Lord,
And my spirit rejoices in God
My Savior,
For he has looked with favor on
the lowliness of his servant.

Surely, from now on all
generations will call
me blessed;
for the Mighty One has done
great things for me
and holy is his name.
His mercy is for those who fear
Him
from generation to generation.
He has shown strength with
His arm;
he has scattered the proud in the
thoughts of their hearts.
He has brought down the
powerful from their
thrones,
and lifted up the lowly;
he has filled the hungry with
good things,
and sent the rich away empty.
He has helped his servant Israel,
in remembrance of his mercy,
according to the promise he made
to our ancestors,
to Abraham and to his
descendants forever.

Joseph stuck his head out of the window. Mary was sitting against the wall of the house singing and snapping beans. “Where did you learn that prayer song, Mary?”

Mary seemed a little embarrassed. “I didn’t know anyone was listening.”

“Well, I was listening and I wrote down the words. I’d never heard them before. Where did they come from?”

Mary put the beans down and stood up brushing the dust from her robe. She walked over to Joseph and through the window she told him, “I made them up months ago while staying with my Aunt Elizabeth and Uncle Zechariah. The first time I sang them they brought me peace. The words still bring me peace and comfort.” Suddenly she bent over in pain and Joseph jumped through the window to her. “I’ll be alright, Joseph. They are just muscles practicing to give birth . . . at least that’s what my mother said.”

“How long have you been feeling these pains?”

“Not long, maybe the past week or two.” There was worry in Joseph’s eyes. “Joseph, please don’t worry. Everything will be all right.”

A fist banging on the front entrance door to the house made them both jump. They walked around, surprised to find Panthera pounding on their door.

When he turned his head to see Mary and Joseph, he ran toward them and said with urgency in his voice, "I need to talk to you inside . . . alone." Joseph led the way and let Mary step into the house ahead of him. Panthera followed.

Standing in the room Panthera said, "We've just received orders that everyone in this area must register at the place of their birth identifying their origin. Joseph, where is your place of origin?"

"I'm a descendant of King David."

Panthera was well trained to know and understand the Judean culture. "That means you must travel and register in Bethlehem, the City of David. You will need to travel there to register within this week." Panthera looked at Mary. "You should be able to travel and register before the baby comes. Plan your trip quickly and get to Bethlehem at your best convenience . . . if that is possible." Panthera took a small sack from his belt and dropped its coins onto the table and turned to leave abruptly. He stopped before stepping out the door and said, "Travel safely."

Mary looked at Joseph and asked, "What did he say?"

Joseph responded with expressive urgency in his voice which Mary didn't understand. "We're going on a trip to Bethlehem. It's not far, maybe seven or eight miles. We can walk that distance in four hours." Joseph's behavior was irrational and intense. He paced and talked as if no one was there until he abruptly looked at Mary and said, "I don't want to be traveling on the road to Bethlehem with you going into child labor. I don't want to be in Bethlehem with you giving birth in a town where we know no one. At least here, your mother will come to our home to help you give birth. Your mother will come to help you. Maybe other women from the Qumran will come and help you. So, we should leave immediately! You're not due to give birth for at least another one or two weeks so we should be safe. Let's get ready to go and I'll tell you why we must go as we are traveling."

Confused, but sensing his urgency, Mary realized that Joseph was extremely concerned about something she didn't understand. She knew it had to do with the Roman soldier and didn't ask any further questions. She went to pack some clothing, food, and water as Joseph headed to the shed to prepare the burro for the trip.

When Joseph brought the burro around to the front of the house, he took what Mary had gathered for the trip and tied it securely to the burro's crude saddle. He lifted Mary onto the burro and began to lead it west toward Bethlehem.

"Joseph!" Mary cried, "Shouldn't we tell my family we are leaving and let them know where we're going?"

Joseph ignored Mary's question and continued walking. For the first time Mary felt as if Joseph wasn't thinking clearly.

She protested again a little way down the path. "Joseph, did you hear me? What's gotten into you?"

"*You*! That's what's gotten into me . . . *you*!"

Mary felt angry and shouted, "Stop this burro right now. I want to get off." Joseph kept walking. "I will jump off of this burro if you don't stop right now!"

Joseph stopped and turned to face her. His face was stricken with fear and Mary didn't understand his behavior. She struggled and jumped to the ground and felt the weight of the baby in her womb drop with a jolt. "I can't believe you are acting like this. Tell me, Joseph, what's going on in that brilliant head of yours?!"

Joseph put his hands up to the sides of his head and dropped his arms down and out. "Mary, you live in a dreamworld! You're only a little more than fourteen years old, but even a fourteen-year-old knows the life-threatening dangers of childbirth!"

Mary yelled back, "I didn't choose to have a baby now! I didn't choose to place you or me in this situation!"

Joseph yelled at her with more intensity, "Oh, I see! And do you think I'm choosing this!? It's not even my baby. I don't know what I was thinking. I thought God would help me keep my promise to you, Mary. You are my almah and I fully intended to marry you and have children with you as guided by our Essene rules. I feel like God doesn't care one iota for me . . . or for us."

Mary yelled back, "Joseph, get a handle on this . . . and you're saying I live in a dreamworld!?! Did you ever think maybe your little plan for life wasn't part of God's big plan? Stop feeling sorry for yourself! You're acting ridiculously, especially for someone a lot older than fourteen years!"

Exhausted, Joseph sat down with his back to Mary. He felt oddly pleased that Mary had spoken to him the way she did. He thought, "We'll be partners all right!"

At first Mary didn't know what to do so she walked and stood next to Joseph, looking in the same direction as he.

"I'd sit down next to you, Joseph, but I'm not sure I would be able to get up again by myself. You show no indication that you would help me so . . . I will say from here that . . . I'm scared too. I know the dangers that come with childbirth and . . . I really don't want to die." Mary's voice was shaking. "Joseph, you have been my anchor. You have kept me steady. Please don't leave me now. Please, Joseph." Joseph stood up immediately and took her into his arms. She reached around him and held him as tight as she was able. "I can hold you too, Joseph. I can be strong for you too."

They both began to weep and their tears released fear and tension. Joseph gained composure first and held Mary a little way from him so he could look into her eyes.

"Panthera came to tell us that a census has been ordered. All of the people living in Israel must register in their places of origin. I am a descendant of King David, so I must register in Bethlehem, the city of David. You are my betrothed wife so you and the unborn child must also register in Bethlehem."

Mary smiled and declared, "Well, you know that I, too, am a descendant of King David so, no matter what, I would have had to make this trip one way or another."

Joseph was intrigued when he realized that he didn't know Mary's full ancestry and to which Israelite tribe she was connected. He asked, "Mary, from what tribe did your ancestors come?"

She answered, "The tribe of Judah."

Joseph stood still and silent as he contemplated the fact that Mary was from the tribe of Judah, as was he. As an Essene he knew that prophesy foretold that the Messiah would be from the tribe of Judah.

"Come," Joseph said. "Let us be on our way. I'm sure we can get to Bethlehem before nightfall, rest through the night, and register in the morning. Then we'll return to our home and wait for the birth of the baby." Joseph put his hand on Mary's round belly and felt no movement. He wondered why there was no movement from the baby, but decided they had enough to contemplate as they traveled west to Bethlehem. Neither he nor Mary knew that no movement and stillness from the baby indicated that the time for the baby's birth was imminent.

THE HILLS OF BETHLEHEM

Eli was a very poor shepherd of little significance and no importance to anyone. Although his lowliness and poverty had made him genuinely humble, he was surprisingly content with his lot in life. He enjoyed his work watching over flocks of sheep even though they never belonged to him. He loved the gentleness and dependency of sheep. The harder work caring for them in the winter months had now given way to warm spring days and nights and the sheep could be led into the wilderness hills to graze on young shoots of grass. This night was still with clear skies. The lambs were resting next to their mothers, tired from the long day of play, and he, too, was tired from their long walks on the hillsides.

Giving in to his own weariness, he leaned against a boulder that was covered with a carpet of soft moss. He gazed at the stars overhead and was surprised to be rudely visited by great emotion. He was overwhelmed. He had never experienced an emotional event like this before. He was consumed with feelings of extreme peace and awesome joy that melted together with feelings of excitement and fear.

Eli's exhaustion won over and he closed his eyes and fell into a deep sleep. As quickly as he fell asleep, he also remembered feeling a sudden, great, and terrifying presence. He couldn't seem to wake up even though he tried. He vividly became aware of a huge, powerful angel of light standing at his feet brandishing a sword. Eli couldn't move as the angel walked around his side to hover over his head above the boulder he rested against. Terror froze Eli's ability to escape as the angel lifted the huge, long sword of light and pointed it down over Eli's forehead. Eli knew he could not stop the angel from plunging the blade through his skull, so he waited in complete helplessness, not able to do anything else.

Finally, even though he was riddled with fear and terror Eli was able to utter, "Please, who are you? What do you want?"

The angel declared in a mighty voice, "I am God's warrior messenger. I am the archangel Michael."

Accepting his fate, Eli closed his eyes, knowing the angel would push the sword through his head. The archangel Michael said in a voice that was as loud as thunder, "Would that you could fly!" Eli opened his eyes as the sword came down upon him swiftly and the blade was driven into his head. To his amazement, Eli felt no pain. Instead, his confusing, mixed emotions dissipated as if the light of the sword drove out all negative thoughts and feelings. Eli sat up and turned to look at the angel. He was not there. He had disappeared but Eli heard a chorus that drew his attention to the distant hills. To his amazement he saw thousands of angels who all seemed to be moving up and down, as if on stairs that reached from the ground to the heavens. All the while they sang in unison, "Glory to God in the highest, and peace on earth, goodwill to all people." Eli recognized the archangel Michael's voice rising above the other voices, saying, "Go to Bethlehem and see this wonder. You will find a newly born baby, wrapped in swaddling clothes, lying in a manger. Go!"

Eli stood up and rubbed his eyes and shook his head. He looked around only to see his flock of sheep lying still under the quiet night sky. He shouted out in an effort to determine where the next nearest shepherd was and heard nothing. He picked up his staff and ran to the well where any shepherd could go and blow the goat's horn to call other shepherds for aid.

When Eli arrived at the well, he was surprised to see several shepherds already gathered there. They were all talking with great excitement. Eli burst into their center and shouted, "I had a really wild dream that seemed so real!" The other shepherds turned to listen to Eli describe his dream. All of them stood and stared at Eli.

Finally, one of the shepherds spoke up saying, "We all dreamed the same dream! We don't understand how this happened, but we're all compelled to go to Bethlehem and see this wonder. We shall look for a newborn, wrapped in swaddling clothes, lying in a manger. Do you want to join us?"

Eli pounded his staff on the ground with confidence and said, "Would that I could fly!"

BETHLEHEM

THE SUN HAD SET and twilight lit the sky. Mary could no longer bear the contraction pains so she asked to be taken down off the burro to walk. Joseph helped her down and they walked with the burro. It seemed as if every five minutes Mary stopped and groaned and breathed deeply. Joseph knew they were close to Bethlehem and much too far to turn back. How stupid he felt. They should have traveled after the birth of the baby but then there had never been any guarantee that Mary would have birthed the baby within the week. She had been experiencing contraction pains that indicated an earlier delivery but not this early. He had never dreamed that his fear would place them in this peril.

Mary stopped walking and cried out again. Joseph placed his hands on her abdomen and felt the rock-hard muscles. It must hurt, he thought. The muscles began to soften and Joseph knew they could walk for another five minutes before the next contraction. The path rounded a cliff-like hill and they both had the town of Bethlehem in their view. They walked a little faster until Mary stopped again and cried out. This time she had tears.

The sun had completely set and darkness had set in. It would be a peaceful still night and Joseph thought that at least God gave them the blessing of good weather. Mary stood up and began to walk as quickly as she could. Joseph knew that at her present pace they would reach the outskirts of the town before the next contraction.

As they came upon the first house of the town Mary bent over in pain again. Joseph ran to the door of the house and he knocked so fervently it gave reason for its inhabitants to not open the door. However, a man in the house next door emerged, hearing Joseph's frantic voice. His evening meal must have been interrupted by Joseph's knocking because he held food in his hand and he spoke with his mouth full of bread. In anxious desperation Joseph said, "My wife is about to have a baby. Please, can you help us get to an inn?" Since the man's mouth was full of bread, he said nothing as he ran to the back of his house. He returned with a small wagon that could hold Mary and allow her to sit up against its side rails.

With the man's help, Joseph and he could pull the wagon while Mary squatted and leaned against its side rail. The burro followed on its own, without Joseph's command, as the men pulled the wagon up several blocks of streets.

"There's only one inn in town so I'll take you there," said the man. Mary cried out in pain and sat with her knees up against her chest. She screamed as another contraction came. The contractions came closer together now. "It won't be a long ride. I'll get you there," the man said.

They stopped at the door of the inn and the innkeeper answered their knocking by saying, "I'm sorry, there isn't any room . . ." Mary screamed. The innkeeper saw what the situation was immediately. "Follow me." He led Joseph, the man, Mary, and their burro to the back of the inn where there stood a nice-sized stable. "For now, let's settle her in the stable. We'll find a way to keep her safe and as comfortable as possible. My wife is a midwife and a good one. She's helped women birth babies for more than twenty years."

Joseph was amazed that the two men did not direct their conversation to him but took control of the situation with a calmness he needed to experience and depend upon. He was scared and uncertain and their confident display of knowledge and control helped him feel as if he was in the presence of angels unaware. Mary screamed again as the two men lifted her from the wagon and placed her gently against a haystack. The innkeeper tied a rope to a rafter above and dangled it down for Mary to hold herself up. Mary grabbed the rope and squatted as she screamed again.

The innkeeper turned to the man who had lent the wagon and said, "Help me get these animals to the other side of the barn." The two men moved and pushed a cow, chased some chickens, and led Joseph's burro and two other burros to the other side of the barn away from Mary. They closed the animals in their stalls and they both started to leave. The innkeeper turned back and said to Joseph, "Stay close to her. Talk softly to her and cool her forehead with that water in the bucket. Here's a rag." He tossed a rag to Joseph to soak in the water. "I'm going to get my wife, then you, sir, can relax."

Joseph took the cloth and soaked it in the water. He sat down close to Mary and ran the coolness of the rag across her forehead. "Mary, try to relax. It won't hurt as much if you let your mind and body relax and rest between contractions." Joseph dipped the cloth in the water again and dripped water onto her head. She seemed to be in a type of trance and she was breathing deeply. Joseph bent his head down, consumed with worry and concern, but he would not let himself lose composure. Softly and quietly, he said, "You'll be fine, Mary. God is providing all that you need. I love you."

In walked a woman who had an air of confidence and cheer. She walked to Mary and said to Joseph, "My name is Beth. You are Joseph and Mary, correct?" Joseph nodded his head. "Joseph, help me take Mary's robe off. It doesn't need to be soiled by the birthing. I'll put this on her for convenience and comfort." Beth held what looked like a large, light cotton sheet. Joseph obeyed and stripped Mary while Beth placed the large sheetlike covering over her head and let it flow beneath her and around her. "Take her robe with you and go outside and wait. I don't think this will take too long." Joseph stood and stared at Mary, who began to scream again with another strong contraction. Beth said with authority in her voice, "Joseph, go!"

Joseph walked outside the barn and felt lost. The innkeeper walked up to Joseph with a hot drink in his hand. "Here, my friend, drink this. It will help you relax, and I'll stay with you until the baby is born."

Joseph heard Mary scream again. The innkeeper said, "Her screaming sounds good and strong. That's a good sign. By the way, my name is Joseph also, but I'm called Joe."

Inside, Beth stooped low to check Mary's progress. She saw that Mary was open all the way and that there would not need to be much pushing on Mary's part to birth the baby. In fact, Beth knew that the greatest danger to both Mary and the baby would be if Mary pushed too hard and too fast. Almost instantly, Beth saw the crown of the baby's head appear and she realized that the baby was most definitely coming too fast. Beth washed her hands and put her hand gently into Mary's vagina and pushed back on the baby's shoulders. She could feel the baby was in the correct position and that there was no cord around or near its neck or shoulders. Beth felt another strong contraction. "Slow it down, Mary. Try not to push so hard."

Mary screamed, "I can't help it. My body wants to push."

"All right, daughter.Your body knows exactly what to do, but sometimes when you're young and strong it does it with a vengeance. We don't want you to tear so you go ahead and push and I will hold the baby back and let the baby be born slowly. That will give your skin time to stretch slowly and not tear."

Mary screamed again. Her scream was louder and sounded more desperate. Beth felt the baby move forward and she gently held it back.

Outside, Joseph was in a panic. He paced and struggled with feelings of hatred toward Panthera. He thought, "That evil soldier did this to my young wife. She was too young to have a baby." Then he thought of the decisions he had made in the past twelve hours and hated himself for taking Mary away from her home right when she was ready to give birth. He justified his decision, remembering that he had decided to leave as they did to avoid this very event and outcome from happening. Another scream from Mary led Joe to say, "That . . . my friend, is the scream of a woman pushing a head through the birth canal. I know that because I've been with many fathers who hear that scream and think the worst. But let me assure you, my wife is the best midwife in *all of Judea*! She's been requested to birth babies in Bethany and Jerusalem. Don't worry. You are in the right place with the right people."

Suddenly there was quiet. It was strange and frightening until a faint cry of an infant was heard. Joe put his hand on Joseph's shoulder and said, "I think the baby's born." Joseph moved to go into the barn and Joe held him back. "No, Joseph, you can't see Mary yet. She must give birth to the sack." Joseph was confused with anxiousness. "We need to give them time," Joe explained. "What they need to do in the time following the birth is almost as important as the birth of the baby. You see, Beth taught me that the sack, in which the baby developed and grew during pregnancy, will pull away from the muscle of her womb and those blood vessels could bleed profusely if it pulls away too quickly. Beth knows what to do. She will massage your wife's abdomen and that will help the blood vessels close. Then she needs to tie the cord and snip it from the baby's belly so there is no bleeding from the baby. Beth will call you in at the right time. Let her take care of your Mary and your baby."

Peace descended upon Joseph and he walked around behind the stable to look out over the hills. He wondered if this was all part of some great eternal plan of which he had no idea or understanding.

In the distance, he saw shepherds walking toward him from the hills. Most of their sheep lingered on the hillside as they walked toward the stable. Then Beth called to Joseph, "She did it! Mother and baby are fine. You can come in now."

Joseph turned from the approaching shepherds and walked quickly into the stable to see Mary smiling, looking down at the baby in her arms. The baby was wrapped in swaddling clothes and Mary was sitting on a fresh bed of straw and hay with her robe on as if nothing out of the ordinary had happened moments before. Joseph walked up to her and bent down to kiss her forehead. Mary whispered, "It's a boy, Joseph."

Joseph took the baby into his arms and said, "Your name is Jesus," as tears streamed down his face. He looked at Mary and said, "You did it. You birthed this child."

She said, "No, Joseph, we all birthed this child. If we had not come here, I would not have been helped as I was. There was no help for me at home. I thank God for the man with the wagon, the innkeeper and his wife, Beth, and . . ."

The bleating of little lambs interrupted Mary as they and some sheep wandered into the stable. Following the sheep, shepherds came in very slowly and knelt before Mary and the baby in Joseph's arms. Joseph placed the baby gently down into the manger next to Mary.

One of the shepherds said, "You would not believe us if we told you what happened tonight and what sent us here to worship your baby. The angels we dreamed about said, 'Glory to God in the highest, and peace on earth, good will to all people.' That is what they said. And now we see."

BETHANY

THE PASSOVER FEAST WOULD begin in seven days. Rachael was thrilled that Benjamin had planned their trip to visit Lazarus in Jerusalem at this perfect, holy time. She praised Benjamin for his thoughtful planning.

"It will be perfect, Benjamin! Jerusalem will be filled with the excitement of the Passover. We can go to the temple and sacrifice there and return to our inn to celebrate the feast that can be prepared for us all. I won't have to do any preparation this year. I can pray and meditate and thank God for my life, our life."

Benjamin smiled sheepishly, knowing that he had not consciously planned the trip to Jerusalem to visit Lazarus to coincide with the Passover. He was excited himself and felt good that all the plans had been made for their trip. Even though it was a very busy time in Jerusalem, Benjamin found and scheduled perfect accommodations for the family's stay. He felt a little dishonest accepting Rachael's undeserved praise, but he figured that the coincidence would serve no purpose if he denied he was not truly part of it.

Levi and Martha were excited as they anticipated the trip to Jerusalem. Even Baby Mary seemed to be aware of something good about to happen because she ate well, cooed, and giggled a lot, and slept through the night without disturbance. It also afforded a good night of sleep for her Aunt Rachael. "She knows we're going somewhere special. I feel she really knows something special is going to happen," Rachael said.

Finally, the day for them to travel arrived. Levi and Martha played and ran around Baby Mary's basket as Benjamin and Rachael packed what they needed for their journey and visit. Levi saw a lizard on the side of the tree beneath which Mary's basket rested. Martha stopped and saw her cousin's fright. "What's the matter, Levi?"

"Look there, above Baby Mary's basket . . . it's a big lizard."

Martha looked and saw what Levi saw immediately. It was a rather unusually large lizard. She thought to herself that it would be a great catch, but before she moved toward the lizard to trap it in her own hands, the lizard dropped into Mary's basket. Levi was horrified. He lunged forward and snatched the lizard off of Baby Mary's face. He stood up and realized that the lizard was squirming in his own grasp.

To his own surprise he didn't throw the lizard onto the ground in fear but stood and watched as it tried to wriggle loose from his hold. "Levi," Martha said, "You saved Baby Mary from that big, bad lizard! You're brave!"

Levi stared at the lizard in his hand and answered Martha, "Yeah . . . I guess I did." He walked to the tall grass and released the lizard, which scurried out of sight. "I guess I'm not afraid of lizards anymore."

"Levi, come here, honey. It's time to get in the cart with Martha and Baby Mary. Stay under the shade of the cart's awning, I don't want the sun to burn your skin."

What an adventure Martha and Levi anticipated, sitting safely next to Baby Mary in the covered cart as their guardian adults led in the front, directing the burros forward. Rachael began to sing a song. The children eventually reclined to nap as the cart's movement over the path gently rocked them to sleep.

Benjamin turned to Rachael and asked, "How do you feel?"

"I feel wonderful," she said. "We're going to Jerusalem. I can't help but feel this is a very important trip for all of us. I know Jerusalem is not far, but do you feel it too? Something special is about to happen."

Benjamin nodded his head. "Yes, I think it's probably more important than you or I may ever realize."

BETHLEHEM AND THE FIRST MARRIAGE CEREMONY

It was late and a chill began to creep into the stable where Mary and Joseph sat with little Baby Jesus. Beth and Joe walked into the stable and Beth asked Mary if she felt she could get up and walk.

"I think I can move and walk."

"Why don't we try and get you up and check out the situation. Joe, help me lift Mary to her feet slowly." Beth was strong and gentle, as was her husband, Joe, and Mary felt secure and good in their presence. Joseph stood up also but was still dazed from the night's events. Beth checked Mary and then said, "You look fine. Do you think you can walk to the inn and up two or three stone steps?"

"Yes," Mary answered and to her own surprise stated, "I actually feel wonderful. Beth, I need to thank you for your gracious help to me and Joseph. As soon as the baby was born, I felt perfectly fine. The contractions stopped immediately, and I felt no pain or discomfort. It's all so amazing!"

"That's how it works. It's a good plan, isn't it? But now I want to take you, Joseph, and the baby inside to stay in a room I have prepared for you."

"I thought there was no room left in the inn."

"Well, things change," said Joe. Joe walked on one side of Mary, Beth on the other. Joseph followed with Jesus in his arms.

"When we get you settled in the bed you need to nurse your baby. Your body will give your baby good things for his body. Joseph, you need to lie down and get some rest. You look like you are in worse shape than everybody here." Beth looked back at Joseph who couldn't even respond. Beth looked forward again and smiled. "I'm convinced the men suffer the worst and longest from this."

Beth led them to a room on the inn's first floor. She helped Mary step in and both Mary and Joseph were stunned. The room was beautifully adorned with sheer drapes over a window that faced the distant hills to the north. Matching sheers fell over a large hay-stuffed bed that was covered in fine linen sheets that invited both Joseph and Mary to lie down and sleep in comfort. Mary and Joseph had never felt linen like this before and wondered where it came from and how it was made.

Against the wall of the room there was a wooden stand holding a large bowl and a pitcher of water. A clump of lye soap was next to the bowl. Two goblets and a bottle of wine accompanied these amenities on a table with two chairs. A platter filled with bread, mutton, and fruit rested on the tabletop. In the corner of the room a pit fireplace radiated a warm glow.

Most stunning of all was that the room was filled with beautiful desert flowers. Joseph stood frozen. Beth helped Mary sit on the bed and walked up to Joseph to take the baby from his arms. A little wooden box filled with soft, clean hay and straw was covered by a soft sheet matching the material on the bed. Beth laid the baby in the wooden box and said to Joseph, "This room is yours to use for four days. All is prepaid and you will be served your meals each day in the dining room down the hall."

Joseph asked, "Who did this for us?"

Joe stepped forward and answered, "A Roman soldier named Panthera. He also wanted you to know that he will be visiting you here two days after tomorrow. He said it was urgent to meet with you so that you, Mary, and the baby remain safe."

Like a typical Roman military soldier, Panthera had knowledge of the baby's birth from informants who were other Roman soldiers. All Roman soldiers were trained and instructed to know what was happening in their jurisdictions at all times. When Panthera had learned that the baby was born, he had used the money he earned as a soldier. He didn't need the Roman army's stipend because he owned wealth from his lost family's estate in Greece. Money was, and had never been, a need or concern for him.

Like a typical new father, Joseph couldn't think straight. He was tired and more confused than he had ever experienced. Beth and Joe walked to the door, and Beth said, "If there is anything more that you need, come and knock on the third door down the hall, and I will do what I can to meet your need and wish." She smiled, walked out of the room with Joe, and closed the door.

Joseph had not moved from the spot where he stood when the baby had been taken from his arms. Mary looked at him and said, "Joseph, please. Bring us some bread and wine and then let me nurse little Jesus. He will go to sleep quickly when his tummy is full. Then we can sleep. I'm so tired."

"From where did all these beautiful flowers come?" Joseph asked.

Mary smiled. "They came from the desert. Didn't you notice that the desert was covered with their beauty as we walked here from home?"

Joseph didn't reply. He walked to the platter of food and took it to Mary. He went back to the table, dipped into a jug filled with wine, filled two goblets, and took one to Mary. They both drank and Joseph sat on the bed next to Mary as they both took bread and ate. "I guess I didn't notice the flowers in the desert," he said, still dazed.

"No, Joseph. Sometimes you're so busy with everything you think is important you forget to live in a dreamworld." He looked at her and she smiled. "It's easy for me. I'm only fifteen years old."

Joseph almost protested but could only laugh. He laughed good and hard. He got up from the bed and walked to the cradle box. He lifted Jesus up, saying, "And you, my Jesus, do you live in a dreamworld? Can you teach me to be there with you?" Joseph laid Jesus in Mary's arms, turned, and walked to the window. He gazed at the night sky and sang an evening prayer.

The following two days were filled with comfort and leisure for Mary and Joseph. Baby Jesus nursed well and slept even better. This evening Joseph stood by the window again to watch the sun set. When the room became dark, he went to the fire pit and stoked the embers and placed more wood on its flickering flames. It bathed the room in a soft glow of light and he looked over at the baby, asleep in the crude cradle. He was a beautiful, healthy baby. Joseph lifted his gaze to Mary, who was also asleep on the bed. She had eaten her fill with him and he felt pleasantly safe and secure, as if the universe coordinated and orchestrated care for all three of them. After they had eaten, Mary had nursed and cuddled Jesus who fell asleep in her arms. Joseph thought, "She's amazing. She birthed the baby and seems to know exactly what to do to care for the baby." Joseph felt pleasantly paternal toward Jesus, which was a surprise to him. The baby Jesus brought unexpected peace to him, and yet he also caused Joseph to fret. When he had watched Mary nursing the baby, he had felt a strange twinge of jealousy. How could he be jealous of a baby? And yet Jesus received more gentle attention and physical affection from Mary than he during their stay in this beautiful room. Somehow Joseph didn't feel this justified his emotional response of jealousy but at the moment he didn't care.

Joseph turned his gaze away from Mary and thought about the scheduled meeting with Panthera tomorrow. Joe had reported that Panthera had stated that their meeting would deal with urgent issues. He worried about this. He knew he needed to trust God and not his own power since everything that was happening seemed to be completely out of his control.

Mary stirred in the bed. "Come to bed, Joseph. I want to hold you."

Joseph sat on the bed and removed his sandals. He crawled into the bed next to Mary, who lay on her side and draped her arm over his body. It was strange not having the great bulge of her pregnant belly always putting space between their ability to come close together physically. Just the feel of her body excited his senses and he longed to be closer still. She turned his head to hers and she kissed him with a depth that cleared his mind of all concerns. She whispered, "Someday, we will be able to make love together, and although that day is not here yet I've been counting. We have thirty more days to wait. Hopefully we will be able to celebrate our first marriage before then." Joseph smiled. "Joseph, I have to say I'm a little scared to make love. It hurt so badly when . . . when he raped me."

"Mary, it will be different for you with me. I'll be your husband and we will move slowly. You will be safe in my love, perfectly safe." He bent over and kissed her on the forehead. Joseph leaned on his back and slipped his hands beneath his head. "Mary, I've been thinking about our relationship. Events have not taken place in the order I always thought they would. What if we celebrate our first marriage tomorrow? We can invite Beth and Joe to witness our vows to one another. We can do it in the desert, on the hills I've been watching since we've come to stay in this room. We can face east and watch the sun rise upon our new life together."

Mary looked at Joseph with a great smile. "Yes!"

Joseph jumped up from the bed and walked down the hall to knock on Beth and Joe's door. When Joseph explained his wish to them, they graciously accepted the honor and told Joseph they would be waiting on the first hill directly behind the inn early in the morning before the sun would rise. Joseph trotted back to Mary, who sat up and asked, "What did they say?"

"They'll meet us at sunrise on the closest hill to witness our vows. They're honored to do it."

Mary and Joseph sat together on the bed and held each other's hands.

"Joseph," Mary asked, "Do you believe in angels?"

"I don't know . . . but I'm finding out that I don't know a lot." Together they lay back to sleep.

Before Joseph fell asleep, he set his mind to awaken before sunrise, but just before the early morning sunrise and the disappearance of the morning star, it was Jesus who awoke them. He was crying. He was wet and hungry. Thankfully Jesus' cry awakened both mother and father, or they might have slept through the sunrise. Mary rose to attend to him while Joseph listened to the birds chattering and singing. The light from outside was dim, but Joseph was aware that the sun would rise quickly. He strapped his sandals on and waited for Mary to finish nursing Jesus. She handed Jesus to Joseph and put her sandals on quickly. Together they walked out of the room, heading toward the first hill north of the inn. Beams of light from the sun began to reach upward into the sky from the east. The flowers of the desert began to open as they walked, and the clouds straddled the sunbeams in bursts of color.

Joseph carried Jesus to the top of the hill and Mary followed cheerfully behind them. To their surprise Beth and Joe were already sitting on the hill, waiting for them and the sunrise. They held goblets and a jug of wine. When Joseph reached them, they stood up. Joseph handed Jesus to Beth and Mary stepped to face Joseph squarely. His right shoulder and Mary's left shoulder to the east. Joe and Beth moved to face them and the sunrise. They waited quietly.

Joseph spoke first, speaking words from the Song of Solomon.

I take you, Mary, as my wife.
I will love, honor, and be faithful to only you,
forsaking all others.
I will be one with you and live with you,
I will share my life with you until death parts us.
You have ravished my heart, my
sister, my bride,
you have ravished my heart with a glance of your eyes,
with one jewel of your necklace.
How sweet is your love, my
sister, my bride!
How much better is your love than wine,
and the fragrance of your oils than any spice!
Your lips distill nectar, my bride;
honey and milk are under your tongue;
A garden locked is my sister, my bride,
a garden locked, a fountain sealed.
Set me as a seal upon your heart,
as a seal upon your arm;
for love is strong as death,
passion as fierce as the grave.
Its flashes are flashes of fire,
a raging flame.
*M*any waters cannot quench my love,
neither can floods drown it.
If one offered for my love all the wealth of my house,
it would be utterly scorned.
O my beloved, Mary.

Mary took Joseph's hands and saw his tears fall. She spoke with innocence and genuine love,

I take you, Joseph, as my husband.

I will love, honor, and be faithful to only you,
forsaking all others.
I will be one with you and live with you,
I will share my life with you until death parts us.
I am my beloved's
and his desire is for me.
Come, my beloved Joseph,
let us go forth into the fields,
and lodge in the villages;
let us go out early to the vineyards,
and see whether the vines have budded,
whether the grape blossoms have opened and the pomegranates
are
in bloom.
There I will give you my love.
The mandrakes give forth fragrance,
and over our doors are all choice fruits,
new as well as old,
which I have laid up for you,
O my beloved, Joseph. (Song 6 from The Song of Solomon)

The light from the sun burst over the hills as Joseph and Mary embraced and kissed. They turned to its light and knelt. All bowed their heads and Joseph spoke a prayer of thanksgiving. Both rose from their knees and looked to the light, then to each other. Jesus cried out and Mary knew his cry was that of hunger. She turned to Beth and took her son into her own arms and walked with Joseph to the nearby tree. Joseph helped her sit down to nurse Jesus as she leaned against the trunk of the tree. Beth sat down near to Mary while Joe opened the bottle and poured each a goblet of wine. Joseph took his goblet, looked down upon his wife and Jesus, and uttered words of praise.

All lingered on the hillside until the sun shined strongly and Jesus had fallen asleep. They walked down the hill and headed back to the inn. Beth paused in front of Mary and Joseph's room and gently hugged Mary.

"I don't know why I feel this way but . . . I think there is something very special about your baby." Beth looked at Jesus sleeping in Mary's arms. "What could it be?"

Mary said, "Maybe you don't need to know or understand fully today. Maybe it will be something that is yet to be revealed."

"Yes, maybe that is so." Beth walked down the hall to begin the preparation of the meals for the day and Joe followed silently. Joseph and Mary walked into their room and Mary placed Jesus onto his bed. He didn't stir.

She and Joseph went to their bed to lie down and rest. Mary fell asleep but Joseph stayed awake as he anticipated the meeting with Panthera.

When Mary awoke from her morning nap, she saw that Joseph was still awake. "Did you not sleep this morning?"

"No, I couldn't sleep. These days of leisure could spoil me and then I'll be sorry. Come, it's almost noon. We need to eat a meal."

As if Jesus could hear and understand, he cried out, ready for a change of wet cloths and more sweet milk for his stomach. Mary responded to Jesus and nursed him for twenty minutes. Joseph waited. When Jesus seemed satisfied, they all walked down the hall to the dining room. Mary realized this was their last full day at the inn and she knew she would miss how Beth and Joe cared for them and served them. More than that, Mary knew she would greatly miss their presence. Together, Mary and Joseph walked into the dining hall and Panthera stood up from a table positioned in the corner of the room.

"Mary," Joseph said as he pulled out a chair for her at a table in front of them, "please sit here with Jesus and eat." Joseph's voice sounded urgent and Mary sat down quickly. Another couple was in the room and the woman came over to Mary to look at Jesus and fuss over him. Meanwhile, Joseph walked out of the room and Panthera followed.

Panthera quickly took the lead and guided Joseph down to the end of the hall to a door leading to a small room which served as a waiting room. Panthera opened the door and waited for Joseph to pass into the room before him. The room contained a small table and two chairs. A lantern stood on the table. There were no windows. Panthera followed Joseph into the room, lit the lantern, and closed the door behind them.

"This room will afford us privacy." Panthera waited for Joseph to sit before he sat. "I'm here to give you and . . . and your family warning."

"Warning from what?" Joseph asked.

"Joseph, in deep respect, I know you are a good man and that you are a learned man. However, I possess greater understanding and knowledge in the world of politics. I'm here to warn you of a political situation that involves you, Mary, and . . . and mostly the infant, Jesus."

"How could a baby affect a political situation?"

"It all has to do with timing. Jesus' birth coincides with perceptions of some that lead to the fact that he may be the Jewish Messiah, your Long-Awaited One. King Herod, who desires the true adoration of all Jewish subjects, has heard of Jesus' birth. Since he believes Jesus has been born, and that he threatens his kingship among the Jews, Jesus and you and Mary are not safe here. King Herod is unreasonably suspicious, and, if you ask me, he is more threatened by his own family. He married eleven wives, and his sons by all those wives have plotted against him and each other for power over Palestine. He is delusional in thinking that Rome isn't aware of his troubles. Rome ultimately remains in political and military control. Rome allows all the territories to rule themselves through political puppet positions, like King Herod. Rome doesn't want trouble, so they will support these puppet regimes to their own advantage. I don't think Rome cares about the birth of a Jewish Messiah, but King Herod is already on the search for Jesus to destroy him."

"What are you telling me?" Joseph paused and took a deep breath. "Are you telling me that King Herod has made up his mind to hunt Jesus down and kill him?"

"Yes. That's exactly what I'm telling you. By shifting his paranoid attention to find the Messiah, he also hopes to unite his family in pursuing Jesus as a common threat to his throne and the continuation of his perceived dynasty."

Joseph was dumbfounded. It all seemed so ridiculous. "Panthera, what do you think we should do?"

"First of all, did you register at an inn in Jerusalem yet?"

"No. We have been resting here and enjoying your generosity."

"Good! I assume you plan to go from here to Jerusalem for the Passover feast and for Jesus' circumcision the day after the feast because that will mark the eighth day since he was born."

"I'm impressed that you have learned so much about our religious, traditional disciplines."

"Thank you. I have spent some time studying your faith tradition and have come to understand some things. Mostly I have been drawn to the Jewish thought that there is One Almighty God. I guess it reminds me of the Roman political mindset. We are taught that there is one Roman Empire and that all control is ultimately Rome's, though each territory is allowed to maintain their local realm of rule. That is why I know that Rome will turn a blind eye to King Herod, no matter how ridiculous his ruling domain becomes. Rome will become involved only if it threatens the power of the empire."

"So, I am to be aware that Herod will be allowed to hunt Jesus down and have him killed?"

"Yes."

"Should we not go to Jerusalem? After all, Herod's palace is in Jerusalem, just a stone's throw from the temple. Should we go home to the Qumran Settlement?"

"No. You should not return home. The reason I'm glad you didn't register yourself and your family here in Bethlehem is that Herod is waiting for information from this census to locate your family. He's waiting to find out where you are and if the baby has been born. He expects you to be in Bethlehem and plans to intercept you here to have the child murdered. But he won't know you are here, or that Jesus is born, until you register. I have arranged for you and Mary to stay at the inn at the plaza directly across from the temple. This inn is a busy inn, and people from all over stay there when they come to Jerusalem."

"I had planned to stay in the Essene Quarters of Jerusalem. There is a small inn there and an upper room used for worship, meditation, and celebration meals like the Passover," Joseph explained.

"No! The Essene Quarters could be a giveaway, alerting King Herod you may be there. Go to the inn we have arranged for you at the plaza across from the temple. The best plan is for you to stay here in Bethlehem this last night and register first thing in the morning. Then leave immediately and go to the plaza in Jerusalem. Everything will have already been paid for, registered, and taken care of. You will be able to celebrate the Passover feast the day after tomorrow at the inn and have Jesus circumcised in the temple the next day in the morning. From Jerusalem, you, Mary, and the baby must leave. You must disappear. Herod will not suspect you to be under his nose in Jerusalem for the Passover. He'll have his palace guards searching Bethlehem when he learns of your registration. When you have fulfilled religious obligations in Jerusalem, he will move his palace guards to the Qumran Settlement in search of Jesus."

"Where will we go from Jerusalem?"

"Egypt."

"Egypt?!" Joseph looked at Panthera with disbelief. "Why Egypt?"

"You will go to Egypt because, just as you are surprised with this, King Herod will never suspect it. I have connections with other soldiers in Egypt who will prepare a place for you to live. They will get you started in your life in Egypt. You speak Greek and will be able to find employment there, I'm sure. You will live there until it is safe to come back to your home and extended family in the Qumran Settlement." Panthera took a purse filled with silver coins. "You can use this money. I know Essenes have no money. You will need money in the place you are going even though you will be near other Essenes there."

"I haven't spent the money you have given us already. I don't need more."

"Take the money. Please do as I suggest. I will make sure to communicate to Mary's family that you are well and safe. I will tell them nothing more so they cannot be indicted by their puppet king."

Joseph sat for a moment and tried to take it all in. Panthera stood up from his chair and waited for Joseph to respond.

"Egypt!?! Where in Egypt are we going?" Joseph asked, dazed.

"You will leave Jerusalem and go to the port town of Joppa. It will take you at least fourteen hours to walk there from Jerusalem. I have arranged for you and Mary and the baby to board a Roman ship that will take you to Alexandria. Do you understand?" Panthera asked anxiously. "Joseph, can you trust me . . . or has my past deed against you and Mary turned you to distrust my efforts to keep you safe?"

"You have proven to be trustworthy, Panthera. I don't believe I have a choice in any of this anyway, so I must trust you. It's difficult for me. However, I will register our family here in Bethlehem and take Mary and Jesus to Jerusalem for the Passover feast, go to the temple for Jesus' circumcision the following day, and leave directly for Egypt." Joseph stood up and asked, "Do you want to see and hold the baby?"

Immediately Panthera became uncomfortable. "No. I can't do that . . . not now." Panthera opened the door, paused, looked back at Joseph, and stated, "May the gods be with all of us."

"May the God of the universe be with you, Panthera," Joseph gently and genuinely spoke.

Panthera left the room. Joseph didn't move from where he stood before he spoke a silent prayer for all of them. When he extinguished the flame from the lantern and walked out of the room into the hall, Panthera was gone.

JERUSALEM

Rachael and Benjamin entered Jerusalem through the Dead Sea Gate and walked past the pool of Siloam and down the colonnade toward the temple. They came to the plaza directly in front of the Royal Portico at the Triple Gate leading into the temple. The children were remarkably good as they watched the action in the city. The activity of Jerusalem mesmerized their senses and, to Rachael's delight, kept them quietly entertained.

Benjamin stopped the cart in front of an inn that faced the plaza of the temple.

"This is where I have chosen to stay during our visit in Jerusalem. We can sit on the front porch of the inn and watch the activity around the Triple and Double Gate leading into the temple."

Rachael leaned over and squeezed Benjamin's arm with affection. "This is perfect, Benjamin!"

"We will celebrate the Passover Seder meal at the inn three days from today. All we need to do is tour the city and offer sacrifice at the temple before then."

"This will be the first and only time I will have sacrificed to the Lord at the Jerusalem temple!"

Benjamin saw Rachael's expression and could not refrain from saying, "I have sacrificed at the temple during the Passover celebration before. I hope you will not be disappointed with some of the temple's activities. People in Jerusalem, and the temple, are just like you and me, Rachael. It will not seem as holy as you may have imagined all these years while living in Bethany. Bethany may only be two miles away from Jerusalem, but Jerusalem has not rubbed off on Bethany, nor has it rubbed off the other way around, in my opinion." Benjamin sighed and looked up at the blue sky. "I think holiness can be found only in the reverent hearts of people. Sometimes there is no reverence here." Rachael looked at him with questioning eyes. "I just want you to be prepared so you will not lose holiness and reverence within yourself." Rachael turned her gaze to the temple looming before them across the street.

"Well, Levi, Martha, let's go into the inn and settle ourselves before we begin to explore this Holy City." Benjamin jumped down from the front of the cart and walked around to the back and helped two very excited children down to the street. He gave each of the children something to help carry into the inn while Rachael stepped around the cart to lift Baby Mary from her basket. Mary was asleep, totally unaware of the action around her. Rachael thought about Mary's emerging personality and recognized that even though an infant, she had a calm disposition most of the time. But she also displayed qualities of unshakable confidence.

They all entered the inn and the innkeeper showed them to their room. There would be enough space and room for all five of them to sleep. The innkeeper explained that the Passover meal would be served on Thursday beginning at six p.m. Benjamin was invited to place his burros in the stable behind the inn and to feed and water them.

As Benjamin returned from the stable to join his little family, he remembered that Rachael was pregnant and he was filled with joy. As he stepped into the inn, he was surprised by the presence of two Roman soldiers. The innkeeper was paying close attention to their instructions.

"It is good you came today. I have only one room left for this Passover festival. It will accommodate two adults and a baby." The innkeeper picked up his writing utensil and asked, "When will this family arrive?"

The soldiers turned and looked at Benjamin. Their pause made it clear to Benjamin he was not to be listening, so he bowed and walked toward his room. As he walked down the hall, he felt uneasy about the presence of the soldiers.

He walked into the room and announced to the family that it was time to go to the market and buy food. He knew the children would enjoy this experience. The market in Jerusalem was larger and much grander than his small stand in Bethany.

Together they began the short walk to the markets. When they arrived at the avenue known as the colonnade, they all felt overwhelmed by the crowds of people shopping. The children remained close to Benjamin and Rachael but were filled with excitement as they looked at all the items available to them. Levi's eyes were certainly bigger than his stomach because he pointed to all sorts of food and squealed that he wanted to eat "that" and he wanted to eat "this" and "that" and "this too!" Martha watched him and laughed. Mary remained asleep in Rachael's sling, held closely to her aunt's chest. Benjamin smiled but couldn't shake wondering about the two Roman soldiers he saw at the inn. Why would they be talking to the innkeeper about a small family staying in their inn?

Rachael stepped up to certain stands and carefully chose items of food for the family. When she felt she had adequately selected what they needed, Benjamin paid the market salesmen and carried the bundle of goods as they walked back to the inn.

"Are you hungry, children?" Rachael asked.

Martha and Levi spoke yes in unison.

Benjamin suggested, "Why don't we eat on the plaza in front of the temple's portico."

Benjamin walked the children to the plaza and sat them down away from the stream of people walking in and out of the temple. It was such a busy place, Benjamin thought. Rachael instructed Benjamin to present the children with the food she had picked for their meal. They all ate and filled themselves with the good things she chose. Surprisingly, Baby Mary didn't stir. She continued to sleep through their entire visit to the market, dinner on the plaza, and return to the inn. Rachael placed her on a bed of straw in the corner of the room and Mary continued to sleep.

"Benjamin, I'm sure Mary will wake up soon and I will need to nurse her. I'll stay here and rest with her. Why don't you take the children into the temple's court and see about finding Eleazar so we can arrange for Lazarus to stay with us while we are here."

Benjamin smiled, "Great idea. Martha and Levi, come with me."

Both children jumped up from sitting around Baby Mary and each grabbed a hand of Benjamin to hold as he led them through the Double Gate into the Court of Gentiles within the temple walls. Benjamin smiled as he felt their excitement radiate from their hands to his.

BETHLEHEM

Joseph woke from sleep before the light of the sun hit the hills. He turned to Mary and woke her with a kiss. "Arise, my love. We must be off to Jerusalem. It won't be a long trip so we can linger and eat breakfast with Beth and Joe before we leave. We will need to register here in Bethlehem directly before we leave."

"What's going on?" Mary asked. "Why was Panthera here and what did he talk to you about? I thought you would have told me last night but you were so distant in deep thought and meditation."

Joseph sat up in the bed and turned back to Mary. He looked so distraught she was compelled to sit up herself. She waited for Joseph to speak.

"Mary . . . I don't know how to tell you this so I will just tell you straightforwardly. Panthera informed me that King Herod in Jerusalem is seeking to murder Jesus. We need to escape to a place where this cannot happen."

"Why would King Herod seek to kill Jesus? How does he even know Jesus has been born?" It seemed too horrible to be true. It also seemed too crazy to be true. "Jesus is just a baby! Why would someone as important as a king waste his time killing a baby?"

"Panthera has access to the knowledge of certain political maneuvers that could affect Rome. He told me that Rome watches Judea very carefully because there is much dissension among the Jews there. Panthera has been aware that our firstborn son is one of the most likely candidates to fulfill the Jewish messianic prophecy. Herod is threatened by the birth of any supposed Messiah. For some reason your circumstances have not altered the belief that Jesus may be the Long-Awaited One."

Mary looked at Joseph and said, "But Jesus isn't our firstborn son. He is only *my* firstborn son. He is the product of Panthera's rape. Surely, even Panthera knows that God would not allow the Messiah to be the biological son of a Roman citizen of Greek descent. After I was raped everybody in the Qumran Settlement knew we would not parent the Messiah."

Joseph placed his hands on the sides of his head. "I don't know, Mary. I feel confused but something inside of me directs me to believe that Panthera knows something more than we are able to know. You know we have been waiting for the Messiah. You also know that it was believed and talked about in the Qumran Settlement that you and I would be the parents to the Messiah. I don't understand the mind of God, but maybe Jesus' birth to us is still part of prophetic fulfillment. Maybe Jesus is the Messiah." Joseph dropped his hands from his head. "In any case, I have no reason to distrust Panthera's efforts to protect the baby. Since he came to us seeking forgiveness, he has also been faithful to us."

"He raped me, or did you forget that little piece of the puzzle? That offense will never go away." Mary snapped at Joseph in anger. "What kind of husband have I married? Who are you being led to trust?"

"I'm sorry you were raped. I believe if Panthera could, he would turn back time and he would not have violated you. Now he tells me your baby . . . yes, *your* baby is in danger and he has solicited my help to keep him safe and alive. Do you love Jesus? Tell me. Do you love that little baby boy?"

"Yes, of course I do!"

"Well, Mary, for some strange reason I love Jesus too. I plan to register him as my son, our son. I will protect him and I will listen to the guidance of something that seems greater than me, or you, or Panthera, or the entire Roman Empire. I see no reason to doubt the possibility that King Herod may think that the Messiah could threaten his perceived power and reign. So, I have decided to trust Panthera and obey his guidance. I'm led by something I can't explain. Sometimes I'm afraid because it doesn't make sense to my own reason." Joseph dropped his head. He sighed deeply. He put his hands back on his head. "My head hurts." He looked up and over to Mary who was watching him intently. "I am sure of one thing. I love you, Mary. I love you. I wonder if my love for you has made me love Jesus too, but then it really doesn't matter. Therefore, I will take the path I feel will protect us all. I'm trusting in Panthera's knowledge and guidance."

"Joseph, wherever you go, I will go. I've made that promise to you and I intend to keep it." She placed her hand on his arm. "I am set as a seal on your heart, as a seal on your arm." Mary pushed him onto his back and placed both arms around him. She brought her lips close to his and he pulled her to him and kissed her. He ran his hands down the sides of her body and moved them over her hips. He pulled her closer still as he kissed her mouth.

"Oh God," he breathed.

Mary felt the physical intensity of their embrace and raised her head. She smiled at him and asked, "Are you praying, Joseph?"

She thought it would make him laugh but instead he said, "Yes, Mary. I'm praying."

JERUSALEM

Benjamin, Martha, and Levi stood together in the Gentiles' Court of the temple and gazed up at its towering walls. The temple was huge and Benjamin had no idea where to begin to look for Eleazar or Lazarus. He looked around at the wandering people in the court and spotted a rabbi. He grabbed the children's hands and intercepted him before he stepped into an inner sanctuary.

"Rabbi! I'm looking for my brother-in-law. He is a rabbi also. His name is Eleazar. My name is Benjamin and this is my son, Levi, and Eleazar's daughter, Martha. Can you help me find Rabbi Eleazar?"

"Of course, I know Rabbi Eleazar well. Come with me." They walked through an entrance of a long wall separating an inner area from the Court of the Gentiles. There were no crowds of people in this inner hall. "This hallway is referred to as the Soreg. We will walk down the Soreg and I will enter the Court of Israel by way of the Women's Court. You can all wait for Eleazar in the Women's Nazirites' Chamber."

The children quietly looked at everything as they entered the Women's Court located directly in front of the Court of Israel's massive entrance. "Wait here," the rabbi said. "I'm sure Eleazar can be found inside the Court of Israel of the temple during this holy Passover week." The rabbi left Benjamin, Levi, and Martha standing alone in the Women's Court. They didn't talk, afraid to make a sound. They turned slowly and looked at all the walls that surrounded them. There were carvings on the walls. One carving caught Benjamin's eye. It looked like a cloud and a pillar of fire. He immediately remembered the two Roman soldiers who had been talking to the innkeeper. He wondered why he couldn't shake their images from his mind.

Eleazar appeared next to Benjamin without notice. Benjamin jumped when he turned and saw him standing in front of him.

"Benjamin, have you and the family decided to sacrifice at the temple and celebrate the Passover feast here in Jerusalem?" Eleazar didn't look well to Benjamin, but the cold reception from Eleazar made any feelings of concern or sympathy from Benjamin fade.

Benjamin responded rudely by ignoring Eleazar's question. Instead, he answered with a question. "Eleazar, here is your daughter Martha. Don't you want to greet her?"

Eleazar looked down at Martha who looked up to him. "Hi, daddy!" she cried. She was genuinely happy to see her father but her surprise indicated that she had actually forgotten she had a father other than her Uncle Benjamin.

Eleazar patted his daughter's head, displaying pitiful awkwardness.

"Eleazar, Rachael and I plan to be here until the day after the Passover feast. We are lodging at the inn across from the Royal Porch and the Double Gate of the temple's plaza. We would like to invite Lazarus to stay with us for the rest of our stay and have him celebrate the Passover feast with us. Your other daughter, Mary, is also here. She is a beautiful little baby girl and she is growing strong. We invite you also to join us for the Passover meal."

"I am very busy this week. I don't have time to visit with family. However, I will send Lazarus to you tomorrow morning and he may stay with you until the day after the Passover feast. If you desire to offer sacrifice at the temple, I suggest you do it early tomorrow morning. The temple is going to become very busy tomorrow . . . I shall make arrangements to take Lazarus to you in the morning. Following the feast, I expect you to bring him back to the temple, here."

Benjamin was irritated. How could a rabbi be so insensitive to the needs of his own children? "Fine, we will all be happy to see Lazarus tomorrow morning." Martha began to jump up and down with excitement. "Martha, Lazarus won't be with us until tomorrow. Can you wait that long?" Martha nodded her head vigorously. Benjamin noticed that his son Levi was doing the same. "Good night, Eleazar," Benjamin said as he extended his hand out to Eleazar, but Eleazar had already turned and retreated, disappearing back into the enclosed Court of Israel.

Model of First-Century Jerusalem
Pool of Siloam by the Dead Sea Gate into Old Jerusalem
Photo taken of model at the Jerusalem Museum, Jerusalem, April 2009

BETHLEHEM TO JERUSALEM

As the morning waned, Mary and Joseph packed and prepared to leave Bethlehem for Jerusalem. Their trip would not be long. Bethlehem was less than three miles from Jerusalem. So, they lingered at a table in the dining hall with Beth and Joe. The sun had risen over the hills and its rays were bathing the room in light. All four sat in silence until Mary reached over to Beth and grabbed her hands. "Beth, you have been more than a mother to me. Sometimes I wondered if you and Joe might be angels. I don't even know how to begin to thank you."

Beth was crying. "No, Mary. I must thank you. It is strange, but in all my years working as a cook and innkeeper's wife, I have been most blessed by my work as a midwife. I've helped a lot of women birth their babies and I have never been able to conceive a child myself. Every time I would witness the birth of a child, I would feel happy for the new parents but sad and empty for myself. But it was not so when your baby was born. I can't explain my feeling about Baby Jesus." She touched Jesus' cheek as he slept in Mary's arms. "I feel like Jesus belongs to us. Not just Joe and me, not even our Jewish race . . . he belongs to all of us . . . and yet I also feel like we belong to him . . . I'm sure I'm not making any sense."

"You are making more sense than you realize, Beth," Mary said tenderly. Mary reached out with one arm and they embraced as Jesus slept peacefully between them.

Joseph stood up and Joe followed his lead by standing up also. He grabbed Joseph's hand. "Sir," Joe said, "It has been an honor to serve you and your family. May God be with you, and wherever you may go, may his countenance look down upon you and give you peace. You will always be in our thoughts and prayers."

Joseph didn't let go of Joe's hand and said, "We have never been shown such loving hospitality. Thank you. I pray that God will grant us blessings allowing our paths to cross again in the future." He released Joe's hand and turned his attention to Mary and Beth, who were still embracing and crying.

He walked close to Mary and gently put his hands on her shoulders, saying, "It's time to go." He looked at Beth and said, "Thank you for helping me, my wife, and my son." She rose and embraced Joseph and softly said goodbye.

Eastern Wall of Old Jerusalem, April 2009
The Islamic Mosque, Dome of the Rock, erected between 685 and 691 CE (AD) on the original site of the Jewish Second Temple, which was destroyed in 70 CE (AD) by the Roman Empire.

Mary and Joseph walked down the hall, leaving Beth and Joe behind in the dining hall. Both lingered and peered into the room that had been their home for four wonderful days. They walked out to the stable and Joseph helped Mary onto their packed burro and led them out of the stable and out to the street. They walked a little distance to the place where all descendants of King David were to register for the census. As they walked, Joseph thought about the fact that Jesus was truly a descendant of King David because he was born of Mary. He thought it strange that it would not count if he didn't declare him as his own son. Maybe if he had not maintained his betrothal to Mary and had not celebrated their first marriage ceremony, he could have registered himself alone and Jesus would not be targeted by King Herod. No. That would have been impossible. He couldn't imagine where Mary and Jesus would be today had he not followed through and married Mary and declared her son Jesus as his son. It dawned on Joseph that it all came down to the undeniable fact that he loved Mary and could not abandon her or her infant son, Jesus. God was certainly directing their path and he had to trust their divine destiny.

The booth to register was not crowded. There were only three people ahead of Joseph and his family. When Joseph stepped up to the scribe, questions were asked and his answers were recorded. The scribe was matter-of-fact and displayed a need to gather the information as quickly as possible.

"Where is your place of residence?"

Joseph answered quickly, matching the scribe's perceived indifference. "We reside in the western quadrant of the Qumran Settlement."

"What is your name and the names of your immediate family members?"

Joseph answered, "Joseph, Mary, and Jesus." The scribe didn't even look up.

"Is Mary your wife?"

"Yes," Joseph answered.

"Is Jesus your son?"

Without hesitation, Joseph answered, "Yes."

"I need the birthdates of all in the family beginning with the oldest member of the family to the youngest."

Joseph answered truthfully and realized that Mary had turned fifteen years old two weeks ago. Without hesitation, he continued to answer the questions asked.

"What is your means of living?"

"I farm our small plot of land for food and work in carpentry."

"Are you from Jewish descendants of King David?"

"Yes."

"From which tribe do you come?"

"The tribe of Judah."

"Do you intend to continue residing in the Qumran Settlement?"

"Yes."

"Are you or any of your blood relatives Roman citizens?"

Joseph didn't know how to answer this question so he simply answered, "I'm not sure of that. To the best of my knowledge no one in my blood relationship is a Roman citizen."

The scribe recorded this answer with a few more strokes of his pen and without raising his head he yelled, "Next."

When Joseph turned to leave with Mary, who sat on the burro holding Jesus and waiting, he was amazed to see the long line that had formed with men and women waiting to register. He gently took the leading reins of their burro and headed north to Jerusalem.

Bethlehem was a small town and it didn't take long to be out of the town vicinity and into the desert. They walked on the path and passed two other traveling parties walking toward Bethlehem. Both were greeted by Joseph while Mary remained silent. As if out of nowhere two Roman soldiers rounded the curve in the path and were walking toward them. Joseph looked carefully and recognized that one of the soldiers was Panthera. He looked back at Mary.

"Don't be alarmed, Mary. It's Panthera and another soldier with him."

Mary drew Jesus closer to her chest and covered her face with her shawl. She wondered when he would no longer cause her anxiety while in his presence.

The two soldiers approached Joseph and Panthera said, "Joseph, Mary, this is Jarius. He is a good friend of mine. He speaks Aramaic. He is helping me help you."

Joseph bowed to Jarius respectfully. Panthera began to officially explain to Joseph what had been arranged for them for the days to come. "You are to go to Jerusalem and you will be staying at the inn directly across the street from the temple's plaza. Arrangements have been made. You are to celebrate the Passover feast there and if you wish you can make sacrifice at the temple beforehand. The day following the Passover you will be able to visit the temple and arrange for Jesus to be circumcised on the eighth day of his life. I did not arrange this because that is something you must do. As soon as he's circumcised you are to leave Jerusalem by the Golden Gate on the eastern wall of the temple, travel north, staying at the foot of the Mount of Olives, and turn west toward the Mediterranean Sea and the port of Joppa, where you shall board a Roman warship which shall take you to Alexandria, Egypt. You will be safe there and there is an Essene colony near the city."

"Egypt! Egypt!" Mary understood the word Egypt. She tore her shawl away from her face and looked at Panthera directly. "Who decided this!?! You? Have you decided we are going to live in Egypt?!" She turned on Joseph and yelled, "You were too afraid to tell me all this, weren't you? I'm not going to Egypt! I don't even know how to speak their language! I can't believe you would let him decide our future!"

Mary's yelling woke Jesus and he began to cry. Jesus' cry turned to screaming. "Come here!" she ordered Panthera. He stood dumbfounded. She said again with more intensity, "I said, come here!" Panthera understood and moved next to her as she sat on the burro. Jesus was still crying. Mary leaned over and placed Jesus in Panthera's arms. She jumped off the burro and stood in front of him and said, "The baby's crying. What are you going to do about it, you big, stupid soldier? Are you going to give us more silver coins bearing the face of your emperor?" She placed her hands on Jesus as he cried in Panthera's arms. "This is life. It's in your arms and you don't even know it. You don't know where to begin to take care of life, not even your own!" Mary walked to Joseph and pleaded, "Joseph, please, please. Don't take us to Egypt. This is absolutely insane!" Panthera didn't understand her words but understood the situation.

Joseph stood still and spoke calmly. "Mary, you told me in the room last night that you would go where I go, be where I am. You said that you were a seal on my heart, a seal on my arm. I don't always know what to do and I desperately try to rely on the guidance of our God. That guidance comes through people. It comes through people . . . people like Panthera."

Mary looked at Jarius, who had not spoken a word, standing at attention. "And you," Mary asked in anger, "who do you think you are?"

Jarius stated in Aramaic, "I'm just another big, stupid soldier, ma'am."

"You're the only one of us who may be reasonable," she shouted and turned abruptly, then turned back to ask him in desperation, "What do you think we should do?"

Jarius looked straight forward, and without expression he said, "I think you, the baby, and your husband should go to Egypt."

Mary glared at him as Joseph interrupted by saying, "Mary, when I was answering the questions and registering us for the census I answered truthfully. Later, I realized I gave information that could lead King Herod to our residence in the Qumran Settlement. We can't go anywhere in Judea while King Herod reigns."

"We can go to live in Samaria or Galilee!"

Joseph looked over to Panthera for help. Jesus had stopped crying and Panthera seemed engrossed with the baby. Finally, he looked up when he realized everyone had stopped talking and all were staring at him. He walked to Joseph and handed Jesus to him and said, "I wish I could say he was my son . . . but he is not." He turned to Mary and said, "Joseph, tell your wife I don't blame her for her hatred of me. I hate myself. But I know what I'm talking about. If you stay anywhere in Palestine, Herod or his sons will find you and murder Jesus. You must go to another country altogether. When King Herod is dead you will be able to return to your home in the Qumran Settlement safely. In addition, I have planned to start a rumor that Jesus and the holy family moved to some obscure little town in Galilee. It will keep King Herod off your trail."

Though Mary couldn't understand Panthera's words, she broke down and wept. "I have no choice, do I?" She looked at Joseph and walked directly up to him. She gently took Jesus in her arms and said, "I never asked for any of this to happen. I feel so powerless." She looked down at her baby. "I feel so used. Dear God, what more can happen to us?" She wiped her tears and sniffled. She looked down at Jesus and prayed, "Lord of goodness and peace, let our son's life be full and abundant according to your will." As tears rolled down and over her cheeks she said to Joseph, "I guess I can only succumb to your plan and go with you to Jerusalem and then . . . Egypt!" Panthera reached for Jesus and held him as Joseph helped her up onto the burro. Mary bent down over Panthera and took the baby from his arms.

Panthera and Jarius gave Joseph a respectful bow as they parted ways, and Mary and Joseph continued traveling on to Jerusalem. For a reason Joseph couldn't explain, when the city's walls came into view, he felt safe. They entered Jerusalem from the road to the Dead Sea. The road led into the city and up the colonnade of markets. It curled around, and the inn to which Panthera had directed them stood directly across the way from the temple plaza. Joseph took Jesus from Mary and helped her down from the burro. No words had been spoken between the two since their meeting on the path with Panthera and Jarius. Joseph walked into the inn and Mary followed.

As the innkeeper was about to show them to their room Benjamin, Rachael, who was holding Baby Mary, Lazarus, Levi, and Martha walked in. The family was noisy and excited. Martha and Levi kept jumping up and down hugging Lazarus. Joseph and Mary stopped in their tracks and turned to watch the excitement.

"Hi! My name is Benjamin and this is my wife, Rachael." Benjamin touched the heads of each child as he introduced them. "This is Lazarus, Levi, Martha, and Baby Mary."

"My name is Mary too," Mary politely answered. "This is my husband Joseph and our son Jesus."

Benjamin went on to explain. "The children are excited because this is the first time they have visited with their brother and cousin, Lazarus, for three months. They'll calm down and be less noisy, I assure you."

Mary walked up to Rachael and leaned over to peek at the baby in her arms. "She's beautiful."

Rachael did the same and gazed at Jesus who was asleep like Baby Mary. "He's so tiny. How old is he?"

"He's five days old today."

"One forgets just how tiny they are when they are newborns. Mary is almost three months old and she is so much bigger in comparison. They grow so fast though. Maybe that's why we forget."

"In any case she's a beautiful baby girl. You must feel proud that God has blessed you with so many beautiful children."

Rachael looked at all the children and said, "Well, actually, Levi is the only one that belongs to me. Lazarus, Martha, and Baby Mary are the children of Rabbi Eleazar. Their mother died in giving birth to Mary. I am their aunt and I feel as blessed to have them under my care as if they were my own."

Mary couldn't help but say, "Well, then you are truly blessed. I'm so sorry their mother died. You and your husband, Benjamin, seem to have the gift of love. I feel so much of it coming from you two."

"Mary," Joseph said, "Come and rest before the evening meal. You and Rachael and their family will have time to visit with one another later."

Mary turned back to Rachael, reached out her hand, and squeezed Rachael's arm. "I'm glad to know you. We'll see one another again soon."

Benjamin told Rachael he would take the children to the Pool of Bethesda to explore and play around, while she also rested and took care of Baby Mary. Joseph and the women walked back to their rooms and were pleased to find that their rooms were next to one another. Rachael walked into her room, and Joseph and Mary stepped into their room.

The room was certainly adequate for their needs. Jesus was sleeping so Mary placed him on the straw and blankets in the corner of the room. She and Joseph sat on their bed and rested together. It was not long before Mary was asleep.

Joseph lay in restlessness. He knew Mary was angry and resentful toward him for taking Panthera's advice. Maybe Panthera was not to be trusted. Joseph prayed and asked that God would help him know what he was to do. He was feeling lost and vulnerable.

Jesus' crying woke Mary and she rose to attend to his needs. As she sat on the bed and nursed Jesus, Joseph rose and walked to the window. The sun was lower on the horizon, indicating that it was early evening. He turned to Mary and walked slowly back to the bed and sat down.

"Mary, I think we need to talk." Mary said nothing. "I've been thinking that it was unfair of me not to have told you the complete plans about our relocating to Egypt for this time. I'm sorry." Mary remained silent. "If we're to travel and settle in Egypt we must be united as husband and wife. These are hard and dangerous times for us and we need to be secure in our love and support of one another. Surely you must know I have made decisions with our safety in mind. I would never choose to live in Egypt if I didn't believe we really had no other choice."

"I could have been part of that decision, Joseph. We could have come to the choice together. Instead, I was left out. You came to this decision with the man who raped me. Do you have any idea how this has made me feel about my trust in you? I told you I'll go to Egypt with you and Jesus. I will keep faithful to my promise as your wife but I can't help feeling lost, and scared, and empty. I will be alone in Egypt, far away from my home and family."

Joseph gently touched her arm and said, "I will be with you." Mary said nothing, ignoring him. "Mary, please," he pleaded, "please forgive me. You're right in feeling betrayed. I'm trying to do the right thing for us and I must remember that you are my partner. I'll try to remember that with my heart, mind, and life from this day forward. I can't go on without you being with me and we being for each other." Mary didn't respond.

Joseph raised his knees to his chest and he placed his head down upon his knees. He felt despair and couldn't believe he had ruined his marriage before their second marriage ceremony and the designation of wedlock. He knew he couldn't go to Egypt with Mary feeling as she did. His mind raced as he contemplated alternatives. He chided himself for placing Mary and Jesus in their present state of danger. Why had he answered the scribe truthfully when he registered himself and his family in Bethlehem? He thought maybe if Mary and Jesus could be separated from his identity they could live somewhere in Galilee under false names. He couldn't even begin to sort out this very real and horrific dilemma.

Then Mary quietly, and surprisingly, said, "I know of no other man that could understand as perfectly as you, Joseph."

Joseph raised his head and looked at her. He was surprised to see her looking at him and her eyes were warm and soft.

"Joseph," she said so tenderly, "I forgive you. I forgive you completely and will not hold this against you. I love you so much! I know I am blessed to be your wife. A man of your wisdom and desire to do what is right is a rare thing to witness. Do not fret about Egypt anymore. We'll go together as a family. God must have some divine purpose for you, and me, and Jesus."

Joseph felt as if he were in a dream as he watched Mary place sleeping Jesus on his little bed of straw. She came back to him and their bed, reaching out to him and pulling him to lie down next to her. He rolled close to her and kissed her with a passion greater than they had experienced before. Their embrace grew with intensity.

"Joseph," Mary said with wonder, "I feel tingly all over."

Joseph placed his finger against her mouth, hushing her to lie still. He moved to rest his head against her chest while breathing as hard and fast as she.

Catching her breath, Mary said innocently, "Well, Joseph, I think we've forgiven each other completely, didn't we?"

Joseph smiled and said, "Yes, Mary. It's a powerful emotion to forgive."

She kissed him on the forehead and moved to the large bowl and pitcher of water placed on a stand. As was her custom before every evening meal,

Mary bathed using the sponge and soap provided. Afterward she clothed herself and walked to the bed to find Joseph asleep. She looked at his face and then studied his body. He was a handsome man and she loved the way he looked lying there asleep.. His body was like hers in many ways, but so different in others. God created a good plan for us, she thought. She leaned over Joseph and kissed him again. He stirred and she gently touched his arm and shook him to wake him.

"Joseph, it's time for our evening meal. I'm sure Jesus will wake soon and need to nurse. Maybe you should wake up too, and we should go to the market and choose food for our dinner."

Joseph opened his eyes and was disoriented for a moment. "I dreamed you . . ." He sat up and whispered, "Something happened here, didn't it?"

"Let's just say we forgave each other and are becoming more like husband and wife."

Joseph stood up and felt modest. "Mary, just now I had a dream. I dreamed Panthera was talking to me and telling me about Egypt. He suddenly changed into a figure of light. It's hard to explain. The figure of light told me to go to Egypt until Jesus was safe. Then the phantom in my dream said that God was with us and we need not be afraid . . . you comforted me before I fell asleep, and now the dream has brought me added comfort." Joseph sat still on the bed with his robe pulled over his body. He wondered if God spoke to people through dreams. Or did God speak to people through His Spirit that was housed in all living people? Or maybe God spoke to people through all of creation in the experience of daily living. Joseph realized he was thinking and wondering again. Mary had helped him understand that it was not good for him to be so often consumed with such obsessive contemplation. Rather, he needed to simply accept the comfort and contentment that came to his soul.

Jesus began to cry and Mary went to him, tended to his needs, and nursed him. As she sat upon the bed nursing Jesus, she was aware that Joseph was bathing himself and dressing.

"Mary, I'm going to the well to fetch clean water for us to use later." He picked up the bowl and pitcher, unlatched the door, and walked out.

Mary sat peacefully nursing Jesus. She thought about how dependent and helpless the human baby was when it was a newborn. She remembered that human babies grew into formidable forces of strength. Their minds were so keen and their intellectual potential afforded them the greatest force for evil and good upon the earth.

Mary's thoughts were interrupted when Joseph banged on the door to be let in. Mary placed Jesus on the bed and knew he was sated because he didn't protest when she drew him away from her breast. She ran to the door and let Joseph in. He placed the fresh pitcher of water on the stand with the bowl.

"I fed and watered the burro. We can walk to the market when you're ready."

"I'm ready," she said. She turned and swaddled Jesus and placed him in a sling to be carried near her chest. They both left the room and walked into the street leading to the market. It was dusk when they arrived and both were surprised that all the stands were still open for business. Mary had never seen such a variety of goods. She and Joseph decided what to purchase for their dinner and walked back toward the inn. When they reached the porch of the inn Mary suggested they eat their meal on the temple plaza of the Gentiles' Court across the street. They walked to the plaza and found a spot away from the stream of people walking in and out of the huge temple.

"It certainly is busy. Are all these people here to sacrifice before the Passover feast?" Mary asked.

"Probably," Joseph answered.

They sat down and bowed their heads to say a private prayer before they ate. Mary began to eat with Joseph and watched the people with fascination. She turned to Joseph and asked, "Are we going to sacrifice at the temple?"

"We must. We are to sacrifice a pair of turtledoves. The law requires that we offer this sacrifice for our firstborn son. Unfortunately, it is also Passover, and although I don't want to sacrifice in this chaos, I must if I am to obey the law." Joseph gazed off to the hills rising above the city's wall. "I traveled here one other time, about three years ago, to sacrifice before the Passover feast. The temple was a madhouse, as it is now. I learned that one actually buys the animal to be sacrificed directly from the temple. But before you can purchase the designated animal to be sacrificed, Roman currency must be exchanged for temple money. I became rudely aware that the exchange was of great discrepancy. The temple cheats people in the money exchange and in the cost of the animal you purchase. They are supposedly sacrificed on the altar of burnt sacrifices in the Court of Israel. The money exchange and the cost for designated sacrifice seemed most assuredly wrapped in deception. I felt horrible after my first experience during the Passover in the temple with all the selling and buying and killing. I'm sure the animal I purchased to be sacrificed was sold and resold to many. I don't mind the concept of one animal's life used for many, I just hated feeling lied to and cheated during one of the most holy festivals of our religious tradition. During the Passover we are supposed to remember our enslavement and deliverance into freedom by God. It seems to me our tradition has given way to the very thing from which we believe God freed us. Because of the birth of Jesus, I will sacrifice and let the deceivers of this temple bear the guilt of their own dishonesty. I'm compelled to obey the law."

Mary continued to watch the busyness around her. "I feel uneasy about all this killing, especially in the temple. I didn't think about it like this until I stood here and watched all these people. Do you think they believe God won't punish them if they kill something for him? Does God want us to kill for him?" Mary stared out over the temple's plaza. "No. Our God is the God of life, not death."

Joseph turned his attention to Mary as she watched the people. He lowered his gaze to Jesus sleeping contentedly against her chest in the sling. He remembered the events of their day and closed his eyes to lift a prayer of thanksgiving to their Mighty God of Life and walked to the money changers' table to buy two turtledoves for sacrifice.

JERUSALEM

Rachael, Benjamin, and the children came toward Mary, Joseph, and Jesus as they finished their meal on the plaza. Lazarus, Martha, and Levi ran up to Mary and knelt down in front of her, wanting to see her baby. They all giggled and tried to touch his hands and feet.

Martha squealed, "Look! Look how little his hands are." She looked up at Mary and with her eyes widened said, "That's how big Baby Mary's hands were when she was born. I remember."

Mary was amused with the children's enthusiasm over Jesus. When she looked down, she was surprised to see that Jesus had awakened and didn't seem to mind the children's noise and chatter.

"I hope we aren't intruding upon your quiet meal. I'll take the children away if you wish. I know how overbearing they can become." Benjamin leaned over and collected little hands, including Lazarus', and pulled them away from Jesus.

Mary said, "No. They're not bothering me or him. Look, he seems to be amused by their touching and laughing."

"So may we join you here?" Rachael asked.

"Please, sit down next to me. How is your little Mary tonight?"

"She's fine." Rachael lifted Mary out of her sling and raised her up. "I've not seen her more pleasant. It's as if she knows she's in a special place with special people. Lazarus, do you want to hold your sister for a while? You must be careful. You may not run with her in your arms."

"Yes. I want to hold her. I'll be careful."

"Can I hold her too?" Martha asked.

"No, Martha. Baby Mary is too heavy for you to hold." Rachael placed Baby Mary into her brother's arms and Lazarus held her with pride.

Martha walked up to Mary and asked, "Can I hold Baby Jesus? He's not too big for me to hold."

Rachael began to protest but Mary took Martha's arms and said, "I think Jesus would like to be held by you. Here. Stand still and put your arms out in front of you."

Levi watched with great anticipation. He wondered if his cousin could really hold a baby without tragedy. Martha obeyed Mary and held her arms out as Jesus was placed into her embrace. Martha looked down at Jesus and smiled. "Look at me, Jesus. I can hold you!"

Levi asked, "When Martha is finished holding Jesus, may I hold him?"

Mary smiled and said, "Of course you may. You're a big boy and I know you'll be very careful." Levi smiled and waited patiently for his turn. Mary gave Martha time to hold Jesus and then asked Martha, "Are you ready to let Levi hold Jesus now?"

Martha didn't look like she wanted to share this luxury of responsibility but said, "All right. I guess it's Levi's turn."

As Jesus was transferred from Martha to Levi, Lazarus came close to Jesus with his baby sister Mary still in his arms. He looked down and said, "Mary seems so happy. She's probably happy because there's someone here who is younger than she." Lazarus paused and thought about what he had witnessed in the temple when he and other students had observed the circumcision of a baby boy named John. "Is Jesus going to be circumcised?"

Joseph answered, "Yes. All Jewish boys are circumcised when they are eight days old. You were circumcised."

"I think it hurts the baby to be circumcised."

"It only hurts for a little while. Later it helps them through life."

"How does it help later?" Lazarus asked.

Joseph looked at Benjamin. Benjamin asked Lazarus, "You watched a circumcision and they didn't teach you why it is done?"

"No," said Lazarus. "They just told us we needed to be quiet and respectful."

Benjamin turned to Joseph and said, "And this is the education a young boy being trained to be a rabbi gets!"

"You sound displeased, Benjamin," said Joseph.

"You could say that." Benjamin turned to Lazarus and told him, "Circumcision is commanded by our God. In your later years of life, you will learn that it also blesses you because it is easier to stay clean. If the foreskin is not removed, dirt often causes the penis to become unclean and . . . well . . . sick. It can become red with sores. Without the foreskin you can keep yourself clean." Benjamin then instructed Lazarus to take Baby Mary back to his wife. Lazarus obediently turned to go to his aunt and Benjamin spoke openly to Joseph. "Lazarus' father is a rabbi but if you ask me, he's a very bad one. When his wife, Martha and Lazarus' mother, died giving birth to Baby Mary, he left Martha and Baby Mary with us and took Lazarus to begin his studies at the temple. Their father has not visited them and neglects even Lazarus who is here studying. Eleazar, no doubt, is a bitter man. It's a good thing my wife loves children so much or they'd have no one to love and care for them. Now my wife is pregnant and I'm concerned that she will have too many children to care for."

Joseph looked at Rachael, who was taking Baby Mary from Lazarus. Mary was lifting Jesus from Levi's embrace. "They're good women, aren't they?"

"Yes. I don't know what I would do without my wife, Rachael."

"I don't know what I would do without Mary. But sometimes I fear that her life would be easier and safer had she not married me."

Benjamin looked surprised and then remembered the two Roman soldiers whom he had seen yesterday afternoon. He had heard enough to know that they were making some kind of arrangements for a small family of three to stay at the inn. Suddenly he realized that this was the family for which they were making arrangements. "Are you and your family in some kind of trouble?"

Joseph stated, "Yes, I believe we are." Joseph and Benjamin stood in silence until Joseph said, "With God's help we'll be fine."

Benjamin continued to stand in a quiet reverence and then said, "I know God will always be present in our lives, especially when there is great need. Sometimes it just seems like his help doesn't come when we think we need to receive it. You and your family will be safe, my brother. I will lift prayers for your family every Sabbath."

Joseph grabbed Benjamin's forearm and looked directly into his eyes. "We need your prayers. Thank you, my brother."

Mary and Rachael called to the children and their husbands. It was getting dark and it was time to return to their rooms at the inn. The two families walked together and said good night.

In the room Mary nursed Jesus and praised him for being such a good little baby. "I think he enjoyed being around the other children. Rachael and Benjamin certainly have their hands full. Did you know that Rachael is pregnant?"

Joseph seemed to be in another world but he was able to hear Mary.

"Yes, Benjamin told me Rachael was pregnant. She doesn't show yet."

Jesus fell asleep at his mother's breast and Mary placed him down on the straw in his own little spot. Joseph came to stand next to her as she rose from putting Jesus down. They stood together and gazed at Jesus. Joseph took Mary's hand and led her to their bed. "We need to sleep also. Tomorrow we will need to buy clothing and supplies for our trip on the Sabbath. We will leave directly after visiting the temple the next day after Jesus' circumcision." Joseph and Mary walked to the bed and sat. They each removed their sandals and Joseph poured water into the bowl he had placed by the bedside. He washed Mary's dusty feet. Then Mary moved and stooped to wash Joseph's feet. Joseph placed the bowl and the pitcher on the stand, extinguished the flame he had lit moments before, and returned to the bed to lie down next to Mary. He was glad to lie down and knew they would both be asleep quickly.

In the darkness of the room Joseph said, "Do you realize that it just so happened that Jesus was born to celebrate the Passover and will be circumcised on the Sabbath following our feast."

Mary responded with a very tired, "Good night, Joseph. Try to stop thinking now and sleep."

Joseph slept very little and woke early. He was surprised Jesus had not cried in the night. He looked at Mary, who was in a deep sleep. Sitting up, he moved to the side of the bed and tied his sandals on. One more day, he thought. They had one more day to be in Judea. He wondered what the future held for them in Egypt. As he walked out of the room very quietly, he chuckled to himself, thinking God must be the author of irony. Tonight, he and his family would be celebrating the Passover feast in remembrance of their ancestors' freedom from Egyptian bondage. Tomorrow, he and his young family would begin their journey to Egypt to obtain freedom for life and safety! Joseph thought that Mary was right. He had to stop thinking.

Joseph headed to the stables to tend to his burro when he was abruptly intercepted by Jarius. "I was instructed to give this to you and encourage you to follow its instructions as closely as they are given." Jarius handed Joseph a piece of papyrus paper and walked away quickly.

Joseph opened the folded paper and studied it carefully. They were to leave by the Golden Gate on the eastern wall and go around the Jerusalem wall until they could begin to travel north. When the city was out of their sight, they were to turn due west to Joppa on the eastern shore of the Mediterranean Sea. Once in Joppa, four soldiers would be waiting to escort them to a Roman warship that would sail them to Alexandria, Egypt. Upon arrival in Alexandria the soldiers were to take them to their temporary home.

Joseph folded the paper and placed it under his robe against the linen tied tightly around his waist. He continued on to the stable and fed and watered his burro. While the burro ate and drank, Joseph calculated in his head that the trip would be approximately 320 miles. Twenty miles would be traveled by land and over 300 miles by sea. Joseph estimated that it could take seven days to complete the journey. He felt hopeful that Mary would be comforted with the news that they would be traveling most of the way by sea. He was not sure she would be pleased to live in Alexandria but it was a large city, filled with cultural diversity. Surely there would be people who spoke Aramaic.

The burro drank its fill and Joseph placed the bucket down. He walked to the room to find Mary and Jesus still asleep. Good, he thought. He felt peace about the trip that awaited them and went to the bed to lie down again only to fall asleep. Jesus woke both him and Mary when he cried out two hours later. Mary jumped up, disoriented.

"What is the hour of this morning? I feel as if I slept a hundred years!"

Joseph also jumped up, startled. He wondered if he had dreamed that he had met Jarius when he went back to the stable. He checked the waist of his loincloth and felt the paper jut out against his fingers. It was not a dream. They were going to Alexandria, Egypt. Telling Mary would need to be done thoughtfully.

"Did you attend to the burro already Joseph?"

Joseph answered and his voice had a bit of a quaver that Mary noticed immediately. After attending to Jesus, she placed him in her sling and looked over the bed at Joseph, saying, "It must be past the tenth hour of the morning . . . Joseph . . . why don't you just talk to me? Tell me what you are contemplating. Speak to me about what you must tell me. Don't worry."

Joseph walked around the bed, sat down on the other side next to Mary, and began to speak frankly.

Model of the Second Temple in Jerusalem
Golden Gate on the Eastern Wall leading down through the Kidron Valley
Photo taken of model at the Jerusalem Museum, Jerusalem, April 2009

"When I went out to feed and water the burro, Jarius approached me and gave me this." Joseph reached under his robe and pulled the papyrus paper from his loincloth. "I know you can't read it because it's written in Latin. It holds instructions for us to leave Jerusalem by the Golden Gate on the eastern wall of the temple. We are to turn and travel north until Jerusalem is out of our sight and then turn west to go to Joppa. A ship will be there to take us to our temporary, new place of residence . . . Alexandria, Egypt."

Mary stared at Joseph. Joseph didn't say anything more. He stood up and waited for Mary to express her thoughts. She said nothing, turned, and slowly sat down on the bed. Then she began to cry. Joseph placed the paper into one of their sacks and moved to sit next to her.

"Please be brave, Mary. We'll be together and we will come home as soon as Jesus is safe."

Mary said, "Jesus will never be safe. I've thought about it a great deal. I've changed the circumstances of his birth a hundred different ways in my mind and I know, in my heart and mind, that Jesus will never be safe. But he must be given the chance to live, and grow, and do the will of our God. If we must live in Alexandria in for that to happen, I am ready." She looked at Joseph. "Joseph, I realized that this really isn't your burden and yet you remain faithfully by my side, by Jesus' side. For that I am greatly blessed and I need for you to know that I do love you more than I can express." She reached out one hand and took Joseph's hand. "Together our love can conquer whatever comes." With her other hand she pulled Jesus close to her as he slept in her sling. "We need to go buy supplies and clothes. The day will be gone before we know it." She rose from the bed and Joseph retrieved their purse of money and both walked into the sun as it shined on the streets of Jerusalem.

They shopped into the afternoon and returned to the inn exhausted. Mary laid Jesus down even though he was awake. He began to cry immediately.

"How am I to pack for our journey if Jesus demands to be held constantly?"

Joseph went to Jesus and lifted him off the little straw mound that was his bed. "I'll take him out for a little while to give you time to pack." Joseph walked out of the inn and crossed to the temple plaza and walked into the Court of the Gentiles. The temple was busy with people everywhere. Joseph walked through an entrance to the Soreg and on into the Women's Court. No one was in sight. He continued walking straight and turned to his right, entering an enclosure he knew was the Court of Nazirites. He knelt in its center and lifted Jesus up. He sang a prayer of praise and lowered Jesus and spoke to him as if he understood.

"Did you know you were born to be a great prophet? You are a Nazirite Essene. You are a keeper of the covenant. You are the Long-Awaited One. Maybe you are the Messiah whom the prophets wrote about and whom God has promised. I am sure God will protect us on our journey to Egypt and home again. We will keep his commandments and trust in his direction for us. I pray I will be the kind of earthly father you need though I feel so inadequate and lacking much."

Suddenly, Joseph heard two men talking outside the Court of the Nazirites and he ran quietly to the corner of the enclosure to conceal Jesus and himself by hiding behind a pillar.

"No. We have not performed a circumcision in the past three days. There are no circumcisions scheduled either. You realize we are in the height of the Passover celebration? I have no time to answer your questions."

Joseph heard one man walk into the Court of Israel entrance. Joseph peered through the entrance of the Court of Nazirites in time to see two of Herod's palace guards exit through the Court of Women and out into the Soreg. Joseph knew they were looking for Jesus and waited a good while before he left the temple to return to the inn.

Mary was angry. "Where have you been? I've packed everything and it is time to join the others for the Passover feast upstairs. Give me Jesus and let me nurse him so he will not disturb the meal when he gets hungry. Maybe he will fall asleep."

Mary took Jesus from Joseph and noticed that he looked frightened. "What's the matter?" Mary asked.

"Nothing . . . I need to clean up before the meal." Joseph turned to pour fresh water from the pitcher into the bowl and he began to wash his hands and face.

The Passover festival lasted seven days and the Passover Seder, or sacred meal, was served on the first and second nights of the celebration, served with various special dishes symbolizing the hardships the Israelites had endured during their bondage in Egypt. The narrative of the exodus was recited, and praise was given for their deliverance. The festival began every year on the evening of the fourteenth of Nisan, the seventh month of the Jewish year. Passover always occurred in the months of the religious calendar, corresponding to March–April. During the seven days of the festival, unleavened bread was used to remind the Jews that there had been no time for the bread to rise when they were called out of their bondage to leave Egypt.

Tonight, Joseph, Mary, and Jesus entered the upper room of the inn together and joined the other guests who were already seated, waiting for them to arrive. The Seder began and the children were reverent, ready to do their parts as the story of the Israelite's deliverance from slavery was retold. Unleavened bread was only one symbolic food to remind all who partook of the event of the Israelites' exodus from Egypt. Salty water and bitter herbs were on the table in remembrance of the bitterness of slavery and the tears of the Israelites. Apples and nuts were mashed together to symbolize the mortar from which the enslaved Israelites had had to make bricks. The bone of a lamb was present on the center of the table to remind all that a lamb had been slaughtered and the blood had been smeared on the Israelite's doors so the angel of death would pass over their homes and not kill the firstborn son of the household. At one point during the meal, one child was always designated to open the door to welcome Elijah in for the celebrative meal. An extra place at the table was always set and left empty, and a goblet of wine was reserved at this place for Elijah, who was expected to return someday soon.

The children were ready to recite and do their parts as were previously assigned. They sat quietly and maintained reverence. At this Passover Seder, it was Levi's responsibility to open the door for Elijah. He did so at the right time. However, when he opened the door and went back to his place at the table to sit, a sudden, strong wind caught the door and slammed it shut with a loud bang! Everyone jumped. The babies, Mary and Jesus, were startled and awakened from their sleep and began to cry. It took a while for Mary and Rachael to calm and quiet them. It was decided that the door would remain closed because the wind continued to blow with a mighty force.

When the meal was over, they all returned to their rooms. Rachael and Benjamin spoke a special good night to Mary and Joseph and there seemed to be an understanding between them without an exchange of words.

THE JERUSALEM EXODUS OF THE HOLY FAMILY

THE SUN HAD NOT risen yet. Mary and Joseph awoke and gathered their meager belongings. Mary lifted Jesus and placed him close in her sling.

"I'll load the burro and we'll travel out of Jerusalem through the Water Gate at the southeast corner of the city. I hope to enter the temple through the Golden Gate by the Kidron Valley near the garden of Gethsemane. Hopefully there will be a rabbi near the gate when we knock to let us in to the Women's Court and through to the Court of Israel." Joseph knew this would be unlikely. Unfortunately, Zechariah was at home, in the Qumran Settlement, celebrating the Passover with Elizabeth and their newborn son, John. If only Zechariah were here, Joseph wished.

Mary looked scared. "At this early hour do you really think we'll find a rabbi?"

Joseph was worried also and said, "God will provide. He's got to provide, there is no other way. I'm sure all the other entrances to the temple are heavily guarded by Herod's palace guards."

Together they quietly walked out of their room and into the hallway. They were greeted by Benjamin, who was standing waiting for them to exit. Benjamin stepped closer to Joseph and whispered, "You're in big trouble, aren't you?" Joseph nodded his head. "We are here to help you and be with you." Out stepped Rachael with Baby Mary, Lazarus, Levi, and Martha. "Tell us what you need."

"I need to take Jesus into the temple to be circumcised. Herod's palace guards are searching for Jesus to put an end to his life. Herod believes Jesus is the Messiah and that he will threaten his reign over Judea someday. After Jesus is circumcised, we need to leave the temple and Jerusalem. We will travel to a distant country as refugees and live there until it is safe to bring Jesus home."

Benjamin touched Jesus as he slept in Mary's sling. He turned to Lazarus. "Go get your father and meet us at the Golden Gate to let us in to the

Women's Court. We will travel out of the Water Gate on the southeast side of the city and walk around the outside of the city wall to the Golden Gate to meet you and your father." Lazarus nodded his head with confidence. He knew exactly where he could find his father and for the first time felt proud that his father was a rabbi. He turned and quietly disappeared.

Benjamin looked at Martha and Levi. "Children, no matter what happens, you are not to speak or make a sound. Do you understand?" Martha and Levi grabbed each other's hand and nodded with a seriousness that matched the situation. "Come." Benjamin led the entire group with Joseph to the stable. Joseph secured their belongings and supplies onto his burro and they all walked south through the old part of Jerusalem known as the City of David. They exited the Water Gate and were relieved to find no palace guards blocking their way. They began their walk going north toward the Golden Gate on the eastern wall of the city. They stayed close together. Mary and Joseph were unaware that Benjamin and Rachael were praying that Lazarus would be there to let them in.

As they walked a dim light rose from the sun and shined on them. When they reached the Golden Gate, also known as the Beautiful Gate, the light shrouded the Kidron Valley and the garden of Gethsemane in golden shades of color. They stood at the huge gate and Benjamin called to Lazarus in a low, quiet voice. "Lazarus! Are you there, son?"

The gate began to open but to all of their surprise there stood an old woman. She was of great age. "Come in! Come in! It's safe. We are ready for our little Messiah. My name is Anna and I have lived in the temple as a prophetess for over fifty years. I have waited for this day for many years and now it has arrived!" She looked at Jesus, sleeping in Mary's sling. "He is beautiful!" She gently touched him on the chest and looked up. She whispered a prayer as they all stood in silence. When she had finished praying, she told Benjamin, "Stay out here with the burro. Try to stay behind a tree in the garden. The rest of you must follow me very quietly. The Soreg Wall surrounding the Women's Court is filled with sleeping guards from Herod's Palace." She turned and led Mary, holding Baby Jesus; Rachael, holding Baby Mary; and Levi and Martha through the Women's Court to the entrance of the Court of Israel. The smell of cooking meat filled their nostrils and Mary remembered that there had been great sacrifices of animals for the past seven days before the Passover feast. This was the smell of animal flesh cooking.

The Nicanor Gate leading to the Court of Israel opened, and out walked Eleazar, Lazarus, and another older man. The older man said, "My name is Simeon." He walked to Mary and took Jesus into his arms. He lifted him up and looked forward into the Court of Israel. It was as if the Holy

Spirit rested upon them both. He explained that it had been revealed to him that he would not see death before he had seen the Lord's Messiah. Guided by the Holy Spirit, Simeon went into the Court of Israel with Jesus in his arms. Joseph, Eleazar, and Lazarus followed him. Just inside, Simeon turned and praised God, saying,

Master, now you are dismissing
your servant in peace,
according to your word;
for my eyes have seen your
salvation,
which you have prepared in the
presence of all peoples,
a light for revelation to the
Gentiles
and for glory to your people
Israel.

Mary and Joseph were amazed at what was being said about Jesus. Then Simeon blessed them and said to his mother Mary, "This child is destined for the falling and the rising of many in Israel, and to be a sign that will be opposed so that the inner thoughts of many will be revealed—and a sword will pierce your own soul too."

Anna placed her arm around Mary and led her to the balcony above the Nazirites' Court. "We will hide above in the balcony." She turned to Rachael and the children and said, "Stay here and do not be afraid."

The men walked into the Court of Israel, and the Nicanor Gate closed behind them. Rachael and the children stood in the center of the Women's Court. They were still and silent what seemed to them to be a long time. Suddenly an infant's cry of pain came from inside the Court of Israel. The infant's scream woke and alerted some of Herod's palace guards who were sleeping in the Soreg hallways.

Three guards entered into the Women's Court and were surprised to see Rachael and her children standing in its center. They began to question Rachael. "What are you doing here? How did you get in here?"

Rachael thought quickly and answered their questions with a lie. "I've come to pray with my children this early morning on the Sabbath. Their father has abandoned us and I fear I have no place to go for help but here. Will you help us? Can you spare some money so that I may buy food and feed my children? Will you please help us?"

"You can't stay here and beg. Leave at once, and take these children with you . . . Wait! You're holding a baby." The guard grabbed Baby Mary from Rachael's arms. Baby Mary screamed. The guard drew his sword. Martha and Levi screamed and Rachael fell to her knees and pleaded, "Don't hurt my child! Please, don't hurt her!"

"Her?" the guard asked. He grabbed the baby by her arm and shoulder and held her up until her wrappings fell to the floor. The other guards laughed.

"It's a female!" one of the guards said. "Go on. Take your baby and get out of here."

Rachael picked up Mary's wrappings and directed Martha and Levi toward the Golden Gate to leave. Baby Mary continued to scream as the guards opened the locked gate and ushered Rachael and the children out. They locked the gate behind them and returned to the Soreg to resume their sleep.

Mary and Anna stood up on the balcony as Joseph emerged with Jesus in his arms. Lazarus, Eleazar, and Simeon followed. Anna and Mary joined them and Mary took Jesus from Joseph and quickly held him to her breast to suckle and comfort him.

"Come quickly now," Anna said. She led Joseph, Mary, and Jesus to the doors of the Golden Gate. She unlocked their massive locks and swung the door open. She walked out with them and Benjamin emerged with their burro. Rachael stepped out from behind some juniper bushes with Baby Mary in her arms, followed by Martha and Levi. Anna held Mary's arms and looked at her squarely. She bent down and kissed the tiny forehead of Jesus and said, "God be praised. Now go and do not linger long. Say goodbye to each other quickly." Anna turned and went back into the temple through the eastern wall and the Court of Women, closing the huge Golden Gates. The locks gave a loud clank as she locked them from the inside.

The two families stood in disbelief, not speaking at first. They all stood in silence as they contemplated the events that had just taken place. It would take time for them to recognize the miracle in which they had participated, not fully able to comprehend the danger they had all escaped. Then slowly . . . with the realization they were all safe, standing together outside the temple, their present state of terror disappeared.

"We must go," Joseph finally declared.

"No." Mary reached out to Rachael and they both began to cry. "I love you as a sister." She turned to Benjamin and touched the side of his face. "You shall forever be remembered as our brother." She looked down at Martha and Levi. "Children, you are brave, strong, and beautiful. I know God will allow us to meet again in our lives." Mary touched Baby Mary in Rachael's arms and whispered, "And you . . . brave little baby girl, you saved my son's life! Sleep in peace . . . Sleep in peace." And Mary wept.

Rachael wept also while Joseph and Benjamin held each other's forearms in genuine love. She said to Mary, "Our home is in Bethany. You will be able to find us when you return to Judea. Bethany is a small town. My heart is so heavy as we stand here saying goodbye. I feel my heart is breaking . . . but we shall see each other again . . . I am certain of this."

Joseph's voice rose above Rachael's. "I pray with confidence and trust that our God of the universe will bless us now, and for all time." Joseph let go of Benjamin and hugged Martha, Levi, and Rachael. He, too, gently touched Baby Mary's head. He turned to Mary, who was still holding on to Rachael's arm, crying. "Come, we must go. Come now, Mary. Let Rachael go. Remember your words that spoke of our meeting again. We shall see them again. Come."

Mary let Rachael go and turned to walk north along the last part of the eastern city wall of Jerusalem with Joseph and baby in arms. She did not look back as Joseph did not look back either. The two families continued to weep as they walked away from each other in opposite directions. Benjamin, Rachael with Baby Mary, Levi, and Martha did not look back either as they walked south along the eastern city wall of Jerusalem. They were weeping quietly as they walked toward Jerusalem's southeastern Dead Sea entrance to safely reenter the city.

The Golden Gate (Beautiful Gate) walled up in the Old Jerusalem Wall, April 2009

JOPPA AND THE MEDITERRANEAN SEA

MARY AND JOSEPH WALKED from Jerusalem to Joppa without speaking a single word to each other. Each thought and believed the other was angry and sad, but in truth, they were filled with fear and uncertainty, not knowing what the future held for them, having to continue trusting the guidance of a supposed enemy, Panthera.

They arrived at Joppa by midafternoon and Joseph was surprised at their excellent time of travel. It did not take him long to guide the family to the correct dock in Joppa. Walking from Jerusalem west to Joppa was a gradual downhill incline to the coast of the Mediterranean Sea so they both saw the water sparkling from a good distance away. They had been silently excited seeing the vast sea ahead them, although they didn't speak of it.

As they stood on the dock looking at the largest ship they had ever seen, four Roman soldiers approached them. One of them asked, "Are you Joseph and Mary from Judea?"

The soldier's voice startled Joseph. He recovered quickly and tried to appear confident by responding with a simple yes.

The soldier explained that he was a friend of Panthera and Jarius. He promised that he and his comrades would see to it that Joseph and Mary were accompanied by them because they were Roman comrades and soldier friends who were familiar with Joppa and sailing. "Have you ever sailed before?"

Joseph felt inadequate and Mary was amused by his apparent lack of experience in this realm. For some odd reason, Mary was more attracted to Joseph when he honestly displayed a lack of confidence. Joseph couldn't hide his inexperience and replied, "The only experience I have had with sailing has been floating my own body on the Dead Sea, so I would assume I am a total novice, ignorant of sailing on a boat of any size. Quite frankly, I don't want to get on that ship. I'm frightened by its size, its supposed ability to be controlled in the water, and the likelihood that it can carry my wife and son safely to Alexandria seems impossible."

The soldier stood silent for only a moment and then burst into laughter. "I like you! You're a Jew, aren't you? I thought the Jews believed they had the personal help and protection of the one Almighty God of the universe. You're not even sure your God will carry you safely in this seaworthy, small ship across a very small part of this great body of water." He laughed again. "You're a good, honest man. It makes me feel like maybe you Jews are human after all." The soldier patted him on the back. "Come with us. Try to trust other human beings, even if they are Roman. You'll be fine."

Joseph, Mary, Jesus, and the burro were guided across a ramp that extended from the dock up onto the ship. On the deck of the ship the soldier allowed them to explore freely. Joseph left the burro and took hold of Mary's hand. They walked to the stern of the ship, which was the farthest from the dock. He and she peered over its rail and could not detect any land underneath as they gazed into the water's depth. One of the soldiers followed behind them. Joseph turned to ask him how deep the water was at this spot.

"It's about fifteen cubits in your way of measuring. Imagine fifteen lengths of your forearm piled on top of one another. That's about how deep it is here. When you sail out it gets thousands of cubits deep."

Joseph stood still and tried to imagine a depth of water that great. Mary interrupted his thought by asking him what the soldier was saying. Joseph looked at Mary and patiently explained what he had told him.

From there, Joseph and Mary were escorted to a lower deck of the ship and the burro was placed in a very tight stall. Water and hay were supplied. They were then walked to another level, or deck, and the soldier showed them their place to sleep. He also explained that when the bell of the ship was rung it was a call to the dining area to eat. He showed them where that place was and ended by saying, "Fair sailing, folks. Depending on the wind, it will take no more than three days to sail to Alexandria. Hopefully the winds will carry us quickly. By the way, you may begin to feel sick because the ship is in constant motion. If that occurs you must get up on the top deck to breathe fresh air. You can also eat some of this." The soldier held out his hand and said, "Go ahead, take some. It's ginger, a spice. Also, if you feel sick you can press these places on your wrists." He exposed his wrists and showed them the places to exert pressure. "A man from the east, far, far away, taught me that. He said they are pressure points that relieve nausea. I tried it and it worked for me. If you feel sick, it may work for you too."

Joseph liked the soldier and was humbled as he became conscious that he didn't know as much as he thought he knew when he lived in the Qumran Settlement. The Roman soldier held his hand out to Joseph, shook it, bowed to Mary, and walked away, leaving them alone to rest in their little room.

From the deck above, it was not long before they heard sailors yelling directions back and forth. The ship began to move away from the dock and Joseph helped Mary, with Jesus in her sling, walk to the upper deck out into the open air. Together they stood watching the shoreline of Joppa disappear. Mary peered to look over the side of their ship and watched the water slap furiously against its sides. She felt as if they were moving more quickly than she had ever experienced before in her life. She and Joseph left the deck only to eat. They sat and watched the sun set before them and Jesus didn't stir or cry until they returned to their little room for sleep.

Mary laid Jesus on the platform bed filled with clean straw and tended to his wound from the circumcision. She applied an ointment that kept the wound clean. Tonight the wound was less severe and was healing quickly. "You are such a good, brave little boy!" Mary rubbed her face on his tiny tummy and ran her hands gently over his little body, massaging him. Jesus cooed and moved his feet as if he were kicking the air. "I love you so much," she whispered.

Joseph watched her as she cared for Jesus and he felt warmth in his heart. "How are you feeling, Mary? We've not spoken since leaving Jerusalem."

"I know Joseph. Although I am dazed from the events that have occurred today and am filled with wonder at our present adventure on this ship, I am content. It scares me to think that I am floating on deep, deep water at a speed I'd never thought possible to travel. However, my wonder cancels out my fear. I'm sad we're going away from our home, everything and everyone we know and love. I never thought I would ever leave the

Qumran Settlement, but here I am, on a boat bound for Alexandria, aching for the familiar smell and feel of my own bed in our home."

Joseph rose from their platform bed and guided Mary to her feet. With Jesus they went to the upper deck into the open air again. The sun had set, and in the darkness Joseph said, "Look up, Mary!"

The night sky was magnificent! The stars seemed to fill the heavens in a way they had filled the heavens at home but their brilliance was contrasted by the blackness of the sea that reflected the stars and moon, appearing to join heaven and earth.

Mary and Joseph watched the sky for hours, and they saw streaks of light fall through its blackness three or four times. Again, Mary could not help but wonder what they were. When she asked Joseph if he knew what caused the brief streak of light, he continued to look upward and shrugged his shoulders.

After a time, they could feel the wind grow stronger and the spray from the sea seemed to splash up more violently. They walked to the back of the ship's deck and looked east where the land should have been. Several other people stood nearby looking eastward. They pointed to something in the sky and talked in hushed tones. When Joseph and Mary followed their pointing, they witnessed another phenomenon they had never seen before. It appeared to them like a bright ball of fire that reflected its light in the water, making everything shine as if it were daylight. Then, to the west, three heavenly bodies in the sky came together ever so slowly. After an hour passed, the three lights joined into one great light, as the ball of fire seemed to follow their ship from the east. Joseph determined that the three heavenly bodies that came together were not formed from three stars coming together, because their light did not twinkle like stars. They were not streaks of light that clashed together, because their light did not burn out. Mary didn't even ask Joseph what he thought they were viewing, because she knew he didn't know. Even so, as the light came together, they were filled with a sense of marvel and fear.

They watched the brightness of the light and finally Joseph said, "It's shining over our home, Mary. We are blessed by its light. It will remind us that we will go home again, someday. Look, it's like a great light shining over . . . Bethlehem." Not taking his eyes off the combined light of the three heavenly bodies, Joseph determined that it most certainly shined down on Bethlehem. As they both watched for another hour, the lights began to separate again, ever so slightly. They continued to move slowly over time, moving in opposite directions to shine over Jerusalem, Bethany, and their home in the Qumran Settlement. Simultaneously they both said in a whisper, "Praise be to God!" as the ball of fire chased them, shining brilliantly in the sea behind the ship carrying them west.

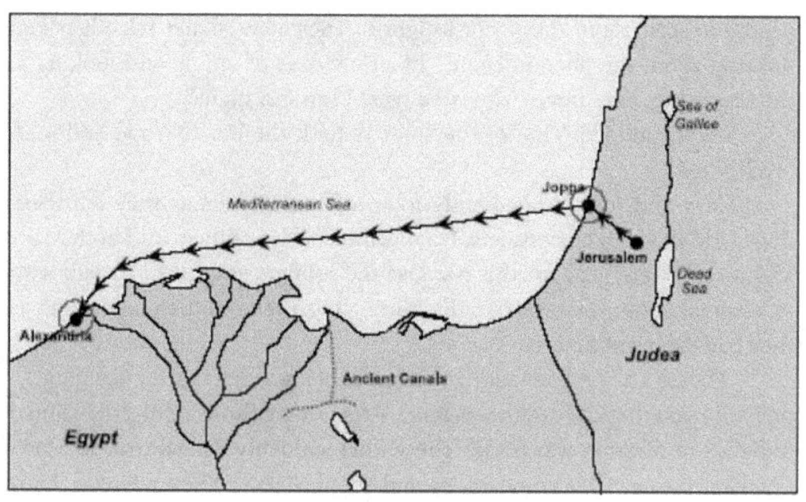

Mary, Joseph, and Jesus's Flight to Egypt

ALEXANDRIA, EGYPT

The trip over the great Mediterranean Sea from Joppa to Alexandria took less than three days because of a rare wind blowing strong from the east. As the ship maneuvered into the Egyptian Royal Harbor under the arched causeway dividing it from the Harbor of Good Return to the west, Mary and Joseph became even more overwhelmed. Alexandria was a huge city. It seemed to rise before them like a great white metropolis, the Brilliant City, as the Romans called it. Mary had surprised herself as she stood on the ship's deck looking out over the busyness of the docks and the city beyond, because she hoped to see Panthera waiting for them on the dock to take them to their new, temporary home in this place. Instead, the four Roman soldiers who had accompanied them on their journey from Joppa to Alexandria stood at the bottom of the ship's ramp with their burro, waiting for them to disembark. Mary and Joseph walked slowly down the ship's ramp and were guided by their four Roman companions down the colonnaded streets along Canopus and the Street of the Soma. The villas they passed were white with marble and alabaster, instead of the dark clay blocks used for building in Judea. The colors and busyness of the docks filled Joseph and Mary with silent awe. It was all so new and exciting, maybe too exciting.

"Did you see those lights join and then, as the boat turned, they appeared to separate in the sky last night!?" Their new soldier friends talked nonstop about the phenomenon. "In all my days of sailing and looking at the night sky I have never witnessed what I saw last night."

Joseph nodded. One of the soldiers took the burro's rope and said, "Follow me."

Mary and Joseph obediently followed the soldiers as they led them down and through busy streets. No one took notice of them and both Mary and Joseph were glad for this because the soldiers continued to talk with excitement about the orbs of light coming together and then separating as they had the night before.

"I heard one person talking about it as being a sign that a great king . . . no . . . he said that a Messiah was born. After seeing those lights I'm inclined to believe a Messiah was born." The soldier suddenly looked over to Mary. He nudged one of his companions and asked Mary, "When was your baby born and where?"

The soldier Joseph liked well said, "What is this, a trial?" He looked at Joseph. "Neither one of you has to answer my nosy friends." Joseph nodded with a thankful glance. The soldier looked at his comrade and said, "Back off. She doesn't understand you anyway."

They stopped at a rather large stone dwelling and handed Joseph the burro's rope. The soldier who had been leading them said to Joseph, "There's a small stable in the back for your burro. It can accommodate more animals but not many more. Here is some money that can be used to purchase bare essentials until you are able to support yourself." Joseph felt irritated. He wondered how much money Panthera felt he needed to give to rid his soul of guilt. Joseph certainly had enough money and his pride was beginning to feel injured. He accepted the money and the soldiers departed, leaving them standing at their new front door.

"Well," Joseph said in a daze, "I'll put the burro in the stable. There is a bench here by the front door. Will you sit there with Jesus and wait for me?" Mary nodded and sat on the bench. "We'll enter the house together."

Joseph walked around the house to the back while Mary sat on the bench, wondering if they would still be able to see the great light in the east from here. She looked at Jesus, who slept so soundly in her sling against her heart. His wound had healed remarkably quickly and she hoped it would be healed completely by the time they settled in Egypt to live, without as much excitement and crisis as they had endured since Jesus was born.

Joseph rounded the corner of the house and approached Mary. "It's quite a nice little stable. Are you ready to go into the house and see our temporary place of residence?"

Together they opened the heavy front door made of a wood Joseph did not recognize. They stepped into the front room and were pleasantly pleased to see a large room with two windows facing the street. The windows had shutters closed over them. Joseph opened one of the window's shutters and light streamed in, exposing a clean, well-swept floor.

They quickly walked through the dwelling and discovered a room for preparing food and another three rooms of good size. A ladder in the main hallway led to four other rooms on the second floor. The entire house was clean and in good repair. Joseph was especially impressed with the tiled roof.

Unfortunately, the house contained only minimal pottery and kitchen utensils. There was no furniture. Joseph immediately went to the stable, where an ample amount of straw was available. He brought in mounds and formed temporary beds in one of the rooms on the first floor and seating areas in the front room.

"Tomorrow I will purchase wood and tools to build furniture for us to use." He looked at Mary and said, "You can think about what needs to be purchased for food preparation and . . ."—he looked around the bare room—"and textiles to soften and warm up these bare walls."

Jesus began to stir and Mary sat on the mound of hay Joseph had prepared for her sleeping. She began to nurse Jesus as Joseph watched on. She looked up at him. "I feel so lonely."

He sat down next to her and comforted her. "I know how you feel. It's been a journey filled with all kinds of new and painfully different experiences and we have no one we know here to help us adjust. Even though there is a community of Essenes in this city, they are all men, but maybe I can befriend a few and you can share in my friendship with them. I guess this would not be proper though."

She looked at him with satisfaction. "That's exactly how I feel!"

Joseph smiled and said, "Well, I guess we're alone together then."

The evening came quickly and Mary placed Jesus down to sleep. She and Joseph ate their meal together and then walked outside into the darkness to look for the great lights shining in the east. The night sky revealed that the three heavenly bodies of light were more distant from each other. The light from each was strong but distinctly separate now, unlike the night before when they had come together in one great light.

Joseph quoted from the Holy Scriptures, "Say unto the cities of Judah, your light has come. O Zion, herald of good tidings; lift up your voice with strength, O Jerusalem, herald of good tidings, lift it up, do not fear; say to the cities of Judah, 'Here is your God!'" (Isa 40:9) They stood together in silence. Peace surrounded them and embraced their souls.

They finally turned and walked together into the house to the room in which Jesus was sleeping. They lay and rested on their mound of straw, using the blankets they had brought from Jerusalem. For Mary they smelled of home and she fell to sleep quickly. Joseph watched her fall asleep and counted the days in his mind. According to the law as written in Leviticus, they had twenty-one days to wait. He thought three weeks seemed too long to wait, but wait he would.

The following weeks were filled with busy times for both Mary and Joseph. They went to the market every day to choose food for their meals. They also purchased reams of cloth to hang in the rooms, giving their home beauty and color. Joseph purchased lumber and tools and began to make tables, chairs, beds, and cupboards. By the second week the house became a home and Mary was pleased with the comfort it supplied. However, her greatest focus was care for Jesus and he seemed to grow every day.

Joseph was able to converse easily with the people living near and around them, but Mary shied away from everyone, knowing she could not communicate. However, that changed one sunny day.

"Mary," Joseph called from the back of their house. "Mary, come here, I want you to meet some people."

Mary walked out and Joseph introduced her to a woman who was older than she and dressed like an Egyptian. Her husband stood next to her and he smiled broadly as Mary approached them.

"Mary, this is Seth and his wife, Mestha. They live in the dwelling three doors down from ours." Mary bowed ever so slightly and smiled. "My wife's name is Mary," Joseph said in Greek. Although Egypt was now a Roman state, previous Greek dynasties ruling and influencing Egypt for over three hundred years had given Egypt the common Greek language. Mary was amazed that Joseph also spoke and understood Greek.

Mestha smiled and said, "Mary."

Mary responded by repeating their names as closely as Joseph had said them.

"Mary, Seth and Mestha lived in Judea when he was a soldier for Rome. He was seriously injured in a battle so Rome released him from his obligation to serve twenty-five years in the army. After his release, they came to live here in Alexandria and have lived here for seven years. He works for a building business in Alexandria now and will introduce me to his employer for possible employment. But the best is that they both speak Aramaic pretty well."

Mary's heart leapt and she spoke to Mestha in Aramaic, "You speak my tongue?!"

In broken Aramaic Mestha answered, "Yes, I think I can remember enough to talk with you."

Mary could not contain her joy and she hugged Mestha. "Maybe you can teach me to speak Greek?"

Mestha smiled and said, "I can try. I think you would certainly be an ambitious student."

It was so good for Mary to hear her native tongue. "Yes! Yes, I would be a good student!"

Seth also spoke in Aramaic, saying, "Then let us set up regular times in the day for you two to meet for your lessons."

Mary learned that Mestha and Seth were both thirty-eight years of age. They had a daughter, twenty years old, named Isis. She still lived with the family. Seth and Mestha spoke about their daughter in Greek and Mary learned later from Joseph that Isis had become ill with blackwater fever at the age of fifteen. She had almost died but miraculously survived and continued to recover, gaining health and strength every year. Seth and Mestha also spoke of their three sons, aged ten, thirteen, and fifteen, who were still living at home and going to school. Seth expressed pride in his ability to afford this opportunity for his sons.

Jesus began to cry and Mary excused herself, leaving Joseph to tell Seth and Mestha they had one son, twenty days old, named Jesus. Seth commented on their son's name and was interested in knowing its meaning and from where it came. Joseph humbly said it was a long story that could be saved and shared for another time.

The afternoon sun had heated the early evening and the new friends bowed to each other and said goodbye. Joseph entered the house to find Mary in the large front room, sitting on the bench he had made. She was nursing Jesus and talking to him softly and affectionately.

Joseph said, "I think the sky will be clear tonight. I'm sure we will be able to see the bright lights again in the east."

Mary looked up and said, "Just speaking to someone who knows my language makes me feel closer to home."

Joseph saw the sparkle in Mary's eyes and he felt joy. He thought to himself that he was happy when she was happy. He believed that maybe there was a possibility for them to be happy, living in peace and joy with Egyptians.

The evening turned to night quickly. As soon as Mary put Jesus down to sleep, she and Joseph walked to the back of their dwelling and searched the eastern sky. The distinct lights were still visible, brightly shining in the east. However, they had moved farther apart. Joseph placed his arm around Mary and she leaned into him.

"I wonder how all of what happened to us in these past recent weeks will end, and where will it lead us?" Mary commented out loud but she spoke as if she were talking to herself.

Joseph moved from his gaze eastward stepping in front of her to gaze into her eyes. He placed his other arm around her, fully embracing her. "I don't know what it all means but I have faith that it holds great importance for us and maybe for our world." He gazed into Mary's eyes, which revealed the reflection of light from one of the bodies of light in the sky. She was lost in wonder and he dropped his arms and turned to gaze at the night sky with her.

Out of nowhere, and much to Joseph's surprise, Mary said, "Take me to our bed and hold me, and do to me what you did while we were staying in Bethlehem."

Joseph was stunned and somewhat embarrassed. "Mary, we did many things in Bethlehem. I'm not sure I know to what you are referring."

"Of course you do! It's on your mind quite a bit in spite of everything else. How many days must we wait until the law will allow us to hold one another and be as one?"

Without hesitation, Joseph surprised himself and said, "Seven more days." He looked down at an invisible annoyance and looked up to meet Mary's laughter.

"I'm learning a lot, Joseph, especially about you. I have not come to only love you, I like you! You're adorable." She grabbed his hands and turned, leading him into their house. She drew him to the front room, took a blanket hanging from the back of a bench he had made, and spread it out on the floor. "Lie down, Joseph," she almost ordered. She proceeded to close the shutters, latched them, and locked the door shut. She lit the lantern on the table and let the soft light fill the room.

"Mary, you know we have seven days yet to wait . . . I can wait . . . Why don't you help me wait."

"You sound scared. For heaven's sake, Joseph, you're nearly twice my age. We are husband and wife. Certainly you can remember what you and I did the day you received the instructions from Jarius?" She removed her robe to stand before him in her thin underclothing, then reached to help Joseph remove his robe, leaving him in his tunic. "I shall never ask you to go against our rules as Essenes, though I think many of them are extreme and ridiculous, obviously composed by men who don't seem to understand the sacredness of marriage. Well . . ." Mary said as she took a deep breath, exhaled, and boldly continued to stand before him in her underclothing "our mothers taught us that the first commandment God spoke to Adam and Eve was 'Be fruitful and multiply.' I'm scared. I don't want to birth another baby.

Actually, I thought I could never endure coming together with you because of the vivid memory and terror of what Panthera did to me. Many of us endure the ravishing of our bodies by soldiers or men who are driven to take us without regard to what it could lead to for us. But this is not true with you, my husband. You are patient and kind, and I wish to be close to you in all ways. I continue to not want to experience some things again because of the trauma and pain it caused me. But we are husband and wife, and I have learned to enjoy physical closeness with you. I know we must wait another seven days before coming together in body, but until then I desire to be close with you now. I wish to hold you. I wish for you to hold me. I desire to hold you and caress you, as you have caressed me."

Joseph was stunned. In his private thoughts he knew he had married the correct woman. He gazed upon her, all of her. She was beautiful. However, he detected she was not as confident as she tried to appear, because she gathered her long hair, which had fallen down over her back, and quickly arranged it to cascade over her breasts and belly and down over the front of her body though she still was clothed in her night clothing.

Slowly, Joseph stood up and gathered her hair into his own hands, rearranging it to fall back over her shoulders, and guided her to lie down with him on the blanket. Mary acquiesced, looking into his eyes, wondering about how this would work in seven days. For the moment, it seemed to be an impossibility for her, even in this moment, but they embraced and experienced gentle caressing. It was as if they both knew what the other needed, and their mutual desire led them in the dance, surprised they knew the steps by heart.

Simultaneously, they both said, "I love you." Joseph lifted his head from her chest and looked at her. Both began to laugh heartily. When they quieted, they looked at each other with gentle peace.

"Joseph," Mary asked, "do you think it's this way for everyone who is in love? I mean, do you think every lover feels what we feel?"

Joseph thought about her question before answering, "I don't know . . . I would guess that two people in love most likely feel what you and I feel." With a distant gaze he added, "It is a wonderful gift to be able to feel this way, don't you think?"

"Yes." But Mary was not done with her questioning. "Will it be different when we actually have intercourse? I know what intercourse is about, but I can't imagine that it will feel good for me. I'd rather keep being intimate with you the way we have been."

Joseph sat up. "I really believe it will be good for you, Mary, as it will be good for me." Joseph understood. The rape will forever be a part of Mary's memory. "We will learn together slowly. We won't jump into it immediately."

Joseph looked at her with a devilish eye. "After all, we still have seven days to wait."

Both slipped on their robes but remained sitting on the blanket that covered the floor.

Mary continued her questioning, asking, "Do you think it's wrong?"

Joseph was not sure he understood what Mary was asking again, and he waited for her to make her question clear to him.

"I mean, well . . . something inside me makes me feel that I am doing something that is not pleasing to God when I . . . you know . . .lie practically naked with you and engage in such . . . pleasure."

"I know what you mean." Joseph paused and thought before he said, "No. It's not wrong or displeasing to God. After all, he created male and female and instructed us to be fruitful and multiply. God created sexual pleasure. When sexual pleasure is used in the way God intended, we certainly reap its gifts for relationship . . . although I think the potential for displeasure to God and ourselves can be as great, or even greater, than the pleasure it can give to us. That's why we hold the law so sacred. It guides us, and by following the law we know we are pleasing God. Thereby we are blessed. So . . . no." Joseph turned and looked at Mary with an expression of love. "What we do to pleasure each other physically is what God wants us to do in marriage. Using the potential for physical pleasure outside of our vows to love, honor, and respect one another in our sacred, faithful marriage could be very damaging and dangerous. It's probably as dangerously powerful as it is wonderfully pleasurable."

Mary smiled and said, "That's exactly what I think."

They embraced each other and Joseph stroked the back of Mary's head. She had beautiful dark hair that made her brown eyes look as if they were sparkling crystals. It was times like this that Joseph couldn't believe he was her husband and they were living safely in Alexandria with Jesus.

Mary interrupted his thought. "What was your mother and father's marriage like?"

Joseph shifted his thoughts to remember his parents. He had loved them dearly and held their memory sacred. "My father, Jacob, left his home as a young man to live in the Qumran Settlement. He followed the discipline of the Essenes and loved God like no man I have ever met since. He was born in Bethlehem and was a descendant of King David from the tribe of Judah. When he left to live as an Essene he chose celibacy, as did most of those within the sect. But something happened to him when he was about the age of forty-five. He had a vivid dream that filled him with wonder. At the same time, it haunted him with anxiety. When I was twelve years old, he confided in me and told me about it. He said that he could not shake the memory of it, witnessing it over and over in his mind. He finally came to accept the dream as a simple vision where he saw two women and a child hovering over a beautiful river. For some reason he knew the river was the River Jordan."

Mary listened and didn't interrupt Joseph's thought. Joseph continued. "After he had the dream, he became disheartened with the Essene sect's rigidity, especially their tendency to honor celibacy. Very few of those within the sect chose marriage so there were few women and children within the settlement. My father was so troubled by this, and the dream, that he left the settlement and settled in Moab, the territory across the Dead Sea from the Qumran Settlement. He worked as a shepherd. He spent a lot of time alone watching the flocks in the wilderness. It was there that he met a woman named Salome. She would always be at the well to draw water for his flock. It was as if she knew when he came to the well for water and she would be there ready to help him. They would talk for long periods of time and my father, Jacob, began to love her for her thoughts, wisdom, and inner beauty. He learned that she was not married but had chosen to remain with her father and mother, caring for them in their old age. When they died, her brother provided for her needs to live, allowing her to stay in the family house. My father was impressed with her unselfish desire to serve others and wondered who would care for her."

Joseph paused and seemed to be thinking of something, looked at Mary, and continued to speak. "My father told me he fell in love with Salome. He had a depth of love for her he had not experienced before in his life. After a while he asked Salome to be his almah and return with him to the Qumran Settlement. Salome expressed mutual love for him but could not accept his offer until she discussed an issue of great concern with her brother. She explained to him that six months prior to my father's request, a young woman named Adah had come to live with her. Adah was pregnant and had run away from her home in Jerusalem. She had fallen in love with a young boy named Hilo, who loved her also, and they had given each other a promise of betrothal. Hilo was the son of a rabbi, and Adah was not acceptable to Hilo's family. Hilo's father refused Adah and did not allow Adah to come and live in their home for the time of their betrothal, as is the Jewish custom. Because Adah was pregnant with Hilo's firstborn child, she was forced to leave Jerusalem, and her own family, to save Hilo from disgrace.

"She traveled to Moab and begged for food during the day and slept in the fields at night. With compassion for Adah, my mother, Salome, took her into her home and cared for her. My father asked how long she planned to care for Adah, and my mother admitted to him that she had not even thought about the inevitable time Adah would have to be sent away to live on her own.

"My father was saddened and asked my mother to take time to pray about what she would decide but that he knew he could not take her and Adah back to the Qumran Settlement to live within the Essene sect."

Joseph sighed. "Do you want to hear all this, Mary?"

"Yes. Go on. What happened?"

"Although my father returned to the well many times after his offer to my mother, she was never there again to help him water the sheep. He spoke to me later about the heaviness in his heart and the great desire to see and talk to Salome again. One night, while watching the flocks, he had the dream again of the two women and the child hovering over the river Jordan. When he awoke, he knew what he had to do. He herded the sheep back to his employer and began to search the area for Salome's home. It did not take long to find. He said when he knocked on the door of her home and she answered, standing before him, he felt as if his heart would burst from his chest. My mother stood before my father in disbelief. 'What are you doing here?' she asked him. He took her hand into his own and told me that the touch of their hands in that moment rushed like a warm wave to their hearts. He told her he loved her and wanted her to be his wife. Why had she not returned to the well to give her answer? Later, they told me they embraced each other and my mother told my father through her tears that she loved him but that she could not abandon Adah and her unborn child. That is when my father understood the dream. Jacob lived with Salome and Adah until the child was born. It was a boy."

Mary breathed in quickly realizing that the baby born to Adah and Hilo was Joseph, her husband. "You're telling me that Jacob and Salome became your adoptive parents!"

"Yes." Joseph's eyes welled up with tears. He looked down and then up again to Mary. "Salome and Jacob adopted me, and Adah returned home to Jerusalem. I don't know what happened to Adah and Hilo but they are my natural parents and they could be alive to this day, somewhere, probably in or around Jerusalem. I don't know if they ever married but I searched for them once. That's the reason I traveled to Jerusalem three years ago. I knew I was going to seek you out to be my almah and I wanted desperately to talk to someone about it. I never found them but I went ahead and asked for your promise to be my almah. You could not come to live with me in my father's home because I had no father. So, your father and I agreed it would be more proper for you to stay in your father's home until we could celebrate our first marriage ceremony."

"What of your parents, Salome and Jacob? Did they truly love each other?"

"My parents were kind, gentle, and loving to each other as they were to me. My father loved me and taught me so much, as did my mother. To me the most important remembrance of them was that love ruled and guided their relationship to each other, me, and our neighbors. My mother told me that her special prayer for me was that I would not have to care for them in their old age, putting my life on hold. My father told me that his special prayer for me was that I would be blessed with the wonder of a marriage relationship. My own prayer, as I grew, was one of thankfulness." Joseph did not continue to speak about his parents until Mary urged him on by gently touching his arm. Her touch brought him back to the reality of his life and he went on to speak after he took a deep breath of air. "My father died when I was sixteen years old. My mother died seven days after my father died. I remember being grief stricken, scared, and devastated all at the same time for many days that followed. Even though I grew up knowing my parents were old, that they would be with me for only a short time in my life, I feel that the love they had for me, and each other, will live forever.

"Slowly, my grief for their loss subsided and I remembered their prayers for me. I began to realize that I could take care of myself, and one day I knew I would choose a partner for life, marry, and have children."

Joseph dropped his head. Mary knew he was shedding tears. She placed her arms around him with the hope of comforting him. She understood his sadness as she thought of her own parents, hundreds of miles away. She wondered if they thought of her and Joseph, not knowing where they were.

He lifted his head and said, "Look at me now. I'm married, with a baby boy, and living in Alexandria, Egypt. Who could have predicted this?"

"Are you sorry you're my husband and Jesus' father?"

"No. But sometimes I must admit that I'm wondering if God really knows what is happening here. It certainly doesn't make sense to me."

"Joseph, were you happy when I accepted your request to be your almah?"

"Of course, I was overjoyed! What a silly question."

"What did you think when you learned I was pregnant?"

Joseph paused before responding. It was difficult for him to answer Mary's question. He was ashamed of his initial thoughts when he learned that his almah was pregnant. He had been going to dismiss her quietly from their betrothal. In an instant he knew he could not lie. He turned to face Mary squarely.

"After news got out that something had happened to you, there were murmurings among the people of our community. I waited and within two weeks your father came to me and explained your circumstance and declared that our betrothal was indefinitely postponed. I was not allowed to see you or talk to you. At that point I didn't know what to think but I obeyed your father and I didn't seek you out to talk to you. Three months passed and I learned you had left to be with your aunt and uncle. After you left, word got out that you were pregnant. I felt the same way I felt when my father and mother died and left me to be alone. I didn't think about how you were feeling until the shock left me and I had to face the circumstances at hand. I didn't understand and was completely confused. Then the elders of our community met and determined that you should be stoned to death. But there was some question over your situation because they couldn't determine whether or not you had consented to lie with someone, or whether you had been raped, as you claimed. Because your father was judged a good man within the Essene community, they allowed you to live, and not be stoned. When I was presented with their decision, I was advised to break our betrothal permanently. I didn't have time to think. I was desperate. I prayed and prayed and prayed that night until exhaustion conquered my ability to think anymore. The next day your father came to me to assure me that the proper thing to do was to follow the advice of the elders. He told me that you would be shunned and would not return to his home. I told him I would quietly break our betrothal.

"The following three months, while you were gone, I was tortured, lost in spiritual conflict. What could have happened!?

"From the start, six months had passed and I lived in constant torment. I wanted to see you. I needed to talk to you. I decided to believe that you must have been raped as you had claimed to the elders. I went to visit your father and pleaded your case to him. He refused to consider the possibility that you had been raped by a Roman soldier and told me to go home and get on with my life without you.

"That night, as I walked home, I remember an owl hooting, almost as if it followed me home. It was as if the Spirit of God was following me in wisdom. When I entered my house, I went back to my sleeping mat and hoped God would grant me sleep. I prayed and confusion continued to haunt my soul. I had lit the lantern and all of a sudden, the light from the lamp became very bright, and then diminished to a flicker that almost extinguished the flame. Then the light resumed its original level. I thought it was odd, but I was so tired, I extinguished the flame and went to sleep. That's when I had the dream about you. The next day I traveled to your aunt and uncle's and brought you home to be with me.

"Mary, I don't regret bringing you home. I am overwhelmed with joy that we are married. Marrying you has been the most correct thing I have ever done in my life. I loved you before you were raped, I loved you after you were raped, and I love you now."

Mary stared at Joseph. She finally stated, "I never could have imagined that all this has already happened to us in our life together, so far. It has been quite a thrill, and much has been unpleasant. I am confident in our love for each other though, Joseph. Even more so, I have peace about my confidence in your love for little Jesus. I never knew you also were adopted. Yet you have spoken of great love between yourself and your parents. I love Jesus but he is my son. I know you will have your own children with me and I wonder if you will love them more than Jesus. There may be more difficulties ahead but I believe God groomed you to be Jesus' father." Mary began to cry, "Joseph, I love you. I love the way you are able to love us." She took his hands. "I'm so thankful for you, my husband. Yet, I'm so angry! I'm angry with Panthera, angry with our community and their inability to offer any support to me, angry with the elders and their ignorance. Most of all I'm angry with my father."

"This is not going to go easily for us, is it, Mary?"

"No, I suppose not."

"We've had a long day. We need sleep. I'm sure Jesus will wake to nurse in the night so let's try to sleep a little before he wakes. Tomorrow, I plan to go with Seth to meet his employer. Hopefully I will find work." Joseph helped Mary to her feet and gently caressed the side of her face. She looked up and kissed him. They turned and walked back to their sleeping room and fell asleep together quickly and the baby Jesus slept through the entire night.

LOVE, LIFE, AND WORK IN ALEXANDRIA

JOSEPH WALKED UP TO Seth's home. He raised his hand to knock on the door but before his knuckles met the wood, the door opened and there stood Seth. He was smiling.

"Good morning! Are you nervous?"

"No. I'm feeling thankful for you. Your employer may give me an opportunity to earn a living, or he may not give me any regard, but I will be with a friend. For that I am grateful."

Seth placed his hand on Joseph's shoulder as they walked. "Don't worry, my friend. My employer may come across to you as harsh initially, but I know him well. It is just a front. He can't keep it going for long. Under his tough exterior, he is fair and unbiased, although I have witnessed him in a rage or two of anger over the years I've worked under his leadership and authority. I'll take you to our place of labor and direct you to him so you can ask about the availability of work. If you speak to him on your own, you will secretly receive his respect from the start."

They had not walked a far distance before they came upon a large structure. Seth explained that this was the building where most of the construction, planning, and drafting took place. Joseph also learned that it was from this building that the workers received their instructions for the labor of the day and many were sent out to sites where construction was conducted.

Seth and Joseph walked into the large building. Seth pointed to a door and explained that it was beyond that door that the employer could be found but Joseph wasn't paying attention. He was spellbound, overwhelmed by the sheer size of the building. It appeared to be greater in expanse inside as Joseph looked around and saw immense tools, instruments, ropes, pulleys, and men everywhere. The workers were busy, focused at their benches and drafting tables. Some were bent over tangled ropes and mechanisms that were unfamiliar to Joseph.

Seth came up behind Joseph, who stood staring at the sight before him, and he turned Joseph by the shoulders toward the door he had previously directed him to go. With a little push from Seth, slowly, Joseph walked toward the door and became more and more aware of his nervousness. When he reached the door, he stopped and glanced back to Seth, who encouraged him to go forward by waving both hands in a forward sweeping motion. With some hesitation, Joseph knocked on the door and heard a gruff voice that simply said, "Come in." Joseph entered, trying to walk as tall as his stature would allow.

The man was looking down at his work on a very large drafting table and said without looking up, "What do you want?"

Joseph lowered his head and said, "I'm looking for a place to earn a living. I was directed to come to you to ask for employment."

The man at the desk looked up at Joseph and studied him from head to sandaled foot. "You're a Jew." He said it as if he were informing Joseph and not as if he were confirming his own realization and surprise.

Joseph humbly replied, "Yes, sir. I am from Judea and have recently moved here with my wife and baby son. Seth, one of your employees, thought I may be able to find work here and brought me today to talk with you about a possibility for employment."

The man stood up, walked to the side of his desk, crossed his arms in front of him, and learned against his drafting table. "What if I told you we don't hire Jews here, we buy them for slaves?"

Joseph confidently but respectfully replied, "I will not cheat or exploit my employer but neither will I work without earning a living for shelter, bread, and drink. Please give me the opportunity to do so."

The man stared at him for a moment and said, "Your clothing . . . why is it so white? Its brightness almost blinds me as the sunlight from my window reflects off of you."

"My garment is woven from a fiber taken from a plant that grows near and around the Dead Sea in Judea. We bleach the fiber after it has been spun into thread. The white threads are laid in the sun for many days before they are woven into clothing such as mine."

The employer was temporarily speechless and then stood up from his leaning. "Your clothing won't stay white and clean working around here. What do you say to that?"

"If you offer me employment, I will wear whatever is appropriate and work to the best of my ability. The garment I am wearing now is made this way to remind me to be clean and ethical from the inside out."

"What do you mean the inside out?"

"The thoughts of my mind, the inspiration of my heart, and the potential for the goodness of my soul are to be rooted in the guidance and love for our God, for myself, and for all others in my life."

The employer stated, "Do you mean your God or, as you said, our God?" Joseph stood before him and waited, saying no more. The Egyptian stood and contemplated Joseph's words and walked around to the front of his drafting table again. He looked down at the contents on the table and shuffled items while he said without looking at Joseph, "All right. You can start work beginning today. I need someone to come and clean and tidy the building after the work of the day is finished. I will pay you . . ." and he wrote a figure of an amount on a piece of papyrus paper and handed it to Joseph, "If that is agreeable to you. Keep that little piece of paper as our agreement. What do you say?"

Joseph looked at the amount and had no idea if it was sufficient for living in Alexandria. He asked, "How many days within the week do you require me to work for this amount?"

"Seven days a week, as is the custom."

"I am willing to work six days a week but I will not work on our Sabbath."

"Oh yeah, Jews remember the Sabbath and . . . how do you say it, you keep it holy?" Joseph watched carefully to see if this potential employer would honor his request to follow his religious conviction and still offer him work.

Finally, the Egyptian employer said, "I like your discipline. It'll serve me well here at work. The job is yours if you want it at the amount I originally offered and wrote on that paper."

Joseph held out his hand to the employer and said, "Thank you. I agree." He realized he had to trust the Egyptian employer and did not find it difficult since he had already learned how to trust a Roman soldier who had raped his wife. Joseph walked to the door to leave and turned back. "Sir, my name is Joseph. What is your name?"

"Amsu." Joseph turned to leave again and Amsu said, "Wait, I'll call for Seth to take you around the building and explain what is done in each area so that you can use your own good judgment as to what needs to be done at the end of each day of work. I suggest you ask each worker what they want, or don't want, cleaned or organized." Amsu walked in front of Joseph, opened the door and called loudly, "Seth . . . Seth, come here."

Seth came quickly and Amsu asked him to take Joseph around to meet the other workers. Afterward Seth told Joseph he ought to go home and come back in by late afternoon to begin his work. He estimated that it would take Joseph six hours to complete the work of cleaning and organizing the building after a workday. Then Seth gave Joseph clear directions home because he had noticed Joseph's nervous distraction when they had walked to work in the morning. Joseph thanked Seth and left to go home. He felt anxious but relieved, pleased that he had employment. When he entered his home, he found Mary sitting in their bedroom nursing Jesus.

She looked up at Joseph and waited for him to tell her what the morning had brought to him.

"I've been hired to organize and clean the large buildings where all the men work in a construction business. The man who hired me is paying me this amount." Joseph held out the papyrus paper with a number written on it.

"What does that mean, Joseph?"

Joseph looked at the numbers again and said, "I don't know."

Mary laughed.

Joseph relayed every detail that had transpired that morning. Mary listened with interest and said she had had no doubt he would be hired because he was such a smart man.

"No," Joseph replied. "Actually, the work that is done at this place goes far beyond my understanding. I'm grateful Amsu could hire me to do anything at all."

"Amsu? Who's Amsu?"

"Amsu is my employer. At first, he presented himself as a mean, unfair employer. Very quickly, it became clear he was a wise, just, and ethical employer. He tested me at first but I wasn't in a position to be defiant or resistant. He hired me to clean the large main building, which is occupied all day by workers. I'm supposed to clean and organize the building at the end of the workday so I'll be working from late afternoon to late at night, six days a week. He honored my request to not work on the Sabbath."

"We'll miss you for the evening, but Jesus and I will be fine. I'm so proud of you, Joseph. We'll all be fine living here. I'm scheduled to meet with Mestha for my lessons in Greek, and now I can leave Jesus with you during that time and give all my attention to the task of learning."

"I'm sure you'll learn without any trouble," Joseph said in Greek.

"What did you say?"

Joseph repeated in Aramaic what he had initially said in Greek, "I'm sure you'll learn without any trouble." He added, "You are a smart woman, and I'm proud of you too."

"Joseph," Mary asked, "where did you learn how to speak and write in three different languages?"

Joseph was still for a moment and seemed to be deep in the thought of a faraway memory. "My father, Jacob, was a very learned man. He taught me Latin and Greek. He taught me with patience and thorough discipline. I also learned quickly because I wanted to please him. I did please him. He always acted impressed with my ability to pay attention and learn. He told me I would never regret knowing more than my native tongue because it would open doors to me I never would expect. He was right."

Mary sighed. "I wish my parents had taught me more. It always seems to me that women are neglected in education. But here I am, in Alexandria, and I'm going to learn Greek. Maybe someday I'll also learn Latin."

"I don't see why not. I'm sure our future will continue to offer us opportunity to learn and acquire all kinds of knowledge."

Suddenly, there was a loud, urgent pounding at their front door. Joseph and Mary immediately recognized Mestha's thick Egyptian accent as she called, "Mary! Mary! Please come quickly to my home!"

Mary gave Jesus to Joseph and they all ran to Mestha's house. When Mary walked into the house Mestha turned to Mary out of breath. Her expression was frantic.

"Isis! My daughter, Isis, is very sick again. She has a fever and she isn't responding to me when I talk to her!"

Mary looked at Joseph, who translated Mestha's urgent words.

"Take me to Isis," Mary said.

Mary was taken to a room where Isis was lying in bed, dripping with sweat and burning with fever. Mary knew the fever indicated something unclean was present in her young body. She looked at Mestha and Joseph and began to bark instructions to them.

"Joseph, let Isis' brother take care of Jesus and go into the fields nearby and look for the goldenseal root. Do you know what that is and how to get it?" Joseph nodded, turned to Isis' eldest brother, and put Jesus in his arms. He disappeared and headed toward the fields near the house.

"Mestha, do you have a tub?" Mestha understood Mary's question spoken in Aramaic. "Fill the tub with tepid water." Mestha shook her head indicating she didn't understand. "Fill the tub with water that is not cold or hot . . . tepid." Mestha understood and left the room and followed Mary's instruction. Mary bent over Isis and removed her blankets and clothing. She waved the blanket over Isis' body to try to cool her in the hope that the fever would break before convulsions grabbed her.

It seemed like an eternity before Joseph returned with a handful of goldenseal root and astragalus herbs he had also found. Mary smiled at Joseph with approval. She covered Isis' nakedness and asked Joseph to come into the room to lift and carry Isis down to Mestha. They found Mestha filling a tub with water. She was crying. Mary let Joseph hold Isis as she comforted Mestha with simple Aramaic words. She felt the water and asked

Mestha to warm the water a little. Mestha took a pot of hot water she had hung over the fire and poured the hot water into the tub of the cold well water and Mary checked its temperature. It was perfectly tepid.

"Joseph," Mary ordered, "Place Isis in the tub. Keep her covered with the blanket." Joseph obeyed and left the room to give the women privacy. Mary and Mestha sat next to Isis. They lifted the blanket that covered her and poured water over her naked body lying in the tub of tepid water. Her fever began to come down. Isis seemed to consciously respond immediately. She opened her eyes and said in Greek that her head hurt. Mary needed no translation. She stood up with the astragalus herb and the goldenseal root and mashed them together in a bowl with hot water and sugar to reduce the taste of bitterness. She returned to Isis and coaxed her into consuming the entire portion she had prepared.

They waited, continuing to pour tepid water over Isis' body. In time Isis became more responsive and Mary could feel that her fever had subsided. She placed the drenched blanket over Isis and called for Joseph to carry her back to her bed.

Once back in her bed, Isis shivered and told her mother she felt better but wanted to pull covers over herself to get warmer. Mary removed the wet blanket and chose the lightest blanket in the room. She placed it over Isis and let her wrap it around herself. Mary felt relieved, knowing the worst was over and Isis' life was out of danger.

Mary looked at Mestha, who was crying again. She walked around the bed and hugged Mestha. She told Mestha that the herb and root would fight off what was making Isis sick and that she should not worry now.

"What did Isis eat last?" Mary asked.

"I fixed a dish with goat's milk and meat," Mestha answered.

Mary gently said, "Mestha, in my faith we are instructed to never mix meat with milk of any kind. It can cause illness."

"But the rest of my family ate and they didn't get sick."

"You told me Isis has survived blackwater fever. She is not as strong as the others in your family. She needs to be careful with her body." Mary knew Isis' body was weakened and could not fight illness or ingestion of unclean food. Mary hoped the words she chose to explain this in Aramaic were understood by Mestha.

Joseph and Mary said goodbye, and Mary said she would come to check on Isis later in the afternoon before Joseph left for work. Mestha smiled and looked at Joseph with a look of gratefulness. They walked home together and Joseph said, "Those boys seemed to know how to handle a little baby. Jesus didn't cry once."

Mary and Joseph spent the rest of the day together. He held and attended to Jesus as Mary finished tasks around the house. Then she left to check on Isis, who was fine, sitting up and sipping broth in bed. From there, Mary went to the market nearby, to purchase ingredients for a wonderful dinner both she and Joseph could eat together before he left to begin his work.

When he returned to the building, the workers were packing up and heading home from their day of labor. Joseph began his labor immediately. He worked diligently and was done within five hours. He hoped he had done a job that was acceptable; however, since this was his first day, he wasn't sure. He was sure he would hear if he didn't meet the expectations of the other workers and Amsu.

The few days that followed proved to be successful. Seth reported to Joseph that everyone was pleased with his work. When Joseph would arrive at work, most of the workers were packing up to leave for the day. Most of these workers had already noticed and expressed appreciation for his work and organizational skills, although some were less friendly. Even so, Joseph was surprised to be accepted as well as he was.

Amsu also recognized Joseph's worth and after his fifth day working, Amsu requested that Joseph come to work a little early the next day to meet with him to discuss Joseph's experience working for him and the other men. Joseph was pleased to receive Amsu's request to meet. He was truly impressed with Amsu's style and skill for management and had already witnessed Amsu's excellent managerial skill with many different workers. He was impressed by Amsu's concern for his employees and his ability to draw out the best in them while displaying support rather than the typical practice of domination and control. Joseph wondered where and how Amsu had developed these talents as an employer and hoped to learn more after he met with him tomorrow.

That night, while walking home, Joseph's mind was filled with many thoughts. As he arrived home, he didn't enter his home immediately but walked to the back of the house and looked to the east. The heavenly bodies of light were completely separated with quite a great distance between them now. He noticed that one of the lights had moved closer to them and would most likely be shining over Alexandria within days. Joseph thought about the past month and lifted a prayer of thanksgiving. He was employed, Jesus was healthy and growing, they had friends, and Mary was learning Greek. Joseph thanked God that Mary was at peace and happier these days. His heart was also at peace. He turned from his gazing at the night sky and entered the house from the back. He knew Mary was asleep so he quietly washed and came to bed to lie next to her. She didn't stir. Neither did Jesus.

Joseph lay still and felt compelled to continue his prayer by thanking God for providing beyond their basic needs. He couldn't help thinking about their life in this faraway place. It was good. He looked at Mary sleeping next to him and thought about the fact that tomorrow would be thirty-three days since Jesus' birth. He knew Mary also remembered and was not enthusiastic about making love with him. He said another prayer asking God to help them overcome fear and dread. He looked at her again and she opened her eyes.

"I'm glad you're home." She reached out to him and held him close. "Tomorrow will be thirty-three days. Please remember that you said we'll move slowly, and learn to love each other properly."

"Hush, shhh . . . go back to sleep and don't worry about anything, Mary." He kissed her on the forehead and closed his eyes, surprised at his own feelings of tiredness. He fell asleep quickly, knowing that little Jesus was sleeping through the night and would not disrupt their sleep.

Joseph woke the next morning feeling well rested. He knew he had slept well because he had not awakened when Mary rose to take Jesus to the front room to attend to him and nurse him. When Joseph came into the room to join them, she smiled and lifted Jesus to her shoulder to burp him.

"Good morning. Did you get a good night's sleep?"

"Yes, but now I'm hungry and I smell bread baking."

"Come," Mary said. "Let's have breakfast and enjoy our time together until you leave for work this afternoon."

Together they ate breakfast, bathed, and clothed themselves. Joseph felt good and anticipated the meeting with Amsu without anxiety.

"Mary, I will be leaving a few hours early for work today because I am to meet with Amsu. Do you think we can eat dinner at noon today and will you stay up for my return home tonight?"

Mary believed she knew why Joseph wanted her to remain awake for his return home from work. "Joseph, please. Can you wait a little longer to engage in our marital . . . intimacy? I'm not ready for this. I need more time to heal from giving birth. So please, let's not try tonight, even if the law declares we can. Can't *we* choose when to engage? Does the law command us when to be intimate, or does it not just instruct how long we must wait?"

Joseph gazed upon Mary and saw her fear and trepidation. He approached her and said, "Come with me." He took her by the hand and led her into their bedroom. He lifted Jesus from her sling and gently placed him in his little bed. Jesus was asleep and didn't stir as he was placed down. He approached Mary and led her to their bed, instructing her to lie down. She did as Joseph directed, but Joseph could detect a hint of fear in her eyes.

"Relax," he gently said. He stroked her face and unbound her hair, pulling his fingers through her locks.

For a moment, Mary closed her eyes, enjoying his touch, but she opened her eyes abruptly, saying, "Joseph, I'm . . . I'm not comfortable lying together with you stroking my hair, face, and neck. Where is this going?"

Joseph, who had lain next to her, propped himself up on his elbow. He looked down at Mary and asked, "Do you trust me? I know what happened to you was a terrible, frightening, painful experience. Giving birth to Jesus was scary also, for both of us. Did it ever dawn on you that we were in the perfect place for you to give birth to your firstborn? We were with Beth, an experienced midwife. You would not have received any help from anyone if you had birthed Jesus at home with me alone. I knew nothing about helping a woman give birth. But we were in Bethlehem. Jesus was born under the best care you could have received and . . . he was born in the city of David, as prophesied! Don't you see! Your son was born in Bethlehem. You did it, Mary. Baby Jesus's head was certainly large, and his body followed in birth through you! He is my adopted son, and you are my wife. I love you . . . I have loved you for many years and now I love your son . . . our son. Trust God . . . trust me. Intimacy between a husband and wife is a gift from God, and we shall be pleasured with it, and you shall birth me children, our children. Please don't be afraid. Please understand our marriage bed shall bring both of us pleasure and bring new life to us as husband and wife." Joseph slowly leaned over her and kissed her. She felt his passion.

"Well," Mary smiled, "I think I can wait until tonight and stay awake for your return from work."

Joseph rolled his head back and laughed. "I never dreamed you would agree so easily, but I promise you . . . it will be good!" He bent down over her again and kissed her, feeling her reciprocation. He got up and left the room, leaving Mary lying on the bed alone. He would wait until tonight, and he hoped he had helped awaken Mary's desire to engage with the same passion he had carried within his heart after refraining from her all these months from their first marriage ceremony. Yet, he didn't regret declaring their first marriage as wedlock. There would be a second marriage ceremony designating wedlock as was the Essene custom, but he also thought that Mary was a remarkable young woman and he thanked God for her.

It was not long and Jesus cried out. He was awake from his morning nap. Joseph walked into the room and lifted Jesus from his bed, and he stopped crying immediately. Mary had gone to the market to purchase food for their dinner at noon.

"It looks like it's just you and me," Joseph said. He walked with Jesus in his arms to the open space in the back of their dwelling. "Does the sun feel good, Jesus? I know, let's visit the burro. He doesn't get much attention these days." Joseph walked into the small stall and held Jesus on the burro's back. Jesus seemed indifferent to the burro and was more attentive in looking at Joseph's face. Joseph noticed this and walked with Jesus to a tree. He sat down and leaned against the tree and cradled Jesus against his propped-up legs. Jesus looked directly at Joseph's face as if he were studying and memorizing his features.

"What are you looking at, Jesus? You've seen me before. I've been here all along."

Jesus' arms waved up and down and he did not stop looking at Joseph. Joseph was pleased with Jesus' behavior and felt emotionally close to the baby he held so tenderly. He lowered his face so Jesus could reach and touch his hair and beard. With an instinct Joseph didn't know babies possessed, Jesus grabbed hold of his hair with unexpected strength. Joseph let him pull as hard as Jesus' little hands could pull and then Joseph gently blew into Jesus' face. Jesus immediately released his hair and began to wave his arms up and down again. Joseph stood up from under the tree and raised Jesus up toward the branches.

"Someday, not long, you're going to be a lot of fun to have around. I hope I'll be able to love you properly. You've already been given a tough beginning in life. But let me tell you something . . . life isn't fair. Don't expect it to be fair, Jesus."

While Joseph spoke to Jesus with tenderness, he didn't know that Mary stood watching from the back door for the last few minutes. When he turned and realized she was witness to his conversation with their one-month-old baby, he turned red with embarrassment.

"Well, he seemed to be listening to me so I thought I wouldn't lose the opportunity," he awkwardly explained.

Mary smiled and walked out to Joseph and kissed him on the cheek. "Just keep talking to him with love, Joseph. I think that's the most important aspect of parenting. At least that's what Mestha told me. She told that to me yesterday, in Greek, and I understood!" Mary acted proud of herself. "Now, I've purchased wonderful food for dinner. Come inside and eat."

Joseph followed Mary to the table and she took Jesus from him. He looked at the table filled with many good things to eat and asked, "What's the occasion? This is a feast, not a lunch."

"It's a special day. You will be talking to Amsu, and, most of all, because I saw you talking to Jesus with tender love." She bent down with Jesus in her arms and with her other arm hugged Joseph's shoulders and whispered in his ears, "And we will make love tonight with a passion we didn't know we had."

Joseph looked a little sheepish,, "I hope I won't disappoint you."

"You can't, I'm convinced of it."

They ate their fill and Mary nursed Jesus, who fell asleep for a long afternoon nap.

"Why don't you nap also," she suggested to Joseph. "It is going to be an important day at work today and, more importantly, tonight we're going to be very busy." Joseph didn't understand at first and then realized to what she was referring and became concerned that her expectations were too high. As if she could read his mind she said, "Joseph, will you stop worrying and breathe a little. Sometimes you act like your skin fits you too tightly." And then she smiled. "Now go, take a nap. I have things to do around here and I will wake you in time to go to work."

Joseph and Jesus had a restful, long nap. When Jesus cried out, Mary woke Joseph up also. He was obviously in a deep sleep because at first, he thought he was at sleep in his own home at the Qumran Settlement. He was happy to see Mary and realized quickly that he was in Alexandria and Mary was his wife. He rose from the bed and washed his face. He dressed properly and found Mary and Jesus in the front room.

"Goodbye, my love. Wish me good fortune. My meeting with Amsu will prove to be important and interesting."

He bent over and kissed Jesus on the forehead and let him grab his finger while he kissed Mary. He stood up and looked around the house, which was clean, tidy, and beautifully decorated. "You are a wonderful mother, and," he looked around the house again, "an artist."

Joseph smiled and walked to the door. As he walked onto the street his heart felt light. It didn't take him long to walk to his place of employment. He confidently walked in, greeted Seth, and approached Amsu's door. He knocked on the door and heard Amsu say in his usual monotone voice, "Come in."

Joseph stepped in and Amsu was working over his drafting table. He looked up and when he saw it was Joseph, he said, "Well, Joseph. Come in. In fact, come here. I want to show this to you."

Joseph came close to Amsu's large table and looked at the papers scattered on top. He picked out one drawing and laid it over the other papers. It was a drawing of a building. It looked magnificent on paper and Joseph thought it would be grand to see it erected and completed in all its glory.

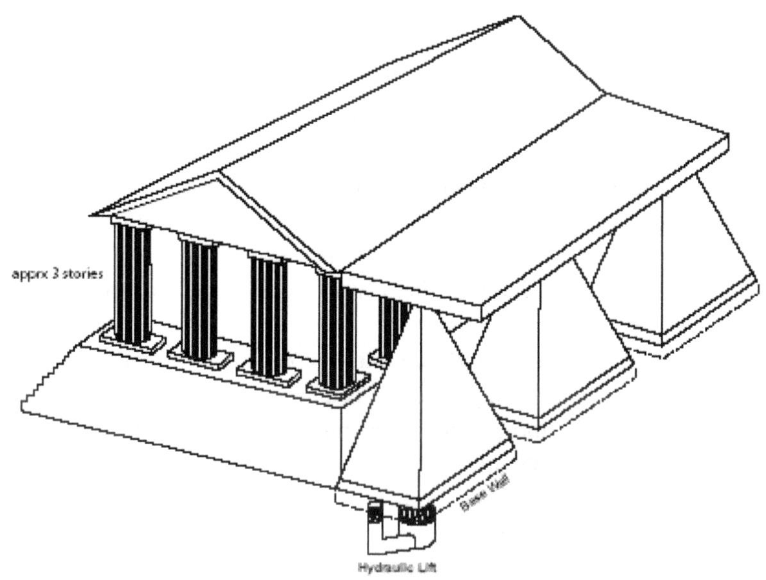

Sketch of the Alexandria Library

"That is a beautiful building! Where does it stand?"

"It doesn't . . . yet," Amsu said. His eyes were sparkling. "I submitted this plan to the commissioners at the University of Alexandria. They want a library built and erected and my plan was chosen. This is a library." He patted the paper and looked at Joseph for his comment.

"Amsu, are we going to be the construction business to build such a building?"

"Yes. What do you think?"

Joseph stared at the drawing and was particularly impressed with the pyramids placed to support the structure in the front. Three pyramids, fashioned after the Great Pyramid of Cheops, whose pyramid tomb had been built sometime three thousand years before, stood as a support to a portico that would span the width of the library building. The three pyramids were not near to the great size of the Great Pyramid but the task seemed formidable, even on paper.

Amsu asked Joseph with excitement, "It will be a great tribute to our Egyptian heritage to build these pyramids, don't you think?"

Joseph finally responded with, "They most certainly will be a tribute. Do you think we have the manpower to do this?"

"I'll hire more men if I have to! That's really what I want to talk to you about. You're a good worker and an honest, intelligent man. I would like for you to become a regular worker and possibly be moved up to the position of foreman. Will you consider working with the men who run the cranes and pulleys? I'll increase your salary."

Joseph stood dumbfounded. Finally, he said, "Yes, I'll continue to work to the best of my ability but you need to know I know more about water and use of its power than I do about cranes and pulleys."

"If you're willing, I would like you to work in this department. You have great ambition and learnedness."

Joseph held out his hand and Amsu grabbed his forearm and said, "Done. Now, do you have any concerns you need to bring to my attention?"

Joseph thought and asked, "With this new position will I still be allowed to observe my Sabbath?"

Amsu waved his hand in the air, "Yes, of course. Go home, Joseph, and come back tomorrow morning to begin work with your new team. You'll be on the same work team as Seth. Come with him tomorrow. He'll show you the ropes." Amsu laughed at his own pun and walked to the door with his hand on Joseph's shoulder. "I'll see you tomorrow."

Joseph left the building and headed home. For some strange reason he was more excited about being home with Mary than the new work he would be doing. When he walked into the house Mary was not in the front room.

"Mary. Mary, where are you?" he called. Mary walked out from the hall with Jesus in her arms.

"What are you doing home so early? Did everything go well at work?"

"Yes. Everything is fine at work." He walked up close to her and asked, "And how are you, my dear?"

"I'm fine but I had hoped to have Jesus down to sleep before you arrived home."

Joseph saw that it was almost twilight and he knew the bright heavenly body of light would be shining.

"Come with me. Let's look to see if we can see the lights in the east." They walked outside and looked east together. The brightest light of the three heavenly bodies was moving west, closer to them. It would soon pass over Alexandria and settle in the horizon of the west for them to see every twilight if the sky was absent of clouds. The young family stood and watched the sky for a long while and then Mary said she would go in to nurse Jesus and put him down to sleep. She would meet Joseph in their bed shortly.

She left Joseph standing and gazing at the sky, shrouded in beautiful colors of twilight. With anticipation and excitement in his heart and mind, he remained staring at the sky and lifted a prayer, "Heavenly Father of the universe, how wondrous is your creation. Guide me and Mary to experience the intention of your plan. You can see into my heart, and you must know how much I love Mary, my wife. But the unfolding plan you have for our love and marriage has been violently disrupted and changed for us both, especially for Mary. She's so young, Lord . . . truly young. She's afraid and unsure of your intended gift of intimacy between husbands and wives. My desire for her is so strong. I don't want to wait any longer to consummate our marriage . . . not one more night. I can't imagine what it has been like for her, bearing a child conceived by a violent rape and then giving birth to her firstborn far away from her home, her mother, her family. Help me be the man who shall love her forever and teach her with all gentleness and patience. She is a daughter of the God who loves her. This world doesn't bring this truth for women to know, but I ask that you grant her love and pleasure that we shall share together until life parts us. Dear God, hear my prayer and have mercy on us with abundant grace, and abounding love showered upon us, beginning this night . . . let this be so, Father, not as the world gives but as our love for you, for each other, and for the infant child, Jesus. Give this for all our living days. Let this be so . . ."

Mary heard Joseph's final words of his prayer and softly called his name, "Joseph, what are you praying?" Joseph came to her, and she was surprised to see his shedding of tears. "Why are you crying? I'm ready . . . my fear is held deep in my heart, which your love has silenced and healed. Come to me."

She reached for him, and together they walked into their bedroom, which was beautifully lit with candles. Joseph felt a greater twinge of excitement looking at their room's preparation for their first time physically alone together, safe as husband and wife.

Joseph stepped forward and lay on the bed, waiting. Mary followed his lead and stood waiting as Joseph whispered, "Just a moment Mary. Stand before me for just a moment." She obeyed, and he said, "You are more beautiful than any sight I have laid my eyes upon," and opened his arms for her to fall into his embrace.

Their physical closeness took them both to a place where they experienced fulfilling satisfaction, which released all fear and pain from their past.

Mary was most surprised by her feelings. She was not afraid or nervous, thinking, "I truly love him, and he must truly love me. How wonderful!"

Joseph smiled as Mary looked into his eyes and dropped her head onto his chest, turning her ear to listen to the strong beating of his heart, which matched hers.

"Joseph, that was wonderful!"

"Yes," he almost whispered. "I feel complete for the first time since before my parents died, only this is better than anything I could have imagined. Mary, I never want to be parted from you, never in this lifetime. I love you with a power and strength I know I can't live without."

Mary giggled, "That's exactly how I feel. I love you, Joseph. I'm sorry life has been so lonely for you for so long but I'm here now. As long as God gives me life you will never be alone again."

They remained lying together naked. Mary said, "Joseph?"

"What, my beloved?"

"Let's do it again."

Joseph looked at her and asked, "Do you mean right now?"

"Yes."

"Mary, I don't know how to explain this to you but I can't do it over and over in the same moment of the night. I need to rest."

"Oh," she said. "So how long do you have to rest?"

Joseph turned to her and laughed out loud. "You are wonderful! Why don't we plan to do this again tomorrow night?"

"All right," she said. She remained quiet for a while and then said, "I guess I didn't really know what I was saying when I said I felt exactly like you. To think I was afraid of this. And yet, we're different as man and woman. What really scares me is that I'm beginning to sound like you. So, I guess we are different and we are also the same."

Joseph smiled and looked at her complete, naked beauty and said, "It all works for good, Mary."

She kissed Joseph and turned on her side to sleep. They fell asleep together, not bothering to cover their bodies. They held each other and they stayed warm in the cool of the evening, not waking until Jesus cried out. Mary rose and clothed herself and left to attend to him. Joseph looked through the window and saw a hint of light from the rising sun. He also rose and dressed and sat with Mary and Jesus as the sun came up for the day.

After breakfast, Joseph said to Mary, "I'm off to work. I'll see you soon," and he kissed her goodbye.

"Goodbye, Joseph. May your day be filled with goodness and success. I'll be waiting for your return."

Joseph grabbed an apple from the bowl on the table and walked to Seth's house. He rapped lightly on the door and Seth met him cheerfully, saying, "Isis is doing well. What did you give her?"

"It's called goldenseal, which is a root that fights unclean things in your body. The astragalus is an herb that does the same thing but it also seems to give energy and strength after a bad fever."

"How do you know all of this?"

"The same way you know all that you know. You learn from people who have gone before or you happen to learn through experimentation."

Seth and Joseph continued to walk together without talking. Joseph ate the apple and offered some to Seth who said, no, he was full. Seth was a big, heavy man and age had caused his muscles to sag, especially in and around his middle. His countenance always presented a pleasant hint of joy but he looked as if he should be eating more apples and less meat. Even so, Joseph had felt comfortable with Seth the first moment he met him and was glad they were neighbors, friends, and now coworkers.

With every week that passed, Joseph learned something new. Everyone at work was busy as the construction of the library progressed. As building proceeded, so did everyone's sense of urgency. Although the construction site was an additional thirty-minute walk from his home, Joseph was always there early. He understood that all the workers had to maintain their highest concentration upon details as equipment was being moved and set up at the site and he faithfully supported and served them as their foreman. The construction would be long and difficult but every day revealed more of the expected glory and magnificence the building would display upon its completion.

THE PASSING OF TIME

Three years and eight months had passed in Alexandria for Joseph, Mary, and Jesus. In that time, Joseph worked hard for Amsu and the construction of the new university library. Mary cared for Jesus, managed the home, and learned to speak Greek. Jesus thrived. Although he was a delightful child, the lessons of life were sometimes harsh for him and his parents. He was speaking Greek and Aramaic interchangeably by the age of three, and often drove his parents to distraction with his relentless questioning. However, his innocence and enthusiasm usually softened their parental irritation and they found themselves often astounded and entertained by his questioning spirit.

A small creek, fed by a spring, flowed behind their house and, as hard as Mary and Joseph tried to keep Jesus from its banks, he always found a way to explore its treasures. Frequently he brought living creatures to Mary or Joseph, who took him back to the creek to release whatever he found. Every time they returned with him to the creek to release his find, they tried to explain that the creatures he had taken from their watery home would die if they were not returned immediately. Whether it was Mary or Joseph, whichever parent was the lucky witness of his new discovery would be obliged to accompany Jesus to the creek immediately, instructing him to release his temporary little captives. Cleverly, without his parent's awareness, Jesus had a way of keeping them involved that afforded him more time at the creek. Both parents tried to instill in him that he was not to explore around the creek alone, ever! Yet, often within the same day, he managed to capture several new and different creatures.

One afternoon, Joseph was home alone with Jesus while Mary visited with Mestha. Joseph dozed while Jesus played with the wooden blocks Joseph had made for him. Jesus enjoyed playing and building with the blocks, but the creek always pulled his interest away from whatever he was doing and lured him to explore the life he found there. Unfortunately, this time Joseph fell asleep. The sound of his deep breathing drew Jesus' attention.

He got up from the floor, stepped carefully over the blocks, and put his face close to Joseph's. "Daddy, are you sleeping?" he whispered.

Joseph didn't respond so Jesus left the room, walked through the kitchen, and ran to the creek, excited to explore again. A rumble of thunder could be heard in the distance and dark clouds were moving quickly over Alexandria from the northeast. Not noticing the approaching storm, Jesus laid his body next to the creek and placed his hand into its muddy bank. He lifted a clump of waterlogged sand and soil to examine its contents. There were many creepy, crawly things squirming everywhere through the mud in his hand. He thought about going in to show his father but his better judgment kept him where he lay. He looked down at his hand and gently poked the different little creatures and giggled as they tickled his hand with their movement.

Another crack of thunder sounded and wind began to blow. Jesus released the plethora of life onto the ground a little way from the bank and became fascinated with their traveling, wondering how they knew what to do as they all began to walk, wriggle, or jump back to the creek. He didn't notice that the creek had begun to rise. The storm in the distance was feeding a surge of water and it was rising frighteningly fast!

"Jesus!" Joseph called from the house, which was at least twenty-five paces away. He saw the water rise quickly above Jesus's little legs and up to his thighs in the time Joseph ran the span of distance toward Jesus, and through the corner of his eye he became aware of a surging wave of water cascading toward the spot where Jesus stood.

The water engulfed Jesus as Joseph grabbed his little hand and pulled him up into his arms. He lifted his child as water surrounded his own legs, rising almost instantly to his chest. Overhead, the clouds burst open with more rain. Joseph struggled to carry him away from the creek's swollen banks and strong current of water.

Soaking wet, in the safety of their home, Joseph lowered his son to stand on the floor and shouted with hysteria, "Jesus! Do not ever, ever go down to that creek without me or Mom! *Do you understand*!?!"

He lifted Jesus, who was now crying, and carried him through the front room toward the bedrooms to find dry clothing as Mary walked in the door.

"What's going on here?" she asked.

Joseph was angry and Jesus was still crying. "Jesus was almost swept away by the creek's storm surge."

Mary ran to the back window to look at the creek and was horrified to see the rushing water. She returned to the front room, confronting Joseph. "Where were you when Jesus went down to the creek!?!"

"No . . . Mary, don't start blaming me!" he yelled.

Mary became angry and matched Joseph's anger. "He's a child. You know how he's fascinated with the creek! How was it that Jesus was down by the creek alone!?!"

Joseph raised his voice further and yelled, "I fell asleep. Jesus was right here next to me, on the floor playing with his blocks. I fell asleep! I suppose that makes me an unworthy father, forever!"

"No," Mary said. "It makes you a neglectful father, and that's worse! Jesus could have been swept away and drowned!"

Jesus had been crying the entire time Mary and Joseph yelled at each other. Now he was wailing, "No, Mommy, no, Daddy!" and his crying was heartrending to both.

Joseph was closer to Jesus, and also dripping wet. He lifted Jesus and embraced him with his whole spirit. "Don't cry, Jesus . . . you're alright! You're safe . . . I'm sorry," he looked at Mary and said, "I should have been watching more carefully. I shouldn't have fallen asleep."

Mary slowly walked across the room to them as Joseph held Jesus. She put her arms around both of them and gently said, "Joseph, you've been working hard. I'm sorry I yelled. The truth is, I also can't keep him from sneaking down to the creek while he is under my care either. It scares me." She took Jesus into her arms. "I'll take Jesus and get him into dry clothes. Why don't you do the same and rest. I'll make dinner and I'll call you when it's ready."

Jesus was no longer crying but his voice shook as he boldly said, "Daddy, you have a very loud voice . . . It's scary."

Later that night, while in bed, little Jesus thought about the day. He didn't understand why his parents behaved the way they had. He knew they were angry but only because of the way they had yelled. Although they seemed to be alright during their evening meal, Jesus felt sad because there had not been the usual happy talking around the dinner table. He just didn't understand and he felt sad.

Quietly, his mother came to him and sat next to him in his bed. Jesus looked at her and stretched his little arms out and around her neck. He began to cry.

"Jesus, Jesus, shhh," she rocked him. "Why are you crying, sweetheart?"

Jesus only said, "I feel sad."

"Well then, I suppose that explains your tears." Mary gently laid him down and brushed his curly dark hair from his face. "And do you know why you are sad?"

Jesus shook his head as tears continued to fall down the sides of his face.

"I think I know why you're sad . . . It's because Daddy and I yelled at each other?"

Jesus nodded his head.

Mary gently brushed the sides of his face with her hands and smiled. "Jesus, sometimes mommies and daddies get angry at each other but then their anger goes away. They stop yelling at each other and they forgive one another." Mary looked up and gazed out of the window at the bright light they had been watching for over three years and felt a pang for her own mother and father. "But they are so far away," she thought. Then she remembered how their arguments had scared her as a child. She looked down at Jesus and said, "Daddy and I are not angry with each other anymore. I'm going to kiss you good night and then Daddy will come to speak evening prayers with you. Now, don't be sad, Jesus. We love each other and we love you." She bent down and kissed his forehead and then his cheeks. "Sleep well, my child."

Joseph appeared above Mary and he placed his hands on her shoulders as she sat up from kissing Jesus. "It's time for evening prayers," he said. Mary stood up and Jesus felt peace fill him as both of his parents blessed him, as they did every morning, afternoon, and night before sleep. Tonight, it seemed more special to him. He smiled as he watched them embrace and kiss each other.

Mary left the room and Joseph sat next to Jesus. "Are you ready to pray?" Jesus nodded his head. "Jesus, we've got to come up with a plan to keep you from going to the creek alone. It's so dangerous! You could have drowned."

"What does that mean, Daddy?"

"If the water had carried you away and covered your head, you would not have been able to breathe air, you would have breathed water. That would kill you. You would die, Jesus."

Jesus didn't understand, but felt he was too tired to ask anymore questions. Joseph saw immediately that his son didn't understand what death meant. He realized he and Mary had been reinforcing his desire to go to the creek to return the little bit of life he had temporarily taken because they always immediately accompanied him back to the creek to release the newly discovered life. All along, Jesus had learned that it was all right to draw living things out of the creek but it was *not* all right to keep them. When he was taken back to the creek to free the living creatures, he did so obediently, always returning with a parent. He enjoyed this the most, being at the creek with the living things and his parents.

Jesus closed his eyes tight, ready to pray. Before all the prayers were finished, he was sleeping. Joseph chuckled and kissed his forehead. "Sleep well, little man," his father spoke in a soft voice.

In bed together, Mary and Joseph discussed the events of the day and decided they must handle the "creek challenge" differently. Joseph explained his theory. He believed Jesus didn't understand that he was not go to the creek alone. They had been rewarding him for finding living creatures by accompanying him back to the creek as soon as he showed his find. Mary agreed. Joseph decided Jesus needed to understand the concept of death for himself as he seemed to understand the wonder of life from the creek.

The following day, in the early evening, Joseph took his son down to the creek. Jesus was thrilled! Joseph instructed him to extract one living creature he could catch from the creek. Although it took time, Jesus finally caught a little fish. Joseph directed him to place the fish on the ground away from the water and watch.

At first, the fish flipped and flopped around vigorously. Slowly it became less active. "You see, Jesus. The fish is going to die unless it goes back into the water. They can't live long out of the water. Look, the fish is almost dead."

"No, I don't want the fish to be dead. We'll put it back in the water."

"You may do that because I'm here with you. But you must understand that just as you must be with Mommy or me to put the creatures you find back into the water, you must also be with me or Mommy when you explore and take something out of the water. Yesterday we almost lost you to a watery grave. We don't want you to die, just like you didn't want that fish to die. Do you understand?"

Jesus put the fish back into the water and watched it swim away. "I can try not to be near the creek without you or Mommy," he said.

"No, Jesus. You can't just try . . . you may not play near or around the creek without me or Mommy at all. Do you understand now?"

Jesus looked over at the creek and then took Joseph's hand. "Why do fish die?"

Joseph sighed. He stooped to Jesus' level and said, "Jesus, everything dies, sooner or later. Everything."

"Will you and Mommy die?"

"Yes."

"Will I die?"

"All human beings die, Jesus. You are a human being. You will die."

"Is it scary to die?"

"No, I don't think it's scary when you die . . . but, for some . . . maybe it is scary. But I don't think it's scary for long. It's only scary if you don't know anything about where you will go when you die."

"Where do people go when they die?"

Joseph looked directly into Jesus' eyes and said, "They go back to God."

"Do all people go back to God when they die?"

Joseph felt exhausted by his son's questioning but this feeling was nothing new to him. He decided to answer Jesus' questions to the best of his ability. "Jesus, I'm not sure how to answer all your questions but . . . we are Essenes. Even though we live far away from home we carry our faith and our traditions with us. I can only tell you what I believe as an Essene. All people go back to God when they die. I also believe that when a person dies, their body stays here, on the earth, and decays away."

"What does that mean?"

Joseph sighed and lifted a prayer that the God of the universe would help him answer his child's questions. "When a body dies, like my arms and legs and all my insides," Joseph touched his chest and arms as he tried to explain, "and decays . . . it means it stops working, and so it is buried in the ground. It mixes with the dirt and ground and changes. It becomes part of the earth and the water. But the human being also has a spirit. It is the spirit that goes back to God to live forever." Jesus was about to ask another question but Joseph quickly raised his hand to say, "God loves you. In fact, God loves the entire universe which He created. He loves people especially. When people die, they do not disappear; they change. We believe that every human spirit is given their time to live so they can learn to be in loving relationship with others, and with God too." Joseph was going to stop there but he saw that Jesus was listening with interest and, amazingly, he appeared to understand. "In this life we can learn about God freely, by our own choice. We can choose to learn about the love God has for us and we can choose to respond to God by loving him back. But the relationship each of us has with God is unique . . . different for every person. Most of all, I think that's what God . . ." Jesus continued listening with fascination, " . . . that's what God desires. He wants to be loved by us as He loves us." Jesus continued to look at Joseph with undivided attention. "So . . . while we live . . . we can learn to love . . . we can learn to love God and each other. He gives us life to learn to love and be loved."

"What is spirit?"

"God is spirit." Jesus looked confused so Joseph tried to explain further. "You can't see a spirit with the eyes of your body, you can see a spirit with the eyes of your mind, and your feelings." Joseph could clearly see that Jesus didn't understand. "Think of Mommy . . . right now, here, as we speak."

Jesus smiled. "You see, you can't see Mommy but you know her by her spirit and your mind can picture her even when you can't see her with your eyes . . . Spirit is like the wind. You can't see it but you can hear it sometimes, and you can see what it does. Look around. Yesterday the wind certainly blew a lot of branches off the trees, and it carried a lot of water that filled the creek with a rushing. Today, the wind is calm, the surging water has receded, and although we don't take notice of the wind like we do when it is in a fury, it's always there."

Jesus innocently looked at Joseph and simply said, "Oh. I'm glad to know that."

He let go of Joseph's hand and started to run back to the house. He stopped, turned back and asked Joseph, "Does Mommy know all this?"

"What do you think?"

Jesus spoke confidently, "Yes, I think she knows. I'm going to tell her that I will never play by the creek without you or her with me."

Joseph was astonished by Jesus' ability to comprehend. His son was certainly more intelligent than he had ever realized before. He remained sitting on the grass in the backyard looking at the creek. He thought, and said aloud, "That wasn't easy. Dear God, what is it going to be like when he's a man?"

REDEMPTION IN ALEXANDRIA

Mary and Joseph enjoyed Alexandria but often spoke of home. They wondered if they would be able to recognize their home, or the families whom they had not seen for what seemed like a long three years. Joseph, especially, was busy with the construction of the library with the other men at work. The front pyramids were ready to be set into the base walls with the portico to be built above. The base walls were constructed and set two cubits under the ground, protruding half of a cubit above the ground to prevent shifting. Each pyramid, made of mortar, weighed 650 tons. The base walls and pyramids were calculated to fit tightly, so once they were dropped into place they were there to stay.

Early one morning, Joseph walked to the work building alone to check on some pulleys he was supposed to bring to the construction site. As he walked into the building, he had an eerie feeling reminding him of a feeling he often experienced when he had first been hired and worked alone cleaning and organizing the building after the workday. He thought he was alone this time also, but before he left the huge empty building to go to the construction site, he heard something drop onto the floor. He turned and looked in the direction of the sound and saw a lone worker at his drafting table and walked toward him. Joseph stood next to the worker, who seemed unaware of his presence as he scribbled numbers and seemed to be calculating something.

Joseph stood and watched, finally interrupting the man. "May I be of service to you? You seem troubled by something. Maybe I can help."

The worker was startled, urgently answering, "You can't help me!"

Joseph was persistent. "Yes, maybe I can."

"I am undone. How can I trust you? You're that Jew Amsu hired over three years ago. What do you know about construction? You work with weights and pulleys."

"Friend, I know some things about construction, though probably not as much as you. But maybe I can help see a solution for whatever problem you're struggling over. I'll not sabotage you. You can trust me."

The worker dropped his head over the papers. Joseph waited until the man lifted his head again and looked at him, studying Joseph's face for sincerity.

Finally, he said, "I've made a terrible mistake in my calculations. The first of three mortar block pyramids weighing 650 tons each, which has taken months to complete, have been dropped into their base wall foundations and one doesn't fit! I made some kind of stupid, simple mistake! The base wall is already set into the ground. We can't change that. The pyramids are to fit tightly within the base walls, which are built two cubits into the ground, extending half a cubit above the ground. The calculations for the base walls are correct. However, yesterday the first heavy pyramid was moved over the base wall with pulleys and ropes, and dropped into place. My calculations must have been wrong. The huge pyramid was dropped into the base wall and is crooked due to my mistake.

"It sits lopsided and must be lifted up and out to be corrected. Only when the pyramid is lifted up and out of the base wall can ropes be secured underneath and around the pyramid and attached to the pulleys on the cranes and moved so it can be corrected to fit into the base wall accurately."

The man looked down at the scattered papyrus over the drafting table. He placed his hand to his forehead. "I have no idea how we can lift the pyramid because there are no places to attach ropes for the pulleys, and no space between the pyramid and the base wall to fit ropes through either! I even thought about possibly digging under the base wall but the pyramid is too heavy. I'm undone. I've tried to think of every possible way to lift this pyramid from underneath and can't come up with a solution."

Joseph felt the worker's anxiety.

"My name is Joseph. What is your name, sir?"

The worker looked up in surprise and then responded with, "My name is Pepi. I've worked here for seven years and this will be the end of me."

Joseph stood deep in thought, remembering the power of water. He contemplated the huge ship that had floated quickly over the Mediterranean Sea when he and his family had traveled from Joppa to Alexandria. He knew the principle that carried the huge ships would not be the same as lifting the pyramid out of the base wall, but he thought about the power of water as a possible clue. He also remembered the water pressure that pushed water up from the underground stream to a basin in his house back at the Qumran Settlement. He knew water had power and something suddenly dawned on him. He had an idea that could possibly work for Pepi. "Back in Judea I used to experiment with different ways to use water power for situations like you are describing. Often, the way water can be used creates a phenomenon of nature."

Pepi looked doubtful. "Like what?"

"Well . . . if we construct something that can sustain water pressure, we can use water to lift. We may be able to lift the pyramid out of the base wall from underneath using water pressure."

"Water pressure created and sustained in what?" Pepi figured he had nothing to lose listening to this unusual Jewish man who seemed to believe he knew what he was talking about. However, Pepi was already distraught and Joseph's suggestion created more confusion and stress for him. Pepi was ready to give up. "What could you possibly be talking about? There is no water underneath that pyramid! It all needs to be torn apart and rebuilt. It's going to take months to rebuild."

"No," Joseph tried to hide his excitement. "Suppose we build an L-shaped, waterproof pipe and connect it to a small waterproof tub like this." Joseph picked up Pepi's pen, dipped it in his jar of ink, and drew a diagram:

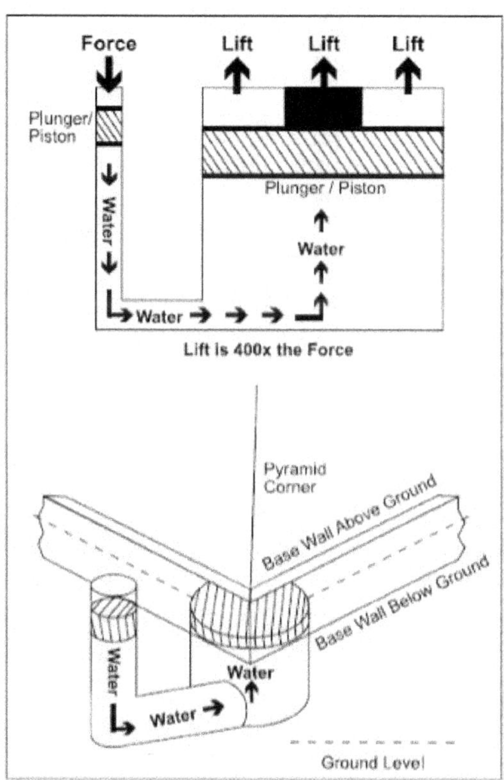

"The pipe and tub could be filled with water. They would have to be strong so no water could escape under pressure. Two watertight plungers will need to be made, one for the pipe, the other for the top of the tub. The plunger that fits tightly into the pipe could be pushed down, forcing water pressure to increase in the tub. The water pressure will have no place to move except up, against the plunger at the top of the tub, which would create lift against the pyramid at the base wall below the ground and also the base wall above the ground."

Papi stared at Joseph's drawing and drew in the plungers. "You mean like this?"

"Yes!" Joseph said.

Pepi stared at the sketch. "We would need four of these 'lifts' to place underground beneath the four corners of the pyramid . . . But how can pushing down on the small plunger create enough water force to lift 650 tons?"

"I believe enough pressure can be created by pushing down on the small pipe plunger. The water spreads and multiplies its force. The water will be forced to go somewhere, and that would be against the only part that can move, the larger plunger. It will also move the only direction it can . . . *up*!" Joseph was excited as he saw that Pepi understood.

Pepi tapped his finger against the diagram and said, "Yeah . . . we could build four of these . . . tunnel under and around the base wall at the four corners of the pyramid and create enough concentrated lift power to raise the pyramid out of the base wall without destroying the construction of either the base wall or the pyramid."

Joseph added. "Once the pyramid is lifted, the ropes and pulleys could be positioned to move the pyramid over from the base wall. The mortar of the pyramid could then be chiseled and altered to fit properly into the base wall. The existing base wall could remain undisturbed, as it is already set into the ground."

Pepi was struck dumb momentarily. "Do you really think this could work!?"

"Yes. I do."

"How do you know this?"

"I've been intrigued with the power of water and the force pushing down on everything on the earth. I've privately tried different experiments that have shown that downward force, causing all things to fall down, doesn't always have the greatest force. You've certainly learned that fact by using all these pulleys and ropes."

Pepi began to feel a sense of relief. Maybe this plan Joseph presented could work and solve the problem created by his mistake.

Joseph said, "Pepi, why don't you go to the construction site and get exact measurements of the depth of the base wall and the rise needed for the pyramid to clear the base wall above the ground and stop worrying. Tomorrow, we'll talk again and design the mechanisms to lift the pyramid out of its base. When the mechanisms are constructed, we can meet with Amsu and inform him. We will talk to him about all of this then."

"Amsu doesn't know about the problem yet."

"Well, he's going to know about it soon," Joseph said. "Now go to the site and try to stop worrying. We'll find a way."

Pepi stood before Joseph and reached out his hand to Joseph. "I don't know how to thank you."

Joseph shook Pepi's hand and said, "You're welcome. Now go."

Pepi walked out in a daze and Joseph returned to his work with the pulleys. A wagon stood ready to use outside to take them to the construction site.

The few days that followed proved to be successful. Joseph and Pepi, together with the help from other coworkers who knew how to construct metal pipes and airtight plungers to fit the pipes and the tub, worked to construct four right-angled, L-shaped water lifts. They were not large. The pipes were made with diameters half the size of a man's fist. The pipes were three times the length of the depth of the tub with a plunger at the top of the tub that would push up against the pyramid, providing lift. The diameter of the tub would be four times the size of the pipe's diameters. The plungers were made of a wood that swelled when soaked in water, which provided a watertight sealing that still enabled them to move up and down within the pipe and the tub.

That night, at home, Joseph wondered about Pepi. For the past five days Pepi, he, and some other coworkers had worked diligently to build four lifts, guided by Joseph's specification. The most important feature was that they be watertight. Each of the lifts would be placed at the four corners of the pyramid, after minimal digging was performed at those corners to fit the lifts down under the base wall. It would not take long to dig a big enough area at each corner to install the L-shaped lifts and secure tubs under the pyramid's corners.

Mary had noticed that Joseph had been working longer hours than usual. He was also quiet and seemed to be in deep thought often. Finally, one morning before he left for work, she asked him about his contemplation.

"You have been in deep thought lately. What are you thinking about?" Mary asked.

"One of the workers at the business made a mistake and now a 650-ton pyramid, built to be one of four erected as the foundational supports for the construction of a large structure, needs to be lifted out of a base wall foundation because the pyramid, due to miscalculations in the cutting of its bottom, doesn't possess the correct dimensions to fit into the base wall already set in the ground. One pyramid was dropped into the base wall and isn't fitted correctly and it seems to be lodged there to stay. The pyramid is crooked with no way to lift it out to fix the mistake. I shared with him an idea I had to create lifts that can raise all four pyramids from underneath. Pulleys and ropes can be attached to move the one lopsided pyramid out and over the base wall and then reconstruction could take place before placing it back into the base wall accurately and tightly."

"Joseph, you're always thinking, aren't you? Do you think your plan will work?"

"Well . . . we'll find out today. Amsu doesn't know about this mistake so I'll support the worker who made the mistake and stand with him when we meet together to tell him this afternoon. I certainly hope my idea and plan will work."

"It will work. I have faith in you, Joseph. More importantly, I have faith in God. If God got us here safely and announced Jesus' birth to the world without Jesus being found by King Herod, I'm sure your 'lifts' will work as you expect them to work. You will certainly have an exciting day today."

"It has not been very exciting for you, lately, has it?" Joseph had noticed that Mary was beginning to show signs of sadness and homesickness because when she did talk, she often spoke of her longing to go home to Judea. "I know I've been busy with work and that I've neglected you. The situation that has really occupied my mind will be over soon. Are you visiting with Mestha and Isis much?"

"Yes. But it is you I wish to be with more. Jesus is growing and keeps me busy but I miss my husband most of all. I know it's a special day. You will be talking to Amsu and there will probably be trouble over the building mistake. I don't wish to add to your stress."

Joseph hugged her from behind and appreciated her understanding. He whispered into her ear, "I'm sorry. I hear you and will change my working trend, which has consumed my thoughts lately. I love you and Jesus more than anything. I know I shouldn't let work intrude upon our love and time. I believe it'll only be a few more days and the problem at the construction site will be corrected."

He kissed her and went to find Jesus. He found him in his room lying awake. When Jesus saw Joseph, he reached for him and Joseph picked him up and held him close. Mary walked to the door of Jesus' room to stand and watch as Jesus' little arms hugged Joseph around his dad's neck.

"Be a good boy for your mother. I'll be home for dinner after work." Jesus nodded and Joseph placed him back on the bed as he turned and watched Mary smiling at them both. She was beautiful to him and for an instant he wondered why he seemed to allow a thought or task consume him and dominate his living. He kissed Mary.

As he left to walk to work with Seth, Mary said, "Good luck, Joseph. I'm sure everything will go well. I'll see you when you come home."

It was the fifth day (Thursday) so Seth and Joseph would not be walking to the construction site. Every fifth day of the week, Amsu had all the workers spend the morning working at the building together in order to keep every worker well informed about their ongoing progress at the construction site.

When he and Seth arrived at work, all seemed normal as expected. However, as Joseph entered the building of their employment, he noticed a tense atmosphere descend upon him immediately. The workers were working diligently but did not move from their stations. Joseph asked Seth under his breath, "What's going on? Why is everyone so tense?"

"Just lie low, Joseph. Amsu's on a rampage. You've never seen him like that. He must have learned that Pepi made a mistake in his calculations and the first pyramid that was dropped into its permanent base wall is stuck and stands cockeyed. We can't build on it as a foundational support for the portico and none of us knows how to get it out of its base wall to be fixed. Amsu is . . ."

From the far end of the building, Joseph and Seth could hear Amsu yelling loudly with shouts of anger. Joseph moved to go toward the yelling and Seth grabbed ahold of his arm.

"No, my friend, don't go near Amsu now. This isn't your problem, although it could set building back to a point that we will all lose money and time."

Joseph ignored Seth's warning and walked past his coworkers straight to Pepi's drafting table. Amsu stood with his back to Joseph and was yelling and flailing his arms. He shoved all the instruments and large papyrus papers off Pepi's drafting table and lunged at Pepi. Joseph caught Amsu from behind and restrained him by holding him tightly, locked in his arms. Amsu was livid.

"What do you think you're doing? Let go of me instantly! Instantly, I tell you!"

"I will not let go of you until you come to yourself. You must calm down and control your anger. You're going to hurt yourself and someone else too."

Amsu recognized the voice and through gritted teeth commanded Joseph to let him go. But Joseph did not let go immediately. Instead, he calmly and slowly asked, "Are you alright? Do you have control of yourself so that you don't do something you may regret later?"

Amsu stood in Joseph's restraint until his breathing slowed. "I am fine . . . now let me go, Joseph."

Joseph let Amsu go slowly, and partially, but it was not yet evident that Amsu had regained composure. Joseph kept his arms around Amsu and said from behind him, "You are angry. But you are our leader. We cannot be led by a leader that is out of control." After saying those words, Joseph let Amsu go completely.

Amsu turned around to Joseph and said, "Who do you think you are?"

"I'm the Jew you hired and wanted for a slave. These other workers are not Jews, and they are not slaves either. This is not the way an employer treats his employees." Joseph couldn't completely conceal his irritation with Amsu and Amsu detected it.

Pepi stood up from the crouched position he had taken below his drafting table. He bravely addressed Amsu, saying, "I know I miscalculated the bottom of the pyramid that was to be lowered into the base wall. I know the pyramid is lopsided and cannot be used as a support for the foundation of the structure. I know we must lift the pyramid out of the base without damaging the base wall and it can be done only by pushing the pyramid up from under the ground and out of the base wall . . . which I think can be done. Joseph explained a way to build lifts that can be placed below the pyramid using water and pressure."

Amsu asked, "What are you saying?"

"I'm saying that with four of these small lifts we can raise the pyramid. Once it is out of the base wall we will be able to attach ropes and pulleys from the cranes to the pyramid and swing it to the side to correct the dimensions of the pyramid's base."

Amsu looked at Joseph. "Does he know what he's talking about?"

"Yes," Joseph said as he nodded calmly.

"Show me on this paper. Draw a plan of these lifts and how they can be dug in place under the pyramid to lift it out of the base wall."

With a pen, Joseph sketched an L-shaped lift, built to be watertight. He explained as he sketched, "The L-shaped lifts have watertight pipes that go down, over, and under to a tub also filled with water under the pyramid. The pipes are joined to the bottom of the tub at right angles. The tub contains a large cylinder-like plunger at the top, which is the part that will be pushed up by increasing the water pressure in the tub. This is what will lift the pyramid. The water pressure is increased when a small plunger is pushed down in the small pipe leading downward, over, and under to the tub under the pyramid in the base wall. This will also increase the water pressure in the tub. The increased water pressure will push the plunger in the tub up. The increased pressure will be powerful. It will push the plunger up against the pyramid from underneath with a force many times greater than the force applied to the water in the pipe. The L-shaped lifts will be set under and against the bottom corners of the pyramid. When the water is put under pressure from the smaller pipes, by pushing the small plunger in the pipe down, the larger plunger at the top of the tub will be pushed upward to lift the pyramid by the increased water pressure from the pipes. The plunger pushed against the bottom of the pyramid must contain a thickness wider than the distance in the tub needed to raise the pyramid above the base wall. If the larger plunger is pushed above the sides of the tub, the water pressure would be lost and the plunger would drop. So, the plunger in the tub contains a width of one cubit, twice the distance of the lift needed from the ground level. We tried to think of everything.

"If we built the lift with watertight pipes, plungers, and tub, the plunger in the small downward pipe would need to push the water down at only a fraction of the weight it will lift on the other side, where the tub plunger will push upward to lift the pyramid. Actually, it will multiply the force by four hundred times to the larger cylinder under the object needed to be lifted. I tested this theory and the lift was consistently four hundred times the force applied to the small plunger pressing down. We can raise that 650-ton pyramid from under the ground with only four small L-shaped lifts."

Amsu stared at Joseph's sketch. "These lifts are right angled and L shaped, so I see that it would take minimal digging to place them under and around the underground base wall to get to the underside of the pyramid. Can we build these lifts and make them watertight?"

Pepi said, "Sir, we have already built them with the help of our metal workers and their expertise. Joseph and I have tested them and they work as Joseph thought they would. We can dig and install them tomorrow. I believe we can raise the pyramid out of the base wall within a day's work if we have enough men digging to install the lifts at the corners under the pyramid . . . underground at the four corners of the base wall."

Amsu was completely calm but could not hide his intrigue of interest. "Joseph, go home and meet us at the construction site tomorrow. I'm asking you to oversee this project."

Joseph said, "Amsu, I will not do this job without Pepi. He knows his mistake and therefore knows what it will take to correct it completely before the pyramid is dropped into the base wall again."

Amsu looked at Pepi. "Well . . . I guess you're back to stay. I'm warning you, I'll also be there to witness this plan. I'm not sure it'll work. If it doesn't work, we'll have to start from scratch and figure out how to tear out the base wall already in the ground to get at the pyramid. If that becomes the case the construction will be delayed for another two or three months and all these workers will not be able to work and move forward in the construction." Amsu looked at Joseph. "I sure hope you know what you're talking about."

Amsu felt awkward but before he left, he said to Pepi, "Forgive me. I should not have lost my temper as I did against you." Amsu turned abruptly and walked away.

The other workers gathered around to hear Joseph say, "Don't worry, I think I know what I'm doing. All of us need to be at the construction site by sunrise tomorrow. Can you be there?" All nodded their heads and turned to go home for the night.

Pepi remained standing with Joseph and said, "I need you to be sure, Joseph. What can I say? You saved my job and maybe even my life."

"Don't worry, Pepi. I'll see you tomorrow at sunrise. Get a good night's sleep."

Joseph was glad to go home early. He knew Mary would be waiting for him and she would be pleasantly surprised at his early arrival. Joseph and Pepi walked toward the exit of the building and before they parted Pepi said, "Joseph, you've been a good friend to me . . . thank you."

"You are more than welcome, my friend."

Joseph turned and walked home quickly. At that moment, for some strange reason, he was more excited about being with Mary and Jesus than seeing the lifting of the pyramid. When he walked into the house Mary was not home. He decided to wash and change his garment. While he slipped the garment over his head, he heard Mary enter the house. He walked out of the bedroom to greet her and she was startled. Jesus was next to her holding her hand and let it go. He raised his hands out to Joseph and said, "Daddy!"

Joseph saw that Mary had been to the market and she was laden with goods in her sling. He approached her to help empty the sling of her purchases as Jesus clung to his dad's legs.

"Let me go so I can help Mommy unpack her purchases. You've both been shopping, haven't you?" Joseph said, and Jesus released his father and began to clap with excitement.

The young family played in the backyard and sat in the sun until early evening. Mary prepared dinner and called Joseph and Jesus in to wash and eat. Joseph took Jesus to the basin he had rigged up with running water. When he released the stop at the end of the malleable pipe made from goat gut, the water poured into the basin. He looked at Jesus, who watched the flow of water with delight. Joseph paused and remembered his father's vision of two women and a child hovering over the Jordan River. Thinking of his father, he felt a pang of homesickness. Then he remembered the huge ship that had carried them on top of the water no matter the depth of water, whether shallow enough to see the bottom or so deep he couldn't conceive their depths. His thoughts gave him confidence, thinking the lifts they built would work.

He looked down at Jesus, who was now standing over the basin, floating different objects in the collected water. He laughed as the rock he held was released to sink. But then he took a small, light wooden cup and placed it in the water to float. Joseph was amazed as he watched Jesus take the rock and place it in the cup. The cup didn't sink under the weight of the rock and he giggled with delight.

"All right, Jesus. It's time to stop playing and wash for dinner. Mommy is probably wondering where we . . ."

Joseph and Jesus heard Mary call, "Dinner is ready. Where are you two and what are you doing?"

"Come on," Joseph said as he wiped Jesus' hands and lifted him to sit at the table for dinner.

The rest of the evening was enjoyed by all. After Jesus was put down to sleep, Mary and Joseph sat in the backyard and watched the sky. They saw three streaks of light and Mary said that she had been thinking about the streaks of light and thought that maybe they were rocks that burned like a candle in the sky. The wind must extinguish their light before they fall to the ground.

Mary contemplated the phenomenon out loud to Joseph by saying, "Maybe they're rocks falling from broken stars into the ocean of air over the earth. As they sink down toward the earth they heat up and burn." Mary rubbed her hands together rapidly and said, "Like the heat you feel when one object rubs against another object."

"But the air isn't an object," Joseph proclaimed. "Surely, a rock couldn't fall through the air to create enough heat to burn up?" Joseph asked.

Mary leaned back against Joseph and said, "No, I guess not. But I was just thinking about it and it's only an idea."

Both retreated to the bedroom. They made love and they realized that their passion was changing for each other. It was no longer as intense as they had experienced at first. Now, lovemaking satisfied them peacefully, much like the calm of the water behind the stern of a moving ship.

They fell asleep in each other's arms.

Morning came fast. The first hint of light awakened Joseph. He dressed quickly and kissed Mary as she continued to lie in bed.

"If the lifts work, I'll be home before the evening meal."

Mary said, "They'll work. I love you."

Joseph walked to Seth's house to begin their journey together to the construction site. They walked for forty-five minutes when they turned the corner in the street and came upon the grand building site. Although the building was in no way complete, it gave promise to be colossal and magnificently decadent.

In the front of the structure were three square stone walls protruding from the ground, but the first square wall contained a crooked pyramid. The pyramid was of great size and its weight could easily be estimated to be over 650 tons.

"There's the mistake. What a shame. It's hard for me to even look at it," Seth said as he walked around the pyramid and saw that there was no room for any rope to be placed under and around for it to be lifted up and out of the base wall by pulleys. Its correction seemed impossible.

Joseph also walked around the pyramid like King David must have walked around the fallen Philistine Goliath. He looked up to the pyramid's crooked apex and began to feel doubt about his plan.

As if appearing from nowhere, other workers descended to the site from all different directions. Some had even come on horseback. Pepi must have arrived earlier and waited alone for others to arrive. He approached Joseph with nervousness and said that he had the four lifts ready to be installed under the pyramid at the four corners. Joseph recognized Pepi's need and took the lead by organizing the workers into four teams and explained the procedure to each of the assigned team leaders. He outlined and explained instructions for what needed to be dug out, down, and under. The lifts would be placed properly from the outside, down, under, across, and up, digging out enough space to fit the tubs under the four corners of the lopsided pyramid. To explain clearly, Joseph drew a detailed diagram in the dust to illustrate how the digging needed to be done. The leaders understood and began the work with their teams.

Before the sun was halfway to high noon the lifts were in place and they were filled with water. Joseph examined each lift for placement, watertightness, and levels. He told the leaders that success was critically dependent upon the equalization of lift and the expedient placement of ropes under and around the pyramid once it was lifted from the base wall. Cranes were placed over the pyramid. Ropes and pulleys were strategically attached to the cranes, ready to secure the pyramid and move it away from the base wall as soon as the lifts worked their power.

Amsu rode up to the site on a small two-wheeled chariot pulled by a beautiful black horse. He stepped out of the chariot and walked up to

Joseph. Pepi stood close to Joseph as he gave the leaders final instructions. Joseph continued by explaining that he and Pepi would be standing at the opposite corners of the pyramid, giving direction to evenly apply pressure to the small pipes by pushing down on the plungers of the protruding watertight pipes. When the plungers were pressed down, the water pressure would increase in the L-shaped pipes, and pressure would be distributed to push the large plungers upward in the tubs directly under the pyramid's four corners.

"Does everyone understand what they will be doing? Remember, this is a coordinated effort and each man must be alert to the directives from Pepi and me. I am counting on the men who work the pulleys and the cranes to be ready when the pyramid is lifted to do what they know how to do once the pyramid is lifted out of the base wall. You will notice that there is a large rock cut to equal weight at each corner, to be placed on the plunger to push the water down in the small pipes of water. The weight of the rock must be allowed to push down on the plunger, increasing the water pressure evenly. The trick will be to evenly increase the water pressure with all the lifts. It will take ten strong men at each corner to lift the 815-pound rock and lower it onto the pipe plungers as directed. Do you all understand?" Joseph looked at all the workers and closed with words of encouragement. "We can do this, together. Mistakes happen all the time. What counts is how we are able to resolve the mistakes constructively. That's what we are about as construction workers, as brothers, and as human beings, right?"

The workers all responded affirmatively and were anxious to see the lifts work. Amsu seemed most anxious, but he remained silent and watched as Joseph, Pepi, and the rest of the men took their places.

It was as if time became suspended, captured in anticipation. Everyone was ready. Joseph said a prayer as Pepi took the lead and instructed each team of ten men to lift the rocks at their corners and hold them over the top of the plunger poles sticking out of the pipe. Suddenly, Pepi's aura became strong and confident. He clearly yelled out his direction. "On the count of three, lower the rock evenly according to the direction of Joseph's and my hands . . . One . . . two . . . three!" Joseph matched Pepi's descending hands and the workers lowered the weight of their rocks onto the plungers evenly. Hopefully the water pressure in the lift was being increased slowly enough and distributed evenly to the larger plungers in the tubs to create lift underneath the pyramid.

At first, the men heard the sound of rock rubbing against rock. It was unbelievable. Slowly, but most definitely, the pyramid lifted above and out of the base wall. It seemed to hover as men hurriedly crisscrossed ropes underneath the pyramid. The ropes were threaded through and tightened over the pulleys, and together, manpower applied force to secure the pyramid in a cradle of ropes attached to pulleys and cranes above. They moved the pyramid by swinging it over and away from the top of the base wall. The pyramid was moved to the side of the base wall and set on four large rocks so the pyramid could rest above the ground, enabling it to be worked on and easily maintain attachment to the pulleys and the cranes with ropes again to be moved back and lowered over and into the base wall. It happened slowly, and every man held his breath as the huge pyramid dangled in midair.

Amsu stood still and silent as the workers cheered and congratulated each other. In a loud voice that rose above the din, Pepi said, "We're not done yet, men. I'm grateful to Joseph and all of you for your faithfulness, which has made it possible to correct my mistake, but the real celebration can follow when the rock cutters correct the dimensions of the bottom of the pyramid and we have successfully dropped it into the base wall. We'll need everybody's help. I believe we can complete the task by this afternoon."

Pepi handed the job over to the rock cutters and consulted with them to insure exact dimensions.

Amsu stood with his arms crossed over his chest, standing like an unmovable statue in the same spot. He remained silent and his expression was that of disbelief. Joseph walked over to him and his voice brought Amsu to the reality of the moment. "I'm relieved that the lifts worked."

Amsu looked at Joseph and said, "No you're not. You knew it would work, didn't you?"

"No. I wasn't sure it would work but I believed it would work. Sometimes faith works more powerfully than we're able to accept."

"You could say . . . maybe . . . our God," Amsu moved his finger pointing back and forth to himself and Joseph, "had something to do with what I just witnessed?"

Joseph smiled, "You could say that . . . and believe it. The Creator of the universe put these physical laws into place and I believe they are as important, and as real, as ethical or spiritual laws. It's not magic, Amsu."

Amsu finally turned his stare to Joseph and said, "If someone had told me that I would hire a Jew to clean and organize . . . and he would then rig up a plan that would save us months of work and great amounts of money . . . I would have laughed in disbelief."

Joseph didn't respond except to reach out his hand and take Amsu's forearm with firmness.

The rest of the workday for the men went well. They were enthusiastic and inspired to get the pyramid back into the base wall. By midafternoon they believed the pyramid's dimensions had been adjusted to allow a tight fit into the base wall. After rechecking, Pepi gave the order to remove the lifts and fill in the small square holes at each corner where the lift tubs had been placed. The ropes placed around and underneath the pyramid were still attached to the pulleys on the cranes. The pyramid was lifted up by manpower, pulling on the ropes attached to the pulleys. They swung the pyramid into place above the base wall. Slowly, it was lowered to inches above the base wall and positioned to be dropped into place. The ropes were ready to be cut and the pyramid was expected to fall tightly within the base wall, secure and straight.

Joseph watched as the ropes were simultaneously cut and, as was hoped for, the pyramid dropped into the base wall with a thud that vibrated in his bones. The men lifted a roar of cheers as the pyramid stood, erect and straight.

Seth and Pepi ran up to Joseph and each embraced him. Pepi's eyes filled with tears as he said, "Six days ago I believed my life was over. I feel like I've come alive again. Thank you, Joseph!"

Amsu stepped up to Pepi. "You did well. You are a valuable worker, and I'm seeing that all these men are also good, faithful employees. You have saved us time and money and you will receive a generous bonus in proportion to the money saved." Amsu turned to Joseph. "You will receive double the bonus. Seth, tell all the workers here they, too, will receive a bonus of payment for their work here today. Tomorrow is the seventh day (Saturday) and it will be a day off from work for everyone."

Amsu looked at Joseph as if he needed a word of approval and Joseph obliged, saying, "I have never, in all my working days, worked for an employer as fair, just, honest, affirming, and generous as you. I am blessed by you, Amsu."

Something changed in Amsu's countenance that day, and it remained changed in his heart in the days that followed.

THE JUDEAN DESERT

Anne and Joachim climbed the path to the home of Zechariah and Elizabeth. When they arrived, they saw five-year-old John sitting in the wheat field. His little face turned to watch his aunt and uncle approach the house. Although he was quite young, John knew something was terribly wrong. He knew his mother was sick and he felt confused over his father's inability to help her. John was glad to see his Aunt Anne and Uncle Joachim, but he did not run to them from the wheat field. Instead, he sat among the wheat and gazed at them. Anne spoke to Joachim, calling attention to him, "Look at John, over there, sitting in the wheat field." Joachim turned his head to spot John. "He's a beautiful little boy but he is a strange child. He's been alone too much. To me, he looks like a little ghost, waiting for something, I don't know what."

Joachim gave no response but watched John as they walked. Suddenly a rather strong gust of wind blew the wheat that fanned little John's wild, curly hair. John remained in the wheat field as Joachim and Anne entered the house.

Zechariah was sitting alone at the table and he looked old and tired. When he saw Anne and Joachim, he said, "Please, Anne, come and see Elizabeth!"

Anne followed Zechariah to a room and came close to Elizabeth, who was lying on a bed of straw. When Anne knelt next to her sister, Elizabeth turned her head and tried to smile.

"Did you see John outside somewhere?" she asked.

"Yes, we saw him sitting in the wheat field," said Anne.

"Good, I'm glad my sweet little boy is close to home today. Sometimes he goes out in the morning and he doesn't return to the house until after dark. I've not taken care of him properly lately. I'm so sick. I can't keep my hands and arms from shaking. Zechariah is riddled with pain also, and finds it hard to move. My little John is on his own most of the time." Elizabeth began to cry.

"Don't cry, my sister. Joachim and I are here. We will help you."

Elizabeth continued to cry. Through her tears she said, "Do you remember our own mother? She was sick like I am now. She didn't live long after her shaking became terribly severe and she couldn't walk any longer. That's where I am with this sickness now. I'm afraid I'll not live too much longer and I'm so worried for my son. Zechariah is old and ill also, and he doesn't know how to take care of a little boy, especially a little boy with John's energy."

Anne had cared for many people with different ailments, but she didn't know what to do for this ailment. She didn't want to face the fact that her sister was dying, and there was nothing she could do to help.

Anne reached out and tenderly held her sister. "Elizabeth, I promise you I will be there for your son and husband should you pass on from this life. I will raise your son in my home. He will have brothers, sisters, nieces, and nephews close by. You and Zechariah will not be abandoned. Neither will John be abandoned."

Elizabeth smiled. She felt true comfort. "You have always been filled with grace, Anne. Thank you."

Anne stood up and went to prepare a meal for the family. However, when the time came to eat the meal no one could find John. Zechariah wasn't concerned by his son's absence. It was a common occurrence.

View of Bethany from on top of Mt. Zion in Old Jerusalem, April 2009

BETHANY

Rachael and Benjamin sat together after they knew Mary, Martha, Levi, and John had fallen asleep. Even so, they talked in soft, low tones to one another. There was trouble in Judea, and it always seemed to translate into their deep concern for the future life and safety of the children.

"I can't believe King Herod continues to be so threatened by the birth of a supposed Messiah. To think he's crazy enough to continue his search for the child after four years! Benjamin, do you believe what I believe?"

Rachael's question was not a mystery to him. "Yes. I believe Baby Jesus is the Messiah. But I also believe that God will protect him, Mary, and Joseph. I believe they'll return to live in Judea again, and Jesus will fulfill his calling to be our Messiah."

Rachael lowered her eyes and sadly said, "I don't think they'll be coming back for a long time, at least not until King Herod's threat to Jesus is dead. That may not be until Herod dies. And then we'll still be under the oppression of his sons."

Benjamin sighed. "You may be right. King Herod is sick with suspicion and fear. Making the situation worse, I'm concerned about the mounting tension over his fortification of Masada. The radically violent Sicarii are using Masada as their base for raiding and pillaging Roman *and* Jewish settlements alike. Even the Jewish Zealots are in opposition to the Jewish Sicarii. And yet Masada is the fort that King Herod supports and spends our tax money to reinforce. I think it's leading to more bad trouble. King Herod seems to be so confused. His warlike mindset thinks the Messiah must be a militant who will chase Rome's presence out of Judea and all of Palestine. At the same time, he sees the true Messiah as a threat to his dynasty. Can't he see that Rome has ultimate control and that he's only a puppet ruler?"

Rachael whispered, "I don't think Jesus was born to be involved with Rome, Masada, or any political force. I think the Messiah will do something greater than Masada, Jerusalem, Israel, Rome, or even the world. I'm not sure, but I think the Messiah will save us and give something important for us and the distant future . . . He'll be a spiritual gift beyond our ability to understand now . . . I just keep remembering little Jesus and all the coincidental actions in the temple the last day we were with him, Mary, and Joseph. He was such a beautiful baby boy . . . Benjamin, do you realize our family, including Baby Mary, had something to do with Baby Jesus' escape?"

They sat in thoughtful silence together for a moment until Benjamin asked Rachael how she was feeling. She had given birth to their second son, John, and although he was very happy about having four children in the house, he was concerned, because she was pregnant again.

"I feel fine and well," Rachael said. "Baby Mary initially had a rough time of it after our son John was born. Much of my attention was taken from her, but she loves her brothers and sister, and has become a great help to me as have Martha and Levi. John is also showing signs of independence and this new baby will be no extra trouble, just another blessing among us."

Benjamin became more thoughtful and serious as he said, "I've noticed that Baby Mary is a strong child, in body and soul, and has a spirit of independence. I don't think we'll have to be concerned for Mary, even when she learns the circumstances of her own birth." He glanced at Rachael with a heart full of love, taking her hand, lifting a prayer for Mary, Joseph, and Jesus, wherever they may be, and thanked God for their lives and abundance.

View of Bethlehem from on top of Mt. Zion in Old Jerusalem, April 2009

JUDEA AND MASADA

PANTHERA AND HIS FELLOW soldiers knew there would be more skirmishes between the Jews and their Roman presence in Judea. The buildup at the fort Masada could be watched in the distance from their tent camp. As the walls around Masada seemed to be expanding and built up on top of the plateau in sight, Panthera continued to believe that it was no threat to the power of Rome. He realized that their Roman presence was orchestrated by the Roman powers that be. Although at first he had not been concerned over the possibility of a Jewish revolt in Judea, he was beginning to feel unsure as Masada seemed to be more fortified and active every day. Each of the commanders of the legions in their tent camp informed them that they were to expect trouble, especially now that the violent, radical Jewish group known as the Sicarii were present and based at Masada.

Panthera comforted his own fears and concerns by trusting the intelligence of the Roman Empire. If it came to battle, he felt confident that their training and battle technique far outweighed any Jewish attempt to rise up against them.

Everything changed one early evening. Since it was the Jewish Sabbath, Panthera's Roman tent camp was quiet and subdued. No one expected trouble on the Sabbath. The soldiers were eating their evening meal when they all heard a loud cry from the guards at the south and east gates of their camp. Panthera and his comrades were disciplined and trained, knowing exactly what to do. They stopped whatever activity with which they were involved, and grabbed their gear and weapons. Within moments they were in formation outside the tent camp trenches protecting the tent camp's south and east walls. They took their places to establish the unique military Roman tortoise formation. In the shape of a tortoise shell the men moved forward with their metal shields over their crouched bodies. They moved forward toward the enemy for hand-to-hand battle while the crossbow archers stood behind their formation, firing arrows for an offensive advantage.

Panthera was filled with adrenaline that excited him and, unfortunately, led him to make a mistake. Rather than trusting the instructions called out by the "seers," he stood up to determine the distance of their approaching enemy. When he stood up, an arrow shot from the archers behind found its mark in Panthera's right side, taking him down to the ground immediately. His comrades continued to move forward, careful not to step on him but not stopping to help him. Panthera knew they were doing what they were trained and required to do in active battle.

Instantly, Panthera's body became riddled with excruciating pain. He found it hard to breathe and he knew he was injured seriously. At first everything seemed unreal to him. He felt he was dreaming and that this was not reality. He dared to raise his left hand over to try to assess his injury. The arrow had entered his body diagonally from the back, coming out at his right side. When he had fallen to the ground, the arrow must have broken off in his back, leaving the rest of the arrow jutting out in front through his body. The arrow extended out from his right front torso. His instinct told him to pull the arrow out from its tip, forward, straight through. No, he thought. He remembered his training and he would obey. He pulled his shield over his body, and with all his strength against the pain, he pulled his legs under the shield as much as possible. He waited.

Later, the battle was classified as another skirmish. There were no casualties and only one injury. When the attacking Sicarii retreated up the cliffs to Masada, Panthera was retrieved and carried by stretcher back to the tent camp. He was taken to the infirmary and a doctor examined his wound.

"I need a surgery knife, cleansing fluid, bandages, and wine." The doctor shouted orders to assistants, who brought what he asked for quickly. The doctor poured a brimming goblet of wine and helped Panthera drink it all.

Panthera was thankful for the little relief from pain it served him. However, the relief was short lived.

The doctor continued shouting orders as he rolled Panthera on his left side to examine the wound where the arrow had entered. Without hesitation, he cut open the area where the arrow went into his body from the back to examine the broken end of the arrow in his body. He needed to determine the condition of the arrow's end so he could pull the arrow out from the front without causing more damage, should the point of breakage be shattered and splintered.

"The gods must be watching over you," the doctor said. "I will cleanly clip the end of the arrow that is not deep inside your back to create an even better streamline and pull the arrow through you and out of the front of your chest. It appears the arrow has not struck a rib but it may have nicked the right lower lung. Hopefully no fever will develop." The doctor asked the assistants to hold Panthera securely on his side. He walked around the bed and said, "Panthera, this will hurt but try not to move. I'm going to take the arrow out of your body from the front. Are you ready?"

Panthera felt nauseous and gripped the assistant close to him with a tight hold. He nodded his head and turned to focus his eyes on the assistant's sandaled feet. The doctor pulled with one strong tug and removed the arrow from Panthera's body. Panthera screamed. As air rushed into the wound, he felt pain greater than he had ever experienced before. The doctor began to attend to the wounds, both front and back, which were bleeding. He compressed bandages against the bleeding wounds and wrapped swaddling material around his torso to hold the bandages on the wounds in place.

The assistants removed Panthera's clothing and moved him from the platform bed he was lying upon onto a stretcher. When they moved him, Panthera felt lightheaded and sicker than before. They covered him with light cotton sheets and carried him to another room. He was placed on a bed and when they lowered the stretcher onto the bed Panthera groaned and passed out from the pain. The doctor followed the assistants and looked at Panthera.

"Good, he's unconscious," the doctor said. "Hopefully he'll be out long enough to get a good rest." He looked down at Panthera and noticed that his face and body were glistening with sweat. He touched Panthera's forehead and said, "This one may be a goner. He is hot with fever. Place cool compresses on his forehead, under his arms, and behind his knees. I'll be back to see him in the morning."

The doctor walked out of the tent room shaking his head.

Masada National Park, Israel 2009

The Roman Empire in the Age of Augustus

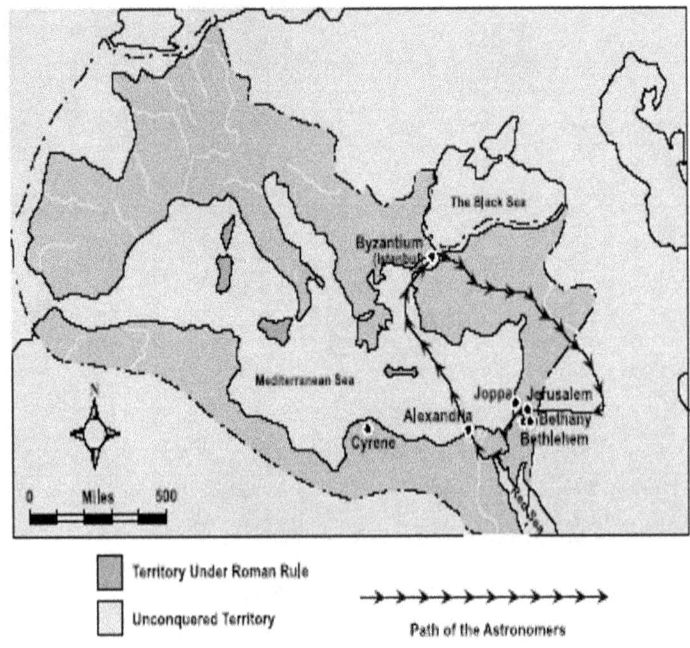

BYZANTIUM

Caspar, Melchior, and Balthasar were learned astronomers who lived and studied the stars and sky from Byzantium. Byzantium used to be a great city within the Persian Empire, but lost its renowned status with the fall of the empire and the birth of the dominant Roman Empire. However, wars and rumors of wars never quiet the advancement of knowledge and this was true for these three astronomers who never lost sight of their calling in life to constantly study the movement of heavenly bodies in the dome of the day and night skies. They were able to track fireballs with long tails of light known as comets, and accurately predict their passing above Byzantium. They understood the workings of lunar and solar eclipses. They knew that the brief flashes of light that burned out quickly in the night sky were large rocks falling to the earth, burning up before they reached its surface. They knew the difference between heavenly bodies that were lit up due to self-generation of light and those that were lit up due to reflected light from other stars or suns. Most importantly, they knew that at certain, rare times, the heavenly bodies that reflected light from the sun would align and appear to be the brightest light in the night sky, to eventually separate again and shine to their own previous level of brightness.

Their learnedness also incorporated their knowledge of folklore and legends. They understood the importance of folklore and legends and allowed them to carry significance that was not ignored. The three were quite excited as they witnessed the aligning of three reflective heavenly bodies in the east, far beyond them. Their calculations turned out to be miraculously accurate and they were compelled to believe it as a sign that a great leader had been born somewhere near Jerusalem. They were driven to follow the sign, to find the great leader who had been born. They longed for peace and the return of a world that would allow Byzantium to become the great city of knowledge and growth it had promised to be before the fall of the Persian Empire. They believed the leader born in Judea the night the heavenly bodies came together would become the greatest teacher of the world. Their determination to find him and give him their gifts, support, and homage could not be subdued or squelched.

Together, three and a half years after the great shining light had appeared in the east, Caspar, Melchior, and Balthasar left Byzantium to travel to Jerusalem and the surrounding cities of Judah. They believed they would be led to the King of kings and the Prophet of prophets. It didn't matter to them how long their journey would be or how far their search would take them.

THE QUMRAN SETTLEMENT

ANNE AND JOACHIM VIGILANTLY visited Mary and Joseph's vacant home. They took care of the house and the surrounding yard but, after three years had passed, the fields and garden grew freely. It didn't take long for what had been a wheat field and vegetable garden to change and grow into a wild tangle of desert vegetation. Mary's parents felt obligated to care for the home and the small area around the walls of the house. This visit was not a long visit. After sweeping and dusting the interior of the house, Anne and Joachim sat in the front room. They sat together in silence for a long time.

Anne spoke and broke the silence they held. "Where could they be, Joachim? It's been more than three years since they disappeared." She began to cry.

Joachim stared at the cloth hanging on the wall as if he were studying its beautiful pattern and colors for the first time. "I don't know where they went and am not sure why they left in such a hurry without telling us where they were going. However, Joseph is a smart and wise man. I'm sure Mary's safe with him. He took Mary away for a reason and I trust his reason. I believe he took her away to keep her, and her unborn child, alive . . . and safe. I also believe I've been a stupid man, swayed by the rigid attitudes of this settlement. Mary must have given birth to a baby boy and named him Jesus, Emmanuel, God is with us." Joachim walked to Anne and knelt at her feet. He wrapped his arms around her waist and sank his face into her lap. He looked up. Comforting her, he said, "Don't cry for long, my beloved. It is Elizabeth's family that needs our help the most now. There is no one to care for John. However, in the end, we will all be together again."

BYZANTIUM AND THE CITIES OF JUDAH

THE THREE WISE ASTRONOMERS made slow progress in their travel to Jerusalem. They traveled east and south and entered Israel and the province of Judea after traveling over eight hundred miles of desert, mountains, and plains. It took them six months to reach Israel. When they entered the city of Jerusalem, they requested an audience with King Herod, whom they believed could surely help them in their search. King Herod was delighted to receive them and they talked about the event of the unknown prophet's birth for many hours. All the while, King Herod portrayed a false concern for locating the infant who had been born the night in which a great heavenly body of light had moved with a star-stretched tail from the east and settled over Bethlehem. The infant born that night would now be a child of four years. Herod professed that he also wanted to find the child, to guard and protect him so he could grow into adulthood to fulfill his divine calling. He implored the three men to return with news should they successfully learn about the present location of the child and his family. The king revealed that he knew the child was born in Bethlehem but that his parents were from the Qumran Settlement. He knew this because of information gathered during a census registration by the child's father indicating this fact. The three astronomers knew the next destination in their search was Bethlehem.

Caspar, Melchior, and Balthasar departed from Jerusalem to make the short journey to Bethlehem and promised to return to discuss their findings with King Herod.

"I think he's a liar," Caspar declared as the three camped under the stars in the fields of Bethlehem that night.

"I agree," said Balthasar.

"There was something about his intense need to find the baby four years ago. His intensity has not subsided and it seems to be rooted in fear, not rejoicing. If we find the child, I'm inclined to avoid returning to King Herod with a report. His purpose is most certainly shrouded in deception and I can't trust a man, especially a leader, if he deceives." Melchior had stared ahead as Bethlehem came into their view from atop their camels. "One thing I did learn is that there is only one inn in this little town of Bethlehem. Since the child's parents were travelers from the Qumran Settlement, I'm certain that the inn is the place we must visit to find further direction before we travel on and leave this area."

The inn was easily found in Bethlehem the next morning and all three dismounted their camels and walked into its entrance. Joe emerged from a door and asked the astronomers if he could serve them.

"Yes." Melchior displayed a genuine demeanor of gentleness and intelligence. "We have traveled here from Byzantium and have just left from an audience with King Herod. We are in search of truth, and hope that you can be more helpful than King Herod."

Beth came through the same door and stood next to Joe, who said, "I'm sure King Herod can be of greater help to you than we. We are just innkeepers in this small town and don't have occasion to acquire information of any importance."

Balthasar stepped forward. "You judge yourself wrongly. It is from common, everyday people like you through which protected truth can evolve. We, too, wish to find truth and must rely on both of you to help us. King Herod is of no consequence to our search. We have decided he is not truthful and therefore cannot be trusted. Will you please talk to us and decide if you can trust us?"

Joe looked at Beth and silently received her willingness to listen to them. "Come with me," Joe said. He led them into a room with tables and directed them to sit at the only table that could seat more than two or four people. The five sat down while Joe remained standing and he asked if they needed food and drink. The astronomers declined, asking only for water. Joe brought five goblets to the table and placed a pitcher of fresh, cold water down before them. All three poured the water into their goblets and drank quickly.

After drinking and releasing a long, satisfied sigh, Caspar began, "We are astronomers and have studied the day and night skies for many, many years. Four years ago, in late March and early April, three heavenly bodies aligned themselves to create a great light, shining in the east. From our calculations it shined directly above Bethlehem."

Balthasar continued. "Legend holds that when a heavenly phenomenon of this magnitude happens it is an indication that a great spiritual leader has been born. We believe that happened here."

Melchior put his hands on the table and looked at Beth and Joe in earnest desire. "We have traveled very far in our search for this leader and we don't even know his name. All we know is that he was born in Bethlehem four years ago. Can you help us in our search? We wish no harm to him or his family. In fact, we wish to give him gifts. These gifts will serve him well in his lifetime."

Beth and Joe sat silently. They wondered if they dare share what they knew. Beth spoke first, and with confidence. "I believe and trust you." She turned to Joe. "I'm going to tell them what we know."

Joe leaned back in his chair and nodded his head.

"About four years ago, at the time you have described, a young woman and her betrothed husband came to our inn. She was pregnant and it was her time to deliver the baby. The baby was born in our stable. After the baby was born, shepherds came to praise the baby. The shepherds reported that they had seen the great light in the hills while keeping watch over their sheep. Angels in their dreams had directed them to the stable where the baby was born. The shepherds left after worshipping the newborn and we brought the couple and their new baby into the inn to stay for four days. In that time, she and he married on the nearest hilltop. Her name is Mary. His name is Joseph. The baby was named Jesus."

Joe added, "He is also called Emmanuel, which means . . ." At the same time, with Joe, the wise astronomers said, "God with us."

Joe stared blankly back at Melchior, who seemed to him to be the leader in their quest. "How did you know that?"

Melchior didn't answer his question but implored Beth to continue with more information.

"A Roman soldier named Panthera came to our inn and paid us for Mary and Joseph's stay. He was quite mysterious and he came to the inn only twice in those four days of their stay. The first time he just gave us money to cover the cost of the young family's food and lodging. The second time he and Joseph talked privately in an enclosed room so I don't know what was discussed." Beth paused and her countenance evoked loving memory. "We came to love them and were honored when they asked my husband and me to witness their marriage vows. They left early on the fourth day and we have not seen or heard from them since."

Balthasar leaned forward with Caspar in deep thought.

"A Roman soldier named Panthera?" Caspar said, "We must find Panthera. He must know something about this family. Finding a Roman soldier assigned to this area will be easy!" He looked at Melchior with excitement. "The brightest heavenly body separated and moved west. The other two moved northeast and southeast. I'm sure that will be a confirmation of their whereabouts sooner or later."

Melchior asked Joe, "May we stay in your inn for the night and refresh our animals in your stable?"

"Of course, yes, you may. We have entrusted you with precious information but I think we were certainly directed by God to do so. I'm sure you won't share anything that could return to King Herod. He is still trying to find the child and we believe he wants to kill him."

Melchior said, "You may be assured that we will not expose the child to danger. We will leave early tomorrow morning and travel to the nearest Roman tent camp to try to find Panthera."

THE ROMAN TENT CAMP IN JUDEA

THE COMMANDER OF PANTHERA'S legion was sitting at a table studying a map when Caspar, Melchior, and Balthasar were escorted in before him. The Roman commander didn't look up immediately from what he was studying but when he did, he was taken aback at the sight before him. "Where did you come from? What do you want? Who are you?"

Caspar introduced himself and his traveling comrades. He explained that they came from Byzantium and were following the path of three heavenly bodies that had aligned and shined over Bethlehem four years ago. Since then, the heavenly bodies had separated. The most prominent light of the three could be seen on the horizon in the west as the sun sets. Balthasar interrupted Caspar and said, "We have traveled far following this phenomenon. We believe it holds great significance for the world. We are looking for a Roman soldier named Panthera who may be able to direct us correctly in our search."

The commander chuckled with guardedness. "The things that happen in Judea never cease to amaze me. Unfortunately, Panthera was seriously injured yesterday in a skirmish with the Sicarii. We expect more trouble and Panthera needs to get out of here. Since he has no family or home, we have kept him here but he is delirious with fever. We expect him to die. I don't think he's in any condition to talk to you."

Caspar stepped forward. "Please, sir. We must talk to him. We are willing to take him out of here tomorrow with us, to a place where he can be cared for and receive a chance to live beyond whatever injuries ail him. If he is delirious with fever, it means he needs some medicine to help the fever go away. I have a potion that will help fight the fever instantly. In time he can heal and return to your army to continue serving Rome."

"What kind of potion are you talking about?"

"It comes from a root and herbs mixed together."

The commander had heard of this potion before but he put no faith in its healing power. He stood and walked closer to the strange men who were dressed like royalty. "Why do you wear all that heavy clothing in the desert? Doesn't it make you hot?"

"No. It actually keeps the sun and hot air off our bodies. When the cold comes at night, we wrap the clothing tightly around our bodies to keep warm." Caspar answered the commander's questions with respect and hoped he would grant their request to take Panthera with them.

"I can't be worried about every soldier who falls in battle. Many have already fallen and many more will follow. There are things that must be recorded before you take him." He shook his head and said, "He's going to die anyway." The commander sighed, walked to the opening of the tent, and yelled for an assistant, who responded quickly. "Take these three men to the recorder and have it recorded where they will be taking Panthera." The commander looked at the astronomers and corrected his statement, "Excuse me . . . it can be recorded when they know where they are going."

The assistant looked confused, crossed his chest with his fist to the commander, and walked the astronomers out to another tent, where they spoke with an official who recorded important information about injured soldiers.

"Where do you plan to take Panthera?" he asked. He, too, was looking down at his work and didn't look up immediately. He looked down to write in the scroll before him.

Caspar simply said, "West."

The Roman official looked up and was surprised to see three kingly-looking men standing before him. He didn't know how to respond to their report so he said, "West!" and then asked, "West where?"

Caspar said, "We plan to take Panthera west to an unknown place because we ourselves don't know yet. We need to talk to Panthera and determine where he would like to be taken. We will act as his family now."

The official stared at them and looked at the assistant who stood at attention. Addressing the assistant, he asked, "Can you tell me more about this situation?"

The assistant said, "No, sir. Just that Panthera's commander gave the orders that these men were to take Panthera . . . somewhere."

The official shrugged his shoulders and wrote the information down on the scroll. He looked up and his expression indicated that he had an idea. He said to the assistant, "Go and ask Jarius to meet with these men. Maybe he can add some clarity to this situation. After you talk to his friend you have permission to take Panthera with you. Remember, he is a Roman soldier and once he is healed and well, he is to be returned to this tent camp to finish his assignment."

The assistant led Caspar, Melchior, and Balthasar to the infirmary. Only one soldier lay on a bed in the tent so the three astronomers walked directly to Panthera's bedside. Panthera was wet with sweat and he breathed slowly. His eyes were closed.

Jarius was escorted into the tent also and he approached Panthera's bed. He didn't look at the three strange men standing around the bed. He simply asked, "What do you need to know?"

"We want to find Mary, Joseph, and Jesus. We want to take Panthera to them to stay, be cared for so he can heal. Can you tell us where they are?"

Jarius said, "They're in . . ." He paused. Then he looked at them and asked, "Who are you?"

Balthasar answered, "We are astronomers from Byzantium. We know the Messiah was born in Bethlehem and that the young family was taken somewhere where the child Jesus can grow in safety, away from King Herod. We are friends of the holy family and we are friends to you and Panthera."

Jarius moved his stare from the three astronomers to Panthera and said, "Alexandria, Egypt." He looked back at the three men and said, "Take care of him. You need to know his little brother and mother were murdered by a Persian soldier. His father died soon after he joined the Roman army. He has no family I know of." Jarius looked down at Panthera with genuine love for a friend. "You also need to know that Panthera raped the holy child's mother. Panthera is the natural father of Jesus. I believe Joseph will allow Panthera to recuperate in their home, but it will be hard for the mother, Mary. I just thought you needed to know." They stood in silence for a while and Jarius continued, "You are from Persia, aren't you?"

Caspar answered with understanding, "We are all from God. Please, friend, you must trust us."

Jarius said, "I think I already have." He turned and walked out of the tent and turned his gaze toward the cliffs and the fort of Masada. He thought, "When will it end?"

ALEXANDRIA, EGYPT

JOSEPH WALKED TO WORK with a heavy heart. He and Mary continued to hope and pray for another child that did not come. Jesus was past the age of four years and needed a brother or sister even though he was a bright and beautiful child who filled their home with joy. Oddly, it was not enough for them, especially Joseph. He wondered what was keeping Mary from becoming pregnant. As he walked to work one morning, he was in deep contemplation about this. His good friend, Seth, who walked with him to work every day, knew Joseph was once again in deep thought.

"Well, Joseph, come out with it."

"Come out with what?"

"What is occupying your mind this morning?"

"Nothing," Joseph said. For the present, he believed these thoughts needed to remain private. They walked the rest of the way to work and Joseph went to his station and said nothing more to Seth. Seth accepted his friend's treatment because he knew that when Joseph was in deep thought it was no use to try to interfere.

After the situation with Pepi and the pyramid, Joseph had been promoted to a high position in Amsu's construction business, and he served Amsu well. There were many times when problems with construction would arise and Amsu would turn the problems over to Joseph and the men placed under his direction. The present problem on Joseph's mind could not be resolved with equations, calculations, or reason. It had nothing to do with his work. Joseph was plagued with the question "Why is Mary not pregnant?' He thought about the accepted attitude in which problems with pregnancy were always attributed to the female. But Mary had already conceived and delivered a healthy baby boy. It couldn't be a problem with her. Could it be a problem with him? What a thought. Men are not the source of fertility problems . . . or maybe they could be he questioned. It had never dawned on him until now that the problem could be with him.

Joseph didn't accomplish much at work and felt more anxious about his quandary as the day progressed. Walking home at the end of the workday, Seth noticed his friend was still bothered by thoughts. He cautiously tried to reach out to Joseph with kind and gentle support.

"Joseph, you are still so troubled. Many times in my life I, too, have contemplated troubles and have learned that the only choice I had to lighten my burden was to share them with a friend."

They walked on in silence and Seth felt he had offered Joseph what he could. Finally, as they turned the last corner in the road to reach Seth's home Joseph said, "I'm worried because Mary isn't getting pregnant." They walked in silence until they reached Seth's front door. Seth didn't go in but stood and waited for Joseph to say more. "I never told you but . . . Jesus is not my natural son." Seth was surprised with this information but hid his emotion so Joseph would continue. "Mary was raped at fourteen by a Roman soldier. It was he who impregnated her. I married her after Jesus was born. In the Essene discipline, I can't celebrate a second marriage ceremony, or wedlock, until she conceives and bears me a child."

Joseph fell silent again. Seth asked with no judgment in his tone, "Why?"

Joseph looked at him as if he had been far away and had just returned to their conversation. "What do you mean 'why'?"

"Why can't you have a second marriage ceremony? I never heard of such a rule."

"It's from the rules within the Essene sect of which both Mary and I are a part. We may be far from home but I can't forget my religious convictions."

"Do your religious rules dictate that you break off your marriage, or is it a choice you can use to divorce Mary?"

Joseph smiled and felt stupid. "Of course, one is not required to break off the marriage if the wife cannot conceive to the husband. It is up to the husband to make that decision. If his wife cannot conceive and bear his children, he can divorce his wife and seek another. I don't want to leave Mary and Jesus. I don't have to leave Mary and Jesus. Besides, living in Alexandria, Egypt, Essene rules do not influence the people here. They will not judge me or Mary if I stay married to her. Besides, in my heart I feel it must be my fault that Mary isn't pregnant. She has already successfully conceived and birthed a child."

Seth remained quiet, making sure Joseph said all that he needed to say. "I was remembering a time when Mestha and I were having the same problem in our marriage. Isis was born to us and it was over five years before she conceived our second child. She became pregnant with our third child almost too soon. When I think back to that difficult time in our marriage, my wife couldn't seem to be able to conceive again. I also remember that our lives were filled with stress. The circumstances of our stress seem so unimportant now, but at the time, we were both riddled with anger and bitterness over an issue that involved the work of forgiveness. You see, I had been injured in battle and the Roman army tossed me out like I was a worthless rag. In reaction to their treatment of me I came to Egypt to live. At first it was very hard and there were times it got so bad, we depended on the mercy and generosity of others for food and shelter. I was having a hard time finding employment because I couldn't speak or understand Greek. I raged inside, blaming Rome for getting me into this predicament. Then I came to my right mind and realized that it was I who drove me and my young family to be in this situation, not Rome. I'm not saying Rome treated me well, or that it was all right for my country, which I had served faithfully, to treat me this way. But, as soon as I forgave and let go of my rage against Rome, my life began to fall into place. I found a job, acquired a home for the family, began to earn money to buy what we needed, and believed that a greater power than Rome would provide. It was then that Mestha became pregnant again."

Joseph listened carefully and understood the insightful message he received. He asked himself if he had forgiven Panthera and Rome, or even King Herod. He contemplated the possibility that he still held an unforgiving heart against his home and the community in which he grew. Most of all he wondered if he had forgiven God, whom he believed had taken his father and mother from him at too young an age.

Joseph turned to place his hand on Seth's shoulder. "You're a good friend, Seth, and a good man . . . even if you were a Roman soldier once." They laughed. "Thank you, Seth, thank you."

Joseph turned and walked the short distance to his own home. When he reached his front door, he heard strange voices coming from within his home. Instead of entering, his curiosity and caution kept him still, listening and trying to place the voices from his memory. He could not, but when he heard Mary's voice in distress, he opened the door immediately and found it hard to believe what he saw before his eyes.

Three stately men, dressed as royalty, stood before him in his house. On a stretcher lay an injured man . . . Panthera. Young Jesus was crouched in the corner of the room as if he were hiding. When Jesus saw Joseph, he ran to him and hugged his legs. Joseph bent over and picked Jesus up to hold him close as he walked over to Mary, stood next to her, and embraced her with his other arm.

Jesus said in Aramaic, "You're strong, Daddy."

Joseph turned his head to Jesus and kissed his cheek. "What's happening here? Are you alright, Mary? I heard your voice from outside the door and you sounded upset."

"These men claim they are from Byzantium. They have been charting the movement of the stars that came together and shined over Bethlehem when Jesus was born. It's taken them four years to watch the stars and travel here and they say they are here to see Jesus. In their search they talked to King Herod, Joe and Beth, and finally Jarius, who sent them and Panthera to us."

Jesus raised his little arms up in the air and shouted, "Yeahhhh!"

Joseph put Jesus down and stooped to his level and said, "Jesus, this is a serious situation. We need for you to be quiet and calm."

"Yes, Daddy, I'll try to be quiet but I can't be calm." Jesus proceeded to run around the astronomers until he stopped in front of them and looked up at them. All three regal men knelt before Jesus. Their kneeling stopped Jesus abruptly. He turned to his mother with wide eyes and said, "Why did they do that?" Mary stared at the three kneeling and told Jesus to be still. Jesus said, "I guess this is a really, really serious situation," but he mispronounced the words "serious" and "situation." It made Joseph smile.

All three men remained on their knees. Melchior said, "We come with gifts for the child." From under his cloak, he brought forth a beautiful box, placed it on the floor in front of Jesus, and said, "Frankincense."

Balthasar brought out from under his cloak another beautiful box and said, "Myrrh."

Caspar quoted the Jewish Holy Scriptures from Isaiah, saying: "And I went to the prophetess, and she conceived and bore a son. Then the Lord said to me, Name him Maher-shalal-hash-baz; for before the child knows how to call 'My father' or 'My mother,' the wealth of Damascus and the spoil of Samaria will be carried away by the king of Assyria.

"The wolf shall live with the lamb, the leopard shall lie down with the kid, the calf and the lion and the fatling together, and a little child shall lead them" (Isa 8:3—11:6).

Caspar opened his cloak and held in both hands a large box, which he placed on the floor. Jesus stared at the box and didn't move while Caspar proceeded to open it, revealing its contents. It was filled with many gold coins.

Panthera groaned. Balthasar got up from his knees and walked over to a saddle he had brought in from his camel. He took a vial from the saddle and went to Panthera, coaxing him to raise his head to swallow whatever it contained. Panthera could not hold his head up long enough to finish its contents. He groaned again and started to cry softly.

Jesus' attention was drawn to Panthera and he moved next to his stretcher. He stroked Panthera's head and innocently said, "Does it hurt? Don't cry. We'll help you."

Mary surveyed the room and said with resolve, "Well, I guess I need to prepare some food for everyone." She turned and left the room to enter the kitchen. She pulled Joseph to follow her. When they were out of their unexpected guests' hearing, she said, "What are we going to do, Joseph?"

"I think we need to feed them and allow them to spend the night. I can bring in enough straw to make them comfortable. Fortunately, they speak Aramaic and Greek." Joseph thought to himself that they probably spoke Latin also. "Do we have enough food?"

"Yes. We have enough food but what about those gifts? What about Panthera? I think they intend to leave him here with us!"

"Mary, we need to talk with these men and understand the circumstances at hand. Prepare the food and we will talk over the meal. I'll go out and prepare a room for them to rest and sleep. We can put Panthera in the room with them. He seems to be very ill from injury. These three astronomers from Byzantium must have been trying to doctor him while traveling. That won't work."

Mary spoke with an intensity that expressed more than anger. "When these three men decide to leave, they must take Panthera with them anyway. I don't feel I can be in the same house with that man and I don't want Jesus around him. As for those gifts . . . I don't think we should accept them. This all seems so strange!" Mary was preparing food as she talked and her movement was filled with emotional action that indicated angry distress.

As Joseph watched, he judged that his wife continued to harbor hatred for Panthera. He decided Mary's hatred may have been justified at one time, but now, her hatred displayed the fact that she had not truly forgiven Panthera yet. Joseph silently and secretly believed that Mary was still a slave to her negative feelings. Therefore, he foolishly freed himself from any involvement or guilt in the matter of her inability to conceive. He dismissed any previous thought that it may have been he who maintained an unforgiving heart. After having heard what Seth told him, Mary's behavior easily changed his mind from thinking that he may have been at fault for any error present in his heart and mind. He felt vindicated and accepted the thought that he did not need to correct any wrongness in his spirit. It was not he that kept them from the blessing of her becoming pregnant by him. Now he believed the wrongness of spirit dwelt in her heart and it was she who had not forgiven Panthera. It was her unforgiving heart that prohibited conception. He determined that she was not spiritually free. He wanted Mary to become the woman God wanted her to be, but that was shrouded in his belief of his new, personal revelation.

As these thoughts passed through Joseph's mind and spirit, he was nagged by a vague feeling that his thought process was mistaken. He suspected that he didn't own fullness of understanding. He chose to ignore that he may have been acutely responsible for a contrite heart, mind, and spirit. He couldn't grasp or determine that, in truth, the blatant flaw was present in his own thinking. Although this unconsciousness on his part continued to haunt his being, he refused to allow the discomfort to lead him to move out of the way of God's spirit working in Mary's life. His ego lured him into ignoring this feeling, and instead he believed he needed to help his wife see the truth of her own wrongdoing. This thought strengthened his determination to "save" his wife from her unforgiving heart. He decided to help her by directing and teaching her so she could become all he thought she was meant to be.

"It is obviously very hard for you to have Panthera in our home. I, however, am ready to carry out what God directs us to do for Panthera. If the three astronomers intend to leave him here, I will accept him and care for him. I will expect you to tend to Panthera also." Joseph walked behind Mary who was mashing apples and nuts with unusual vigor. He placed his arms around her and whispered in her ear, "You're so angry. I love you even when you're angry." He tried to kiss her neck but she pulled away from him. He accepted her rejection and walked out to the stable to gather mounds of hay and straw to prepare soft beds for their guests.

When Joseph stepped out into the back of the house he was taken aback when he saw three huge camels. He stepped into something soft and knew by the odor it came from the camels. As he looked down, he realized the entire backyard was scattered with droppings from the camels. Now Joseph felt a surge of anger. He could give his wife advice; could he accept it for himself? Gingerly, he avoided the piles everywhere and entered the stall and began to gather clean hay. His burro began to bray and he said aloud, "I know. They're nasty, dirty animals but we will have to accept their presence for a little while. The first good rain will clean their droppings. We must remember they're God's creatures too." He said it but he didn't believe it yet.

When Joseph was finished preparing a room for the astronomers and Panthera, Caspar and Balthasar lifted Panthera's stretcher and moved him into the room. Balthasar tried to give the rest of the serum in the vial to Panthera, and Caspar asked Mary for food and drink that he could feed to Panthera. After Panthera was cared for, they all sat together in the large front room and Mary placed the food she had prepared before them. Joseph spoke a prayer and they ate in silence until they were full.

Mary and Joseph noticed that little Jesus was unusually quiet. He sat still through the meal and watched the three strange men eat.

Jesus blurted out in Aramaic, "Are you kings?"

Melchior chuckled. "No, Jesus. We are not kings."

"Well . . . you look like kings . . . and you have gold."

"The gold and other boxes are yours. Does that make you a king?"

Jesus' eyes grew wide. "Mine?"

"Yes, yours," said Melchior.

Jesus stood up and walked to his mother and sat in her lap. She kissed him on top of his head. Jesus looked up and backward to his mother and said, "You can have the gold, Mommy. You and Daddy can have the gold," and he pointed to Joseph.

Joseph said, "Jesus, we don't know if we will accept these gifts the men brought to us. Your mommy and I have to talk about this."

Mary lifted Jesus out of her lap and took his hand. "This has been an exciting day for you. It is time to go to bed and sleep. Come, I'll take you to your room and say prayers with you. Say good night to our guests. You will see them again in the morning."

Jesus was tired and he willingly accepted his mother's instruction. He turned to the men and said, "Good night. Thanks for the gold and other things. Daddy, will you come to kiss me good night?"

Joseph smiled and said, "Yes. Go with your mother, I'll be there to kiss you and bless you good night."

For the first time in a long time, Mary picked Jesus up to carry him to his bed. Jesus enjoyed this treat and wrapped his arms around her and laid his head against her shoulder. As Mary walked out of the room Jesus waved good night to the "kings," who waved back.

Joseph took a deep breath and said, "We have much to talk about but it cannot be done without my wife. Please remain seated while I clear the table and put the remainder of food away properly." When Joseph looked down at the table to pick up plates, goblets, and leftover food, he was surprised to see that almost all the food was consumed and only dishes needed to be cleared and cleaned. He proceeded to clear away the dishes, cleaned them quickly, and had everything put away when Mary came back into the room. She showed her appreciation by thanking Joseph politely.

"Joseph, you need to give Jesus his good-night kiss. He's waiting, but I think he will be asleep very soon."

Joseph went into Jesus' room and sat down next to his bed. Jesus had been turned on his side, looking out the window, but he rolled over and looked at his father. "I was thinking about you and looking out the window.

I hear an owl. Listen." Joseph listened. They heard a soft, gentle hooting, which felt comforting to both of them. "Did you hear it, Daddy?"

"Yes, Jesus, I heard it." Joseph embraced Jesus and kissed him on the forehead.

"Who's that sick man, Daddy? Why is he hurt?"

"Now it's time to sleep. We will talk about everything in the morning. Listen to the owl and sleep well, my son."

Joseph spoke the evening prayers and stood above Jesus' bed, ready to leave the room. Jesus turned on his side again to sleep. As Joseph walked out of the room, he felt overwhelming love for Jesus. He thought about love and the power it held. He felt awe as he contemplated the many different manifestations of love within different relationships. He paused to think about his love for Amsu, Pepi, Seth, Jesus, and Mary. He even thought about his love for animals. He certainly had a greater love for his burro than for the smelly camels. But he remembered that the smelly camels were loved by the three astronomers and how they were relied upon to carry the three men home, which was good. But then he questioned, what about Panthera? Can one love an enemy? Joseph walked into the front room and sat down to talk.

They talked into the early hours of the morning. Mary learned a great deal but was disturbed with their reporting. She learned much about ancient history as the three astronomers talked about the rising and falling of great empires like Babylon, Assyria, Persia, and now Rome. She was spiritually moved by Caspar's quoting from Isaiah about Assyria and the little child that would eventually lead them. She was saddened as she realized that all history was wrapped and riddled in war and violence. Comfort came to her when she heard the words that someday "the wolf shall live with the lamb, the leopard shall lie down with the kid, the calf and the lion and the fatling together, and a child shall lead them." She knew these words well and remembered them from her own father's teaching and reading from the Holy Scriptures and the prophetic writings of Isaiah.

As the three astronomers talked, they explained that they believed Jesus was "the child" that had led them so far. Although he was born from the violent crime of her rape, they confessed that they believed he would grow up to be a great prophet and Messiah. They described Panthera's history and appealed to Mary to forgive and understand. They asked her and Joseph to keep Panthera and nurse him back to health. They insisted that their gifts be accepted and that the myrrh be saved for Jesus' burial someday. They alluded to many other great events yet to be revealed in history. They said that peace would surely come through the teaching of Jesus and that through him mercy would kiss justice for all time for those who believed what he taught. They stated, with confidence, that Jesus' teaching would most certainly reveal true salvation in life for the human soul.

When they had finished talking, Joseph told them they would care for Panthera and accept their gifts with gratitude.

Finally, they all retreated to their rooms to sleep for the remainder of the hours left in the night. Mary lay next to Joseph and turned on her side so her back was to him. She seemed to fall asleep instantly. Joseph detected that something was not right with her, but his own exhaustion took over.

Light from the morning sun came too quickly. As usual, Jesus alerted his parents to rise by walking into their bedroom saying, "Good morgging!" Although Jesus was a brilliant child, learning to speak Greek, Aramaic, and now Latin, he tended to misplace the sound of the last syllable of a word somewhere into the middle of the word. Often Mary would be amused as she listened to him say "bakset" for basket, and "waps" for wasp. Although Jesus displayed his typical joyful demeanor, this morning Mary and Joseph rose with a solemn attitude. Mary went to the kitchen to prepare food for breakfast.

Jesus tugged on Mary's garment and asked, "Can I wake up the kings?"

"No, I'm not quite ready for anyone. I'm still preparing breakfast. You can wake them up with Daddy when it is time." Mary paused before saying, "Jesus, I don't want you to go near the sick man. Do you understand?"

Jesus stared at her and said, "Yes, Mommy."

Joseph walked into the room and Jesus ran to him. Joseph picked him up and walked next to Mary. She turned away from him and said, "Please wake our guests. They wanted to leave at an early hour. I think they said they needed to board their ship for the journey home before high noon."

Joseph definitely felt Mary's hostility. He walked to the "kings'" room with Jesus in his arms and rapped on the door.

"Come in." Joseph recognized Balthasar's voice. He opened the door and saw that all three men were packed and ready to leave. Melchior and Caspar were attending to Panthera. Melchior asked Joseph if food could be brought to Panthera. Joseph responded by telling them all to come for breakfast. He would see to it that Panthera was fed.

The three astronomers came and sat before the food Mary had prepared. Little Jesus sat between Balthasar and Caspar. "Are you going home today? You don't have to go home yet. You can stay to play in the creek we have in the back of our house. The water is reeeeal cold!"

"That would be fun, Jesus, but we must go to get on a ship to take us home. If we are not there to get on the ship it will leave without us."

In innocence Jesus asked, "Who will take care of that man who is hurt?"

Caspar genuinely liked Jesus and was not surprised that this child would show concern for another as he had. "Your mother and father have agreed to take care of the man."

Jesus looked at his mother who stood over a wooden table cutting goat cheese. To Jesus she appeared to be cutting the cheese with unnecessary vigor.

The three astronomers rose from the table and bowed to Mary. Melchior said, "You are a holy woman, blessed by God. We thank you for your hospitality. We will never forget this honor, to meet you and your child. Please accept our genuine gratitude."

Mary simply said, "You are welcome."

They turned to Joseph. "My brother, may the God of the universe continue to bless you and keep you, and your family safe. We are forever in your debt." Caspar turned to Jesus and said, "Jesus, will you come here and hug me goodbye?"

Without hesitation, Jesus hugged each of the men in turn. "I have been with kings!" he said with delight. "Will you come again?"

Balthasar said, "We will all be together again, I'm sure of it."

The men finished packing their camels and Joseph walked to the back of the house to help them check the camels' saddles for secure fastening. The men mounted the camels and bowed as they moved away from Joseph. Caspar turned back and gave one last wave to Joseph, who returned his gesture with a final wave as he stood in the yard and looked around at the mess. He looked up at the sky and could not detect one cloud that could give an indication that there may be rain. He sighed and looked at the house. He saw Mary moving in the kitchen cleaning up after their meal. He knew she was angry about something and he was hesitant to address it with her. He had to be at work in one hour. This could not wait so he walked to the back entrance and confronted Mary.

"You are obviously upset. What's wrong, Mary? You've been upset since last night."

"Joseph," Mary stood straight from wiping the table. The cloth she had been using was left crumpled on the table's surface. "I will not allow that man to be in our house alone with me."

Joseph appealed to her and his words angered her more. "Mary, he is sick and injured. He may die. We can't turn our backs on him now. Look what he has done for us since . . ."

"Since he raped me!? Joseph, I will not . . . *no*! I cannot feed, care, clean, protect, and nurture that man! How could you have agreed to care for Panthera to those three men without first privately consulting with me!? I'll be the one who will have to attend to him, alone, with only Jesus in the house with me while you are gone to work!" Joseph tried to say something but her voice rose above his. "You may be a good man of God, Joseph, but you're different than me! Your life experience is different than mine! I will not live under your judgment or spiritual guidance! I am a good woman of God. I may not know as much as you but I know how to hear the spirit of God within me even if I am a woman! What do you think I was doing as I grew up in the Qumran Settlement? You act as if I had been sitting around watching pigs grow fat!" Joseph winced. He knew Jewish Essenes would never allow pigs in the settlement. She continued blasting her anger after she released a low, guttural cry. "I will submit to you as a wife, but it ends there! I am called by God to submit to a voice that transcends your voice, and I will obey God's!"

Jesus started crying. He ran to Mary crying. Joseph said nothing and Jesus started crying harder. He clung to Mary. Mary bent over and picked Jesus up, kissed him gently on the head, and whispered, "I love you." She walked up to Joseph and handed Jesus to him and then she turned and walked out of the house.

Joseph stood dumbfounded. Jesus was still crying in his arms. "Where's Mommy going, Daddy? Go get her before she goes far," as great tears ran down his cheeks.

Joseph held Jesus closer to himself and sat down. "Shhhh . . ." he whispered. He felt lost. He rocked Jesus to try to calm his crying. He thought about the words Mary had thrown at him. He began to process the situation. She was right. He had agreed to taking care of Panthera without giving a thought to consult with her. He wondered how he could be so stupid. She must have also sensed his judgment of her all this time. At first, when they experienced difficulty conceiving, he had assumed it was a physical problem with Mary. It had taken him more than two years to realize that it could not have been due to her physical problem. After all, she had already conceived and gave birth to Jesus. After talking to Seth, he had decided that maybe his own unforgiving heart prohibited the conception of a baby. But then he changed his mind and believed that Mary couldn't conceive because she had a spiritual problem and had not forgiven someone. When he had walked into his house the day before he had thought that God was showing him that Mary certainly needed to forgive Panthera more fully. He believed God had presented her with the opportunity to actively forgive him by caring for him, here and now. Her words echoed inside his mind. She had yelled at him. She had said, "I will not live under your judgment or spiritual guidance." He knew she meant what she said.

Jesus had not stopped crying and his wailing rudely dragged Joseph back to the reality at hand. He looked at Jesus and stood up, carrying Jesus back and forth across the room, trying to comfort him. From the other room Joseph heard Panthera cry out for help. He walked with Jesus still crying in his arms to Panthera to find him covered in his own mess of vomit and urine. Panthera couldn't seem to move and he groaned in pain. Joseph placed Jesus down and his son cried all the more. He picked Jesus up again and looked down at Panthera. "I can't help you right now," he said. He walked back to the kitchen with Jesus crying and clinging to him. As he walked with Jesus he began to think. He needed to find Mary. He needed to ask for her forgiveness. He needed to figure out where Panthera could be moved to be cared for properly. He needed to . . . before he could finish his thoughts, Mary stepped into the room with Mestha and Seth.

Jesus cried out with joy, "Mommy!"

Mary came to Joseph and took Jesus from his arms. "I went to our friends and asked them if they would consider taking Panthera into their home and attending to him."

Seth said, "Well, Joseph, I guess we're going to be late for work. Mestha, Isis, my boys and I would be glad to take care of Panthera. Why don't you and I move him to our home now? We'll leave for work from there."

Joseph looked at Mary. She said, "Go on. Go to work. We'll talk tonight."

As if in a trance, Joseph and Seth walked to the room which Panthera presently occupied. Panthera appeared to be either asleep or unconscious but when Seth and Joseph picked him up, he groaned. Seth touched his arm gently and said, "Don't worry. You're alright. We'll move you carefully." Seth looked to Joseph and said, "I feel better already. I am thankful for this opportunity to help a fellow Roman soldier. I know firsthand what he has been through."

Joseph and Seth walked to Seth's house, carrying Panthera on the stretcher. They put him down in a comfortable room off the front living room. Isis was waiting to sit with Panthera and cool his brow with water. Seth said, "All right, then, let's be off to work."

Joseph looked at Isis and said, "He needs to be cleaned and he hasn't eaten this morning. Do you feel comfortable doing this, Isis?"

Isis didn't even respond to Joseph but began to attend to Panthera immediately, with gentle hands of care.

Joseph and Seth left to walk together to work and didn't speak another word all day.

At the workday's end Joseph did not walk home with Seth. He walked alone in another direction.

"Where are you going, my friend?" Seth asked Joseph.

"Don't worry, Seth, I'm walking to the docks to look at the sea and think . . . and pray."

Joseph walked slowly. For some reason he needed to see the water of the great Mediterranean. His heart was heavy, and he wanted to be reconciled with Mary. He didn't know how to attain her forgiveness and he desperately needed guidance. As he came closer to the water, he could smell the ocean scents. His memory took him back to the day they had stepped on the ship in Joppa to come to Alexandria. He remembered all the events that had allowed them to narrowly escape the searching claws of King Herod. God had provided for their safety then. He wondered if God would provide what he needed now.

When he finally reached the docks, he looked north over the water that stretched out before him. The sun was setting and the twilight seemed to enchant him. He stepped onto a pier that led over the water for some distance. He walked to its end and felt alone with his God. As he prayed, he began to experience peace. He came to know he could go home and ask Mary to forgive him. He knew he had to tell her that he had also come to understand that it was his spiritual brokenness that may have prohibited their ability to conceive a child together, not hers. From the depths of his soul, he hoped his firstborn son would be the Messiah. He thought of Jesus and dropped his head into his hands and wept. "Dear God, have mercy on us," he cried. He looked back over the sea and embraced the sense of love he felt. Somehow, he felt it surrounded him in his despairing.

Suddenly, he became aware of commotion behind him, on the docks. He saw a slave block he had not noticed before when he passed to walk down the pier. Slaves were being auctioned off and Joseph decided to see what was happening. The slave block was surrounded by men yelling their bids. Joseph was appalled. He wondered how anyone could justify belief in the right to own another human being.

Joseph turned to a man standing near him and asked, "Do they sell slaves here often?"

"Yes."

"But it is near dusk, why would they sell at this time?"

The man looked at him and said with irritation, "It's one less meal they would need to feed them. As soon as the ship comes in with slaves they're sold."

Joseph looked up on the platform and saw a beautiful black woman with her young son dragged onto the block. Her little son must have been four or five years old. They both looked frightened. The auctioneer began his call for bidding and the men present, looking to buy, laughed and shouted, "I wouldn't give camel squat for them." "You'd have to pay me for them." "What good is a woman with a little child? It would cost more to feed them before they could bring a return."

The bidding went on for a while and the men took great entertainment in their jokes. Joseph left. He ran with all his might down the streets from the docks to his home. He entered his house out of breath. Mary and Jesus were not in sight. He stood still, catching his breath. He bent over and leaned his hands on his knees and dropped his head. He felt terrible. When he looked up Mary stood before him with Jesus in her arms. Jesus reached out to Joseph, and he came close so Jesus could put his arms around his neck and he could put his arms around Mary. He wept. He felt Mary's arm move around his middle and she held him as tightly as she could while maintaining her hold on Jesus too.

She let Joseph weep on her shoulder. Slowly, Joseph gained composure and he looked at Mary and said, "Please forgive me, Mary. I can't go on without your expressed forgiveness."

Jesus blurted out, "That's all right, Daddy. You can cry if you need to. I cry all the time."

Joseph took Jesus from Mary's arms, sat down, and placed Jesus on his lap. "Jesus, you don't know why I'm crying. I need to talk with Mommy because I . . .

Jesus finished his sentence, ". . . you need her to tell you she still loves you."

How simple it seemed when Jesus said what he did in his childlike innocence. Joseph smiled at Jesus and said, "Yes. Will you go play while I finish talking to Mom?"

Jesus jumped down from Joseph's lap and ran toward the back door. "I'm going out to talk to our burro. I think he's lonely."

Mary caught Jesus as he tried to run past her. "You can go see the burro but it is almost dark and you must be in the house before night. I have our Sabbath meal ready so do not talk to the burro too long." She let go of him and he ran out the back door as Mary called to him, "Jesus! Be careful where you step. I don't want camel poop dragged into our home."

Mary looked at Joseph, who remained seated and speechless. She walked to him and sat down at his feet. She raised her arms and placed them around him. She rested her head in his lap and he began to stroke her hair. She looked up and said, "What is happening to us, Joseph? I should have never yelled at you as I did. And you didn't come home as you usually do. It's the night before Sabbath. This is not how we should be."

Joseph guided her up from the floor to stand, and then he stood. "I need you to forgive me. I understand what I've been doing to you through my self-righteousness. These past years I've blamed our inability to conceive on you. When I think that you have been the object of my blame, and then I decided that the man who raped you could be in our home, assuming you would care for him, I am filled with shame and have become undone. I realize my guilt and stupidity. I have been completely indifferent to your feelings or needs. I'm sorry. You must forgive me. I don't know how you have managed taking care of Jesus and our home, as well as everything else you do. I don't know what I was thinking when I decided you could take on the care of an injured soldier, let alone Panthera."

"Done," Mary said. "However, you need to know that I forgave you when I figured out how to solve my problem. As soon as I remembered that Seth had also been a wounded Roman soldier, I knew they would take Panthera in and care for him."

"When did you think of that solution?"

"While I was yelling at you, about the time I said I knew how to hear the spirit of God within me. I believe I was directed by God just in time."

Joseph asked again, "I need to hear your words now. Do you forgive me?"

She reached out to him and kissed him long and deep. "I forgive you, Joseph. I love you and Jesus. Together we will be able to endure any challenge that may come our way."

"I love you, Mary."

The back door opened and Mary looked out the window. The twilight was gone and night was upon them. Jesus could be heard entering the house from the rear and climbing up onto his chair at the table in the kitchen. He called out, "I'm ready for the Sabbath. Let's pray and eat."

FROM ETHIOPIA

The next day Joseph and Mary woke late in the morning. Jesus also slept later than usual. They were all worn out from the day before. When Joseph opened his eyes from sleep, he thanked God for the Sabbath. As he relaxed, anticipating the entire day of rest with his family, there was a flash of lightning and a loud roll of thunder. Jesus ran into his parent's room and jumped on top of Joseph.

"Don't be afraid, Jesus. It's just thunder. It announces that a storm is coming. We'll be safe together in our house."

Another clash of lightning and thunder rattled through their house. Jesus put his hands on his ears and sank his head into Joseph's chest. Mary walked to the window and looked up to the sky. She reached for the shutters and closed them tight. "I'll go and close the other shutters around the house. It's going to pour!"

Joseph pulled Jesus closer to him and said, "Now, Jesus. Let's listen for the rain. I'm glad it will be raining. It will wash away all the messes the camels left for us."

Jesus looked at Joseph and his eyes revealed the moment he comprehended to what Joseph was referring. After an expression of understanding Jesus laughed with a laugh that brought Mary back to the room and into the bed. Although she had no idea why Jesus was laughing, his laughter was contagious and she couldn't help laughing too.

Jesus said, "Are you talking about the smelly poop the camels left?" Joseph tried to hold back his laughter so as not to encourage Jesus. He tried to say yes without laughing but it seemed to have an opposite effect on Jesus. Finally, Joseph gave up and joined their laughter as the rain began to fall with a vengeance.

Their laughter calmed and Mary suggested they speak their Sabbath prayers in bed together. When their prayers and meditations were finished Mary rose to prepare breakfast.

Joseph got up, washed, and dressed quickly. "Come, Jesus. Let's help Mom make breakfast." Both headed for the kitchen and together the family prepared breakfast. As they ate, Mary suggested that this should become a tradition for their family. "Everyone should help with the Sabbath breakfast," she said. Joseph nodded and then Jesus nodded.

After breakfast was finished, the young family walked into the front room. It was still raining and Jesus began to play with the wooden objects Joseph had made for him. Jesus loved playing with the wooden shapes, especially when he was not alone. At this moment he enjoyed both parents' undivided attention and he felt happy and safe. Mary and Joseph watched as Jesus built with the shapes and they expressed approval with words of praise.

"I walked to the docks last night after work to look at the sea."

Mary turned her attention from Jesus to Joseph. "What did you say, Joseph?"

"Last night I walked to the docks and out over the longest pier. The evening twilight was spectacular. The sky to the west was streaked with red, violet, and pink." Joseph sighed and his eyes looked at the wall as if he could not really see. "I was standing on the end of the pier when I heard men yelling behind me. As I walked back to the docks, I realized they were conducting a slave trade. Men were standing around the slave block bidding for people being sold into slavery. They dragged a beautiful black woman and her son to the block and the men started laughing and joking about bidding for her and him. Evidently, they were worthless because she was a woman and he was just a child. It was horrible. I left and ran all the way home feeling sick. I thought of you and Jesus and your incredible worth to me. I was still sad over our situation . . . their mistreatment on the slave block was unbearable."

Mary didn't respond but Jesus was listening. "Didn't the little boy have a daddy?"

"No, he didn't have a daddy," Joseph said to Jesus.

Jesus got up from the floor and crawled onto Joseph's lap and asked, "Why didn't the boy have a daddy?"

"Because sometimes things happen in life and either their daddies can't be with their children or don't want to be with their children."

"Why wouldn't a daddy want to be with his children?"

"Jesus, there can be and are many reasons. For this little boy, he was probably taken away from his father and brought here to be sold to whoever bids the most money. Then they become workers for the man, or men, that bought them."

"Can the man who buys them be the daddy to the boy?"

"I suppose, if he chooses to become a father and good master."

"Why don't we buy them? We can use the gold that the kings gave us!" Jesus was getting excited. "The mommy could help my mommy . . . the boy could be my brother . . . and we could play together! You and mommy want another baby that would grow up to be a boy or a girl anyway!"

Joseph looked at Mary sheepishly. "I guess we haven't been too secret about our desire to have more children."

"No, Joseph . . . you have not. Despite it all, I have never been worried that you would send me away and find another wife." In the distance rolls of thunder rumbled. "Joseph," he looked at her in shame, "I'm pregnant."

Jesus jumped off the lap of Joseph and ran around Joseph and Mary shouting, "Yeahhhh! Yeahhhh! There's going to be a baby. We can have another little boy and have a baby too! Yeahhh!"

Joseph sat in disbelief staring at Mary. He started to say something and his mouth dropped open, staying that way, as Jesus began to dance between them. Another loud crack of thunder brought Jesus to his father.

"The thunder still scares me but I'm getting used to it," Jesus said. He climbed back onto Joseph's lap. Joseph finally closed his mouth and looked down at Jesus. He hugged Jesus and stood up with him in his arms and slowly walked to Mary.

He asked, "How far along are you?"

"Three months. The baby will be born in our holy month of September. I've prayed that this baby will be a boy, mostly for you, Joseph. If it is a boy, he will be born according to the rules that our Essene faith requires of a Messiah. Also, since I have conceived to you and have carried the baby three months, we can celebrate our second marriage and wedlock."

"Why . . . why didn't you tell me before?"

"Joseph, I had not yet carried the baby three months. The chances of miscarriage are greater in the first three months. But this baby seems strong and is growing well. I often feel tired and overwhelmed with caring for Jesus and the home. I knew I couldn't care for Panthera also. When you went ahead and told the astronomers we, or should I say, *I* would nurse Panthera back to health, I knew I couldn't do it. You didn't talk to me before you told them we would help Panthera. If you had talked to me, I would have told you then."

Joseph put Jesus down and pulled Mary to her feet. He picked her up and spun her around as he laughed with joy. He placed her back on her feet and kissed her with great love. Jesus stood and watched his parents with delight. He proceeded to tug at Joseph's garment.

"Daddy, it stopped raining. Can we go and bring that lady and her little boy home?"

Joseph looked at Mary and asked, "What do you say? I think you need help around here and Jesus would have a playmate."

Mary smiled, "I'd love to have another woman in the house. She could be like a sister to me. I'm sure she would be a great help. I don't want her to be sold as a slave to some owner who may not love them properly. I know you would honor them and provide proper protection for them. This is a big house. She and her son could use the four rooms on the second level for their living."

Joseph said, "What about the gold? Should I use the gold to bid for them?"

"Yes, use all of it. I don't even want it hiding in the house. Besides, human beings are worth far more than gold. Bring them home, Joseph."

Joseph stood still and realized that the rain had stopped. He reached for his cloak and said, "It is the Sabbath. What better day than to free them. Although," he paused, "they could have been sold last night and I'm not sure they will be bidding today. I'm going to go anyway. Jesus, do you want to come with me? After all, it is your gold. The astronomers gave the gold to you."

"But I gave the gold to you and mommy. I want you to use it the right way."

"Well, do you want to come with me?" Joseph asked again.

Jesus grabbed his little cloak and declared, "Yes, before they're gone."

"What do you say, Mary? Will you come also? I'm sure the woman and her child will be less afraid in the presence of another woman."

Mary grabbed her cloak and the three walked out the door toward the docks.

When they arrived at the docks the slave block was empty and devoid of bidders. Joseph led Mary and Jesus around to a building where he had seen slaves taken in and out at the auction the night before. When they entered the building, their eyes needed to adjust to the darkness. As they were able to see, they saw three doors in front of them. Joseph leaned forward to listen to determine which door to rap upon. Behind the middle door he heard voices of men so he knocked on the door loudly enough to interrupt their talk. The door opened and a rather dirty man said, "What do you want?" His teeth were rotten and the stench from beyond him wafted past him.

"I was here last night and a young black woman and her son were presented on the block. The men were joking with worthless bids. Are those two people still within your care?"

"We don't *care* for anyone around here. What are you talking about? We sell slaves! Yes, the woman and her child are here but the bidding for them will not start until the arrival of another slave ship. We may be able to sell them with the new group that is coming."

Joseph respectfully inquired about the anticipated time the next slave ship was to arrive. The man with the rotten teeth said, "By noon, today," and he looked at Jesus. "What are you doing bringing a little kid like that around here?"

"He is our child and he is anxious to befriend the woman's little boy."

"What? Are you crazy? Are you going to let your little boy be a friend to a slave?" He gave Joseph a suspecting eye and added, "I suppose you're going to be a friend to the woman?" Joseph understood the accusation and stepping aside he said, "This is my wife."

Embarrassed, the man asked, "Where are you from? You sure don't look Egyptian."

"We are from Judea but have lived in Alexandria for some years now."

"Well, you look like Jews, for sure. You need to get with the Egyptian way of life around here. Making friends with slaves is not one of our practices." He closed the door.

Joseph turned and led Mary and Jesus out of the building and into the sun that was now shining on the water. The brightness blinded them for a short time and Joseph suggested they travel to the market and purchase food for their lunch and dinner. He looked at the sun and figured they had at least two hours to wait so they meandered among the goods being sold in the market. After Mary chose food for them they found a shaded place on soft grass to eat their lunch. Jesus played after eating and Mary and Joseph leaned against a large tree, watching Jesus. Both Mary and Joseph were filled with peace and they felt a completeness that also gave them joy.

"When shall we celebrate our second marriage ceremony, Joseph?"

"When would you like to celebrate it?"

"The ceremony should take place next week, on the Sabbath. Jesus' birthday is next week also and we could combine the two events into one celebration. I'm sure Mestha, Seth, and their children would come. You could invite Amsu and his family, and Pepi and his family. I would also like to invite the family living next to us. Since I learned to speak Greek, the wife and I have become rather close friends. I've not talked with her husband much, so I don't really know him, but he must also be included as one of our guests."

"Then it is done. That's when we will celebrate. Next Seventh day Sabbath. It's perfect."

"I feel so happy, Joseph."

Joseph reached and placed his hand on her abdomen and kissed her lightly on the cheek. "I feel happy too."

Jesus ran up to them and shouted, "Look what I can do." Jesus tumbled forward and then tried to stand on his head. "Well, I did it before when you weren't looking."

"Jesus, come here. I need to tell you something." Jesus obeyed immediately. "We are going to go back to the docks and it will be bad because you will see people being sold like things you can own. Mom and I do not believe this is how people should treat people. However, I need for you to be very quiet. You must stay close to your mother. I will walk up to the slave block and bid for the woman and her little boy."

Jesus nodded and they gathered their purchases and walked toward the docks again. This time the slave platform and block were surrounded with men and loud noise. Several men were dragged to the block and sold as the highest bids were shouted out and claimed.

Finally, the black woman and her child were dragged to the block. They had chains on their legs and hands. As had happened the night before, laughter rose from the loud men, making jokes with their bidding. From the distance where Mary and Jesus stood Mary began to cry. She remembered being taught about the prophet Hosea and could not help but see a similarity captured in the scene she was witnessing. Mary had been taught about the prophet by her father, who had read to her from the Holy Scripture. She remembered being told that Hosea's unfaithful wife left him and their children. She was drawn to the arms of other lovers. Her life became a downward spiral to disaster and many years later, she was brought to the slave block to be sold. Her purchase was to pay for her debt. But the bidders made fun of her and laughed at her, devaluing her worth to nothing. Although Mary remembered being taught that Hosea's wife, named Gomer, represented Israel and her unfaithfulness to God, she saw another point from her own perspective. She saw the worthlessness of women if they were not loved, married, and bearing children. She recognized the same in the black woman on the block.

In the scroll of Hosea, the prophet Hosea showed faithfulness to his old, worthless, unfaithful wife by placing a sack of silver on the slave block to buy Gomer back and restore her worth. Mary wondered if the black woman and her child would feel worth after Joseph placed their sack of gold coins on the platform.

"Why are you crying, Mommy, because of the chains on them?" Jesus asked.

"No. Just watch what Daddy is about to do." She picked Jesus up for a better view.

They both watched as Joseph pushed his way to the front of the platform and yelled with a voice everyone could hear. "I bid this sack of pure gold for her and her son." A hush moved through the chaotic crowd. "Can anyone bid more than this amount?"

Little Jesus said, "That's the gold the kings gave us!"

"Yes, darling. Would you rather keep that gold or free the mother and her child to come and live with us?"

"I want them to come and live with us! I want a brother and another mother!"

The slave auctioneer came up to Joseph and said, "Let me see what you have in that sack." Joseph dumped the sack of gold coins onto the platform. The slave auctioneer picked up one of the coins and examined it closely. He picked a second coin up and did the same. He ran his fingers over the coins and spread them out to see if they were all alike. "These coins are ancient gold coins from the Persian Empire!" He stared at Joseph and said in disbelief, "You can have her and the boy for a lot less than *one* of these coins!"

Joseph said, "Gold, silver, or any precious metal taken from the bowels of the earth can never equal the worth of human life, but I offer this gold to assure the freedom of this woman and her child to come home with me. Again, can anyone here outbid me?" Not a sound rose from the crowd. Joseph said, "Remove their chains."

The same man with the rotten teeth bent down before the woman and her son, to free them from their fetters. He removed the chains and dropped them on the platform. The sound they made dropping onto the wood echoed through the surrounding docks. Joseph jumped up onto the platform and approached the woman. In fear she clutched her child and drew him close as he came near to them. Joseph reached out his hand and waited for her to take it. At first it seemed as if she would remain, like a frozen statue on the block. But the silence of the crowd, and the softness she detected in Joseph's eyes, gave her courage to take hold of his hand. With Joseph leading her she stepped off the block, holding her son tightly in her arms. She followed Joseph to the edge of the platform. Joseph helped her and her child jump down from the platform to the ground. The crowd of men parted to let them walk through. They walked up to Mary, who placed her own cloak around the woman while Joseph took her son's hand, and then Jesus' hand, to walk home.

When they arrived home Joseph and Mary guided the woman through the front entrance and into their front room. Jesus walked up to the little boy and stood, looking at him. Jesus turned to Joseph and asked, "He can't talk our words, and I can't talk his words, yet." Jesus turned to the little boy and pointed to himself and said, "Jesus." He then pointed back to the little boy and waited.

After a little time had passed the boy put his hand on his chest, looked at his mother and said, "Yemane." He touched Jesus' chest with his finger and said, "Jesus."

Jesus excitedly clapped his hands while running circles around the woman and her son, shouting with pure joy, "*Yes*! You said my name and I said your name, Yemane!"

Mary stepped before the black woman and pointed to herself, "Mary."

The woman lifted her hand slowly and touched her chest. She finally said, "Ghidai." She looked at Joseph and pointed to him.

Joseph understood her question and said, "Joseph."

Her eyes widened with recognition. She said, "Ab . . . ra . . . ham, Isaac, Ja . . . cob, Jo . . . seph, Mo . . . ses."

Joseph and Mary nodded. Ghidai waited for them to say her name, and her son's name. Then she said, "Joseph, Mary," she put her hand on Jesus' head, "Jesus . . . Emmanuel."

Joseph and Mary were amazed. Mary looked at Joseph and said, "Where do you think they're from and how does she know those names?"

Joseph asked slowly, "Cushite?" When Ghidai nodded her head Joseph said, "They must be from Ethiopia. That's on the other side of this great land mass. Egypt borders the Mediterranean Sea to the north. Where she comes from would take many days of travel. Her country borders the sea going to the Far East."

"They must be hungry and tired. Joseph, will you prepare a room for them with hay mounds, straw, and blankets for now. We will prepare the second floor for them later this week but right now they need to wash and eat and lie down to sleep. I'll get Ghidai a garment to wear. Jesus, after you show Ghidai and Yemane where they can wash, will you pick a garment to give Yemane to wear. He's bigger than you but I think one of your garments will fit him until his mother and I can make new clothes for them."

Mary put the food they had bought that afternoon out on the table and set a plate and goblet for each of them. She picked a garment she thought would fit the best for Ghidai and when she came back to the table, they were all standing present. Mary placed the garment over Ghidai and let it fall to the floor. Joseph reported that the room was supplied with enough hay and blankets for ample comfort. Jesus announced that his hands were "all clean" as he raised them up to be examined. Yemane followed Jesus' lead and held up his hands also. He was wearing one of Jesus' garments and Mary was pleased that her son showed loving, unbridled generosity.

Joseph sat and the rest sat after him. Joseph spoke a prayer and they all ate to their fill. Afterward, Mary showed Ghidai and Yemane to their temporary room and took Jesus to his bedroom to speak his prayers and meditations before he went to sleep also. As Mary leaned over Jesus to kiss him good night, Joseph came into the room and sat on the bed to kiss and bless Jesus too. Jesus looked very tired and closed his eyes. Before he fell asleep, he said, "I will play with Yemane tomorrow. We will learn each other's words tomorrow."

"Sleep well, my little man," Mary said as she stroked Jesus' curly, dark hair. "I'm proud of you and how you delight in living." She rose from the bed and walked toward the door.

Joseph lingered back and bent down to kiss Jesus on the forehead. He stared down at Jesus and thought about the new baby growing in Mary's womb. He couldn't forget that Mary said she had prayed that the baby was a boy and that he would be born in the holy month of September as designated and dictated by Essene practice. Maybe the child in Mary's womb was to be the long-expected Messiah, not Jesus. He looked at Jesus sleeping and felt uneasy. He was doing it again, thinking he knew the ways of God. He bent down again and kissed Jesus and stood straight to look out the window. Another Sabbath was gone and the day had certainly been filled with events that promised change. Joseph lifted a prayer thanking God for life and love. He knew life and he knew love. But he did not know or understand the ways of God. Secretly he hoped the baby boy to be born to him and Mary would be the Messiah. He fantasized about returning to Judea and the Qumran Settlement with his natural son bearing the calling to be the Messiah. But as he turned his gaze down to the sleeping child Jesus, something ached in the depth of his being. The black woman, Ghidai, had touched Jesus' head and called him Emmanuel. The astronomers from Byzantium had knelt before him and honored him with more than gifts. They had honored him with faith that had brought them far to find him. They had spoke of him as growing to be the prophet of prophets. Even King Herod had displayed an imagined, or real, faith in Jesus' importance because he fervently sought to kill him. Joseph did not turn his gaze from Jesus as he thought. He finally turned and walked out of the room to look for Mary. He felt a great need and desire to talk to Mary.

He found her in their bedroom and she was crying. "What's the matter? Why are you crying?"

"Oh, Joseph," she said, "It's been quite a day. I have so many different emotions circling around in me. Do you think we should send Ghidai and Yemane home to Ethiopia? We may have used gold to pay for their freedom from slavery, but they will forever be viewed as slaves here."

Joseph thought for a moment and said, "Why don't we let them live here with us for a time and then let them decide what they would choose to do."

Joseph's solution was completely acceptable to Mary. "I know I said I prayed that the baby I carry be a boy, but I'm really not sure. I know you want a son, born under the correct rules designated by our religious Essene order, but we have no control over the sex of the child. I believe that's up to God. Or maybe it's just chance . . . like casting lots."

"Mary, I am thrilled we will have a child together. I will accept with joy whatever he, or she, will be." Joseph felt as if he was being somewhat dishonest. He sought to talk to her about his thoughts about the coming of the Messiah and realized this was not the time to confide in Mary about his hopes and dreams. Besides, she seemed to know what he was thinking and feeling already.

They undressed, washed, and climbed into bed. After Joseph extinguished the lamp, the room seemed unusually dark. The night sky was overcast and it was a new moon. Both lay together, still. Mary's voice broke through the darkness with a question. "How could Ghidai have called Jesus, Emmanuel?"

"I wondered about that too. I know that Moses' second wife was a Cushite woman. Ever since then there has been a connection between Israel, Egypt, and Ethiopian tribes. It is no surprise that she knew the names Abraham, Isaac, Jacob, and Moses. They must also know about the expected Messiah. But when she called Jesus Emmanuel I . . . well, I became amazed. Why would she have called our child Emmanuel?"

"Why would anyone call him Emmanuel?" Mary whispered in the dark. Together they reached out to each other and lay waiting for sleep to come.

Ghidai also lay awake next to her sleeping child. Never in her most impossible dreams did she expect to be filled with good food, lying, clothed in beautiful garments, ready to sleep in a safe, cozy room with blankets on soft, clean hay and straw. She looked out into the darkness through the open window. The door to their room was not locked. She and Yemane could easily slip out into the dark night, she thought. But she felt safe here. She felt her child was safe. She wondered if she should follow through with her plan to escape and find her way back to Ethiopia together with her son. She would never forget the terror she had felt when the fighting had started in their village. Her husband had been killed and she and Yemane had been dragged onto a ship that sailed many days and weeks. South at first, then east, and finally north they sailed, on a dreadful journey that ended in Egypt. She had believed all would end for her and her son in certain death. Then, she thought of the man Joseph, and his wife and child, Mary and Jesus. They had brought her and Yemane to their home and shared food with them at their table. Something drew her to the child, Jesus. She had no answers to the questions in her mind that night but she allowed her exhaustion to lead her into sleep, deep sleep. She and Yemane would still be in Joseph's home when the morning came and she was comforted.

Joseph woke first and looked over to Mary, who appeared to be in a deep sleep. She looked beautiful! His heart filled with love for her and he didn't want to disturb her sleep. He moved out of bed carefully and quietly to wash and dress. He took a box out from its hiding place in a dressing table he had made. He had built the piece of furniture with a special hidden compartment to hold valuables. When he opened the box, he was reminded that he had quite a lot of money. He thought about all the money Panthera had faithfully sent each month by way of traveling soldiers from Judea to Alexandria. Since he had an income from working for Amsu they never needed to use the money Panthera sent. Maybe they would begin by using some of Panthera's money to buy wood for furnishings he would build for Ghidai and Yemane. Mary knew where to find the money and he would encourage her to use whatever she needed for textiles she could use to sew into clothing, and food and wine as she would purchase for their second marriage celebration. The Sabbath would be here again and he felt excited as he took an ample amount of the money and replaced the box into the compartment.

He went to eat breakfast and was surprised that even Jesus and Yemane had not awakened. After he was finished eating, he walked back into the bedroom to kiss Mary. She stirred and he said, "I'm off to work. I'll invite Amsu, Seth, Pepi, and their families for our second marriage and wedlock celebration. You need to go shopping and purchase what Ghidai needs to sew clothes for herself and Yemane, and buy food and drink for what you think we need for the celebration. I took money to buy wood and will return home after work to take the burro to retrieve my purchase. I plan to have their beds built by tonight. I love you, Mary."

Joseph kissed Mary and she said, "Calm down, Joseph. You're not going to be able to work properly until you calm down."

"I'm excited but by the time Seth and I reach work my feet will be back on the ground." With that he turned and was gone.

Mary thought, "This will be a good week."

The day progressed and Mary tried to explain to Ghidai that she was going to the market to purchase goods. Ghidai acted as if she understood and motioned that Jesus could stay home with her and Yemane. Mary asked Jesus if he would feel comfortable alone with Ghidai and Yemane, and Jesus said, "Of course, Yemane and I need to explore the backyard together, especially the creek."

"Jesus, I want you to watch and obey Ghidai. You may not explore the creek without her presence. You must be careful around that water. It may be shallow but it can still be dangerous."

"All right," Jesus answered. He turned to Yemane and said, "Come on."

Mary looked at Ghidai and said, "I won't be too long." By the look on Ghidai's face Mary was confident she had understood.

Mary enjoyed her day shopping. She bought beautiful cloth for Ghidai and Yemane. She bought thread and needles to use for sewing. She bought bottles of wine and dried fruit and meat, flour and sugar. She was glad she had brought the burro to help her carry all her purchases home. The burro also seemed pleased to be with her on her shopping trip. As she headed home with her goods, she reviewed in her mind, deciding she would bake this week and buy perishable goods Friday evening.

When Mary came home, Yemane and Jesus were sitting on the floor in the front room playing together with the wooden shapes Joseph had made for Jesus. Jesus looked up at his mother and ran to her to hug her around the legs. Ghidai entered the room and immediately saw that Jesus was hugging Mary and preventing her from moving. Mary's arms were full of goods and Ghidai gently pulled Jesus away from his mother and began to take the goods from Mary's arms and sling.

"Ghidai, come and see." Mary walked into the kitchen and was surprised to see lunch laid out and ready to be eaten. Mary put the bottle of wine, fruit, and other staples into the cupboard. She proceeded to spread the cloth selections she had bought in front of Ghidai. Ghidai ran her hand over the textiles and cooed with delight. Mary gave Ghidai the thread and needles made from the bones of fish and pointed to Yemane and then back to her. She lifted the cloth and placed it into Ghidai's arms. Ghidai's eyes welled up with tears as she looked at Mary and placed one hand on her own heart. She then directed Mary to sit down and eat and simply called Jesus and Yemane to the table. When they came to the table, she examined their hands and sent them to wash. Mary looked at Ghidai and put her hand on her heart as a gesture to express her gratitude toward her also.

The boys ran in and presented their hands to Ghidai, who spoke to Yemane, directing him to sit down. Jesus followed Yemane's lead and sat down also. They ate together but Mary talked with Jesus, and Ghidai talked with Yemane. When they were finished, Ghidai looked to Mary and expressed with body language that the morning had gone well while she was gone. Mary responded in the same way and thanked her for her care of the children and the house. Ghidai bowed and began to clean up the dishes they used for lunch. Mary intervened and indicated that she would clean up from lunch and take care of the boys. She directed Ghidai to take the cloth she had bought and feel free to use her time as she wished, maybe to sew clothing for herself and Yemane. Ghidai bowed and smiled as she took the cloth, needles, and thread and went to her room.

Mary called the boys in from their play outside after she finished cleaning the dishes and put them away. She instructed the boys to lie down in the front room to take a nap. They obeyed and fell asleep quickly. Mary proceeded to begin baking for their second marriage ceremony and accomplished more than she anticipated while the boys slept and Ghidai sewed.

Joseph returned from work and was still excited about making furniture for Ghidai and Yemane. He came into the kitchen as Mary was finishing her baking. Yemane and Jesus had awakened from their nap but played quietly in the front room until Joseph walked in. They followed him into the kitchen.

"Something smells good in here," he said. He kissed Mary. "I'll take the boys and the burro to collect the wood I purchased and begin to make beds for Ghidai and Yemane. I think I'll be able to finish their beds tonight. What's for dinner?"

Mary gently pushed them all out of the kitchen. "Just go and do what you need to do. I'll have dinner ready when you return."

With Ghidai's help, Mary was ready to present dinner when the boys and Joseph returned. Mary and Ghidai worked side by side, and they both felt as if communication flowed easily between them even though words were not used. Mary was truly appreciative of Ghidai.

After they all shared the evening meal Joseph went directly to work on the construction of the beds. The boys helped. Yemane and Jesus worked at handing wooden boards to Joseph up through the opening to the second floor. Then they climbed the ladder and stayed with Joseph, watching him work and display his carpentry skills as he made the beds.

Mary and Ghidai sat in the front room. Together they worked on the clothes Ghidai had begun to sew. Mary learned from Ghidai as she sewed and Ghidai learned from Mary as she showed her what she knew about weaving shawls and blankets. They enjoyed each other's company and smiles.

As night began to fall Joseph came down with the boys and announced that the beds were ready to be filled with hay and straw and covered with blankets. Ghidai was shown that the space on the second floor was her place with Yemane. When everyone climbed the ladder to the second floor with Joseph, Ghidai looked at the beds and tears came to her eyes. Joseph misinterpreted her tears and tried to explain that he would be making more furniture for them but she would have to be patient. But Ghidai placed her hand on her heart and then placed it on Joseph's chest. She looked at Mary, who smiled and said, "Joseph, she is overwhelmed with gratefulness." Mary looked at Jesus, who was standing, holding Yemane's hand. "It's time to sleep. Jesus, come with me to your room and Dad and I will say good night."

Joseph, Mary, and Jesus descended the ladder. Before going to Jesus' bedroom, they washed in the basin that Joseph had rigged to bring a flow of water from the stream that flowed approximately ten cubits under their feet, in the ground. As they washed Joseph said, "I plan to get water to run up to the second floor for Ghidai and Yemane. It won't be hard."

Mary looked at Joseph and touched the side of his face. "I love you and who you are, my beautiful husband. Do you know that?"

Joseph smiled and answered, "Yes, but keep reminding me." He bent down and lifted up Jesus, who was not washing but playing in the water. "All right, little man, enough. Off to bed we will go." He kissed Mary and said, "I'll see you in our bedroom."

Mary knew what Joseph meant and was pleased. It had been a good day and she looked forward to love with Joseph. They were not disappointed when they fell into each other's arms. Their lovemaking was always filled with pleasure and tonight was no exception.

Upstairs, Ghidai lay awake and listened to the deep breathing of her son. She knew he had had a fun day with Jesus. She wondered if he would always remember the terror and carnage he had witnessed in their village. After the fighting was over, she couldn't block remembering how they were captured and dragged away from what was left of their home. They had been taken to a large ship and chained in the lower deck. There was only a small opening in which they could see the water and bit of sky as the ship sailed to unknown destinations where there were always more people, and some children, added to their numbers in the lower deck. The new people chained in the lower deck never spoke the language that Ghidai understood. She knew they were sailing farther away from home and she was frightened for herself, her son, and their future.

The days that followed had been days and nights filled with horrible events that crowded her memory and ran together in hopeless obscurity. But Ghidai couldn't shake a specific memory to make it disappear, even now, in the safety of her present circumstance. She worked to drive it from her mind.

While chained to each other, and to links attached to the boards they had sat upon, two men would often come down to their deck and each would take a woman of their choice to some place above. Ghidai understood what was happening and every time they came to take their pick she would crouch down and babble as if she were insane. They never took her and it was worth the endurance of cockroaches that crawled over her face and into her hair. The rats had to be avoided, however, so she would not lower herself to the deck's floor when she detected their presence. She diligently protected Yemane by instructing him to roll up into a tight ball and sit very still at the end of the bench when she fell to the floor.

One terrifying night, there had been a great storm. The ship moved violently up and down and side to side. Water began to fill their deck. She believed they occupied the lowest deck so as the water rose, she became greatly alarmed, realizing they would be the first to drown. When the water rose to their waists, she had prayed that God would take them quickly. She was most distraught over the loss of her son's life. "Take care of him, my Lord and my God!" she had prayed, speaking the words out loud. Suddenly, the two men who had often come in the night to take their choice of women appeared and grabbed ten women and their children. They were dragged up the stairway to the upper deck and Ghidai had heard their screams as they were thrown overboard. The remembrance of this event was forever locked in her head. She remembered seeing through the small hole of the ship's window a flash of lightning. Through the small opening, she had watched as one of the women and her child fell into the raging sea. She had held Yemane against her chest and placed her hands over his ears and eyes.

Not long afterward, the two men had returned to their deck and ordered the ones left to bail water with the containers given to them. Yemane and Ghidai worked hard bailing water through the small opening next to them. As they bailed the storm subsided. All that was left of the water was a shallow puddle when they were ordered to stop bailing.

Through the night the waves had become more and more calm and Ghidai embraced Yemane, humming a song to him until she was sure he had fallen asleep. In this night, her child's breathing couldn't block out the memory of the women and children screaming with terror as they had been thrown overboard. She remembered she had looked out the small opening after the calming of the raging storm and sea to see the moon reflecting on the water. Her heart was pounding and she began to whimper and then began to cry outright. Her crying turned to loud wailing and screaming.

Joseph heard Ghidai's wailing first and rose quickly to pull his garment over his head while Mary did the same. Mary followed Joseph out of their room, down the hall, and up the ladder to Ghidai and Yemane's room. Yemane was sitting up crying, twisting the corner of the blanket in his hands.

Joseph bent over Ghidai and held her by her shoulders. She began to swing her arms, hitting Joseph in the face and chest. "Ghidai, Ghidai, you're here. You're all right. Ghidai, it's me, Joseph! It's Joseph!"

Yemane cried out, "Mama! Mama! No."

Joseph encouraged Yemane to come close to his mother and she turned to look at her son. Recognition finally came. She grabbed Yemane and looked at Joseph and Mary. With tears in her eyes her voice shook as she asked, "Joseph? Mary?" She began to talk in her native tongue but her body language pleaded for forgiveness. Joseph approached her slowly and held her until her hysteria subsided. He carefully and slowly took Yemane from her grip while Mary came close and held Ghidai. Mary said her name softly and rocked her back and forth.

Little Jesus climbed into the room and asked, "What's happening. Yemane, why is your mommy crying?"

Joseph said, "Mary, lie down with Ghidai and sleep with her. I'll take the boys to our room and sleep with them until the morning light comes." Mary nodded her head and helped Ghidai to lie down. She lay down next to her and stroked her forehead until she was asleep.

As Mary and Joseph fell asleep, they both wondered what horrors Ghidai and Yemane must have survived. Both prayed the same prayer asking God to bring emotional and spiritual healing to their souls.

Morning came and although the night before had been filled with dark memories for Ghidai, the sun shined with unadulterated brightness. Mary rose and looked at Ghidai, who was still sleeping. She rose and went down to find Joseph. He was in the kitchen eating fruit and bread. He was in deep thought.

"Good morning," Mary said.

He jumped a little, as if startled, and then looked at Mary and reached out to her. She came close and allowed him to place his head against her soft bosom. There were scratches on his face from Ghidai and the night before. She could tell they would heal quickly and knew that Joseph was thinking about the trauma Ghidai and Yemane must have endured.

"Can you handle this, Mary? I mean, surely this will not be the only outburst we will experience from Ghidai."

"Joseph . . . Ghidai's help to me yesterday certainly surpassed the trouble caused by her outburst. She is a human being who has been through incredible, terrifying, and dangerous experiences. Already, in this short time, I feel love for Ghidai and Yemane. It's only been two days that she and Yemane have come to live with us. They will be fine and so will you, Jesus, and I." She bent down and kissed the three scratches on his face. "Go to work. I'll have the evening meal ready as soon as you come home so you will have time to make another piece of furniture for Ghidai and Yemane. You are a wonderful carpenter and the pieces you make are beautiful. I plan to go the market again with Ghidai, Yemane, and Jesus. I will have her pick two pieces of cloth to hang on the walls in two of her rooms upstairs. For the rest of the day, after lunch, she and I will bake and prepare for our celebration that is now only four days away."

Joseph rose from the table and smiled. "If you are all right, I am fine," he said. He hugged her and kissed her and left to meet Seth to make their daily trip to work.

The day progressed as Mary planned. Ghidai found a textile with a pattern that seemed to remind her of something. She chose the same pattern to be hung in two rooms. When they came home from shopping Mary helped her hang the cloth in both rooms up against the walls. Ghidai seemed pleased, smiled, and hugged Mary.

After lunch the boys were placed in the front room for their afternoon nap and Ghidai and Mary baked. Mestha entered through the back door to meet Ghidai and ask Mary if she should bring anything to the celebration.

"No, Mestha. I want everyone to just come and be our guests on this very special day for us."

"Well, we'll be there." Mestha paused before she continued, "Panthera is not doing well." Mestha waited for Mary's response.

"I'm sure it is hard work for Isis to give him vigilant care?"

"No . . . in fact . . ." Mestha paused again.

Mary stopped what she was doing and gave Mestha her full attention. "What are you trying to tell me, Mestha? Come out with it."

"She loves him. Isis loves Panthera. Mary, he loves her. They talk constantly. She tends to him with tenderness and love. I would never have believed this could be possible if it was not happening before my eyes, in my house. Seth sees it too. He is pleased because Panthera is a Roman soldier as he was."

Mary stood in disbelief. "Mestha, how can two people fall in love so quickly?"

"If they are to love one another as partners . . . how can they not fall in love quickly?" Mestha paused again and then said, "Mary, I know what Panthera did to you but that is the way of a soldier. Rome encourages their young soldiers to rape. He was doing what he was ordered to do . . ." Mary glanced at her with disdain.

Mestha took Mary's hands into her own and said, "Please, Mary, you are my friend. I do not wish to insult you. But Isis is my daughter . . . she loves him. Please give me assurance that what had happened to you is forgiven and past. Surely God will use everything for his great goodness to be done."

Mary looked down. Mestha and Ghidai watched as she walked to the window and looked out. She sighed deeply. She thought of Jesus and turned around slowly. “Mestha, tell Isis and Panthera they are welcome to be present at our second marriage ceremony this Sabbath.”

Mestha approached her and said, “Mary, I know how to sing the wedding prayer. May I sing it at the ceremony?”

“You know the wedding prayer song?”

“Yes. Please allow me the honor of singing it for you and Joseph.”

“Yes, Mestha, I would be pleased and honored.” Mestha and Mary hugged each other and without another word Mestha left the same way she had come.

Mary returned to her work with Ghidai and did not seek to communicate until Joseph came home. He came in to greet Mary and Ghidai but took the boys upstairs immediately to work on the making of more furniture. Mary and Ghidai finished preparing dinner. Mary called up to the boys and Joseph. She asked them to wash and come to dinner.

While eating, Mary appealed to Joseph’s attention. “Mestha came by this afternoon.”

“Oh, did she? What did she have to report?”

“She told me that Isis has fallen in love with Panthera and he loves her.”

Joseph stopped eating and looked at Mary with an inquisitive expression.

“I told Mestha that Isis and Panthera were welcome to our celebration. She in turn asked if she could honor us by singing the wedding prayer. I’m very pleased that the prayer can be sung so I told her we both would be honored by her singing a prayer from our home and faith tradition. What do you say?”

“If it’s all right with you, it’s very well with me. I, too, would appreciate the wedding prayer sung at our marriage ceremony.” Joseph looked at Jesus, who was eating. Jesus looked up at Joseph, smiled, and redirected his attention to Mary. “What do you say about Panthera and Isis?” Joseph proceeded to ask Mary.

“I am at peace with it, Joseph. I hope Isis and Panthera will learn to love each other and remain faithful until death parts them. I believe they are both capable of this calling. But Jesus will remain my son. He will also remain your son.” Mary rose to take her plate to the sink. Ghidai followed Mary and began to remove the pottery from the table to be cleaned. When Joseph stood the boys popped up from their chairs and ran to the second floor in anticipation of continuing wood work and carpentry. Joseph walked to Mary and asked, “Are you sure you are accepting of Panthera’s presence at our marriage ceremony?”

“I’m sure, Joseph,” she said softly. “Go, the boys are waiting for you. Go finish your carpentry work.”

Joseph completed a table, two chairs, and a standing wooden shelf. When Mary and Ghidai came to see his completed work, Ghidai clasped her hands together and spoke words that certainly expressed appreciation. She moved the table against the wall by the hanging cloth, placed the chairs under the table and the shelf against the opposite wall.

Mary, Joseph, and Jesus bowed good night and descended the ladder to their own rooms. Jesus seemed more anxious than usual to lie down but he fell asleep before his prayers were completed. Mary kissed him good night and Joseph also went to kiss him good night but Joseph found a sleeping child. Once again, he lingered and gazed at Jesus. He was a beautiful child and the love he felt seemed to constantly grow stronger. He walked back to his room and found Mary fast asleep. "Good," he thought. "She needs her rest."

Joseph climbed in next to Mary and fell asleep before his prayers were finished. The night was still and everyone in Joseph's household was in deep sleep. Suddenly there was a rapid banging on the door. Someone was hitting the door with great urgency. Mary and Joseph rose to respond and were surprised that the din did not awaken anyone else in the house.

Joseph opened the door to meet Isis' panic. "He's going to die. Please help me, Mary! He's going to die!"

Mary stepped around Joseph and said, "Isis, who is going to die?"

"Panthera. He is very hot with fever and he's having trouble breathing! Please help us, Mary."

Grabbing her shawl, hoping it would ward off the night's chill, Mary came back to the door and told Joseph she would be home as soon as possible. Joseph stepped aside and let his wife pass and run to Panthera with Isis.

When Mary stepped into the house Seth and Mestha were waiting in the front room.

Seth said, "I'm afraid it may be too late for Panthera."

Isis screamed, "Don't say that! Don't you dare say that!" She proceeded to run into Panthera's room to fall on her knees next to his bed. Mary followed her.

Mary touched Panthera's head and felt the hotness sear through her fingers. She had never felt such a strong fever. Maybe Seth was correct in saying it may be too late for Panthera. She bent down close to Panthera and witnessed his labored breathing.

"Panthera . . . Panthera, can you hear me . . . Panthera?" He didn't respond.

Mary removed her shawl and told Isis to bring boiling water and a sharp knife. Isis obeyed and Mary began to remove clothing and blankets that had been wrapped around him. She thought, "Can't they tell he's hot with fever? Why do they cover him with so much clothing and blankets?"

When Isis returned Mary placed the sharp knife in the boiling water. "The knife must be clean. Go boil more water so we have it on hand as we need it."

Isis left the room to boil more water while Mary stripped Panthera and began to cut the cloth bandages to remove them from his body. As she removed the bandages, layer by layer, she smelled the unpleasant odor of damaged, stale flesh. Each bandage seemed more stained with blood and pus than the one before. Finally, she removed the last bandage that had been placed directly against the wound. She dropped her head and closed her eyes. She had never before seen such a neglected wound.

Isis came in with more hot water and Mary asked, "Isis, when was the last time you changed these bandages?"

Isis stared, blankly. "I didn't know the bandages were supposed to be replaced. Those are the bandages the wise astronomers put on him." She began to cry seeing Panthera's wound and realizing that it was her neglect that may be the cause of Panthera's death.

"No crying!" Mary ordered with kindness. "We've got work to do and you must do exactly what I tell you to do." Mary tried to hide her own dread and frantic sense of urgency. "Go to my house and tell Joseph we need the myrrh given to us by the astronomers." Isis turned on her heels and disappeared. "Panthera, you've got to show me strength. I need to see your will to live. You're a soldier. You can do this. It won't be easy, but you've got to fight for your life." Mary knew he couldn't hear or comprehend what she was saying because of his delirium, but she spoke in Greek with the hope he could obtain some small comprehension.

Mary began to soak the soiled bandages in the boiling water. Isis had boiled and brought pots and buckets of water and placed them all over the room. Mary took some clean cloths and placed them in another pot of hot water and pulled them out and held them in the air to cool down. She began to carefully clean the wound on his chest. Panthera immediately responded with painful crying out. Mary didn't stop her work at cleaning the wound. She dreaded as she thought and remembered that they would need to turn him over to clean the wound on his back also.

"Please, stop. Please, God, make her stop," Panthera moaned.

Mary didn't stop. Her heart began to pound wildly in her chest. She knew she must continue to cleanse the wounds completely. Isis came into the room out of breath. She held the box that contained the myrrh and frankincense.

Mary ordered Isis to take the cloths she had used to wash out Panthera's wound and boil them in water for a good while. She explained that the stains would not be cleaned out but the boiling water would make them clean enough to use again. "Keep the supply of clean cloths ready for me to use." Panthera whimpered in pain. Isis obeyed, though she wanted to sit by Panthera and comfort him. Mary sensed Isis' desire and said, "There will be time to comfort Panthera, but not now! Not until we clean his wounds thoroughly and have him rebound with clean bandages." Mary continued to clean Panthera's wound. "You are going to be all right, Panthera. Just keep breathing. You can do this."

When she felt satisfied that Panthera's wound on the front side of his chest was free of all pus and dead flesh, she took the frankincense and rubbed it into the wound as gently as possible.

She called for Isis who came quickly. "Ask your father and brother to come here and help us gently roll Panthera onto his left side so I can begin cleaning the wound on his back."

Isis ran out of the room and returned instantly with Seth and her brother. "We need to roll Panthera onto his left side. Isis and I will lift him from his shoulders. You and your father will need to lift him from his hips and gently move him onto his side."

Everyone listened to Mary and went to the spot where they could follow her instructions to turn Panthera.

"Are you ready?" Mary checked. "If your hands are placed where they need to be to lift Panthera, we can turn him carefully, hopefully without causing him to suffer too much more pain." All the participants nodded their heads, ready to do their part. "All right, we will move him together. One, two three, lift. Turn him carefully and put him down gently."

Panthera was lying on his side and Mary began to remove the bandages from the wound on his back. Fortunately, the wound was not as large so there was less flesh to clean. Mary began to work again. She felt tired, unsure that her work would prove to be successful in her effort to save Panthera's life. As she cleaned away at the wound Panthera said, "Please, no more," and he began to cry softly in pain. Mary kept cleaning and began to cry also. She felt she couldn't go on. The air in the room felt thick and smelled of rotting flesh. She became lightheaded and thought she might faint.

Suddenly a blast of cool fresh air blew into the room from the window. Panthera fainted and she cleaned the wound without fear that she was hurting him anymore.

When the wound was cleaned thoroughly, Mary rubbed a generous amount of frankincense and myrrh in and over it, as she had done to the wound on his chest. Together, with Isis, her brother, and Seth's help, they removed Panthera from the dirty bed and placed clean bedclothes stuffed with fresh straw under his motionless body. Mary let Panthera lie naked on the clean bedclothes as the cool breeze moved across the room from the window and out the door. Seth and Isis' brother left the room to go to bed themselves. They, too, felt exhausted from this ordeal.

Isis stood over Panthera and caressed his face with a gentle swipe of her hand. "I love him, Mary," she said with tears in her eyes.

Mary surprised herself when she answered Isis' statement with, "I love him too. I don't love him like I love Joseph, but to my surprise, I love him. I want him to live. I never thought this was possible." Mary seemed to be speaking to herself and for her purpose alone.

After sitting in silence for a while, Mary rose and began to cover the wounds with the clean bandages Isis handed to her as she needed them. Mary felt that the wounds had been exposed to the air long enough for his body to form their own, natural, dry closure. After working and wrapping his wounds, she covered him with a light sheet. Then, to Isis' wonder, Mary laid her hands on Panthera's wounds. She held her hands motionless against him on the different parts of his body that had been wounded. She whispered prayers. When she finished praying, she lifted her hands and looked up at Isis. His fever was still present. Mary told Isis that she could use a cloth dipped in cool water to cool his brow, under his arms, and behind his knees. Isis gladly attended to Panthera as Mary dropped her tired body onto a mound of clean hay and straw provided for Panthera's bed. It was then that she realized the extent of her own exhaustion.

Panthera began to come to consciousness and Mary rose to place her ear against his chest to listen to his breathing. When she heard the rattle of air within his chest as she listened, she knew the night was not over.

"Help me pull him up to sit," Mary said. Together she and Isis pulled him up by his arms to a sitting position. Panthera became completely conscious of his surroundings and asked to be left alone.

"No, Panthera. Isis and I are here to help you. I know this is extremely painful and hard for you, but you are going to live. You must cooperate with us. You must! I need for you to sit up with all the strength you have. Breathe in and out deeply, and cough." Panthera let his head drop onto his knees which he had painfully brought up to his chest, close to his body for balance. It gave him more pain and he groaned.

He tried to obey Mary and take a deep breath. Sharp pain struck him again, and it took his breath away. "No, I can't. I can't," he said. His eyes were full of tears.

"Yes, you must. Come now, take a deep breath," Mary implored.

"Please, Panthera. Do what Mary is telling you to do. We'll take deep breaths together. Now breathe with me." Isis took his hands into hers and breathed in deeply and then expelled the air. Isis shook his hands gently. "Come now, Panthera. Breathe with me." Isis' voice quivered and she fought back tears. She took a long, deliberate, deep breath in and held it in as she squeezed his hands, indicating that he must breathe in deeply also. He looked at Isis and made an effort to breathe in as deeply as she had.

Mary praised his effort, "That's it, Panthera. Good job! Breathe in again, only, this time breathe more deeply." Although Mary was exhausted, she spoke with as much enthusiasm she could draw upon.

Panthera tried to breathe as deeply as he could. "Yes. You're doing it! Now cough. Go on cough."

Panthera forced a cough and cried out in pain again.

Mary lifted his head with her hands and looked straight into his eyes. "Breathe again and cough. I know it hurts but we must loosen the mucus that is caught inside your chest. Do you understand me?"

He breathed again deeply and forced himself to cough. He felt mucus in his chest and coughed again. This time some greenish mucus came up into his mouth. Mary grabbed a cloth and told Panthera to spit the mucus out onto it. "We're not done yet, Panthera. Breathe in deeply again and hold your breath while I pound on your back.

"No. Please, no more. Please, Mary. I need to lie down."

"Panthera, do what I say. Go on. Breathe in deeply and hold your breath." Panthera obeyed and his expression indicated that the pain may take away his consciousness again. "Don't give up, Panthera. I want to see the Roman discipline of a soldier. Do you hear me?" Panthera let out his breath and coughed. More mucus came up into his mouth. As he spit the mucus out into the cloth Mary held, she said, "Breathe in deeply and hold your breath now." He obeyed. Mary moved around to his back and pounded it, avoiding the wound she had cleaned. This time Panthera coughed quite a bit and mucus continued to spew forth from the inside of his body.

Mary drove Panthera to continue the breathing, pounding on his back, and telling him to keep coughing. Every time Panthera obeyed, more mucus emerged in his mouth to be spit out. Mary coaxed and encouraged Panthera to continue the hard work. It seemed to go on for hours but Panthera obeyed Mary's insistence. His effort was accompanied with constant tears of pain and exhaustion.

Isis stepped up to Mary and said, "I'll do what you are doing. You are exhausted and we must not forget about your health and the health of your unborn child." Mary stepped aside, grateful for Isis' offer to take over the pounding on Panthera's back.

As Isis continued the work with Panthera, Mary drifted into a semiconscious state. She was drawn back to a memory of her mother when she was a very young girl. Her little baby brother, Joachim, had been very sick with a fever and was suffering with labored breathing. She remembered her mother doing to Joachim what she was now doing for Panthera. She had helped her mother through the night, but when morning came her little brother had died. Great grief had filled their home and her father, Joachim, had buried his youngest and last baby, who bore his name, at the bottom of a hill beyond a wheat field. Mary vaguely remembered the greatness of her father and mother's grief, but now she believed that, should Panthera die, she could not bear it.

Deep in these memories, Mary cried out for her mother and became aware that Panthera was also crying out for his mother. She rose and walked to him and encouraged him with comfort. "Your mother is near, Panthera. She gave you life. Let her memory give you comfort and strength. We are almost done. Let me see you breathe in deeply again and cough." Through tears, Panthera breathed in deeply and coughed. Very little mucus came up to his mouth and after he spit out the little that did come, Mary and Isis helped him lie down. Isis sat close to him and cooled his head with a damp cloth. Panthera fell into unconscious sleep and Mary also sat down to sleep.

"Isis, maybe you should rest now while you can. We'll wait for the morning light and see how Panthera fares."

"No, Mary. I can't sleep. I will attend to Panthera, but please go home and sleep in your home. If I need you, I'll come and get you. It will be dawn very soon. Go to your home and husband and sleep."

Mary knew there was nothing more she could do. She rose and placed her shawl around her shoulders. Isis walked over to her and placed her arms around Mary with deep gratitude and affection and said, "I know I am older than you, but I feel you have been more like a mother to me and Panthera than a friend. You have wisdom beyond me. Thank you, Mary. Thank you for Panthera. We love you."

Mary gently placed her hand against Isis' face and turned to walk home. When she entered her house Joseph was in the front room sleeping on the floor. Mary walked over to him, bent down, and awakened him. He awoke with a start.

"Thank God! You're home. Are you all right, Mary?" Joseph asked.

"Yes, I'm fine but I'm exhausted. I don't know if Panthera will be alive when the sun comes up, but I have lifted a prayer to God asking that his life be spared." Joseph stood up, walked close to Mary, and picked her up off her feet. He cradled her in his arms and carried her to their bed. He gently placed her down to sleep. He lay next to her and pulled the covers over her body and held her close. She fell asleep next to her husband in peace.

Morning came and went. Joseph had left for work and Ghidai took care of the boys, not waking Mary until she awoke on her own in the midafternoon. She woke suddenly and was disoriented. She thought she was at home with Joseph in the Qumran Settlement. She sat up and decided she would go to see her mother and began to dress quickly. Reality hit her like a lightning bolt. She heard the voices of Yemane and Jesus, playing in the front room. She remembered she was pregnant with Joseph's first child. She also remembered she was in Alexandria, Egypt. Most importantly, she remembered she and Joseph were to celebrate their second marriage this Sabbath and was happy to realize this celebration would bring them into holy wedlock. She became overcome with emotion as she sat on the bed and cried until she could cry no more.

As she continued to weep the door opened slowly and Ghidai emerged with dates, oranges, olives, and something hot to drink. Shyly, Ghidai presented the fruit and drink to Mary, as she gently placed her hand on Mary's in a clear gesture of care and empathy.

"Shalom," Ghidai spoke the word with love.

Mary smiled and felt deep gratitude. She reached out and softly embraced Ghidai saying, "Shalom, my sister. Where are the boys?"

Jesus ran into the room and jumped into his mother's arms, asking, "Is the poor man better?"

Mary smiled as she watched Ghidai's son Yemane follow Jesus' lead, jumping into his mother's arms, laughing and kissing her. Ghidai reprimanded the boys and ordered them both to go outside and play. There was no doubt that Ghidai felt their enthusiasm displayed outside behavior. As the two little boys were directed outside, Mary began to eat and drink. It had been a very long, difficult night but something rejuvenated her spirit. She was anxiously awaiting for the seventh-day Sabbath and the celebration of her and Joseph's second marriage into wedlock.

THE QUMRAN SETTLEMENT

ANNE AND JOACHIM WALKED the distance from their home to Elizabeth and Zechariah's home. When they arrived, little John was nowhere to be seen outside, giving Anne a sense that something was not right. They walked into the house and found Zechariah and John sitting on the floor. Both were weeping.

Zechariah looked at them and through his tears he said, "Elizabeth is dead. I'm not even able to bury her properly. She died yesterday afternoon and I could not carry her body out and bury her before the sunset." He placed his head in his hands and wept with deep sobs of grief.

John jumped up from his father's lap and ran out the front door. Anne tried to catch him but couldn't. "Let him go," Zechariah said. "He finds comfort in God's wilderness."

Anne walked to Elizabeth's bedroom and found her body lying on the bed. Her face displayed peace and this comforted Anne. She moved quickly and gathered oils from the kitchen and began to massage her body and prepare it for burial. Joachim had gone outside to the place Zechariah designated for her burial. He understood that it was not possible to bury Elizabeth in the place where all Essene women and children are buried because the circumstances surrounding Elizabeth's death prohibited the travel and arrangements. Therefore, Joachim continued to finish digging in the ground for Elizabeth's body to be laid not far from their house. Zechariah joined Joachim's effort to dig and realized he was not able to finish. When Joachim was finished preparing the grave, he walked slowly back to the house to find that Anne had Elizabeth's body prepared for burial, wrapped in large, white cloths. As Anne and Joachim carried her body to the grave site, Zechariah spoke the priestly prayers for burial. As Elizabeth was lowered into the grave, John emerged and stood still to watch and listen as his father spoke.

"You were my beloved partner in life. I remained faithful to you as you remained faithful to me." Zechariah continued to speak through his weeping while John moved next to his father and took his hand to hold tightly.

"I love you, Elizabeth. You gave me our son in your old age, as Sarah gave Abraham a son in his old age. My honor, respect, and love for you will be with me for the rest of my living days. God have mercy on us all."

After Elizabeth's death, John was moved to live with his Aunt Anne and Uncle Joachim. They, with the support of other relatives, placed Zechariah at the residence for aging, widower rabbis, in Jerusalem. Zechariah died three months later and received the proper burial rites of a high priest. At the ceremony of Zechariah's burial, Anne felt great sadness and made a dedicated decision to care for their son John, always allowing him the freedom to be in the wilderness as he wished, always allowing him to their home whenever he chose. John grew in strength and wisdom and the extended family enjoyed his presence among them.

PREPARATION FOR THE ESSENE SECOND MARRIAGE CEREMONY FOR MARY AND JOSEPH

MARY LEFT HER BEDROOM and Jesus ran to her and jumped up into her arms. He hugged her tightly. "You're up from sleep, Mommy! I already ate lunch. Are you sick?"

"No, darling, I was up all night helping that man you saw on the stretcher. He is very sick."

"Is he going to die, Mommy?"

Mary looked at Jesus and was intrigued by his accepting attitude of death. It was as if Jesus comprehended death as having no enduring consequence. "Jesus," she asked, "what do you know about dying?"

"Daddy always talks about his parents who died. I think when someone dies, people are sad, because they won't see them anymore. I think everyone dies. The one who dies is not sad. I think they know they are about to be changed. Yup, that's what I think."

Mary looked at Jesus with wonder and then said, "Well, I must go see the man that might die, and I must be ready to comfort the people who would be sad and miss him if he has already died."

"Can I go with you?" Jesus asked.

Mary remembered the fact that Jesus was the natural son of Panthera and felt it would not be right to deny either of each other's meeting this afternoon. "All right, Jesus. You must be a very good boy and be calm and kind to Isis and the man whose name is . . ."

"Panthera," Jesus said.

Mary didn't even bother to ask Jesus how he knew Panthera's name. His little ears seemed to hear a lot. "Let's go. Ghidai," Mary called. "Jesus and I are going to check on how Panthera is doing at Seth's house."

Ghidai peered around the door from the kitchen and smiled, indicating she understood. Yemane remained on the floor in the front room playing with building objects of wood Joseph had made for him and Jesus, adding to the already elaborate set he had made before for just Jesus. Luckily, Yemane and Jesus shared everything well.

The walk to Seth's house seemed unusually long. Mary walked slowly and held Jesus' hand. Many questions and thoughts raced through her head, like what if Panthera died after she left him and Isis; how did Jesus know about death the way he displayed; why had the astronomers not changed his bandages and cleaned Panthera's wounds properly; why did she feel like it was not until now that she could forgive Panthera and love him? Wind tunneled down the street between the rows of houses and caught Mary off guard. Her shawl wrapped around her face and tangled around her shoulders. She stopped to remove its blinding affect and was suddenly confronted with a whirlwind of understanding. She decided she could accept Panthera's death if he had died. She remembered the wind in the fig grove by her home, when something had revealed to her that she would become pregnant with a special child. Mary looked down at Jesus, who looked up to her, waiting in patience. Her anger toward Caspar, Melchior, and Balthasar disappeared as she remembered that they had left under the assumption she would be caring for Panthera, not Isis, who knew nothing of care for his condition. Yet, in the end she did care for Panthera through the most critical time of his ailing injuries. If he was dead, she knew she would have to wrestle with grief and guilt. Above all, she had never thought she could ever love her enemy, the man who had raped her, but she did love him. Jesus' patience gave way and he tugged on Mary's garment. She snapped out of her thoughts and said, "I'm sorry, Jesus." She stooped to his level, looked at him, and said, "I'm so afraid Panthera died after I left early this morning. I'm dreading going to find out."

"Oh, Mommy, I think Panthera is fine." Jesus hugged her around the neck. "Don't be afraid. It's just like thunder, it can't hurt you."

When they reached the home of Mestha and Seth, Mestha opened the door and stood before them with a broad smile! "Come in, come in! The wind is blowing in with you," Mestha said cheerfully.

Mestha took Mary and Jesus directly to Panthera's room. Panthera was sitting up with Isis. Both were smiling. Jesus ran up to Panthera and squealed. "Are you feeling better? You look better!"

Panthera reached out and took Isis' hand and then stroked Jesus on the head. "Yes. I'm feeling better."

Mary stood frozen by the door. Panthera looked at her and said, "I did what you said and you made me well."

"No, Panthera, you made yourself well. I'm so glad you're fine!"

He looked at her and raised Isis' hand to his mouth to kiss it. "I've never felt better. Are you really glad I'm fine?" Mary nodded to him. "I'd say that's a miracle."

"Yes, it is," Mary agreed and came close to Panthera's bed, next to Jesus.

With delight, Jesus said, "I'm glad you're better too!"

"So am I. So am I," said Isis.

Mary told Panthera he needed to rest and drink hot drinks to help loosen any mucus that could collect in his body again. "Keep coughing and breathing deeply. Isis, you must clean his wounds and change the bandages every day. Please douse the wounds with frankincense. It helps the healing and keeps the wounds clean."

Isis nodded and Panthera took a deep breath to show off. Mestha came into the room with hot soup for Panthera, who said, "I'm actually hungry and feel I can eat again."

Jesus watched Panthera eat the soup with ravishing fervor. "Is that soup good? Do you need someone to eat with you? I don't like soup that much but maybe Isis can eat with you."

Isis rose from her place and returned with a bowl of soup for herself. She sat next to Panthera. Jesus smiled. "Good," he said.

Mary took Jesus' little hand and said, "We need to go home now and let Panthera rest. They will be at our house for the marriage ceremony on the Sabbath."

Jesus obeyed and he and Mary turned to go home. At the bedroom door Mary stopped and turned to say, "Panthera, God has truly blessed you and all of us."

The following three days were spent in preparation for the ceremony. By sunset on the sixth day (Friday) everything was completed. Tomorrow morning all that would need to be done was the placing of wine and food out on the appropriate tables.

Joseph had completed the building of a cupboard and a special piece of furniture with a secret compartment that he revealed to Ghidai alone. She was thrilled with her new home and family. She, too, was excited about the upcoming celebration and had a grateful heart for Mary, Joseph, and Jesus. Yemane also displayed a security he didn't have when they had first come to the house. From the very first day, he played well with Jesus and seemed to take on the role of a bigger protective brother.

There were no more outbursts from Yemane or Ghidai, and Joseph felt pleased that she seemed to be secure and strong in spite of the trauma she had endured. He also possessed great gratitude for Ghidai and Yemane helping all of them. So, when Joseph returned from work late on the sixth-day (Friday) afternoon he walked into the house to find Ghidai sitting on the floor with Yemane and Jesus in her lap. They all looked up at Joseph when he entered and smiled. Jesus and Yemane left Ghidai's lap and hugged Joseph's legs.

"Where's Mary?" Joseph asked. Ghidai placed a finger over her mouth and then pointed in the direction of their bedroom. Joseph found Mary lying on the bed dozing. "Well, well, well. How is my lady of leisure?"

Mary sat up and said, "Fine. I'm ready, Joseph. I'm ready to be in holy wedlock with you." She stood up and came to his open arms, "I love you so much!"

"I love you too." He spun her once and held her while looking out the door of their bedroom into the hall. He continued to hold her as flashes of memories raced through his mind. He saw his mother and his father. He saw Mary, dancing in the rain when she was four years old. He saw Joachim and his stone face as he refused to believe Mary had been raped. He saw Anne, sitting at his table in his home at the Qumran Settlement pleading for him to understand her circumstances. He saw Zechariah and Elizabeth holding Baby John. In his mind's eye he saw the face of Anna the prophetess, and Simeon, lifting Jesus up with tears in his eyes. He saw Beth and Joe, the shepherds, Rachael, Benjamin, and the children, Lazarus, Martha, Levi, and Baby Mary who would be a baby no longer. He remembered Jarius, Panthera, and the friendly soldiers who had brought them to this house. He pictured Amsu and Pepi and many of the other coworkers with whom he worked. He remembered the three astronomers and saw images of Ghidai and Yemane laughing. They all seemed to radiate light in his mind. When he opened his eyes, he saw little Jesus standing in the doorway watching him hugging Mary. He smiled at Jesus, who smiled back and shrugged his little shoulders, turned and tiptoed away. Joseph held Mary more tightly and felt that all was truly good.

THE SECOND MARRIAGE CEREMONY

THE SUN BURST FORTH, bathing the morning in light. It would be a beautiful day. Joseph rose and walked to the window in the front room. He opened the shutters and the light poured into the room and filled it. He walked to the other shutters and opened them also. The light was dazzling. He turned and saw Jesus standing quietly in the doorway. Joseph smiled, crouched down, and opened his arms to Jesus. Jesus took his inviting cue and ran into his embrace. Joseph lifted him up in a close embrace and said, "Look, Jesus. Look at the sun coming up to shine all its glory on us."

Jesus looked and the light from the sun reflected in his eyes. He looked at Joseph and said, "I like the sun, Daddy. It makes me feel happy. Does it make you feel happy?"

"Yes. It makes me feel happy, especially today, because today Mommy and I will become husband and wife until death parts us."

"Does that mean you will be my mommy and daddy forever?"

"Yes, as long as we are alive and forever in eternal memory."

"But you're not going to die, ever."

Joseph sat down and placed Jesus on his lap and began to explain to Jesus, as best he could, that he had also believed his parents would be alive with him forever but that they died when he was still a boy. He talked about how sad he was when his parents died but in time, he learned to accept the ways of the Almighty God. "When my mother and father died, I felt very alone. I didn't know that God had a plan for me to have a wife and then a son. Now we have Ghidai and Yemane, and Mommy's going to have another baby. I'm not alone."

"Where are your mommy and daddy now? Even if they are dead, they must be someplace."

Joseph smiled and said, "I believe they are someplace. But where they are, I'm not sure right now, so I don't know."

"Sometimes, do you cry because you miss them?"

"Yes. Sometimes I cry because I miss them but I don't stay sad because God brings us new life and new people to love, with a promise we shall all be together again."

Jesus sat still on Joseph's lap for a moment and then hugged Joseph saying, "I'm here and I love you. You can wait to see your parents again, can't you?"

"Yes, Jesus. Yes." They sat together in silence and Joseph felt a kind of peace he had not experienced before. He held Jesus and Jesus fell asleep in his arms. He laid his own head back and dozed until he heard Ghidai and Yemane in the kitchen. Mary came into the front room and motioned for Joseph to stay still with Jesus. She whispered, "I'll begin getting ready for our celebration. I love you." She kissed her fingers and touched his mouth. He gladly obeyed her.

The afternoon came quickly but all was ready. Amsu and his family were the first to arrive. He carried a piece of papyrus and explained that he had registered them as lawful husband and wife, as was the custom in Egypt. Mary and Joseph were pleased and honored by his gift. Pepi and his family came shortly after Amsu and presented Mary and Joseph with a fine bottle of wine. Pepi instructed them that it was not to be opened until after their first anniversary. He brought out a musical pipe and explained that he would supply music with one of Seth's sons, who played a stringed instrument. Pepi's three children gave Jesus a birthday gift of a toy boat. They ran to the creek with Yemane to check its seaworthiness. Mary's friend Qadesh, from next door, arrived with her husband, Nua. They congratulated them with a loaf of bread.

As the guests moved through the house, they spread out into the yard space in the back. Mestha, Seth, and their three sons entered. They walked to the back of the house and placed a structure up and adorned it with beautiful fabric, which they draped over its top and sides.

"Mestha, the canopy you created is beautiful! Thank you so much!" Mary exclaimed.

"A beautiful canopy for a beautiful couple," she said and stroked Mary's cheek with her hand. She hesitated and then said, "Isis and Panthera are sitting in your front room."

As Pepi and Seth's eldest son began to play their instruments Mary and Joseph retreated to their bedroom and placed their dazzling white garments on for the celebration and exchange of vows. When they walked out, they both turned and entered the front room to greet Isis and Panthera. Isis spoke her congratulations in Greek, which Mary now understood well. They embraced. After looking back at Panthera, Isis proceeded to walk out to the back of the house where the other guests were gathered.

Panthera struggled to stand before Mary and Joseph and they could see this caused him great physical pain. When he finally established security, using a wooden cane to support and steady himself, he spoke. Mary listened to the sound of his words and understood his emotion, although he spoke in his native tongue, Greek, which Mary also comprehended in every word.

"I give you great honor on this day of your wedlock. I . . . I am constantly tortured with thoughts about what I had done to you." It took all he could do to muster the courage to look at Mary to say, "Now that I am in love with a woman from whom I do not ever wish to be parted, not ever . . . I . . ." Panthera could stand no more. He sat down and began to weep. Mary and Joseph stood still before him and allowed him to finish what he felt he needed to say. "I don't know anything except that I love Isis. She has given me life by caring for me this last week. My fever is gone but I know more healing must happen. As I lie and wait for my body to heal, I'm plagued by what I've done in my life . . ." He looked at Mary, saying, ". . . to you. I know you graciously forgave me when I saw you in your home and I want to believe it's genuine." Panthera directed his words to Joseph and spoke in Latin, knowing Mary would not understand. Joseph didn't translate their meaning to Mary. "The boy . . . Jesus . . . is he . . . is he yours, or is he mine?" Panthera looked to Joseph with deep regret.

Joseph saw no intention on the part of Panthera to take Jesus from them so he translated, telling Mary what Panthera had asked, and answered, "He is your natural child, but he is my son."

"I am going to marry Isis before I return to Judea to finish my assignment. Isis will travel with me to Judea when I am well enough to return. She will stay near the tent camp where I will be stationed and we will see each other often. I will be faithful to her alone. I love her and she has declared her love for me. We will not have children because her illness from the blackwater fever has made her incapable of bearing children. I accept this. I love her greatly and it has cancelled out my desire for children of my own. I feel I don't deserve children. I long for her. Today, I, too, will give my silent vow to be faithful to her until death parts us." Panthera's eyes welled up with tears. "May I please see the child Jesus and give him this gift?" Panthera took from his belt a large gold coin and held it out in his hand for Mary to see. "Please, let Jesus accept this gift from me and let me touch him and hold him in my arms."

As Joseph finished telling Mary what Panthera said, she placed her hands over her face. She never thought there might be a chance that Panthera would take Jesus from them. She wanted these horrible possibilities to end. She realized that she had often pretended that Jesus was conceived from Joseph but knew this was not true. As she stood with her face covered by her hands, she saw a flash of light though her eyes were closed. The flash of light compelled her to understand that Joseph was the true earthly father of Jesus, not Panthera. She realized that Joseph was the father who had remained with her and Jesus from his conception. He protected them and loved them. He was Jesus' father both relationally and spiritually. Mary lowered her hands from her face and turned to Joseph. In Greek she said, "Take Jesus to Panthera so he can give his gift to him." Joseph turned and left Mary and Panthera in the room alone together. Mary stepped closer to Panthera, who found it hard to look at her again. She placed her hands on his head and said in Aramaic: "May the Lord bless you and keep you. May he make his face shine upon you and be gracious to you. May he give you peace, now, and for all your living days, Panthera." Then in Greek she said, "Let this be done between us. Let Jesus love and live with his earthly father, Joseph. When he is older, he will be told the truth about his conception. He will also be taught about the power of forgiveness and he will not hate you, as I do not hate you."

Jesus ran into the room without Joseph and announced, "Daddy told me to come in here to see the man that was hurt." As soon as Jesus saw Panthera sitting up before him, he approached him and said, "You're getting better every day, aren't you?"

"Yes, I feel better every day that passes. Come here, Jesus, I have a gift for you." Jesus came close and Panthera reached for Jesus' hand and placed the gold coin in his palm.

Jesus turned to his mother and said, "More gold, mommy." He gave the coin to his mother and asked her, "Can you take it for me?" Mary took the coin from Jesus and prompted Jesus by saying in Aramaic, "What do you say to Panthera?"

Jesus ran to Panthera and hugged him. "Thank you!"

Panthera held Jesus longer than usual and began to cry. Jesus didn't seem to mind and patted his back with his little hands. When Panthera finally released Jesus, he stroked Jesus' hair and said in Latin, "You are the blessed child we have all been waiting for to bring us the message of truth and life."

Jesus said innocently to Panthera, "I'm learning your words, too, but I still don't know what you said."

Panthera looked at Mary and then said to Jesus, "I love you." With a distant look, from a time long ago, Panthera said in Greek, "Go play." Jesus understood and turned to run outside.

Mary caught him and asked him to find his daddy and ask him to come in to help her help Panthera to the backyard for the ceremony under the canopy that Seth and Mestha had prepared.

Joseph came to her quickly and together they helped Panthera stand and walk to a place where he could sit in the yard. Mary was pleased when she realized that Ghidai had set the food and drink out to enjoy after they spoke their vows. She looked at Ghidai and nodded a thank you.

Seth's son and Pepi began to play a song that invited the guests to gather around the canopy. Even the children came and stood reverently. When everyone was in place and still, Joseph turned to Mary and said: "You are my betrothed, my bride, and now my wife until death parts us. I will be faithful to you and walk beside you in life; forsaking all others, I will cling to only you."

Mary said to Joseph, "You are my betrothed, my bridegroom, and now my husband until death parts us. I will be faithful to you and walk beside you in life; forsaking all others, I will cling to only you."

Mestha sang the wedding prayer as her son accompanied with a stringed instrument. Her voice was beautifully clear and all stood mesmerized by her gift of singing. Amsu stepped forward with two goblets of wine and gave one each to Mary and then to Joseph. Mary and Joseph drank the contents and threw the goblets against a rock close to them. The goblets shattered into a thousand pieces that mixed together and looked like sand on the ground. Everyone cheered and Pepi began to play a joyful tune on his pipe. The children ran for the food that had been set on the tables while Ghidai poured wine for anyone holding an empty goblet.

The festivity continued for hours and Joseph was amazed that Amsu and his wife danced so well. Qadesh and Nua also danced well. They both seemed to take joy in trying to teach the children to dance. Surprisingly, the children learned quickly.

Qadesh looked at Nua and asked, "Wouldn't it be wonderful to have children of our own?"

Mary noticed that Nua snapped at Qadesh and declared, "I am the one who will decide when to have children."

Jesus danced with the most joyous emotion as Yemane danced with his mother. Mary danced also, and Joseph tried. Mary told him that he needed to stop thinking about how to dance and just dance. She kissed him as he tried all the harder and she simply said, "I'm glad I never chose you to be my husband based upon your ability to dance."

Joseph answered back, "Well, if I remember correctly, I chose you because you could dance. Now I see that it is not your ability to dance that drew me to you, it was your sense of inner freedom."

When the sun started to set the guests began to leave. All had a good time and Mary felt as if the memory of their second marriage ceremony would remain in her heart for a lifetime. As Joseph helped Seth take

Panthera home Isis approached Mary and simply stated, "Thank you for your forgiving kindness."

Mary embraced Isis and whispered into her ear, "Love him well, and be faithful to him."

Ghidai cleaned up after the wedding as Jesus and Yemane continued to play with the boat in the creek. She finished the work of putting all things in their proper place and told Jesus and Yemane to come in, wash, and go to their beds. They were happy to obey. Ghidai came to Jesus first and sat with him while he said his prayers. She kissed him on his forehead and said what she had practiced to say in Aramaic, "Happy special day!" Jesus smiled with happy acceptance, kissed Ghidai, and turned on his side to sleep.

When Ghidai climbed the ladder to the second floor she found Yemane fast asleep. She bent down and kissed him and went to her bed. She, too, fell asleep quickly.

Mary and Joseph took their gowns off and lay down together naked. They kissed each other and touched each other and loved each other until they both fell asleep filled with peace and complete satisfaction.

LONGING FOR HOME

ALTHOUGH LIFE WAS GOOD for Mary and Joseph, they often wondered about Ghidai and Yemane. Both were learning Greek quickly, and Joseph made a point of it to speak Aramaic just in case she chose to stay with them as part of their family and return with them to Judea. In truth, Mary loved Ghidai and Yemane, as did Joseph, but it was Jesus who displayed the greatest love and affection toward both. He had certainly accepted Ghidai as an aunt, or more like a mother, and he loved Yemane like an older brother, respecting him most of the time but standing his ground when he needed.

Two months had passed since they had brought Ghidai and Yemane to their home and Mary was concerned that if given the opportunity they would choose to go home to Ethiopia. Joseph had told Mary that he would give Ghidai the choice to go after one month but he hesitated because Mary's hope for their permanence as part of the family was so strong.

It was evening, the boys were asleep in their beds, and Ghidai was in the kitchen putting the pottery from supper in their places in the cupboard. Joseph and Mary were sitting in the front room and Mary was feeling very tired. She was five months pregnant and movement had become cumbersome but not impossible. She knew she could manage the house and take care of Jesus too, but she wouldn't choose to be without Ghidai.

"I will talk openly and honestly with her," Joseph said. "We must be prepared to let her return to her home if she chooses. We can always hire another to help you and be with us."

"That's not the point. I can do what needs to be done around here. With Isis gone to Judea with Panthera, Mestha and her boys would always be ready and willing to help me if I needed extra help . . . Joseph, I love Ghidai. I love Yemane. Most importantly, Jesus loves them."

Joseph stared at the floor as he listened to the sounds of the pottery being put away. "Mary, we need to give the choice to them. We can't keep them because of our desire. We need to think about their desire."

"I know . . . I'm ready to give them that choice. They're not ours to keep." Tears fell as Mary reached out for Joseph's hands. "I never thought that love could hurt so much."

Ghidai walked into the front room drying her hands on a small cloth. She saw that Mary was crying and stepped close to her. She sat down and placed her long fingers on Mary's cheeks to wipe her tears away. She asked gently, "Why do you cry?"

Mary took a deep breath and said, "Ghidai, Joseph must talk to you about something."

Ghidai looked at Joseph and stood up. "No, Ghidai. Sit down, please."

Ghidai moved to another spot where she could sit and see both of their faces.

Joseph sighed. He wasn't sure he could explain what he needed to say in simple terms because he knew Ghidai was not yet completely fluent in any language he spoke. He prayed and began. "Ghidai, Mary, Jesus, and I love you and Yemane very much." He looked to see Ghidai's reaction. She smiled and placed her hands on her own heart and reached out and touched Joseph and Mary.

"We hope you're happy here . . . with us?" Ghidai nodded but her expression changed. She looked at Joseph with an inquisitive expression, as if she was not sure why Joseph was talking this way.

Joseph cleared his throat. "Ghidai. When you came to our home, Mary and I decided you should be allowed to go back to Ethiopia if you wanted to go home. I will pay to make sure you and Yemane make it home in safety if you choose to go." Ghidai didn't move. She tried to process his words and was not sure she understood.

Joseph tried again. "Ghidai, you are free. If you want to leave us you are free to go home. You may go home . . . to Ethiopia. You may go home with Yemane. I will make sure you get home if you want to go."

Ghidai said softly, "We go home? Yemane and I go home?"

Joseph said, "Yes, Ghidai. If you want to."

Ghidai stood up and said, "I go to my room now. I go to think, yes?"

"Yes, Ghidai, go and think."

Ghidai turned and walked slowly to the hall. She glanced in to look at Jesus sleeping. She thought about how hard he and Yemane had played. She closed her eyes and saw his beautiful face, laughing, squealing, and expressing delight when he and Yemane discovered a new lizard or bug near the creek. She opened her eyes again and Jesus had not moved but she could hear his breathing and it comforted her. She turned to climb up the ladder to the second floor and looked in on Yemane. She felt a surge of love build in her chest. Something urged her to believe that these two young boys must be together. Joseph was offering her freedom. Freedom for what, she wondered? She remembered her life in Ethiopia. She remembered her husband. He was not a man like Joseph. He had made her work hard and he used to hit her and shake her if he was displeased with her. He had done the same to Yemane. Even so, when the fighting between tribes broke out, she was traumatized when she saw her husband fall to the ground with a spear in his chest. As they had dragged her and Yemane away, they didn't spare her but pulled her past the body of her husband lying on the ground. She remembered seeing that he was not dead. He was groaning.

She wondered if the God of Abraham, Jacob, and Isaac expected her to return to Ethiopia. What if her husband had recovered and was alive. Didn't Yemane deserve a father? She closed her eyes again and remembered how Joseph showed the boys how to cut wood and make it fit together. She saw Joseph laughing, playing together with the boys, often placing them on the burro's back together for a ride into an imaginary adventure. She loved Joseph and his gentle love for all of them. How could she take Yemane from this family? How could she take herself away from this family?

Early the next morning Ghidai rose to go and begin to prepare food for breakfast. She thought everyone was still asleep but when she entered the kitchen Mary was standing over a small basket of eggs she had collected. Mary looked up at Ghidai and said, "Peace be with you, Ghidai."

Ghidai walked up to Mary and threw her arms around her neck and began to cry. Mary reciprocated and held her tightly. "You don't have to go, Ghidai. Don't go, please don't leave us. I love you."

"I love you too, Mary."

Jesus walked in and climbed onto his usual chair that was made to raise him up to the table. Although it took him a little while to maneuver his placement facing the table he looked up, smiled, and said, "Let's eat brefskit."

Yemane was at his place before Joseph sat down. When he did sit down, he looked at the women and asked, "Was a decision made?"

Ghidai looked back at Joseph and said, "Your God is my God. Your people are my people. Your home is my home." Joseph looked at Mary, who was smiling with tears in her eyes.

That night, when the children and Ghidai were asleep, Mary and Joseph had a very serious talk about going home themselves. They had been gone for almost five years and Mary wondered if King Herod was no longer a threat. Joseph confided in her that he received news about Judea constantly. King Herod was still alive and well, contributing to the buildup of his palaces and Masada. Joseph knew they couldn't return home safely yet. As Joseph fell asleep, he thought about home and the Qumran Settlement. He wondered if Mary's family and the rest of the community had given up on waiting for their return. Dear God, he prayed, please let the baby in Mary's womb be a boy! He fell asleep before he could think of anything more.

THE BIRTH OF SALOME

THE MONTHS SPED BY and Mary was very close to the time of her delivery. Joseph continued to go to work but there was a plan to alert him to come home quickly should anything start to happen. Her time did arrive. It was midmorning. Seth's son ran to get Joseph when Mestha told him to bring Joseph home from work. She would be joining Ghidai to help with the delivery of Mary's baby. When Joseph arrived, he heard Mary's cries and remembered what it had been like when Jesus had been born.

Ghidai came out of the bedroom where Mary was and met Joseph as he walked into the front room. He asked, "Is everything all right!?!"

Ghidai smiled and said, "Yes." Mary cried out again and Joseph looked at Ghidai as if she didn't really know. Ghidai said, "Joseph, calm down and let life happen." She walked into the kitchen and Joseph walked closer to the door of their bedroom.

Ghidai came back and Joseph asked, "Where are the boys?"

"They are at Mestha and Seth's house with their eldest son." Joseph was impressed with Ghidai's almost instant ability to speak Aramaic and Greek so clearly.

"I want to be with Mary. Can I be with her?"

Ghidai smiled and said, "She is your wife. I would ask her if I were you."

Joseph walked into the bedroom and Mestha was attending to Mary, talking softly to her. Joseph knelt down next to the bed and said, "Mary, it's me, Mary. May I stay with you?"

Mary cried out again and Mestha looked to see if the baby's head was visible.

"All right. It won't be long now, Mary. Breathe deeply, that's it."

Mary yelled, "I have to push. I've got to push."

Mestha looked again and said, "Push if you must. I think you'll be fine. Go ahead and push."

Mary cried out with great effort and Joseph thought maybe they shouldn't have anymore children. It seemed too hard on the woman. Mary screamed.

"Mary, everything is all right. Go ahead, push . . . that's it. Here comes the baby!"

Suddenly the baby was in Mestha's hands. "Mary, Joseph . . . You have a beautiful baby girl!" Mestha took the baby, and she and Ghidai cleaned it together by rubbing salt over its little body and then rinsing it with fresh water. The baby was wrapped in clean cloths. Mestha brought the baby to Mary, who was no longer screaming in pain. Mary reached out and took the baby and held her close as Mestha and Ghidai waited for the afterbirth to be born. Then they massaged Mary's abdomen to calm and prohibit further contractions. Joseph stood and watched in awe as the women worked so skillfully.

"Joseph, do you want to hold your new baby daughter?"

Joseph looked at Mestha and said, "I need some fresh air. I'll be in the back." He turned and walked out of the room and out to the backyard. He moved under the tree and sat with his back against its trunk and looked up at the sky. He thought, "Why, God? Why have you given me a daughter now?" He had truly wanted a son. He had been fantasizing for months that they would return home and he would be able to present his son with pride. He leaned his head back and sighed. He didn't notice the trail of ants walking up the tree trunk. His leaning interrupted their path and the next thing Joseph felt were red ants crawling up his neck and biting ferociously as they moved up toward his head. Joseph jumped up and swatted at his neck. Some of the ants had found their way down his back and he jumped and twisted as he tried to rid his body of their nuisance.

Ghidai came to the backyard holding the little baby girl. "Joseph, Mary is sleeping now. She and the baby are fine. Do you want to hold your new firstborn?"

Joseph could not help himself. "No, Ghidai. Not now, please. I'm thinking."

Ghidai stood with the baby in her arms and said, "When I was growing up, I used to think the most important parent to me was my mother. Now, as a woman, I see that it was my father who gave me the strength that I have. He loved me and my sisters. God never granted him a son but it didn't seem to change his heart as he loved us and made us feel as if we had worth and importance." She paused and seemed to be searching for the correct words to speak. "You are the more important parent to this little girl. You can give her the message that she is important to the world because she is important to you, her father. Please hold your daughter. You need to give her a name

. . . I need to go and get Jesus and Yemane and bring them home to meet this new little girl." Ghidai stood and waited humbly before Joseph but Joseph said nothing.

"Mary had been abandoned by her father when she needed him most and he even took her name away and gave it to her sister."

Joseph looked at Ghidai with surprise. "How do you know that?"

Ghidai answered, "She told me." Ghidai hesitated and then with courage asked. "Joseph, do not delay giving your daughter a name . . . a name that shall never be taken from her."

Joseph sighed again. One lone ant on his neck gave him a bite. He slapped his neck and looked at Ghidai, feeling shame. "Give my daughter to me." He took the baby girl into his arms and truly looked at her. Unexpectedly, he felt a sudden surge of love that could not be held back. He looked up to Ghidai and said, "Go get the boys and tell them they have a new baby sister named . . . Salome, as was the name of my dear mother."

Ghidai turned with joy and ran to Mestha's house to bring Yemane and Jesus home to meet their sister. She knew they would be thrilled, more thrilled than finding a new lizard or strange beetle near the creek.

That night Joseph talked with Mary as she sat in bed nursing Baby Salome. "I'm pleased with the name Salome," she said. "It was your mother's name. You honored our daughter with your mother's name."

Joseph sat next to her and pulled the covers back to see Salome's little face. She was a beautiful baby. He was her father. Yet he felt unsure about fathering a daughter because he was used to having Yemane and Jesus. As if Mary understood his thoughts she said, "Joseph, you will be a wonderful father to this little daughter. I hope you are not terribly disappointed that I did not birth you a son."

Joseph was honest. "I was hoping for a son but I think God may have another plan that I need to accept. Although it is hard for me . . . but when I held Salome, I knew God had blessed me beyond my own ability to understand. Let me take Salome and place her down to sleep. We need to sleep because she will be up within a little while to nurse again. I remember how that goes."

Joseph took the baby from Mary, who turned and fell to sleep instantly. Joseph held his daughter for a long time and then placed her in the cradle he had made for Jesus when he was an infant and went to his bed to sleep also. Before his eyes closed, he prayed a prayer of thanksgiving but also asked for help to love his daughter properly.

Jesus and Yemane were thrilled to see Baby Salome again the next morning. After Mary had nursed Salome, she promised the boys that they would be allowed to hold her. Ghidai had to guard their parents' bedroom door because the boys were threatening to run in and disrupt Baby Salome's nursing. Finally, Joseph came out of the room and sternly instructed both of them to wait in the front room. The baby would be brought out to them when she was finished eating. Jesus and Yemane ran into the front room and sat down. Joseph followed them and said, "I'm serious. If you don't calm down you will not be holding Baby Salome."

Jesus looked at Yemane and said, "This is a serious situation. We need to calm down." This time Jesus pronounced the words perfectly.

Yemane nodded his head in agreement.

The door opened and Ghidai walked up to Yemane with the baby in her arms. "Yemane, you are the oldest so you will hold her first. Jesus, I want you to pay attention to how I will place Salome in Yemane's arms. Yemane, you need to stay seated and keep her in your arms the way I place her. She is only one day old and if she were to fall, she could be hurt very badly."

"I told you this was a serious situation," Jesus said again. Jesus watched as his new sister was placed in Yemane's arms. Yemane smiled down at the baby. Jesus sat patiently waiting for his turn, which finally came.

"She's so tiny!" Jesus exclaimed.

"When you were born you were also tiny," Ghidai smiled as she watched Jesus play with her fingers. He held her carefully with one arm to free his other hand to play with her little hands.

"Her hands are so tiny too." Jesus had calmed down completely and said, "Someday you will grow up like me and Yemane. We will play with you and teach you everything!"

Ghidai took the baby from Jesus' arm and instructed the boys to wash, dress, and come for their breakfast. Joseph had been standing the entire time behind Ghidai. He was watching the boys' reaction to Salome. They were genuinely happy a little girl was born. To them it was a baby, a new human being, and she held no rank of importance based upon her gender. Neither did the boys show any judgment about her gender. They loved her and accepted her with open, excited arms. Joseph felt shame.

Ghidai detected his shame and she said, "Joseph, I think it will be a long time before any culture realizes the full worth of a female. For now, I guess we have to learn it one father and brother at a time. I'd say Salome has a good start."

Joseph smiled sheepishly and mumbled that he was going to work. He left without saying goodbye to the boys or Mary. Ghidai stood alone in the front room and prayed that he would come to understand the mighty goodness of God apart from his own delusional desires. She also prayed that God would grant them another child and that both Mary and Joseph would be blessed with a son. It seemed so important to Joseph. As she finished her prayer the door opened. It was Joseph.

"I forgot to say goodbye to Mary and the boys."

Ghidai smiled as he passed her to find Jesus and Yemane. He yelled to the boys and they yelled goodbye to him. He came to his own bedroom door and walked in to say goodbye to Mary. He found her crying.

"Why are you crying, Mary?"

"Oh, Joseph, you wanted a boy. Is it my fault the baby is a girl?"

Joseph sat still close to her. With his hands he wiped her tears and said, "I can't deny I was hoping for a son first. But in the years we've been living here, I've learned so much. I've also made mistakes in my thinking. I know God is teaching me." He paused. "I think he's trying to teach me that His ways are not my ways, and His thoughts are not my thoughts. I love you, Mary. That is foremost in my heart. I also love Jesus and Yemane. You could say I already have two sons. I know I will love Salome with the same strength I loved my own mother. Please be patient with me."

Mary held his hand and asked, "Do you hope for and want a son who will one day be the Messiah?"

Joseph lowered his head and then looked at her. "I'm ashamed, Mary. Yes, I wanted to return to the Qumran Settlement with the Messiah . . . my son."

Mary whispered, "You already have that."

Joseph was struck with this thought and he bent over and kissed Mary. "I'll see you after work. Ghidai has everything under control. Sleep when the baby sleeps and rest as much as you can. Having babies doesn't ever seem easy." He kissed her again. He walked out the door to meet Seth and went to work.

The days grew into months and Joseph refrained from sexual intercourse with Mary for forty-four days as required by their law. After waiting Joseph and Mary were very much ready to share intimacy and physical pleasure again.

THE TENT CAMP AND JERUSALEM

WHEN PANTHERA'S RECOVERY WAS complete, he and Isis were legally married in Egypt. However, his recovery dictated that he had to return to Judea and rejoin his legion. Although the army supported marriage, wives had to live separately from their husbands. Panthera therefore would return to the Roman tent camp, in the desert between Jerusalem and Masada, while Isis would live with the wives of other soldiers in Jerusalem.

As soon as they disembarked from their ship in Joppa and traveled the twenty-six miles to Jerusalem, Panthera left Isis in the inn across from the temple and reported to his tent camp. When he walked into the commander's tent, he crossed his chest with his fist and said, "Panthera, reporting back from injury leave, sir."

The commander looked up at Panthera and stood up to walk around his desk to examine Panthera more closely. "By the gods, you recovered from your injuries! Are you well?"

"I'm completely well, sir. I'm also married."

"Did you marry an Egyptian girl?"

"No. But she has lived in Alexandria for most of her life. Her parents are Roman and her father had served in the Roman army."

"Good" was all the commander replied. The commander sent Panthera to their doctor for an examination, to confirm that he was ready to return and resume military duty. When the doctor saw him, his face turned white, as if he had seen a ghost. He had been sure Panthera would die at the time he was taken away by the three strange men who dressed like Persian kings. Yet, here stood Panthera, alive, well, and strong.

The doctor told Panthera he could take five days to be with his bride in Jerusalem and report back to the tent camp afterward. Panthera walked out of the infirmary and searched for Jarius.

Jarius was found, playing dice with three other soldiers. When Jarius saw Panthera he jumped to his feet and heartily embraced Panthera. "My God, you're alive! How are you? Were you in Alexandria all this time?"

"Yes, and I've taken a wife."

"So have I! She's an Israelite! She lives in Perea, and I'm with her every other week for three days at a time."

"My wife is Roman, but she was born in Judea and grew up in Alexandria. She is waiting for me in Jerusalem. I received five days to be with her before I must report back for duty."

Panthera suddenly and spontaneously embraced Jarius again. "I can't wait to meet your wife, Jarius. Congratulations!"

"Same to you, my brother who once was dead, but now has come back alive!" Jarius became somber and said, "Panthera, things are getting worse around here. The Sicarii are mounting resistance against the Roman presence and there is fear that there will be battles. Maybe if King Herod would die, things would calm down. He secretly supports the Sicarii and thinks no one knows. Even his Jewish subjects are aware that it is their tax money to him that feeds the Sicarii. It's not good."

"Well, I'd say it's all in God's hands and time."

Jarius laughed. "You sound like my wife. That's exactly what she would say."Jarius displayed a distant glance and returned quickly by saying, "This is not my week to be with my wife. You go ahead, Panthera. Go be with your wife. I'll see you in five days." As an afterthought Jariussaid, "Wives are most certainly wonderful gifts in life?"

"Yes, indeed they are," Panthera answered and paused before saying, "Well, I'll be on my way then, to my love." Jarius and Panthera embraced again and Panthera turned to leave for Jerusalem

Panthera undertook the journey back to Jerusalem with great anticipation, to be once again with his new bride. Their passion was a wonder and a blessing to them both. The modesty, fear, and hesitation that he knew marked some marriages was not an issue for him and Isis as a married couple. Perhaps it was the weeks of forced intimacy between nurse and patient. Whatever the reason, their physical connection was powerful.

When he stepped into their small room their reaction to each other was immediate and intense. Their long embrace was disrupted only by the hurried shedding of clothing. Her beauty and absence of shame at her nakedness pleased and aroused him. Their lovemaking was brief but powerful, like a sudden summer storm. They pleased each other. Panthera, whose previous experiences with aggressive sex had been so distorted and tortuous, was now experiencing marital sexual intimacy with one woman whom he loved and knew loved him.

He took a deep breath and looked into the eyes of his lover.

"Are you hungry?" he asked.

"You mean for food?" she replied.

And they laughed together. He stood to dress himself and as she looked at his young, strong, healed body she closed her eyes to keep his image safe in her mind. Silently, she wished he was not a soldier. But the beautiful young Isis and her soldier husband fed each other their fill.

THE EGYPTIAN DELTA

Days turned into weeks, mounting into months and years for the holy family, Ghidai, and her son in Alexandria. During the passing of time, Yemane and Jesus grew in age and wisdom. They began to venture farther away from the house more frequently, in search of adventure. It was as if the wilderness was their teacher now, and at the ages of nine and eight, respectively, Yemane and Jesus usually explored farther into the delta desert that spread west, beyond their home and the creek in their backyard. The land stretched out, unexplored and ready to be discovered by the two young boys, who operated as if they were the first and only explorers of this region.

One night it rained very hard and the following morning the boys ran out to see the creek swollen with fast-moving white water. Yemane and Jesus saw the challenge and began to look for a way to cross the raging water so they could resume their exploration beyond.

As they stood by the creek ready to implement their plan to cross, two other boys from their community joined them and they decided to help each other in their quest. The other two boys were Egyptian and older than Yemane. One of the Egyptian boys looked at Yemane and then at Jesus and back to Yemane. "You're really black. Where did you come from?"

Jesus stepped in front of Yemane and said, "He's from Ethiopia, a faraway place in Africa, but he's my brother."

"Oh, yeah, well, where are you from?"

"I've lived here all my life but my parents are from a place called Judea, in Palestine."

The other Egyptian boy said, "Come on. Are we going to try to cross this creek or stand around all day talking?"

The boys decided they could not step into the water to cross the raging stream because the current was too strong. Yemane noticed that a large branch from a nearby tree spanned the width of the stream. He pointed it out to the others and their adventure began. The Egyptian boys climbed up the tree first. Jesus followed and Yemane came last. They all made it to the branch. From this spot, standing on the branch, the water below looked more dangerous. None of them revealed their fear outwardly.

"You go across first," the Egyptian boy in the lead commanded Yemane. Yemane obeyed and although he was afraid, he was successful. He stopped on the other side of the branch where he could have jumped to the ground on the other side of the stream. Instead, he waited and said, "I'll stay here so if you need to reach for someone to help you, I can grab ahold of your hand."

"Good idea. You're smart. I'll go next." The first Egyptian boy inched across the branch on his belly like a caterpillar. Near the end of the branch, he reached for Yemane and stood up to walk the last stretch holding onto Yemane. He jumped to the ground and called his friend to come next.

The other Egyptian boy was a little larger and his weight caused the branch to bend down closer to the water. With Yemane's help he made it safely to the other side and jumped to the ground also.

Yemane looked at Jesus, who was the youngest of the four. "Come on, Jesus. You can make it."

The Egyptian boys also encouraged him to move across the branch. They knew that more adventure awaited them in the delta desert and they were anxious to get started. Jesus began to slide across the branch on his belly but the weave in his garment kept catching and snaring on the branch's bark. He felt compelled to go forward but knew he would not be able to continue the way he was moving. He very carefully stood up on the branch to walk across the distance to Yemane.

"No!" Yemane yelled to Jesus. "You're going to fall."

Jesus looked up to Yemane and smiled. He had already calculated and saw that he was able to grab onto another branch overhead. He walked the distance and reached Yemane. Together they jumped to the ground on the other side of the creek and their exploration of the desert began.

The boys began their walk together but they were unaware of a potential danger. The desert they walked upon was part of the Sahara Desert, which eventually spread east to meet the Egyptian Delta where the Nile River split into many veins of water, creating a fertile marshland. This huge delta was formed and maintained by the rivers that emptied into the Mediterranean Sea. With the desert to the west and the delta to the east, when a hard rain fell across these two areas, the water would often randomly pool under the sand of the desert and mix with mud from the delta, turning it into treacherous, camouflaged, sinking ground. Fortunately, none of the boys inadvertently stepped into the sinking sand hole that lay directly before them because they were warned by the terrified bleating of a goat in distress. The goat was caught in one of the pools of quicksand. They knew they could have easily walked into this natural trap had the goat not warned them by its bleating. As they came closer to the goat, they saw that she wasn't sinking. However, she was stuck. If she were not rescued, she would die in a few days. The quicksand hole would hold her tight even as the pool of water below dried and became like solid mortar. One of the Egyptian boys knew this and warned the others.

"Don't go near that goat. You'll get stuck too, if you do." He explained that they were not to approach the area near or around the goat.

"We can't leave the goat to die!" Jesus said.

"I'm not going near it," said the larger Egyptian boy. "Besides, it's just a goat."

Yemane turned to Jesus and said, "I think he's right. We need to stay away from that goat."

"No. We've got to do something," Jesus said. "Yemane, help me think of what we can do."

Yemane stood unable to think of anything. The two Egyptian boys agreed that what Jesus seemed determined to do was too dangerous and they left, abandoning Yemane and Jesus with the screaming goat, following their path back to the creek to go home.

"Jesus, come, let's get out of here," Yemane pleaded.

"No! We need to help the goat."

Yemane resigned himself to the fact that Jesus was not going to acquiesce. He looked around and saw some rocks and old branches from trees that must have grown there from years ago. "Come on," he said. "I have an idea."

Yemane explained his idea, which involved the placing of rocks and branches that could provide a crude platform near the goat. Together they could lie on the branches and lift the goat up and out of the quicksand onto the mat of webbed branches and sticks.

Both worked diligently as they built a bridge with rocks for a foundation and branches placed as close to the goat as possible. They approached the goat and worked with all their strength to lift the animal from its stuck position. Finally, they freed the goat's front legs and the goat was able to lift the rest of its body out of the quicksand and onto the mat of branches.

The goat ran off and Yemane said to Jesus, "If that goat gets caught in another quicksand hole, we're not going to rescue it!"

Jesus didn't respond but watched the goat run free and he smiled.

Yemane said, "Jesus, we better get home. It's probably time for lunch."

When they returned to the creek the water had subsided to its shallow status and they walked through, bending down to rinse sand from their hands, feet, and face.

When they entered their house, they found Ghidai in the kitchen preparing lunch for them. She didn't look up from her work, telling the boys they needed to wash and come to eat. Yemane and Jesus didn't speak of their morning adventure.

Something changed for the boys. Before, the creek had served as a barrier for Jesus and Yemane's adventures, but no longer. After the rescuing event of the goat, Jesus and Yemane often ventured past the site of the goat's entrapment and became familiar with the wilderness a good distance beyond. Jesus often looked across the desert's expanse and saw what he thought were mountains in the distance and wondered about them. He couldn't tell how far away they were but he longed to explore their secrets. Would there be waterfalls and caves to be explored? Would there be wild animals or exotic birds? Often, he would sit and stare at the mountains and think that someday he would find the answers to his questions.

One morning, very early, Jesus was awakened by the rising sun and felt a very strong urge to try to reach the mountains. He woke Yemane. "Get up, Yemane. It's going to be a beautiful day. Today I want to explore farther than we have ever explored before. I want to go to the mountains we can see in the distance beyond the creek."

Yemane grumbled but rose from his bed and dressed. No one else in the house was up, so together they quietly went into the kitchen and packed food into a small cloth sack. Then they slipped out the back door and waded across the creek. The water was so cold it made their feet ache. By the time they reached the desert their feet and sandals were dry.

"This looks like a good place to eat," Yemane said.

"You and your stomach! You just can't do anything unless it's full, can you?" Jesus asked. It was obvious that Jesus had a plan for the day and he didn't want to carry it out alone.

"You know something, Jesus? Everybody that ever lived, lives, or will live in the whole wide world eats."

"Yeah, but not like you. Most people can have an empty stomach for at least a little while when they're awake." Jesus smiled as he spoke.

"All right!" Yemane said, "Why don't you tell me what you have planned for us while I finish my breakfast?"

"Well," said Jesus with enthusiasm, "I've always wanted to go to those mountains and explore them. We may find a cave, or a waterfall, or even wild animals."

Yemane looked toward the distant mountains, as Jesus had declared them to be, and decided they were really just hills and he didn't hesitate to say, "Those aren't mountains, Jesus. They're just big hills."

"Wait, stop, shhh . . ." Jesus exclaimed. "Look over there."

"What?" Yemane looked in the direction Jesus was pointing. There sat a lone dove. "It's just a dove."

"No, look again. It's a dove alright but it's sitting still by another dead dove."

Sure enough, as the boys came close the living dove did not fly away or move. It stood on the ground motionless, waiting for something.

"Why won't it fly away?" Yemane whispered.

"I think the dead dove is its partner and the living dove won't leave or fly away without its mate."

"Well, if it won't fly away it's going to die sitting there waiting. How long do you think it will sit there and wait?"

Jesus said with sadness, "I think it will sit there until it dies too."

Both waited and watched the dove. It didn't move.

"I know," said Yemane, "I'll scare it away." Yemane ran toward the dove and yelled loudly.

"Stop it, Yemane! Stop it. All you're doing is scaring the dove to move a little way away. See . . . it's coming close again to its dead partner. Come on. Let's go. Maybe it will fly away on its own after a while. Let's start walking toward those mountains."

Yemane and Jesus began walking toward the hills. After walking for three hours, they determined that they were no closer from when they began. The mountains were too far away so they turned around to head back, retracing their steps carefully. As they came close to the place where they had seen the doves, they were very thirsty, which made them glad they had walked during the morning hours while the sun was not strong.

It was close to the noon hour when they came to the site of the doves. Yemane said, "I sure hope that dove isn't still there by its dead mate."

No sooner had Yemane spoken the words than the boys came upon the same dove. It was still holding its vigil next to the body of its mate.

"Maybe we should bury the dead dove," Yemane suggested.

"No," Jesus said. "We need to leave the dove alone and go home."

They walked the remaining distance home, quenched their thirst at the creek, and cooled their faces and necks with the cold spring water that fed the stream. They were surprised they had become so thirsty. As they walked into the house Ghidai, Mary, and Salome were sitting at the table in the kitchen eating lunch.

With obvious irritation, Mary asked, "Where have you boys been? You've been gone since before the sixth hour this morning!"

"We went exploring beyond the creek and into the desert," Jesus answered.

"That's not a desert! It's a delta and there are dangers you two wouldn't know how to handle. Now, come and eat lunch. Jesus, you will be inside for the rest of the day."

Ghidai spoke sternly as she informed Yemane that he also would be spending the rest of the day inside.

Yemane protested briefly. "Jesus woke me early this morning and told me to go with him to explore beyond the creek . . . and then . . ."

Ghidai interrupted her son's protestations of blame and quickly silenced him with the wave of her hand. "You're ten years old, Jesus is nine! You can offer no excuses for participating in such dangerous play. No more needs to be said."

Ghidai was angry and Jesus regretted leading Yemane into trouble. He turned to her and touched her arm. "Ghidai, I did coax Yemane into going on this adventure with me. I'm sorry."

Ghidai hugged Jesus and held him close for moments before she reached out to her son and hugged him. Mary watched with pleasure as Ghidai said, "I still love you both but it doesn't mean what you did will be all right. Never walk out into the desert or delta beyond the creek for longer than it takes you to become thirsty. Always take water with you. When you become thirsty and you drink your water you must turn around and return. Do you understand?"

Jesus and Yemane nodded their heads and were resigned to staying inside for the remainder of the day.

Both boys napped in the afternoon and were happy to hear Joseph talking in the kitchen when they awoke. Unfortunately, Mary informed Joseph about the boys and their foolish adventure. Jesus and Yemane couldn't see that Joseph was smiling as he listened attentively to the details. Ghidai and Mary confronted Joseph with expressions of disapproval that communicated to him he was taking it all too lightly.

During the evening meal little was talked about. Ghidai instructed Yemane to help clean up after the family was finished eating and Jesus followed his mother into the front room. She was weaving on the loom she and Joseph had made. The loom was a vertical loom. Mary had orchestrated its construction, combining the models of the Egyptian loom with the loom they were familiar with in the Qumran Settlement. Jesus watched as she wove another linen garment. She was a master at the loom and had perfected techniques that enabled her to weave wool also. She could weave twills because she had developed a way to throw the shuttle from selvage to selvage, thereby making wool and linen garments with no seams. Her weaving was meticulous and the garments she produced were admired by all.

Jesus enjoyed watching her throw the shuttle back and forth between the webbed threads. After each throw of the shuttle, she would shift the threads on the loom and move the weft down to tighten the weave. Rows of even patterns changed the separate threads into a woven complexity of beauty.

Finally, Jesus asked, "How did people ever figure out how to make looms and weave cloth?"

Mary stopped her work and said, "Many people believe myths that explain that the spider was given permission by the gods to reveal the secrets of weaving. However, I believe God gave human beings the ability to watch, learn, and create. Maybe the spider helped lead people to figure out how to build a loom to weave, but I prefer to believe that these great creative tools are part of the relationship extended to us by God through all of creation. If we open our eyes we will see. If we open our ears we will hear. If we open our hearts to be aware of the Almighty God, we will be with God in this life experience and we will create as God has created. After all, we are made in His likeness and image."

Mary began to weave again and Jesus stood still and continued to watch. Mary sensed he needed to talk to her so she threw the shuttle for one last line of thread to be tightened against the existing weave with the weft and placed the shuttle on the floor next to the stretched linen on the loom.

Mary looked at Jesus, who asked, "Are you still angry with me?"

He had asked with genuine humble penance so she could not help but say, "No, I'm no longer angry with you, mostly because you are alive and safe. Walking out into the delta desert as far as you did without water was not a safe thing to do, Jesus."

"I know now, and I won't do it again," Jesus promised. He continued to stand before his mother and she asked him again what he wanted. "When Yemane and I were walking toward the mountains, just beyond the creek we came upon two doves. One was alive, sitting next to another dove that was dead. I decided they must have been mates and the one that was alive was holding a vigil for the one that was dead. Yemane tried to scare the living dove to fly away but it would only move out of his reach for a while and then return to the side of its dead partner. We gave up on coaxing the dove to fly away and began our adventure and walked until midmorning toward the mountains. When we realized we couldn't go any farther we turned to come home. Six hours must have passed when we came upon the doves again. The living dove was still sitting next to the dead dove. I felt sad but there was nothing we could do so we came home." Jesus paused and looked out the window. He determined that there were still two hours of daylight left before nightfall. "Will you go with me to the spot where the doves were to see if the living dove is still there with the dead one?"

Mary gently touched Jesus' cheek and rose, moving away from the loom. She went into the bedroom to find her shawl. She said to Joseph, who was sitting playing with Salome, "I'm going across the creek a little way with Jesus. He wants me to see something. I'll be right back."

Joseph smiled at Mary and said, "Another adventure? Be careful. It'll be dark soon."

Mary walked into the kitchen and Jesus was standing by the back door ready to go. Both walked toward, and then across, the creek. Mary felt Jesus's sense of urgency. They walked in silence until Jesus came upon the site. He stopped and waited for his mother to come up next to him. Two turtledoves lay dead before them. Jesus tried to hide that he was crying. He knew two doves were not of great importance but he couldn't stop his sorrowful emotion. Mary wrapped her arms around her son and said, "My dear, you've had a difficult day today, haven't you?"

Jesus's muffled crying turned into weeping. "Jesus, Jesus, what are you so upset about? Come here." Mary led him to a large rock and they both sat. Mary never took her arms from around Jesus and she let him cry as they sat. The sun began to sink below the horizon.

Jesus's crying began to subside and he moved from his mother's hold and began to talk about his feelings.

"Those doves were like partners in life. When the one died it was as if the one left living also died. Mom, are doves partners for life, like you and dad?"

"Yes, Jesus. Those were turtledoves and they become partners for life, but not like me and Joseph."

Jesus sat up straight. "What do you mean not like you and dad?"

Mary took a deep breath and said, "Human beings often are not partners with one other person for life. There are cultures in which it is acceptable for a man to have many wives. Look at our own Israelite culture. Moses had four wives. King David had many wives, or concubines, as they were called."

"Why is it that the man is always the only husband or partner for the woman but he can have many partners? Why can't a woman have more than one husband?" Jesus asked.

"Oh, Jesus, you often ask very difficult questions . . . I think it has something to do with having babies. If there is only one husband, as the woman's partner, her faithfulness to him assures that her children are his. A woman doesn't have to guess at which children are hers because they are born from her body and there is no question or doubt about which baby belongs to her. If she were allowed to have many husbands at the same time, there would be no way to determine who was father to which baby." Mary wrapped her shawl tightly around her shoulders and shivered. She knew her shiver was not due to the coolness of the evening. "I can only tell you what I know and believe." She looked at Jesus, trying to determine if he was ready to hear about love, marriage, and sex. She began to explain things to Jesus with discomfort but her feminine confidence supported her to continue. She told him about females and their monthly cycle of bleeding. She explained about men and their ability to excrete semen. As they sat on the rock together, Mary explained that men and women can reproduce and have babies together through the act of making love. Since Jesus seemed to be accepting of her descriptions and explanations, she shared the information fully. Many laws about the way men and women are to function and behave sexually were written in the scroll of Leviticus and Mary suggested that Jesus ask Joseph to cover these parts of their Holy Scriptures. "I need for you to talk about this with your father because I don't accept some of the teachings in our faith tradition. It may be wrong for me to share my personal beliefs and thoughts because they may be contrary to God's word." She sighed. "I wish more females were included as the interpretation of God's word was defined. What you will be taught will be men's interpretation, not women's interpretation." Her voice became low and soft. "I often long for an understanding of God from a woman's perspective. It may be wrong of me to wish for that." Mary looked down and Jesus knew she was shedding a tear.

"Mother, I know you are my mother because I was born from your body. I don't know who my father is unless you tell me."

Mary looked directly into Jesus' eyes and asked, "What are you saying? Joseph is your father."

Jesus didn't take his eyes from Mary's face. Courageously he said, "I know and understand more than you are able to see or believe I am capable of knowing. You may think I'm just a young boy that doesn't need to know anything yet. You're wrong. I don't know completely about how babies are made but I know they are born from a woman's seed and something from a man. What I wonder about is which man started me in you."

Mary didn't answer. Jesus looked up to the sky, which had begun to show different colors from the horizon up into the darkness of the approaching night sky.

"I love Joseph as my father but I know another man had something to do with my being born." He turned to look at his mother again and said, "I'm ready to hear about my beginnings. I'm ready to hear your beliefs about love, and marriage, and sex. Please tell me."

Mary and Jesus sat on the rock as the sun set completely and darkness surrounded them. Mary held nothing back from Jesus and answered every question he asked. When there was no more to say Jesus whispered, "Thank you, Mom."

Mary sighed and put her arm around Jesus and whispered back, "Is it better to know?"

Jesus leaned his head against Mary's shoulder and answered, "I don't know. I feel a little . . . sad and confused." Jesus sighed and choked back tears as he thought about his mother, his father, and Panthera. Oddly, to himself, he felt anger surge in his veins but knew this emotion was not appropriate for this place and time with his mother. He worked at trying to change the subject by saying, "I know I want to be married when I am old enough to take a wife. I want only one wife for all of my life. I hope she will love me because she wants to love me, not because she has to love me." Jesus' mind seemed to shift thought from marriage and family to wars and soldiers. "I don't want to be a soldier. I don't care about fighting and power. I don't want power. I want peace and love . . . and you and Dad have shown me how peace and love between a man and a woman can happen . . . against all odds!" Jesus looked up toward the sky. The clouds that made the darkness of the night greater cleared away and stars peeked out to shine. "I know we're Essenes, and male Essenes don't usually get married but it is the desire of my heart to be married. I believe God gave me that desire." Mary gazed at her son's profile, which was shrouded in the darkness and hard to see. However, it was not dark enough to see he was shedding tears again.

Mary suddenly felt warm inside and said, "When you marry, I will give your wife the loom and teach her how to weave." Jesus and his mother fell into each other's arms and embraced under the stars, giving both a long moment to take in gentle, sweet peace that passed both of their complete understandings.

LEARNING IN ALEXANDRIA

Salome was growing quickly. She was a pleasant child at four years of age and she rarely cried. She was regularly entertained by the boys and she acted as if she longed to be with them constantly. She was running faster now and she tried to keep up with Yemane and Jesus when they ran in the yard. She fell often but Jesus would always pick her up and put her back on her feet and coax her to run and catch him.

Joseph and Mary's life was full. They enjoyed Salome, the boys, and Ghidai, who was a great help to Mary. One evening, while Mary and Joseph lay in bed together after making love, Mary turned to Joseph and ran her fingers over his forehead and around his face. Joseph wondered to himself about her and how she seemed to know what gave him pleasure in so many ways.

He whispered, "I love you, Mary. I feel like I can't say that enough to you."

Mary was almost twenty-four years old and she still maintained youthful beauty. Her hair was long, dark, and curly. Her olive complexion was flawless. Her figure was slim but full. It was the beauty of her dark-brown almond-shaped eyes that held the greatest attraction while revealing the developing wisdom beyond her years.

"Joseph," she said. "I'm pregnant again."

She stopped running her fingers over his face as he turned to look at her. It never dawned on him that this would happen again in Alexandria. He wanted a son but had comforted himself thinking his firstborn son to Mary would be born in Judea. Salome was just over four years old . . . In an instant, he realized that Mary had just told him she was pregnant again and he placed his arms around her and pulled her on top of himself. He took her head into her hands and kissed her on the mouth with deep love.

"Do you feel all right?" he asked.

"Yes. I've not had the morning sickness that I had with Salome. I feel great!"

"How many months are you?"

"Three months. This child will also be born in the holy month of September as Salome was," Mary said as she looked for a hint to Joseph's thought.

Joseph leaned back and put his hand on his head. He realized that work around the house with the children was increasing by the minute. Even with Ghidai's diligent and skillful help, he knew the boys were becoming quite a handful.

He also knew Mary had told Jesus about Panthera. Ever since, both he and Mary had noticed a change in Jesus' attitude and behavior. He seemed to be more contemplative and had small episodes of anger. Thankfully the outbreaks didn't last long, but had given reason for both parents to become concerned.

Joseph lowered his hands from his head and announced, "The boys need to go to school. I'll see about that this afternoon. That will keep them busy and they need to begin to learn all that they can learn while they are young."

"I'm glad you feel that way. Do you think Yemane will be accepted in school?"

"I'll be paying for their schooling. I don't expect a school to turn down a potential student who has a paying patron. The school is dependent upon money for its existence."

Joseph was true to his word. That next afternoon he left work for a while to inquire about schooling at a nearby institution of learning. He registered a ten-year-old Ethiopian and a nine-year-old Israelite. Although he sensed coldness from the man who took the information for registering the boys, after Joseph paid for six months of schooling in advance, the man gave him an emblem of acceptance and told him the boys were to report to school at the beginning of the following week.

Joseph returned to work feeling a bit unnerved and angry toward the registrar's attitude. He hoped attendance at this school for Yemane and Jesus would offer both boys an education without discrimination. He felt less worried when his friends at work assured him that it would be fine.

"Besides," said Seth, "my boys are attending that school and I'll instruct them to look out for your boys. If you are not satisfied with their treatment just report it to Amsu. He's a man of great influence and he relies on these schools to train and supply well-educated young men and potential employees."

That evening, while eating dinner together, Joseph announced to the boys that they would be going to school in a week. He told Yemane and Jesus he planned to take them to the school to visit and meet their teachers.

"I'm going to school too?" Yemane asked.

"Yes." Joseph became somber as he went on to say, "Both of you may receive poor treatment because you are not Egyptian but you must not return evil treatment with evil."

"What should we do if they try to fight with us?" Yemane asked.

"I'll be here to help you decide what must be done, but if someone tries to fight with you, don't fight back. If they become seriously violent, move to a person of authority very fast. If there is no person you can turn to for help, sit down and roll up into a ball and do not move."

"God will give me the words to speak to them so that their violence will stop, or God will tell me to be silent and stand firm," Jesus said with a recent, typical air of anger and self-righteous confidence.

Everyone at the table looked at Jesus. Even Salome squealed and clapped her hands. Jesus continued eating and ignored their temporary staring.

Jesus continued, "You know something, I think there would be less fighting if a school would let girls be there."

Joseph sat quietly and then finally said, "Well, maybe you're right, but I've seen girls fight also."

"I haven't," Jesus said with a biting tone that surprised Joseph. His tone certainly invited a provocative attitude, and Joseph didn't ignore it as he usually did, always hoping Jesus would return to his loving attitude.

"Jesus, what's got into you lately? You seem filled with anger and you display a bad attitude that is not acceptable." Joseph was visibly provoked to irritation.

Usually, Jesus respectfully retreated and acquiesced to Joseph. Not lately. Instead, he pushed the chair he was sitting on out from under himself and stood up. "Why would you order us *not* to defend ourselves if someone is attacking or hurting us?" Jesus was angry, and his eyes were filled with tears of rage.

Joseph was astonished. Everyone at the table sat holding their breath. Finally, Joseph responded in calmness. "It would not be pleasing to God if you were to return violence for violence. Your behavior right now is not pleasing to God either. Dismiss yourself from this table and go some place until you regain composure."

Jesus stormed outside, and Joseph stood to follow him. Mary reached for Joseph and appealed to him, "Joseph, no, please let him be alone for now."

Joseph sat down at the table and finished his meal. No one spoke. The tension was unbearable. Joseph continued to eat, banging his goblet and utensils against the table and plate. Finally, he finished eating, and he stood up from the table and walked out of the door Jesus had used to leave. Jesus's plate still rested on the table filled with food. Mary, Ghidai, Yemane, and Salome remained seated at the table. They didn't speak a word, but Salome began to whimper with fear and sadness. Although Yemane couldn't understand Jesus' behavior either, he leaned close to Salome and patted her shoulder in an effort to comfort her.

Joseph found Jesus standing by the creek. He was staring at the ground. Joseph walked up behind him silently and then stepped to his side. "What's going on with you, Jesus?"

Jesus didn't answer.

Again, Joseph said, "Jesus, I asked you a question. What's this all about?"

Jesus didn't answer. "Jesus, this is blatant disrespect and disobedience of me, your father and . . ."

Jesus turned on Joseph and yelled, "You're not my father!" He sat down and began weeping. Joseph walked next to Jesus and sat. He didn't say anything as Jesus continued to weep. Joseph felt lost and prayed for guidance. He raised his head from prayer and watched the fish swimming happily in the creek. Slowly Jesus ceased his weeping and sniffled intermittently. He didn't look at Joseph and said, "You're not my father. Mom told me what happened to her and now I know that Panthera is my father. I'm not stupid. I knew all along something was missing in this whole story about why we came here to live . . . and my birth in Bethlehem . . . I just don't . . . I don't understand . . . How could you have let this happen to my mother? Why did you allow her to end up in a situation where she was alone to be raped? Why? She was your almah. She should have been in your care in your home with your parents . . ." Instantly Jesus remembered that Joseph's parents were dead and that Essene rules would not allow an almah to live with her betrothed husband unless there was a father present in the home. Suddenly, Jesus realized that his mother could not have been with Joseph even if they had chosen to live together as a betrothed couple. She had had to remain under the care of her own father until the first marriage ceremony. Jesus finally looked at Joseph and then dropped his head and started to cry again. "I hate Panthera. I hate him! Why didn't you do something, Dad?"

Joseph very calmly and quietly said, "I did. I married your mother and adopted you as my son."

"That doesn't change anything!" Jesus screamed at his father. "Panthera got away with rape, you didn't marry a virgin, and I will always be illegitimate!"

"Maybe you're too young to understand this," Joseph said softly, "but . . . there is the 'letter' of life and there is the 'spirit' of life. Do you really believe your mother wasn't a virgin? Do you feel as if I'm not your father? Do you know, spiritually, there is no such thing as an illegitimate child?"

Jesus stared out across the creek and over the delta desert. Joseph continued. "As human beings, we all go wrong somewhere, but we have the blessing of forgiveness and redemption. Because we have that blessing, God can take the worst possible situation and turn it to His will in ways we can't comprehend or imagine."

Jesus looked back at Joseph, and Joseph could feel that Jesus felt badly still. He was breathing deeply and every now and then a tear fell.

"You wanted a son instead of a daughter when Salome was born. If I am your son, spiritually, why were you hoping for another son so desperately?" Jesus was speaking with difficulty through his tears.

Joseph smiled and shook his head. Finally, he responded, "Yes, Jesus. You're right. The truth shows, doesn't it?" Joseph couldn't look at Jesus as he said, "I still want a natural son. I'm ashamed of that truth but you're too smart for me to deny it. What can I say?" Joseph took a deep breath and looked out beyond the creek. "I need forgiveness just like everyone else. Every day I try to let God guide my thoughts, desires, and ways. Yet . . . well . . . it's difficult. However, I never thought it was possible for me to be able to forgive some of the offenses perpetrated against me, but I have. I have to believe God will forgive me always. I believe people in my life will forgive me too."

Jesus sat in silence, thinking with intensity until he couldn't think any more. He looked at Joseph again and said, "I'm so hungry."

Joseph stood up and extended his hand to help lift Jesus to his feet. "Maybe you need to go in and finish your meal. I would be so happy if you ate and felt filled up. Maybe the Jesus we've come to know and love would come alive again and return to us. You've not been yourself lately and I, for one, miss the Jesus I have reared from infancy."

This time when Joseph smiled, Jesus gave a hint of a smile in return.

When Jesus and Joseph walked into the house and to the table, the rest of the family had already finished their meal. Jesus' plate of food was still on the table and Yemane and Salome sat with Jesus as he finished his dinner. Afterward, Yemane and Jesus ran out to play in the twilight. At one point in their play, they pretended to be soldiers and fought using sticks as swords. As Jesus moved around in their imaginary battle he looked up and saw a great light on the horizon. He called, "Dad! Dad, come here. I want you to see something."

Joseph walked out to the backyard and Jesus pointed to the light. "What's that?"

Joseph looked at the familiar light and told Jesus the story of the three lights that had joined together and shined over Bethlehem when he was born. "After coming together, the three lights began to separate again to different parts of the sky. The brightest of the three settled in the west and can now be seen above the horizon whenever the sun sets. But more amazing than that, when you were born there was a great ball of light moving quickly across the night sky with a tail of light, stretched out, coming from the east, as if it were a ball of fire, beginning in the east and moving west mysteriously."

Yemane and Jesus stood and looked at the light, not knowing that the brightness of its shining came from a planet reflecting the sun's light. As the sky darkened, its light always shined with greater strength and brilliance, more than any other heavenly body in the heavens until the moon rose. Both sat on the grass and watched until the firmament was completely dark and the moon moved and shined above them. Joseph left them in the yard to sit and watch and called them in to get ready for sleep later than usual.

After Yemane went up the ladder to go to bed, Mary came in to say prayers with Jesus. She looked at him with great love and said, "Jesus, I'm going to have another baby."

Jesus reached out his arms to hug his mother and when she moved back away from him to sit up, she asked, "Do you know how much I love you? You will always be my firstborn son and you are very special to me."

"I know, Mom. I love you too."

"Do you feel, sometimes, that there are too many other things for me to do and I don't have enough time for you?"

"Not yet. But I think with another baby maybe Dad will feel you won't have enough time for him, not me. I like babies." Jesus paused for a moment and said, "I think Dad likes babies too. We'll all be happy with the coming of this new baby to our family!"

"Good night, darling."

"Good night, Mom. See you in the morning."

Mary went directly to the backyard where she found Joseph sitting against the wall of the house gazing up to the night sky. She sat next to him and tucked her arm through his. It was a warm night but she felt comfort snuggling against him. They watched the sky and in a moment they both witnessed another streak of light that flashed and disappeared almost instantly.

"I was thinking about what you had said over four years ago," Joseph said to Mary.

Mary was still looking up toward the sky. "What was that, Joseph? I can't remember what I said a moment ago, let alone four years ago."

"You had said that you thought maybe the streaks of light in the sky were rocks that had fallen off of stars and that as they fell into the ocean of the earth's air they burned up. You rubbed your hands together, felt the warmth it created, and then thought that maybe the rocks rubbed against the air to burn like a candle."

"Well, maybe I thought about that, but I don't remember now." She gazed up at the sky and said, "I wonder where Caspar, Melchior, and Balthasar are when you really need them." Both laughed.

Joseph looked at Mary and said, "I didn't really listen to your idea and encourage you with your thought that time you spoke. I told you that the air is not an object that could rub against a rock and burn it up. I'm sorry I kept you from your thinking. We're sending the boys to school and I've been to school and I realized that you never got to go to school. Even young Jesus made a comment about girls needing to go to school." Joseph paused and then asked, "Mary, do you want to go to school?"

Mary chuckled. "Sure, maybe before I had children. I have Jesus and Salome to care for now. In less than six months, there will be another baby. I have no desire to go to school at this point in my life." Mary thought and asked Joseph, "However, I would like to learn to read Hebrew. Could you teach me how to read Aramaic and ancient Hebrew? I always wanted to read the Holy Scriptures even though my father taught me their lessons for life. But I'd like to decide for myself what they teach."

"I'll do that. I'm sure you can learn sometime in between my working hours, you giving birth, nursing, providing care for Jesus, Salome, the house, and we can't forget Yemane. When I think of Ghidai I realize that she is really a gift from God to us, is she not?"

Loud yelling came from next door. Then there was screaming. Mary jumped to her feet.

"Joseph, that's my friend Qadesh screaming! She must be in trouble. Please, come with me to her aid."

Joseph also rose to his feet. He and Mary ran to their neighbor's house. The screaming continued as Joseph banged on the door. There was a crash and then silence. Joseph paused and looked at Mary, who displayed great concern. He began to bang on the door more forcefully. Finally, the door flung open and Qadesh's husband, Nua, opened the door with unnecessary fury.

Nua stood at the door and Joseph asked, "Is everything well here? Mary and I heard screaming and a loud crash. Do you need help?"

"No. We don't need help. We're just having a little disagreement."

"Who's having a disagreement?" Mary asked.

"My wife and I are having a disagreement. This is not any of your business!" Nua shut the door. Mary and Joseph stood by the door for a moment and heard no more sounds coming from inside the house.

"Let's go home, Mary." Joseph took her by the arm and they walked the small distance to their own front door. Ghidai stood in the front room. She looked worried and was wringing her hands in nervousness.

Mary approached Ghidai and asked, "Are you all right, Ghidai? Come here and sit down. What's the matter?"

Ghidai sat and began to cry. Joseph said, "I'll check on the children. Please stay with Ghidai, Mary."

Mary was going nowhere. She placed her arm around Ghidai and gently said, "You know what is happening next door with Nua and Qadesh, don't you?"

Ghidai nodded her head. "It's happened to you, hasn't it?" Mary gently said.

Ghidai said, "Yes, back in Ethiopia. My husband . . . all the husbands would hit their wives. Some would beat them severely, and even when the women died from their beatings nothing was done. There is no help for women. We are doomed creatures. We are always subject to our men. I thought every home was like my home until I came to live here with you and Joseph. Now after hearing Nua and Qadesh I'm afraid. What if he comes to hurt us?"

"He won't do that. Joseph would not allow it." Mary turned, and she saw Joseph standing in the doorway to the room.

"All the children are fine and have not been awakened by the commotion," he said. He walked and sat on the other side of Ghidai. "I'm sorry your husband hit you and beat you, but you are here now. Don't be afraid." Joseph asked Mary to take Ghidai to her bed and stay with her until she was asleep. "I'm going next door to talk to Nua."

Mary helped Ghidai to her feet, and they climbed the ladder to her place. Joseph walked out and over to his neighbor's door. After wrapping on the door softly, he was surprised to see Qadesh answer. She held a covering over her face, and Joseph gently reached for her hand to lower the cloth, exposing her face. Her face was bruised and bloody. Her lower right lip was swollen and bleeding. A clump of hair was missing from her head. Joseph could tell by her injuries that more bruises would be evident in the morning. He wondered about the rest of her body, but she seemed to move her arms as if they were not injured.

"Qadesh, do you need help?"

Qadesh didn't answer Joseph's question but glanced back into the house as if to indicate the location of Nua. Finally, she said, "He's asleep now. We won't be bothering you with noise anymore this evening. I'm so sorry."

Hiding his anger Joseph said, "Qadesh, you have nothing to apologize for; your husband must apologize to you. Come to our house and spend the night. In the morning you will be able to decide what you can do to give yourself permanent safety and resolve this issue with Nua."

"No. I'll be fine. Thank you, Joseph," and she slowly closed the door.

Joseph stood at the closed door in disbelief. He had had no idea this kind of trouble happened between married couples. In this night alone he had learned of two more such situations. Evidently, Ghidai was a victim of abuse from her husband—and now Qadesh. He was at a loss and didn't know what to do. He wondered if he should bang on the door again. Maybe Qadesh deserved Nua's abuse . . . *no* . . . no one ever deserves such abuse, he thought as he walked back into his own home. He remembered how he had held Amsu back from hurting Pepi when Pepi had made a potentially costly mistake. Should he go and force Qadesh to leave her husband? Joseph thought that he needed to talk to Mary. He walked into his house to the foot of the ladder leading to the second floor and called for Mary gently.

Mary came to him quickly. When she reached the last rung of the ladder she jumped down and asked, "Is Qadesh all right?"

"No," was Joseph's reply. "She opened the door when I knocked and she held a covering over most of her face. She refused my help and said that Nua was asleep but not before I saw her beat-up face. She apologized for the trouble and said she would be fine and closed the door. I waited at the door trying to decide what to do. I didn't want to wake Nua up so I came to ask you what you think we ought to do."

"I don't know what to do, Joseph. I've been aware that there has been trouble in Qadesh and Nua's marriage but I never thought it escalated to physical violence. Just now, before Ghidai fell asleep she told me that this happens often with many married couples. I think Qadesh will be fine tonight. Tomorrow morning Nua will leave for work and Ghidai and I will offer help to Qadesh."

Joseph couldn't help recalling a story in the Holy Scriptures about a young girl who was abused, abandoned, and killed by a gang of men. He had no access to the Holy Scripture and there were no synagogues in Alexandria to check the reading for accuracy. He remembered it was a story found in Judges (19). It was about a girl who had run away from her husband. Although the girl in the Scripture's story was interpreted to have been a proud, ungrateful second wife, Joseph remembered that she was reported to have run away from her husband to return to her father and he believed there was more to her running home than the story portrayed. He always wondered why it was interpreted that the young wife was at fault for her destiny and death. It seemed to Joseph that she had wanted to get away from her husband for a reason other than what he had been taught. In this case she had not gotten away. Her husband had come after her, forcing her home with him. On their journey home they had stayed in a town, where he turned her out of the house in which they were guests for the night. She had been attacked and raped by a gang of men who had continued their abuse and torture of her through the night. The next morning, she had crawled to the front door and begged for help from her husband, who ignored her and left her to die. He had then taken her body home and cut it up into twelve pieces. He had sent a piece of her body to each of the twelve tribes of Israel.

Joseph had originally believed this story in Scripture must have been allegorical, but as he lay in his bed that night, he began to understand that it held a teaching of even greater significance. It took him a long time to fall asleep because he felt a sense of great doom looming over Qadesh, Nua, and all of them.

When morning came, Mary insisted that Joseph go to work. She would watch for Nua to leave for work because Joseph had not seen him leave his house yet. As soon as he left, Mary decided she would retrieve Qadesh to their home. Mary assured Joseph she and Ghidai had a plan that would allow her to escape from her husband and give her a new life.

Joseph trusted Mary's wisdom and left as she had asked him. He continued to feel uneasy about the situation. He instructed Mary to send for him as soon as she needed help. They decided that Yemane could run to Joseph's place of employment to summon him if they needed help because Yemane knew where Joseph worked and he was a fast runner.

Ghidai and Mary woke the boys and Salome to feed them breakfast. Afterward, Salome was sent to Mestha's home. The boys stayed with Ghidai and Mary, who spoke with an urgency they understood. She explained that a very sad and serious situation had happened the night before to their neighbors Qadesh and Nua. The boys were told that Nua had beaten Qadesh. Together they were going to help Qadesh go to a place where she would be safe. Mary instructed Jesus to stay against the front room wall with Ghidai and Yemane. Ghidai instructed Yemane to stay alert and watch her carefully. If she pointed to him, it was a signal for him to go out the back entrance and run to get Joseph at work.

Finally, at midmorning, Nua left his house. As soon as Nua was out of sight, Mary went and knocked on her neighbor's door. Qadesh answered, and Mary saw her bruised and swollen face.

"Quickly, Qadesh, come to my house." The women entered Mary and Joseph's home and Ghidai offered bread and fruit for Qadesh to eat.

Mary sat in front of Qadesh at the table in the kitchen and let her eat. When she was finished eating Mary reached out to Qadesh and took her hands into her own. Mary led her to sit with her in the front room. The boys followed and showed great obedient discipline to Ghidai and Mary.

"Qadesh, how long has this been happening?" Mary asked.

"It started from the very first week we were married. I remember Nua came home from work and found me napping and he hit me and pushed me around, saying he never wanted to see me napping during the day again. I obeyed him. But he would always find another behavior or action of mine that angered him and he would lash out at me. Lately, he seems to get angrier and more violent with me. I'm scared. I don't know what to do."

"Can you go home to live with your father and mother?"

"My father died. I have only a brother who is married. My mother lives with him and I know he can't bring me to live with him in his home also. He has children."

"What about an uncle?"

Qadesh's eyes lit up. "Yes, I have an uncle who lives in Pelusium. I can go to him, I'm sure." Then Qadesh said, "But Nua will never let me go. If I leave, he'll come after me."

Mary insisted, "You must leave now. Don't go back to your house, not even to pack. I will give you money to go to Pelusium. You will go to the docks and find a ship that can take you around the delta from Alexandria. While you wait for the ship to take you, you must hide. Hide in a room at an inn near the docks. You must leave quickly. I'll get money for you." Mary ran upstairs to take money from the secret compartment in the piece of furniture Joseph had made. She took plenty, knowing it would cover any cost for her trip. She hoped it would provide her safety. When she came back into the front room, she asked Qadesh, "Will you find a way to contact us and let us know you are safe with your uncle?"

"Yes," Qadesh said. She looked at Mary and said, "I'm scared, Mary. I'm scared."

The door to the front room crashed open. It was Nua. He had kicked the door in and Ghidai pointed to Yemane immediately. Yemane ran to the kitchen and out the back entrance. He had never run faster. He wished Joseph was not at work. He wished Joseph was home taking care of them. Yemane was scared. Nua looked mean and angry.

Mary stepped in between Nua and Qadesh. "Nua, please, sit down and we'll give you something to eat and drink to calm you. I'm sure we can resolve this problem without anyone getting hurt."

"Shut up, Mary! She's my wife and you're interfering with us and our marriage! Is that what Jews do? Interfere with people's marriages?"

Jesus released the tight hold he had had on Ghidai's arm. Ghidai looked at Jesus and moved to hold him tightly against her. It wasn't enough. Jesus blurted out, "Don't tell my mother to shut up! You hurt Qadesh. You're not a good husband! You're a bad husband!" Jesus remembered the goat, stuck in the sinking sand. He looked at Qadesh and felt she was like the goat. He called out to her and said, "Don't give up, Qadesh. You can get unstuck!"

Ghidai grabbed Jesus and turned his head into her chest to quiet him. Nua took a step closer to Mary.

"Get out of the way, Mary. I'm taking my wife home."

Mary stood confidently and said firmly, "Nua, you are not making sense. You have hurt your wife and you can't take her home now. You will end up hurting her and yourself more. Sit down. We can talk."

"I'm warning you, Mary! Get out of my way."

Mary didn't move from her spot. She looked Nua directly in the eyes. He couldn't take it anymore. He looked away. He seemed to be studying the room. He looked back at Mary and then lunged for her. He grabbed her and threw her onto a bench that was covered with hay underneath the upholstery of cloth. Mary wasn't hurt, but she was frightened.

Jesus broke free of Ghidai's hold and ran straight for Nua. He tackled Nua at the knees and brought him to the floor. Ghidai was upon Jesus in a flash and pulled him off Nua, who was stunned and hurting from his fall. Qadesh jumped up from her place and ran for the door, but Nua was faster. He intercepted Qadesh at the door and dragged her to the floor. He began to slap her across the face. He pulled her, along with himself, up from the floor. They had both fallen in their struggle and this time he grabbed her by the hair and lifted her body with the strength of one arm. Qadesh screamed. Ghidai and Mary tried to pull Nua's hands free from Qadesh's hair without success. Nua pushed Ghidai aside and then shoved Mary. Jesus was livid and paused to think of a way he could help. He thought of biting Nua's leg when he saw a broom leaning against the wall. Jesus grabbed the broom and used it to swing against Nua. He hit Nua three times before Nua caught the broom in his hand and pulled it from Jesus' grip. He swung it around and warded off Mary and Ghidai. They all stood frozen for a moment and Nua threw the broom to the other side of the room. He looked at Mary and said, "You're going to regret this."

Mary pleaded with Nua as he turned to grab Qadesh again. "Nua, please, don't you remember your vows of love to Qadesh? Don't you remember the wedding celebration Joseph and we had five years ago? We had a good time, didn't we? We've been good neighbors all this time. Please sit down. Don't hurt your wife any more. Haven't you learned that when you hurt your wife you hurt yourself as well?"

Mary's pleas were not heard. Nua turned to Qadesh and with his teeth ground tightly shut he said, "This is your fault. You will pay." He shoved Qadesh against the wall and began to strike her about the head and kick her in the abdomen.

Mary and Ghidai tried again to pull Nua away from Qadesh when the door opened and in came Joseph, Pepi, Seth, and Amsu! The four men easily pulled Nua off Qadesh, who slumped to the floor. While Amsu held Nua back, Joseph and Seth lifted Qadesh to the bench. Mary and Ghidai brought cool water and began to attend to her wounds. Yemane stood next to Jesus and asked him if he was afraid. Jesus looked at Yemane and said, "I was scared before. I'm not scared anymore."

Joseph came back to face Nua as Amsu held him so he couldn't move. Pepi and Seth waited behind Amsu while Joseph said, "If you don't want more trouble than you already have, I suggest you leave this house right now and do *not* come back. Is that clear to you?"

Amsu let him go with a little push toward the door. Nua walked out and Joseph closed the door. The men turned and looked at the women. They were busy attending to Qadesh, who was crying softly.

In a timid, lost voice Qadesh said, "I just wish this would end. But it will never end. Not as long as I'm alive."

Mary said, "Qadesh, now stop talking that way. We need to follow through with the original plan. Look around, Qadesh. These men will help you."

Qadesh looked at all four men and said, "Thank you. Thank you."

Jesus fought through the crowd of adults hovering over Qadesh and placed his hands on her bruised face. He told her, "Don't give up . . . You can't lose hope. We're all here to help you."

Qadesh smiled faintly and embraced him. "What a dear young man you are, Jesus."

It was decided that Qadesh would go home with Amsu. Pepi escorted Amsu and Qadesh to Amsu's home, and she spent the night with him and his family. The plan was that Amsu would then take her to board a ship and sail to Pelusium. Fortunately, Nua couldn't interfere with her plans to sail away, and it was assumed that she arrived safely to live with her uncle in Pelusium.

Mary and Joseph never learned that Nua had learned where Qadesh planned to go. She had been murdered by her husband, killed on the road from the Pelusium Port to her uncle's home. Her uncle had never known Qadesh was coming, and her body was never recovered.

LEARNING IN JERUSALEM

ELEAZAR WAS RAGING INSIDE. "You took food to the leper colony! What were you thinking, Lazarus! You went into the presence of the unclean! Do you understand the seriousness of your violation against the law? Weren't you taught that you are never, ever to associate with the unclean? You have committed a grave sin!"

Lazarus said nothing as his father berated him. However, he thought to himself that he didn't regret bringing food to the colony. The people in the colony were hungry and they were completely dependent on the kind offerings left by merciful people. He was going to be a rabbi someday and he could not agree with the temple's teaching that a rabbi should remain separate and not respond to the needs of those who were ill. Rather, he felt he should always show the compassion of God to any and all whom he may encounter. It was his own idea to visit the colony and take food but Lazarus's mistake had indicted two of his classmates who had joined him.

Eleazar recognized that his son was not listening to him carefully. He became more enraged. He swung his arm and slapped Lazarus against his head. The blow was strong enough to knock him to the floor. When Lazarus slowly sat up again, he fought back tears and would not satisfy his father's rage with crying. He placed his hand on his ear and felt a warm trickle of blood.

Eleazar saw that Lazarus was bleeding but couldn't bring himself to comfort his son. Instead, he accused Lazarus of lacking character. Eleazar believed Lazarus didn't possess the necessary qualities or discipline to become a Pharisee.

Fighting his tears, Lazarus held his ear and said, "I don't want to be here anymore. I want to go home."

"And where do you think home is, Lazarus?"

"I want to go home and be with my sisters and cousins and Aunt Rachael and Uncle Benjamin." His anger toward his father helped him successfully hold back his tears.

"Enough . . . ! Enough!" Eleazar shouted. "I'll send you to your Aunt Rachael and Uncle Benjamin's house, but you will only stay with them for two weeks!"

Eleazar turned and walked out of the room as Lazarus laid his head down on his bed. Finally, alone, he released his emotion and wept bitterly. He felt as if his sadness would last forever. He prayed but felt that God had forsaken him. Maybe his father was right. Maybe he should not have gone to the colony to share food with the leprous. His mind was confused.

SCHOOL IN ALEXANDRIA

YEMANE AND JESUS STAYED close together the first months of school, interacting with no one. Yemane openly admitted he didn't like school. He would have rather explored outside and played and learned the lessons of life he felt he needed to learn. He was a hard worker and enjoyed physical accomplishments. He found it difficult to sit in school and use only his mind as he learned. But his complaining about going to school was quickly silenced as his mother admonished his complaints and fervently tried to instill in him an attitude of gratitude for the great opportunity and fortune he was given by Joseph to receive formal education.

Unlike Yemane, Jesus loved school. He needed no coaxing or encouragement to give all attention and gratitude both to his father or his teachers, whom he had come to love and honor.

Together, Yemane and Jesus would walk to school in the morning and together they would return to their home in the afternoon. Ghidai faithfully packed their lunches. It was at lunchtime that Yemane felt a depth of love for his mother. Every time he ate the wonderful food she had packed every day for him and Jesus, he clearly comprehended the love he held for his mother. He thought about how she had protected him and nurtured him in his lifetime. He was her only child. Although he realized that he loved Mary, Joseph, Jesus, Salome, and his friends, nothing surpassed the love he felt for his mother.

Often Yemane wondered about his father. He tried to remember his father but found instead that he thought of Joseph and wondered if his father was like Joseph. But he doubted this possibility because every time he questioned his mother about his father, she replied that he was not alive. She did inform Yemane that when she had lived with him as his wife, it would have been better if he had died sooner than he did. "The only good that came from your father was you, Yemane." She always said that when he asked about him so he asked no longer.

Jesus's love for his parents also grew stronger and matured. His mother had wisdom and intelligence that often seemed to Jesus to be greater than his father's. She accepted and confronted his questions with confidence. His father would often shy away from his questions or he would acquiesce to his mother. Interestingly, she would answer his questions with answers that provoked more thought. However, before their going to school, Joseph had taught both him and Yemane every day. By the time they went to school they had attained a good foundation for excellent fluency in the speaking and reading of Aramaic, ancient Hebrew, and Greek. They knew the history of the Israelites and knew the Torah well.

School in Alexandria focused upon the teaching of math, Egyptian history, and the speaking and writing of Greek and Latin. Jesus helped Yemane in his academic studies and the boys became closer in brotherly love as time went on. It was no wonder that Jesus and Yemane stayed close together during their first months of school in Alexandria. At first, the other Egyptian boys ignored them and didn't include them in any activities, not in the school building or on the grounds where they went to play during breaks from study. Then at a time during a play period, the two Egyptian boys who had previously accompanied Jesus and Yemane across the swollen creek and into the desert approached them.

"What's your name again?" the larger boy said to Jesus. They both held slingshots and had obviously been playing the popular game of shooting clay birds they had made. When a stone from one of the slingshots was hurled and hit a bird, the bird shattered nicely. Yemane and Jesus enjoyed watching them play and they were quite impressed with the skill of some.

"My name is Jesus. What are your names?"

"My name is Hapy."

"I'm Nefertum."

They stood looking at one another until Jesus said, "This is Yemane."

Hapy ignored Yemane and invited Jesus to use the slingshot and try hitting a clay bird. Jesus gladly took the slingshot and aimed carefully. He shot a stone at one of the clay birds and his rock missed the bird.

"Here, try again. You came close," Hapy said.

Jesus took careful aim again and Nefertum told him to aim a little higher because the stone would arc downward as it flew toward the clay bird. Jesus took Nefertum's advice and released the stone with accuracy, smashing the bird into pieces.

Hapy declared, "Good! It's fun. Isn't it?"

"Yes. It's Yemane's turn now," Jesus said as he turned to give the sling to Yemane.

Nefertum snatched the slingshot from Jesus. "No. He's too black. He can't play with us.

Jesus was stunned. "I've played with Yemane my whole life. He's my brother."

Nefertum said, "We don't care. We won't play with him."

"Then neither shall I play with you without Yemane. I think you're just afraid he'll be better at shooting the birds and you won't have any more birds to shoot. I'll make more clay birds for you and bring them to school tomorrow if you let Yemane play with us."

Hapy and Nefertum looked at each other and then at the few birds they had left. "Can you bring them to school soon?"

"If you let Yemane try to shoot three of your birds, I'll make ten clay birds and bring them to school tomorrow," Jesus promised.

Both Egyptian boys agreed and gave the slingshot to Yemane. "We don't want to waste our stones so you can try once." Hapy whispered to Nefertum, "I bet he won't be able to hit one anyway."

Yemane took the slingshot and aimed. The first release of the stone shattered one of the clay birds and ricocheted to shatter a second bird.

Nefertum exclaimed, "Wow. You hit two birds with one stone!"

Jesus patted Yemane on the back. "It was a lucky shot," Yemane humbly replied. "I don't think I could do it again if I tried."

"There are two birds out there," Hapy said. "Try to do it again."

Jesus looked at Yemane and gave him a look of confidence.

Yemane lifted the sling and took a longer time aiming. He released the sling and once again was successful at shattering two birds with one stone.

Hapy and Nefertum cheered. "You did it again! Can you teach us to do that?"

"Sure," Yemane said as all the students were called in and Yemane invited Hapy and Nefertum to their house. "We'll practice after school if you want to. We'll meet you at the end of this school day."

Hapy and Nefertum, Jesus, and Yemane agreed they would meet after school.

The afternoon lesson in school intrigued Jesus beyond the experience of shooting the stones at clay birds. The instructor talked about the great pharaohs from ancient Egyptian history. Jesus listened intently and learned that when a young boy was designated to be a future pharaoh he was placed in a tomb where he was suffocated to the point of death and then resuscitated. It was a mathematical calculation that insured that the young boy would not die permanently but would be allowed to remain dead long enough to experience the afterlife. This trained and contributed to the future pharaoh's rule to be administered with a justice and wisdom beyond the understanding of this life experience.

He also learned about how the ancient Egyptian magicians knew how to hold asps with a specific grip that kept them safe from being bitten with a venomous bite. They also knew how to apply perfect pressure at a point around the neck of the snake, causing the snake to stiffen like a wooden rod. Jesus couldn't wait to return home to talk to his father about these new discoveries of knowledge.

When Jesus and Yemane came home after school that day, it was raining very hard. They entered the house dripping wet and were instructed to go directly to their rooms and change into dry clothing. After changing into dry clothing, Jesus stood by the back kitchen window and watched the rain fall as he patiently waited for the sound of the front door opening and his father's return from work. Yemane came to stand and watch the rain with him and together they witnessed the little creek turn into a torrent of fast-flowing white water again.

"I wonder if that spot in the desert will turn into another sinking sand hole," Yemane said.

Jesus was in deep thought and kept looking at the water swell in the creek as the rain fell. Finally, the front door opened and Jesus ran to meet Joseph. "Dad, I've got to talk to you about something we learned in school today!"

"All right, Jesus. Let me get out of these wet clothes and greet your mother first."

Joseph found Mary in the extra bedroom with Salome. Jesus stood and watched as his mother played a game with his little sister's hands, which, though he watched intently, he didn't understand, but he sat down next to them, kissed Salome on the head, and turned to Mary. He placed his hand on her abdomen and the baby within kicked a strong kick. He wondered if it hurt his mother as Joseph entered the room, asking Mary how she was feeling, and Mary responded with "I'm fine but tired."

"I love you. If you need to, go lie down now. I'll take Salome, and Ghidai has already started preparations for dinner."

Mary said, "I think I'll do that, thank you."

"You seem sad, Mary. What's bothering you?"

"Oh Joseph, I fear the worst. I asked Qadesh to let us know when she reached her uncle in Pelusium and she's been gone for more than two months now and I haven't heard anything. I fear she is dead."

Joseph gently kissed her forehead. "We did what we could. God will see that there is justice, whatever has happened and whatever will happen. Please, go rest and don't worry."

Mary stood up with Joseph's help and walked to their bedroom as he bent down and lifted Salome. "My goodness, you are growing to be a beautiful young girl!" Joseph said to her. She giggled and hugged Joseph around the neck. "Come, I think Jesus needs to talk about something." He carried her to the front room and Jesus followed them to sit with his father, waiting as patiently as possible for a boy of nearly ten years old.

Joseph sat next to Jesus and asked, "Now what is this that you need to talk to me about?"

Ghidai called Yemane to help her in the kitchen and he left Jesus and Joseph as Jesus began to relay what he had learned in school. Joseph listened with interest and then thought. He asked Jesus, "Well, what are your thoughts about what you learned today?"

"I'm glad I learned that when someone is hurt and not breathing you can get them to start breathing again by blowing air into them. You can press on their chest to get their heart pumping again too."

"And what do you think about the ancient Egyptian magicians causing poisonous asps to become stiff like sticks?"

"I don't think it's magic. I remember you told me about Moses being told to lift a snake and it became like a rod and then God told him to throw it on the ground and it returned to be a living, moving snake again. When you told me about that, I thought it might have been God doing magic. Now I think it was God's wisdom that knew Moses wouldn't be hurt by the snake. God may have been teaching him to face the magicians in Egypt with confidence. It turned out that when Moses did confront the Egyptian magicians and their snakes, Moses' snake swallowed their snakes. The story isn't magic, it's a likely possibility." Jesus leaned against Joseph in thought. "I'm not sure why, but I feel a different kind of closeness to God lately. It's as if God allows us to be a part of his actions and doesn't do anything we can't come to understand."

Joseph put Salome on the floor and turned to Jesus. "I think you are growing and learning just as God wants you to grow and learn. Trust your God, Jesus. Trust your God by trusting yourself. God is in you. He's in us all. Different life experiences for all the different people who ever lived, or will live, make trust and faith grow differently in each of us, but that difference doesn't mean God is not there at work in every human being. Always remember to love God with all your heart, and mind, and soul. And love every person as you love yourself."

Jesus surprised Joseph as he moved closer to him and leaned his head against his arm saying, "I'm so glad you're my dad. I love you." Joseph put his arm around Jesus as they sat together. "You made another baby in mom. I like having brothers and sisters. We're getting to be a big family."

"Yes, we are," said Joseph.

Mary rested before she came to the dinner table to join the growing family. Joseph spoke their prayers and they ate a wonderful meal prepared by the loving hands of Ghidai. "Do you know what I appreciate these days? I don't have to tell Yemane and Jesus to wash before eating. They're doing it on their own." Ghidai said. "Salome, I want you to start washing without a reminder also."

Salome smiled and said she would. Mary sat down and although she felt tired, she was filled with loving joy transcending her tiredness. As they remained sitting at the dinner table, the rain kept pouring down.

By the time dinner was over and the eating utensils were put away, the long afternoon rain had stopped. There were two hours of light left in the evening and Yemane and Jesus ran out to play in the backyard. "Don't go far, boys," Ghidai called after them as they ran out. "You will need to come in soon for bed, you have school tomorrow."

Without hesitation, Jesus ran to the swollen creek's edge. Yemane followed and warned, "Don't even think about going across this to go into the desert to that quicksand hole."

Jesus ignored Yemane and started climbing the tree to cross the river by walking on the branch that spanned the width of the raging water.

"Didn't you hear what I said?" Yemane yelled. "I'm going to go into the house and tell your father and mother what you're doing."

"Yemane, just stay there and watch and make sure I don't get stuck in the sand hole. If I do get stuck then go tell my father and mother."

"Jesus, please don't do this . . . I'm not going with you! Do you understand, Jesus . . . Come back here!"

Yemane watched as Jesus jumped from the branch to the other side of the creek and cleared the water. He turned and ran out into the desert toward the place where he and Yemane had saved the goat. As Jesus had suspected, a flock of doves were caught in the quicksand. Seven birds were flapping their wings, wildly trying to free themselves from the sand. Jesus knew they were in trouble because he had seen them land on the quicksand in the middle of the storm as he had carefully watched through the back window earlier. Trusting and waiting for the rain to end through dinner, he was determined to set them free. Without stopping to reexamine his plan, he moved rocks around the edge of the quicksand hole and laid branches over the rocks and around the hole close to the struggling birds.

"Don't worry. I'm here to help you," he told them as if the panicked birds understood. He remembered the experience when he and Yemane had found the doves in the desert less than a year ago. One dove had lain dead while its partner remained close to it on the ground, holding a vigil and guarding it without fail until it also died in the extreme afternoon heat of the desert. Jesus looked at the doves that were caught in the sand hole and then at the other birds sitting and waiting for their partners to be freed. Carefully he stretched his body over and across the branches, moving closer to the doves that were struggling to free themselves from the sucking quagmire that held them captive. He gently reached out and pulled one from the sand and tossed it softly to solid ground. It walked around a bit and shook the sand from its wings. There were six more birds to free. Yemane could see what Jesus was doing and he shook his head, wondering what was wrong in Jesus' head!

Out of nowhere, Hapy and Nefertum appeared at Yemane's side. Nefertum saw Jesus in the distance and asked, "What's Jesus doing?" Yemane didn't answer. Rather he continued to watch with intensity. Nefertum and Hapy also watched and could see that Jesus was lifting birds out of the sand and placing them on solid ground and they both assumed he was making clay birds to bring to school the next day.

After Jesus freed all seven from their trap, one by one the birds flew away, some with their waiting partners, up into the sky and over the heads of the boys.

"Wow! Did you see that? Jesus's clay birds came alive! How did he do that?" Hapy asked in amazement.

Yemane looked at Hapy and shook his head but decided it wasn't worth it to explain to his new Egyptian friends what really was happening. He was more concerned about Jesus' safety. He yelled, "All right, Jesus, get out of there. I'll meet you to help you cross the creek by way of the branch. Get over here, now!"

Jesus could be seen inching his body away from the quicksand hole on the branches he had laid down. When he backed up to solid ground he stood up and ran back to the branch hanging over the creek. Yemane didn't wait for him to crawl back over the wild water on the branch but climbed the tree to the branch and lowered his hand to lift Jesus up onto the hanging limb. With Jesus and Yemane on the limb it dipped down and the leaves were brushed by the fast-moving water in the creek. Together they spanned the bridge the tree branch supplied and this time Yemane walked upright across the branch like Jesus had. They climbed down the trunk and stood on the ground to face Hapy and Nefertum.

From the house the boys heard Jesus' mother cry, "You boys need to come in and get washed for bed now."

Hapy and Nefertum continued to stand and stare at Jesus.

"I've got to go in the house now. See you tomorrow. Oh, I can't bring ten clay birds tomorrow because of the rain and . . ."

Nefertum finished Jesus' sentence, "And they all flew away anyway."

Jesus turned and looked at Yemane. He shrugged his shoulders. He and Yemane left the two Egyptian boys standing alone speechless.

The next day a rumor spread throughout the school. Hapy and Nefertum told everyone that Jesus could make birds from mud and sand, explaining that miraculously he did something to make them come alive. Jesus received a lot of attention but he didn't necessarily like it. He had just talked to his father about the difference between real life and magic. He tried to tell Hapy and Nefertum that the birds were living when they had become stuck in the quicksand and he had just freed them. The boys needed the myth, however, because it certainly provided more intrigue and mystery. It also brought them personal fame and attention in the school as they insisted that their friend, Jesus, had power to give life.

So, Jesus did his best to ignore the new false fame and tried to go about his business of learning, especially when the history lessons about ancient Egypt were being taught. In the lessons, Jesus wondered why there was no mention of the Israelites, their slavery, and their freedom from the pharaoh. Given the commotion he already felt responsible for in the school, he decided to wait and ask his father at home.

Already feeling responsible for the distracting excitement of the day, Jesus patiently waited as this school day seemed to progress slowly. Finally, school ended and Jesus ran home with Yemane. Yemane went directly out to play while Jesus waited for Joseph to come home from work. As Joseph entered the house, Jesus intercepted his father before anyone else. "Dad, Dad! I need to talk to you!"

"Let me find your mother and kiss her hello. I also need to hug Salome and greet Ghidai and Yemane."

Jesus sat on the bench in the front room with controlled impatience. Finally, Joseph came into the room and sat down next to Jesus and said, "You have my undivided attention now."

Jesus talked quickly and with excitement while he explained what he had learned about Egypt's ancient history. "Dad, the teacher never talked about the Israelites, or Passover, or their slavery, or their escape through the Red Sea. He didn't teach about the plagues or the firstborn son dying in a household if the blood of a lamb was not placed on the doorframe. I was going to say something but decided to come home and ask you."

Joseph sat in silence for a while. He sighed and looked at Jesus. "We talked about magic as opposed to reality the other day. Jesus, I can only tell you what I have come to understand and you need to know that it may not be physically and factually correct. As you grow you will need to learn and decide for yourself."

Jesus looked at his father and said, "But I don't know enough to make decisions for myself now. Tell me."

Joseph felt tremendous responsibility and discomfort. It almost seemed too great for him and he realized that Jesus was not even ten years old yet. He feared and wondered what it would it be like for him when Jesus was eighteen, or twenty-four? Mary walked into the room and detected her husband's quandary.

"What's going on here?" she asked.

Joseph looked at Jesus and said, "Why don't you speak of what you have just said and ask your mother what you asked me."

Jesus repeated to her what he had questioned with Joseph about the great exodus of the Israelites from Egypt and explained that the event was never mentioned by his teacher as he taught and they studied ancient Egyptian history.

"Oh, my goodness, Jesus," she replied. "You certainly think deep thoughts." She sat on the other side of Jesus and with more confidence than Joseph she spoke. "I don't think God makes magic happen but there are mysteries. Mysteries can be understood but not without the help from the Spirit of God. Mysteries are not magic, but they often appear to be magical. The Israelites were enslaved, as we all are enslaved to our own state of humanness. Whether or not the Israelites were actually slaves in the sense of being owned by Egyptian masters does not matter. The importance lies in the faith we hold, which supports a belief that the Israelites were people called by God to bring ethical truth into the midst of human existence. The law was given to them, and us, to be displayed in our lives as examples to others. Many years have passed and the details of the Israelite historical events have become obscure. The mystery lies in the fact that we remember the story of the exodus and we observe the law given to Moses, as a gift from the great Creator of the universe for all people. Jesus, we are Israelites. We understand that we are chosen by God to be witnesses to the great Yahweh to our world. Our lives show that there is a God who loves us, cares for us, and guides us. Because I believe that, I also choose to believe we were slaves at one time within the Egyptian Empire and were led by Moses to freedom. That freedom is the freedom that comes to us even today if we are open to the guidance of God. We are taught from the scroll of Deuteronomy that we are to love God with all our hearts, minds, and spirits, and we are to love each other as we love ourselves." Mary jumped. "Come here, Jesus. Feel this." She placed Jesus' hand on her abdomen and Jesus felt the child within kick and punch.

"Does it hurt, Mom?"

"No, but it makes you take notice. In a little less than three months there will be another baby with us." Salome ran into the room and jumped on Jesus.

"Let's play!" she said.

Jesus stood up and let his little sister tug him to the backyard. Jesus turned and said, "Thanks, Mom and Dad. I'm learning bit by bit, but I'm learning."

Joseph moved close to Mary. He put his arms around her and said, "I think you're beautiful and brilliant!"

Surprisingly, the next day in school, Jesus' history teacher, Annon, who never ceased to capture Jesus' attention and interest, spoke of the Israelites. Annon was Jesus' favorite teacher and the youngest among the other instructors. He brought an enthusiasm to his class that the other teachers lacked. Although Jesus respected and liked his other teachers, Annon revealed to Jesus knowledge of events and history that awakened something inside his heart, soul, and mind. Jesus was drawn to Annon and felt greater respect for him because he showed dedication to all his students with genuine kindness and personal thirst for truth.

Finally, that day in school Annon spoke of the Israelites. Jesus felt excitement as Annon taught history like it was an epic adventure. Today, Annon was talking about a Roman military movement to secure their domination and control of Egypt. He talked with animated enthusiasm. "The Romans moved north on ships taking the easternmost branch of the Nile. Finally, they left their ships and marched, following the Necho Canal to the Red Sea. They crossed the border at a place called the Sea of Reeds. The Sea of Reeds is a godforsaken place and the land there is subject to the tides . . . the stench of the place can make you gag and choke. It is the very same place where the Israelites escaped from Memphis many years ago with the renegade Egyptian Moses. The tides control this depressing marshland. It is very flat, and extends across a great expanse. When the tide rolls in, the water is squeezed through these small tributaries. Today, Rome has built permanent canals to direct the seawater to spill over the land farther south to a place north of the Red Sea. When the water rushes in it spills from the canals in huge waves over into the land called the Sea of Reeds. When this happens, the dry land becomes covered with salt water from the Great Mediterranean Sea. It can catch anyone trying to cross the land unaware. It has been known to drown anyone caught there by the force of its waves. This most likely happened when the pharaoh's soldiers tried to follow the Israelites who were leaving Egypt in search of their promised land. The tide must have trapped the pursuing Egyptian soldiers in the marsh and many of them drowned."

Jesus could be silent no longer. He stood and waited for Annon to acknowledge him and give permission to speak.

"Well, well, finally Jesus has something to say. I've been waiting for you to come alive and talk."

Jesus was nervous as he felt the eyes of all his fellow students look at him. Then Jesus's eyes fell upon Yemane, who gave him an encouraging gesture to go ahead and talk.

"Master . . . Annon, you said Moses was an Egyptian renegade . . . I am an Israelite and in our Holy Scripture he is described as a leader, sent by God to lead the Israelites out of Egypt to the promised land. He was not Egyptian . . . he may have grown up in an Egyptian royal family, he may have learned how to be a great leader *from* the Egyptians, but he was an Israelite by birth. He was adopted by an Egyptian princess when he was a baby. When he grew up, he heard God's calling and followed God's direction."

Annon walked across the front of the class with his hands placed together in front of his face in a prayerlike fashion. He turned back around and said to Jesus, "Very good! Well done, Jesus. I knew you were an Israelite, but I never thought you would have the courage to speak up. Good for you! Tell me, what do you think about the explanation about the Sea of Reeds?"

Jesus stood silently for what seemed a long time. All eyes were still turned on him. Finally, he said, "I think you are correct. Of course, Moses would have crossed the shortest distance of a sea in order to get out of Egypt. Although, our Holy Scriptures write that the water was split and the Israelites walked through between two walls of water on dry land. I can easily accept that they crossed the Sea of Reeds at low tide. I need to think about everything else and decide what I believe."

"Ah . . . yes! Then you need to know that there is another natural phenomenon that affects the outcome. It is the wind!" Annon almost ran to the other side of the room. Jesus was intrigued. Annon almost whispered, "The wind . . . ! You see, when the wind blows from the east to the west it can prevent the water, rushing through the canals from the tide, from rolling into the marshland. Sometimes, it has been known to blow the water back . . . back into canals and out to other little rivers in the delta basin. You see, the Sea of Reeds is flat and above the sea level. At times, the wind will blow and actually roll the tidal water back, so it will not cover the land for days. The land actually becomes dry. If the wind blows with strength from east to west and the tide comes in at the same time it will blow the water back in walls of water. It has been reported that the wind can actually blow and split the incoming wall of water from the canals, making a path running northwest by southeast! What do you think of that, Jesus?"

Jesus was in thought but deciphered his teacher's question. "I think . . ." he took a deep breath, "I think I want to go there and see the Sea of Reeds with my own eyes."

Annon smiled a broad smile. Without taking his eyes off Jesus he dismissed the class.

Outside, Yemane and Jesus walked home and talked about school. When they sat down together for their evening meal Yemane took it upon himself to break Jesus' silence and contemplation.

"You should have seen Jesus at school today!" Yemane declared.

Ghidai looked at Jesus and said, "I knew something was up, Jesus. What happened today at school?"

Jesus gave a stare back at Yemane, trying to communicate to his brother to keep his words to himself. Yemane didn't heed Jesus' stare but rather he encouraged Jesus to relay what had happened in their history class.

"Come now, Jesus. How can you not tell your parents and my mother what you talked about with the teacher in front of the whole class?"

Joseph stopped eating and Mary said, "What did you talk about in class today?"

Jesus said nothing. Yemane blurted out and described the entire discussion that had taken place between Jesus and their teacher, Annon. "And he said all this in front of the class too," Yemane reported.

Mary gently said, "How fortunate for you to have such a discussion with your teacher. How absolutely interesting, to think there is a place called the Sea of Reeds and that it can turn into a marshland, a muddy swamp filled with vipers, or sometimes filled with salt water from the Mediterranean Sea when the tide rushes in. What a horrible place to be."

Jesus finally spoke up saying, "I want to invite our teacher to our home for dinner. Can we do that?"

Mary looked at Joseph, who had not begun to eat again. Without hesitation, he said, "Mary, it is up to you and Ghidai. I think I would enjoy the opportunity to talk to one of Jesus' and Yemane's teachers, but it is your decision."

"Of course, Jesus, you may invite your teacher for our evening meal the day after tomorrow, if you would like." Mary felt pride and joy in her son's accomplishments. For some reason she felt his day at school was a great accomplishment of importance.

The next day after school, Jesus approached Annon and graciously asked him to join his family for their evening meal the following day.

Annon was visibly honored. "Jesus, I'm married. May my wife join me at your home?"

Without thought, Jesus knew his mother would welcome his teacher and his wife. "Yes, we would be blessed to have you both share an evening meal with us."

Jesus ran out to Yemane and excitedly told him that their teacher had accepted his invitation. Together they ran home and told their mothers.

The next day progressed all too slowly for Jesus and Yemane. But the evening came and Annon and his lovely wife appeared at their door on time. Joseph greeted them and invited them into the home. Jesus and Yemane stood at attention while Ghidai and Mary introduced themselves to Annon and his wife, Charmion.

Discussion around the dinner table was brimming with interesting topics. At one point, Annon asked, "So, Jesus, if it is alright with your parents and Ghidai, I'll take you and Yemane to the Sea of Reeds to see what it's like with your own eyes."

It was as if Yahweh, the God Almighty himself, jumped in Jesus' mind. "Yes! I'd love to see the Sea of Reeds!"

"Whoa, how far is the Sea of Reeds from Alexandria?" Joseph asked.

Annon stated that it would take them one day to sail to Migdol and one day to walk to the Sea of Reeds, which lies northeast of Memphis. They would need five days to complete the journey and return. Annon admitted he had never seen the Sea of Reeds and explained that he also wished to see the marshland. Their journey would count as educational and he would offer the opportunity to all the boys he taught.

Jesus looked back and forth to his father and mother with serious pleading that they allow him to take this journey with his classmates and teacher, pleading and saying, "I'll be safe to go, and Yemane will be with me!"

Joseph informed Annon that he and Mary would talk about it later and Jesus, along with Yemane, would give Annon an answer tomorrow.

After Annon and Charmion departed, Jesus and Yemane sat quietly in the front room. Joseph went into the kitchen to talk to Ghidai and then passed Jesus and Yemane to enter the bedroom to talk to Mary.

"Do you think our parents will let us go?" Yemane asked anxiously.

Jesus didn't answer. He sat and stared at his parents' door. What seemed like hours had passed. Five minutes later, Joseph emerged with Mary from the bedroom. Joseph looked at the boys and couldn't help grinning. "Yes, you may go to see the Sea of Reeds with Annon. I hope you understand it will be a dangerous trip and you must obey Annon with unfaltering attention and respect."

Jesus jumped up and said, "I will, father!" He hugged Joseph and went to say good night to his mother. Yemane went to find his mother and thanked her. He came to the room to sleep, wishing he could run with Jesus immediately to tell Annon they were allowed to go. But they waited and informed their teacher the next day.

The trip would take place in two weeks. Annon also invited anyone else in the class to join their expedition, but, to Jesus' surprise, only he, Yemane, and Annon would be going.

THE SEA OF REEDS

WAITING TO LEAVE WAS hard for Jesus and Yemane but the day finally came and the three began their trip by boarding a ship that would carry them around the delta to Migdol. They sailed to Migdol in less than two hours. Although Migdol was a small city in comparison to Alexandria, it afforded them a comfortable night's stay.

"Tomorrow we will leave before the sun rises and walk to the Sea of Reeds. We should be able to walk there within the daylight, camp for the night, and rise to see this landmark by daybreak of the next day. I really don't know what we will see because the natural changes of the landscape are unpredictable," Annon explained.

Both boys were up and ready to travel before sunrise. They ate a breakfast of eggs, bread, and fruit and packed enough food and drink for their journey. After walking four hours, a stench like nothing they had ever smelled before invaded their nostrils. No one complained. They had expected this unpleasant part of their planned journey so they continued walking. The stench got worse and Annon explained that it was believed by some of the Egyptians that the stench was the breath of Seth, their god of evil. Jesus and Yemane held the sleeves of their cloaks over their noses and looked at one another with understanding. It made sense to them.

They walked another three hours and Annon stopped abruptly. "We're here . . . I think." As if talking to himself he said, "This is it. It's got to be here. Look down." The ground was dry and cracked. It stretched out as far as they could see. There was no variation in the level of the land's expanse. The horrible stench permeated their sense of smell but it had diminished, as if they accepted its presence. They were tired of walking and glad to believe they had arrived even if they didn't know where they really were. Annon seemed unsure but he chose an area that seemed safe to camp for the night. He secretly chided himself for not having checked the times for high tide at Migdol and calculating their possible effects over the distance they had traveled to this godforsaken land. They all sat together and shared food and drink as the sun set and colored the sky red. Eventually, they were left in an eerie stillness of the night's darkness. Fortunately, they were under a clear sky with no moon. Annon wondered whether this was a good or bad sign, knowing that it was the moon that affected the strengths of tidal surges.

Jesus and Yemane fell asleep quickly and soundly, but Annon dozed on and off, feeling nervous. He was not sure they were safe. If the tide washed into the area they presently occupied, they could be surrounded by angry tidal water almost instantly. Waves of salt water could also possibly reach this far with the potential to literally crash over them. Although he felt he had picked a camping site of safety, where water would not cover them should there be a tidal surge, he was not sure. Everything had looked so flat.

In contrast to Annon, Jesus fell into a deep, peaceful sleep. Later, while sailing back to Alexandria, Jesus remembered a vivid dream he had had the night he slept on the cracked earth of the Sea of Reeds. He had distinctly felt a hand was on his back while a voiceless message seemed to say over and over again, "Do not be afraid, my child."

Near sunrise, Annon was awakened feeling wet. He sat up and looked down. In horror he noticed water trickling beneath them, soaking through the dry cracked land wherever weight was pressing against the land. He looked to the north and to his great alarm he saw a wall of water in the shadowy distance moving toward them.

"Boys!" he yelled. "Get up! Leave everything and run with me."

Jesus and Yemane woke suddenly to find themselves wet with salt water and caked in mud. Jesus looked north and saw the wall of water coming toward them while both he and Yemane followed Annon, all three running as fast as they could. But the ground was now a muddy marshland and it grabbed at their feet with a grip that would not let go easily. The wall of water was moving close. Its speed could surely overtake them and capture them in a salty, watery grave.

Jesus looked up at the sky. Dark clouds and lightning gathered over them, moving very quickly from the southeast. Jesus stopped and turned to look at the wall of water coming from the northwest. He saw that there was no way out.

Annon stopped and also realized that the water could swallow them. He stood and cried out to his god, "Oh, Rah, great god of the world, please hold back the water with your mighty hand now, in this place and at this time."

Yemane had fallen into the mud and Annon knew their only hope was a strong wind from the southeast, which could possibly push the water back north and west in the canals.

Suddenly, with a powerful force of wind, the storm began to blow. Jesus said, "Yes! Yes! I see!" Silently Jesus lifted a prayer he had often heard Joseph pray: "Keep us safe in the palm of your hand so that we may live to do your will."

Annon and Yemane didn't move as the strength of the wind hit them with a blast they had never experienced before. Yemane felt as if the wind could have blown him away had his feet not been stuck in the muddy land. In disbelief and enchantment, they felt the wind move past them and watched it slam against the wall of water moving toward them. Suddenly the water stopped in its path. The wind blew with a force that split the wave on a diagonal track, moving the water to separate, exposing a diagonal path running northwest to southeast. The wind continued to blow the water back, back from where it came. Annon looked around in a panic, hoping to see a sign indicating safe dry land. A good distance away, to the west, his eyes detected elevated land that had no cracks. "Come on, boys! We still need to run!" Jesus and Yemane obeyed. Their feet continued to hit the dry cracked land that crumbled to expose the wet marshland underneath, grabbing at their feet, making it hard to run with any speed but they didn't give up. They continued running until their feet finally fell on completely solid dry land. They saw an elevated bank where the water could not swallow or submerge them even if the wind released the wall of water to crash over and fill the marshland.

They all fell to the ground and began to laugh. They sat up and watched the wind from the storm push northwest. As the storm passed away from them the wall of water regained its surge. Since they were safe where they sat, they stayed to watch the water rush over the marshland before them. Snakes that had remained dormant under the cracked dry earth slithered up from the wet ground underneath to swim in the murky quagmire as they watched in an astonished state of disbelief.

Jesus jumped up. "That was great! That was absolutely great! Who would have thought this sea could actually do this, even today!"

Annon put his hands on his head and he slowly shook his head back and forth. "Jesus, I knew you were a special student but do you realize how close we came to being drowned and swept away? Yemane, are you alright?"

Yemane smiled back at Annon and said, "You must admit it was exciting."

Annon looked at Jesus, asking in a very shaky voice, "Are you alright?" Jesus kept staring out over the snake-infested marshland thinking about the event he had just witnessed.

Annon got up and stood next to Jesus. "I'll never forget you, Jesus, never. I'm not a believing man but it moved me to pray to some kind of god out there." He turned and said, "Well, I think we need to look around this area for fresh water. We can't walk back to Migdol without water."

Jesus continued to stand and look out over the marshland, asking with no alarm, "Did you notice it smells better?" Finally, he looked at Annon and Yemane. He saw they seemed distressed about something. "What's the matter?"

"We don't have any water, Jesus" Yemane said.

"Come along. I think I know where we may be able to find a spring near the Little Bitter Lake. We passed it on our way here. It's not far. I noticed it on the way."

Annon asked, "What makes you think there's fresh water to find near there?"

"I read about it in the Holy Scriptures, in Exodus."

Both followed Jesus. To be sure, there was a spring of fresh water gushing forth from a rock near the Little Bitter Lake. They drank their fill, knowing they had lost any containers to fill and carry with them back to Migdol. Seemingly unconcerned, Jesus began to lead their walk and as they walked together back to Migdol to catch their ship to return home, Jesus had a deep conversation with Annon. Annon explained to him that it was not magic that had allowed the Israelites to cross the Sea of Reeds, it was coincidental timing. Jesus also asked what Annon thought about the Israelites receiving manna in the desert, and the flocks of quail that appeared. Annon told Jesus that, most likely, the manna that appeared on the desert floor was not bread, but a large bread-like mushroom that quickly sprouted in the night. "That type of mushroom still grows today in the desert if all the conditions are present to support the spores to be released and grow. That's why Moses told them to take only what they could eat immediately. The mushrooms spoiled quickly and became toxic. They couldn't be gathered and saved for another day. The appearance of flocks of quail seems quite likely. Many times, flocks of quail have migrated to the south from the Mediterranean Sea's shores. There is no magic, Jesus, only miracles of coincidence, one of which you witnessed in the Sea of Reeds. As time goes by these coincidences grow into unbelievable proportions and sadly, one's reason and logic must be shut down in order to accept their exaggerated interpretation. We all want our gods to take care of us and feed us, don't we?"

Together they made it safely home within three days. They surprised their loved ones when they returned early. Little was spoken about their journey but it had been an important experience for Jesus, which Mary detected but silently held to herself within her heart.

THE BIRTH OF JAMES

THE DAYS TURNED TO weeks. The weeks led to the passing of months and Mary's time to deliver her third child came early one morning before the boys left for school. Jesus was awakened by his mother's scream. He jumped out of bed and met Yemane and Salome in the hall outside Joseph and Mary's bedroom door. Mary released another scream and Jesus opened the door and ran to his mother. Salome and Yemane followed. Mary was lying in the bed and Joseph was holding her hand and placing a wet cloth over her sweating forehead. Jesus and Yemane understood what was happening but Salome began to cry, "Mommy, I want Mommy!"

Ghidai entered the room and walked around the bed and picked Salome up, taking her out of the room. Salome began to cry and reached her arms back to her mother over Ghidai's shoulders. Joseph, Jesus, and Yemane stood still around the bed. Mary began to writhe with pain and Joseph held her down.

"Try to breathe slowly and concentrate, Mary. You'll be all right. You've done this before. Just a little longer and the baby will be born." Mary screamed aloud again and Joseph's eyes filled with tears. Why was this so hard?

Joseph retreated to a chair that had been brought in for him by Ghidai. He put his head in his hands and Jesus knew he was crying. Ghidai pulled his hands away from his head and sternly said, "Joseph, life is a constant challenge. It is a different challenge for each of us. You said that too. I think Mary wants to face this challenge with courage. You can all help her do that now." She reached out to Joseph and pulled him up by his wrists. "Come on. Help Mary be brave in her hour of need."

Joseph stood and walked to the bed and said to Mary, "You can do this. Soon you will be holding this child in your arms and your struggle to give birth will be over. I'm here."

Ghidai turned to the boys and gave strict orders to leave the room. They obeyed and went to sit with Salome. Ghidai checked Mary's progress.

"Oh, my goodness!" she exclaimed. "Alright, Mary. Get ready to push. I see the crowning of the baby's head. Be strong. Obey your body."

Mary's face turned red with exertion. She pushed and let out a low guttural cry and began to push again.

"That's the way to do it! Push again!"

Mary pushed and screamed again. Ghidai moved to catch the baby whose head was already out. In another push the body was pushed out. The pain stopped immediately and Ghidai lifted the baby to Joseph.

"Joseph, why don't you go over to the table that is prepared and clean your new son's body?"

Joseph held his son and couldn't move. It was his firstborn son! Born in September! The holy festivals of Rosh Hashanah and Yom Kippur were about to take place in Judea and his son was born in their midst.

Ghidai attended to Mary and massaged her abdomen, not knowing that this custom actually helped close the blood vessels in her womb. She just knew it helped relax the tired muscles.

"Are you happy, Joseph?" Mary asked. She smiled. "You now have two sons and a daughter! God has blessed you."

Mary had fallen asleep and Ghidai took the baby boy from Joseph to the table and washed the baby's skin by rubbing salt over him, as was the custom. She proceeded to rinse and wrap cloths around the baby and then gave him to Joseph again. Joseph was still shocked. He was given a son!

Ghidai looked at him and shook her head before saying, "I'll send Yemane to Seth and ask him to report that you will not be coming to work today. You need to stay home with your family." Ghidai was sure he didn't hear her but she finished by asking, "What will your new son's name be?"

Joseph said, "James." He held the baby up and praised God. He had James, his firstborn son, born ten years after Jesus. Jesus had been born in March. James was born in the middle of the holy month of September as it was expected that the Messiah would be born. Joseph lowered James and held him close to his chest. It suddenly dawned on him that he needed to locate a rabbi to have his son circumcised on the eighth day of his life. He suddenly felt panicked as he wondered where in Alexandria, Egypt, a rabbi could be found. He felt sure Seth would know. Yes, he would ask Seth.

"Dad," Jesus said standing quietly next to Joseph. Jesus' voice startled Joseph. "Dad," Jesus said again, "May Yemane and I hold James?"

Sheepishly, Joseph said, "Of course, of course." Joseph stood up and handed the newborn child into Jesus' arms.

Jesus looked down at James and felt an instant emotion of love. He looked at his mother who was still resting in the bed and walked next to her. "He's so tiny. Look at his hands and feet." Jesus spoke with genuine awe.

Yemane came up to Jesus out of breath from running to tell Seth that Joseph would not be going to work today. He said, "My turn."

Jesus gently gave James to Yemane as Joseph watched.

Everyone stayed home that day. The boys didn't go to school but stayed close to Salome. Ghidai spent the day attending to Mary and the baby. Joseph sat and held his new son for the better part of the day, releasing him from his arms only to nurse at Mary's breast. The day was different, filled with cheerful tranquility.

The next day everything fell back into somewhat of a typical routine. Joseph went to work, the boys went to school, and Ghidai looked after Salome, Mary, and Baby James. Jesus felt honored to be blessed with another brother. He thought about his own age difference from James. When he would be sixteen, James would be six. He thought that this plan would be fine and he looked forward to the time James would be old enough to follow him like Salome.

It turned out that Seth indeed did know where a rabbi could be located nearby. The circumcision of James was scheduled to take place in their home in seven days.

On the eighth day after James' birth, a man appeared at their front door. Jesus answered the door and didn't recognize the man who stood before him. However, he did recognize the clothing he was wearing, indicating his status as a Jewish rabbi. Jesus invited the rabbi into their home with respect as Joseph stepped between Jesus and the rabbi and talked to him in Aramaic as he led him into the room set up for James' circumcision procedure.

Yemane, Jesus, and the rabbi stood over the table that Joseph had prepared and Joseph brought James to the table and laid him down before the rabbi. Prayers and chanting ensued and the rabbi cut James' foreskin and removed it. James screamed in pain and Jesus remained next to the table until the complete procedure was finished though he was unable to focus on any of the words spoken.

The rabbi left and Mary came to lift James, who was still screaming. She hummed to him and offered her breast for him to suckle and he quieted. Jesus and Yemane said good night and felt ready to sleep so they didn't speak to each other as they walked to their rooms.

As Jesus lay alone in his room, he felt sad and happy at the same moment, not knowing why. He wondered why God commanded this practice of circumcision. He wondered if God was truly merciful and just.

As is the way with life, the new is born and the old passes away. When Joseph returned from work the next day he went to the barn, as he always did, to feed and water their burro. When he came into the little stall he was saddened to see the burro had died. Overcome with too much emotion,

Joseph sat down and cried and cried and cried. The burro had brought them to this safe place, had worked his fields at home, and had carried his beloved Mary home from her Aunt Elizabeth and Uncle Zechariah's. After his weeping subsided, he called Jesus and Yemane out to help him bury the burro's body and thank God for the gift of life, all life.

BETHANY

RACHAEL, BENJAMIN, AND THE children were very happy to have Lazarus home with them. Lazarus was surprised at Martha and Mary's growth. They looked almost like women to him. Benjamin and Rachael now had two of their own children, Levi and Ruth. Although they were younger, they were as much a blessing as Lazarus, Martha, and Mary.

The children were filled with questions for Lazarus. "How long will you be able to stay home? What is the temple like at this busy month of September? Do you ever see King Herod carried through the streets by the palace guard? Do you have a lot of friends?" Of all the questions, not one was asked about their father or Uncle Eleazar. Lazarus was glad for it.

After they ate an evening meal together, the children were sent to bed. Lazarus stayed up to talk to his Aunt Rachael and Uncle Benjamin.

"You have become quite a handsome young man," Rachael praised. Lazarus was seventeen years old and his voice had deepened like a man. However, his countenance revealed his need to be close to his surrogate parents. "How is it for you in Jerusalem, Lazarus?" his Aunt Rachael asked, genuinely filled with thoughtful love.

Lazarus didn't answer immediately. Rachael and Benjamin waited patiently. Finally, Lazarus said, "I hate it! I hate living with my father over the Sabbaths. I feel so lonely in the temple and the studying is grueling. There is no joy. There is no gentle compassion. Every new thing we learn reading the law or the Holy Scriptures becomes grounds for competition. I don't want to go back." Lazarus fought the urge to cry. "I want to stay here, with you and your children and my sisters."

Rachael went to Lazarus and knelt down by him and held him close. "You're so sad." She took his face and turned it to her own. "Does it help to know that your mother would be so proud of you?"

With great sadness, Lazarus said, "I remember her so well. I miss her so deeply. I ache for her every waking moment and it doesn't stop. I remember her clearly. She was like you, Aunt Rachael. She was gentle, and loving, and kind. She filled our home with cheerful peace." Lazarus' expression changed and with resentment he said, "I know what my father did to her. I've studied the law. I hate him for killing my mother. He's a bastard!"

Rachael placed her finger over Lazarus' mouth. "Do not speak that way about your father, ever."

Lazarus placed his head into his hands, covering his face, hoping his aunt and uncle could not detect his tears. Rachael moved close to him again and held him. She began to rock him back and forth gently. "Shhh," she quietly whispered. "Lazarus, do you remember the flowers she gave to you before she died? Do you remember how the desert bloomed in all its magnificent glory the season your mother died? That was God's promise and gift to you. You need a good friend. Do you have any friends at the temple?"

Lazarus shook his head.

Rachael continued to hold him and prayed that a friend would come into his life. She knew he would be returning to Jerusalem in two weeks and was concerned that his sadness was too great for him to bear. "Uncle Benjamin and I will appeal to your father to send you home, here, every Sabbath, for a while. You can certainly walk the distance between here and Jerusalem. Would that help you?"

Lazarus looked up to his Aunt Rachael and then to his Uncle Benjamin, who nodded his head. "We need help around here. With your two sisters and our three children, your presence every week would be a great help to us."

Their invitation to come home every Sabbath cheered him and he hugged his Aunt Rachael and walked to his Uncle Benjamin and fell into his arms. "Thank you."

"You're welcome. Go and get some sleep now. These next two weeks are going to be very busy for you."

Lazarus turned and walked to a sleeping mat in the boys' room. He was careful to be quiet as he lay down and fell asleep, listening to the breathing of Levi and John. His ear often ached where his father had hit him but he was glad to be home.

Rachael and Benjamin sat in their front room for a while and Benjamin walked to the lantern to extinguish its flame. Rachael rose and took Benjamin by his hand and led him outside. She turned to look at the bright light in the northwest that had risen above their heads for the night. Benjamin placed his arm around her and said, "Well, I remember praying for children but I never dreamed it would come like this. It's alright, though. They are all certainly a great blessing."

Rachael said, "I'm glad you feel that way Benjamin . . . I'm pregnant again."

Benjamin looked at her, lifted her off her feet, hugged her, and laughed. "Good Lord, you do give abundantly!"

Rachael looked up into the night sky and prayed: Great God of the universe, please send a good friend to Lazarus. He needs a good friend.

GOING HOME

TIME ADVANCED AND WORD had spread four years ago that King Herod was very ill and would not live too much longer. Among his subjects there was no great sentiment or hope that he would survive. Under his rule, he had built up Jerusalem and its temple, but the tension in Judea and its surrounding area was mounting, and many believed and spoke about this time with hope for the Messiah to come and restore God's shalom.

In Alexandria, Joseph and his family lived well and were loved and respected by all who knew them. Jesus especially had made a positive impact upon whomever he encountered. It didn't seem real to them when they realized they had already lived in Alexandria for ten years. The rumor about Jesus' ability to make living birds from the mud lingered among his fellow students and their parents. However, another event magnified rumors that made Jesus even more unrealistically popular. It happened one Sabbath day and remained indelibly etched in the minds of many who were witnesses. It happened when Jesus, Yemane, and three other Egyptian friends were playing on the roof of Nefertum's house. Their play became rough and a little out of control. The boys were tackling each other and Jesus decided he and Yemane were going to go home. As they descended the ladder to the ground, Hapy and another Egyptian friend named Min pursued Nefertum to knock him down. Unintentionally, they pushed him over and off the side of the roof. As Nefertum fell to the ground below, the boys on the roof were suspended in horror. In the next moment they heard Nefertum's mother screaming for help. The boys climbed down the ladder and stood beside Yemane and Jesus to see Nefertum lying motionless with his mother. She began to wail loudly. Neighbors came out of their houses and tried to pull Nefertum's mother away from her son's lifeless body. Confusion escalated when Nefertum's father and brothers came out to witness the scene. He turned on the boys and yelled, "What happened? Tell me, what happened to our son!"

Hapy pointed to Yemane and said, "He did it. He pushed Nefertum off the rooftop! We all saw him do it, didn't we?"

Jesus stepped forward and walked directly to Nefertum. He gently guided Nefertum's hysterical mother away from Nefertum's body. She surprisingly obeyed by standing up and moving next to her husband. Jesus bent over Nefertum and placed his ear against Nefertum's chest and then up to his mouth and nose. Jesus detected no heartbeat and heard no air moving, indicating he was not breathing. Jesus remembered what he had learned at school about the young boys waiting to become the future pharaohs. He remembered that deliberate suffocation was practiced on these young boys to give them an experience of death in the afterlife. Following deliberate suffocation, the young pharaohs-to-be were revived. Jesus decided to try to revive Nefertum. He placed his mouth over Nefertum's mouth and blew air into his body. Nefertum's chest responded by expanding upward. He blew air into his body again and pressed his chest down to allow the air to expel. He repeated this fifteen times and then began to pump against the middle of his chest, hoping his heart would begin beating again. He pressed the chest up and down ten times and returned to blowing air into Nefertum. Suddenly and most unexpectedly, Nefertum took a loud, long breath under his own power. He began to cough. He sat up and looked completely dazed. He looked at Jesus and said, "What happened?"

Nefertum's father and mother fell on their knees next to their son and began to kiss him profusely. The neighbors watching began to pat Jesus on the back and praised him. Nefertum's father picked Nefertum off the ground and looked at Jesus. "Thank you for my son's life."

Jesus answered, "No, I did what I learned how to do in school."

Nefertum's mother grabbed Jesus and kissed him long and hard on the cheek. Both parents turned and walked into the house with Nefertum in his father's arms as his wife shouted, "Praise the gods! Praise them!"

Jesus looked at Hapy and said, "Why did you blame Yemane for pushing Nefertum off the roof? We were already on the ground to see Nefertum fall." Jesus contemplated this action on Hapy's part and continued to look at him, waiting for an explanation. Finally, Jesus spoke up and said, "You knew Yemane didn't knock Nefertum off of the roof."

Hapy said nothing and Jesus said to Yemane, "Let's go home."

For days after this incident, many neighbors stopped at Jesus' home to talk to Joseph and Mary about their wonderful son. They all discussed the event as if Jesus had special powers. It didn't seem to change Jesus or his parents. However, change did come, and it came abruptly. Not many nights later Joseph had a vivid dream. He dreamed a man, shining with great light, came to him and said, "Get up, take the child, his mother, and your family, and go to the land of Israel, for those who were seeking the child's life are dead." When Joseph awoke from the dream he was greatly moved emotionally and spiritually. He sat up in bed and heard the gentle sound of Mary breathing next to him. Although it was still dark and there were hours yet before the sun would rise, he got out of bed and walked to the window and peered up to the peaceful dark sky, studded with stars that reminded him of jewels. Peace was present in his soul but his mind became troubled as he thought. He knew that Archelaus was ruling over Judea in place of his father and he thought it was not a good time to go home to any part of the Judean area. He thought maybe they ought to go to resettle somewhere else in Israel.

He saw a light flash across the sky and smiled. He looked back to the bed and went to Mary. Waking from sleep, she turned to him.

As she awoke, she was immediately aware of Joseph's acute distress. "What's the matter, Joseph? Are you alright?"

Joseph proceeded to tell her about his vivid dream. He also informed her that he knew Herod's son, Archelaus, had taken over Herod's rule in Judea and he felt they should not return to their home in the Qumran Settlement, which was within the Judean realm.

Mary thought long and still. "Joseph, you just told me you had a dream in which a being of light appeared to you, correct?"

"Yes."

"Who do you think that being was?"

"I . . . I'm not sure. I didn't think of that."

"You have had dreams before. Have you deciphered their significance and guidance accurately before?" Mary smiled at him and they both knew why she smiled.

"I was certainly led in a dream to marry you." He sighed.

"Joseph, you are a man of God with a special calling. Often however, you allow your own thoughts to interfere and oppose the guidance of God. Don't you think God is greater than Herod's son Archelaus? If the being of light in your dream told you to take us *back* to Palestine and the land of Israel, don't you think we can trust to return to our home?" Mary looked at him with confidence. "Joseph, lie down. I'll stroke your forehead until you fall back to sleep. Try not to worry. Haven't we learned together that God will lead us faithfully?"

Suddenly a great wind blew into the bedroom, rattling the shutters. The wind stopped as quickly as it had begun. Joseph and Mary crawled out of their bed and walked to the window and pushed the unfastened shutter open. They both looked up to the clear sky above and a gentle breeze pushed fresh, cool air. Both realized something was about to happen. The very next day a Roman soldier was banging on Joseph and Mary's door. He simply asked, "Are you Joseph from Judea and the Qumran Settlement?"

"Yes," Joseph answered as Mary stood next to him.

"I was sent to inform you that King Herod died more than four years ago. He no longer poses a threat, and neither do his ruling sons, who show no interest in hunting down a potential leader, ruler, or messiah. It's safe to return to your home." The soldier handed them a purse of coins. "This is from Panthera." He left as abruptly as he had come. Mary and Joseph closed the door and looked at each other. Baby James was almost one year old, Salome was soon to be five years old, Jesus was ten years old, Yemane was twelve years old, and Joseph felt like he was one hundred years old, thinking about packing and moving the family home. He knew his home in the Qumran Settlement would have to be expanded to accommodate his larger family and then he wondered about what shape the land would be in. He smiled as it dawned on him that he had decided to obey the guidance of his dream and the presence of light, not fear and dread.

Mary, on the other hand, jumped up with joy and exclaimed, "We're going home! Joseph, we're going home!"

Jesus stood and watched his parents celebrate their joy. In his ten short years of life, they had often spoken about home and their extended family. He had never understood the complete details which would have explained their stay in the only place he had ever lived: Egypt. As Jesus continued to watch his parents rejoice, he silently asked and wondered, "Where is . . . home?"

GLOSSARY OF IDENTICAL NAMES IN NOVEL I

Mary The Mother of Jesus

Mary The younger sister of Jesus's mother Mary, Jesus's maternal Aunt Mary later in the series; from biblical source she is referred to as the "other Mary" and his "mother's sister, Mary the wife of Clopas" (John 19:25b)

Mary Third child and daughter of Rabbi Eleazar, sister to Lazarus and Martha, referred to as Mary of Bethany in youth and later referred to as Mary Magdalene, Mary of Magdala

Mary Firstborn of Issachar and Sarah, the brother and sister-in-law to Mary, the mother of Jesus

Mary Firstborn of Jacob and Joanna, the brother and sister-in-law to Mary, the mother of Jesus